A QUE

"Tell me, Brianna, will the man you marry have to be a paragon of all the virtues?" Christopher asked mockingly.

"No, but it is essential that I respect him above others," she retorted.

"Respect is admirable, but it is no substitute for love, my dear, especially on a cold winter's night," Christopher said. He then added in a purring tone, "I am persuaded it is essential to know what you are turning your back on."

His kiss was pure seduction from the start. Brianna tried to resist, keeping her lips pressed shut, but her protesting brain was betrayed by the involuntary softening of every part of her body that came into contact with his. She was a quivering mass of sensation when Christopher suddenly broke off the kiss, putting her away from him with his hands on her upper arms. Brianna shivered in the cold air and stared at him dazedly.

"Do you still prefer respect to love?" he demanded, his eyes gleaming.

THE LOST HEIR

by

Dorothy Mack

Ⓞ
A SIGNET BOOK

SIGNET
Published by the Penguin Group
Penguin Books USA Inc., 375 Hudson Street,
New York, New York 10014, U.S.A.
Penguin Books Ltd, 27 Wrights Lane,
London W8 5TZ, England
Penguin Books Australia Ltd, Ringwood,
Victoria, Australia
Penguin Books Canada Ltd, 10 Alcorn Avenue,
Toronto, Ontario, Canada M4V 3B2
Penguin Books (N.Z.) Ltd, 182–190 Wairau Road,
Auckland 10, New Zealand

Penguin Books Ltd, Registered Offices:
Harmondsworth, Middlesex, England

First published by Signet, an imprint of New American Library,
a division of Penguin Books USA Inc.

First Printing, July, 1993
10 9 8 7 6 5 4 3 2 1

 REGISTERED TRADEMARK—MARCA REGISTRADA

Printed in the United States of America

1

"What happened to you?"

Mr. George Cardorette put down the pen with which he had been making entries in a large ledger and got to his feet without haste, pushing his heavily carved chair away from the even more ornate desk at which he had been performing his labors. Three steps brought him to the middle of the small room where the business of the estate was conducted, by which time he had completed a survey of the somewhat disheveled appearance of the man whose unheralded entrance had interrupted his work.

A strong likeness existed between the two men with the newcomer being a somewhat younger and more finely drawn version of Mr. Cardorette. Both possessed luxuriant heads of hair so dark as to appear nearly black, but where the elder's wavy locks were sternly disciplined, the younger's curled riotously, falling over his wide brow to the detriment of his dignity. Both had the rich olive complexion that bronzed at the first kiss of the sun and straight black brows that could lend a stern aspect to their expressions at times. Mr. Cardorette's cheekbones were less pronounced than his cousin's, his jaw was more squared, and his eyes were a decided brown rather than the changeable hazel of the younger man's. Christopher Cardorette, the sixth Earl of Ashleigh, stood an inch or two below his cousin's six-foot stature and was decidedly less bulky, though his broad-shouldered frame and well-muscled thighs belied the slim elegance of his person as turned out by one of the master tailors of the realm. Mr. Cardorette, on the other hand, wisely did not aspire to a sartorial elegance that his massive chest and powerfully built arms denied him outright. He preferred his coats cut generously enough so that he could shrug himself into them unaided. And he never failed to stigmatize his cousin as a dandy and a fop in retaliation for the earl's frequent sighs of despair when he studied Mr. Cardorette's raiment through the quizzing glass he affected as an integral and—to his cousin—annoying part of his attire.

At the moment, however, the earl's customary elegance was

sadly diminished, thanks to the cumulative effect of dirt on his dove-gray inexpressibles, a jagged rent in the left sleeve of his claret-colored coat and, worst of all, a deep scuff mark on one of the expensive Hessian boots that his valet took an inordinate pride in keeping in a constant state of effulgence. Nor had his person escaped the ravages of whatever mishap had befallen him. His cheek and jaw were begrimed and there was an ugly scrape on the back of his left hand. All this Mr. Cardorette had assimilated by the time he stopped close to his cousin and repeated his question in a concerned voice.

"What happened to you, Kit?"

"The offside wheel went flying off the curricle going around the curve near where the Fairleigh Road joins the one from the village, and I went flying into the ditch. I missed cracking my head open on the milepost by a couple of inches."

Mr. Cardorette's black brows elevated in horrified disbelief. "A wheel came off a vehicle from the Ashleigh stables? Grimstead will go off in an apoplexy. I would not wish to be one of the grooms or stable lads under his direction at this moment. Did you hit a hidden stone or something to shear it off?" he asked over his shoulder as he walked over to a side table where he poured a tot of brandy into one of the glasses on a silver tray.

The earl shook his head. "No, nothing like that. Fortunately my chestnuts took no injury when they stumbled, and I had my groom with me. Whitby is bringing them home. I came ahead, thanks to the kind offices of a farmer who was passing in a gig."

Mr. Cardorette returned with the glass of brandy which he thrust into his cousin's hand while he took his arm to lead him to a chair. The earl bit off an exclamation of pain, paling perceptibly as he jerked away.

"What is it, Kit? Have you hurt your arm?"

"Shoulder," muttered the earl, downing half the contents of the glass in one gulp. "Wrenched it when I landed. It's nothing serious."

"Sit down," Mr. Cardorette commanded, wrestling a chair from in front of the huge desk closer to the accident victim. He stared down into the earl's pale, perspiring countenance. "Are you sure it's not a dislocated collarbone?"

"Quite sure." The earl eased himself into the wing chair, leaning his head against the high velvet back with a sigh of relief. "Whitby checked me over thoroughly before he'd let me leave the scene. Don't you fuss over me too, George. One devoted nurse-maid's more than enough for a man of seven-and-twenty."

"Ingrate." Mr. Cardorette's stern features relaxed into a small smile as he headed back behind the desk and took his own chair again. "You don't deserve Whitby's devotion—or mine."

The earl's lips twitched in response but he persisted. "I ceased being Matt's little brother and your young cousin six years ago when I went into the army, George."

This statement was expressed in the gentlest of tones and the speaker's countenance reflected his customary good humor, but Mr. Cardorette's eyes lowered to the ledger on the desktop for a second before he met his cousin's steady gaze again, while a self-deprecating twitch distorted the corner of his mouth momentarily. "If you are tactfully reminding me that you are quite competent to manage your own life, Kit, I assure you it was not really necessary." He shrugged his bulky shoulders beneath their dark blue covering, rippling the woolen fabric of his coat. "I became so used to doing everything for Matt that I suppose it's difficult to break the habit."

"I saw little of Matt from the time I went off to Cambridge, and you two, being the same age, were probably closer than he and I anyway, despite the fraternal tie." An elusive sadness touched the earl's features briefly. "It's strange, isn't it, George? That once unbridgeable four-year gap in our ages seems trifling at this stage. Was it a case of never really growing up with Matt, or was it simply that as the heir he was always toad eaten and catered to by everyone until in the end he couldn't do anything for himself?"

"A little of both perhaps," Mr. Cardorette replied with another shrug. "Matt was sports mad and he avoided this place as much as possible while your father was alive. They never did deal well together, as you probably recall." He looked up and the earl nodded.

"My father considered him a mindless fribble, not to put too fine a point on it, and since he detested all forms of sport himself except hunting, he had little tolerance for Matt's youthful enthusiasms for sporting pursuits . . . or others."

"You mean women?"

Again, the earl nodded. "Matt was twenty-five and I one-and-twenty when I joined the army. His petticoat adventures had already cost my father a packet by that time. I fondly remember one particularly rapacious little opera dancer who actually followed him here the summer before my last year at Cambridge." A reminiscent little smile played about his lips.

"That was before my time at Ashleigh. I was acting as secretary to Lord Malvern in the Foreign Office at that point. I'd have given a lot to be a fly on the wall when Uncle Herbert was accosted by Matt's opera dancer," George added with a gleam of humor.

"Alas, it was not my privilege to be present during that fateful interview, but I was later told by Matt that the atmosphere was surprisingly cordial between the two protagonists. My father had no moral objection to rapacity or to people playing the cards they were dealt. What he couldn't stomach was stupidity. He could abide a successful rogue, but he had nothing but contempt for a fool. He warned Matt that he'd paid to extricate him from that sort of situation for the last time and told him he could damn well marry the next ladybird who got her hooks into him."

"Matt wasn't a fool but he needed to be liked by everyone. He was open-handed to a fault, and people took advantage of his good nature as I quickly found out when I came here after your father died."

"The fact that he could never seem to gain my father's approval or respect was no doubt behind a lot of his youthful follies. He gave up trying early on and went in the opposite direction, falling into one scrape after another, whereas I just went away to an arena where the standards, though strict, were not capricious and unfair." The earl had looked a trifle abstracted as if trying to clarify the past for his own benefit, but now he pinned his cousin with keen hazel eyes. "Matt had been in full possession of my father's estate for over two years when he was killed in that accident. Did he not settle into the role after a while?"

"To some extent he did, of course, but Matt depended on me and others to smooth the course of his life. He didn't wish to concern himself with the details of estate management, so I handled all such matters for him." Again he glanced down at the ledger on the desk before completing his thought. "Naturally I continued to deal with everything here when he overturned his curricle and it took you so many months to sell out of the army."

"Napoleon's escape from Elba upset a lot of people's plans. Knowing you were fully capable of carrying on here in the meantime, I decided to stick around until we finished the job we'd begun in the Peninsula."

"You've had time to find your feet by now, Kit. You are already more conversant with the actual day-to-day running of the estate than Matt was after two years in possession. You may well feel able to dispense with my services by now. I certainly won't fault you for deciding to save the extravagant salary Matt insisted on making me."

"Unhappy, George? Perhaps you are getting bored now that I

am gradually taking over the reins. Shall I set you to cataloguing the library or some other monumental undertaking, like compiling a family history so you'll feel you are earning your stipend?"

"No, no," his cousin said with a chuckle. "I just want you to know you have only to indicate when my presence is no longer necessary, and I shall look around for a suitable position in London."

"My dear George, surely Ashleigh Court is large enough to assure us adequate privacy if we should grate on each other's nerves occasionally."

"I was thinking more in terms of your upcoming marriage, actually. Your bride may not wish to start off her married life with a permanent boarder under her roof."

"I was under the impression that you and Lady Selina were good friends."

"We are friends; I like and admire her immensely, but women do not generally invite their friends to share their homes, especially new brides. There are adjustments to be made, routines to establish—"

"Afraid we'll fight like cats and dogs and embarrass you, George?"

"You are being deliberately obtuse," his cousin declared.

"Yes, I beg your pardon," the earl said, smiling with a great deal of charm. "I appreciate your tact and delicacy, really I do. Matt will have been dead for a year on December fifteenth, and a fortnight later I shall be marrying the woman who would have been his wife had he not killed himself while engaged in a curricle race on an icy road to win an impulsive wager. It's a piquant situation to say the least. Shall we leave it that we'll play it by ear, standing ready to make those adjustments you spoke of if they become advisable?"

With this Mr. Cardorette had to be satisfied, for the earl heaved himself out of his chair, wincing as he jostled his injured shoulder. He held up his good hand and warned lightly, "No, don't say it, cousin. I have no intention of calling in the medical profession or taking to my bed, and every intention of joining you presently for dinner."

With a smile of singular sweetness, the earl then exited from the office, leaving his cousin staring after him, a thoughtful expression on his countenance.

Some three hours later the two were sitting at table taking their time over their port when Pennystone, his lordship's butler, en-

tered the dining room in his usual stately manner and came to
stand near the head of the table.

"I beg your pardon, my lord, but there is someone without who
desires to see you."

"At this hour?" Raising his eyes to the butler's impassive face,
the earl inquired, "Is it one of the neighbors, Pennystone? Why
did you not send him along here?"

"The caller is a stranger to me, sir. A young woman."

The earl's keen hazel eyes examined the unrevealing face
above him for further clues. Finding none, he ventured, "A be-
nighted traveler perhaps?"

"As to that, sir, I really couldn't say, but the young woman
asked specifically to speak with you."

"Shall I take care of the matter for you, Kit?" Mr. Cardorette
asked, putting down his glass.

"Stay a moment, George. Does this young woman have a
name, Pennystone, and is she attractive?"

The barest flicker in the butler's eyes acknowledged his lordship's mischievous intention and quite properly ignored it. "I believe the young lady would be considered comely by most people,
sir, and she gave her name as Llewellyn."

"*Miss* Llewellyn, Pennystone?"

"Yes, sir."

"In that case, George, though I thank you for your selfless offer
to act as my deputy, I believe this may be one of those onerous
duties I really should undertake personally." The earl got to his
feet, cast a wicked grin in his cousin's direction and followed his
butler out of the room.

"Where did you put Miss, ah, Llewellyn, Pennystone?" he
asked when the man walked past the small reception room off the
main entrance hall and proceeded toward the back of the house.

"It was my impression that the young lady was perhaps not
feeling quite the thing, sir, so I put her in your study where there
is wine and brandy if you should consider it advisable to offer her
a restorative."

"If I'd known you were intent on subjecting me to the
vagueries of a vaporish female, Pennystone, I'd have turned her
over to Mr. Cardorette, be she ever so attractive," the earl complained in an undertone as the butler opened the study door and
stood back for him to enter.

Christopher took two reluctant steps into the room and stopped
short, devoutly hoping his bemused state was not reflected on his
countenance, for Pennystone's description of Miss Llewellyn as

"comely" had ill-prepared him for the lovely creature who stared at him from a pair of outsize eyes the intense green of emeralds. For the space of a missed heartbeat his brain shut down while he feasted his eyes on the symmetry of a classically oval face containing, in addition to those extraordinary eyes, a perfect little nose and the most kissable mouth it had ever been his privilege to discover. Sanity returned in the next instant and with it the power of discernment. He saw the girl, for she was little more than that despite her all-black costume, was deathly pale; that she was in fact looking not at all the thing, to paraphrase Pennystone, even apart from the paralyzing shyness that seemed to grip her on confronting his presence. She had turned a shade paler, if possible, as he came closer, and concern for her gentled his voice as he urged, "Please sit down, Miss Llewellyn, here in this comfortable chair. Are you ill? Shall I call your maid?"

The omission struck him all of a sudden and he cast a lightning glance around the room for an attendant who should have been present.

"I . . . I don't have a maid and I am not ill, just tired from traveling so many hours."

"Then if you have been traveling, you must be sorely in need of refreshment. Pennystone, bring tea for Miss Llewellyn."

"Very good, sir."

"Oh, no, please do not trouble!" the girl cried in distress as Pennystone withdrew at a nod from his master. "I did not mean to cause you any bother, sir," she explained. "My errand will not take very long. The landlord's son kindly offered to drive me and bring me back to the inn before dark." Her voice trailed off as her host turned his back on her to pour out a glass of something he then carried to her.

"Miss Llewellyn, you shall discharge your errand to me after you have recruited your strength with this brandy and the tea that will arrive shortly. No, do not argue," he insisted, smiling at her kindly. "Trust me that you will feel much better able to explain the matter that has brought you an apparently great distance to seek me out when you are feeling more yourself. Now, don't say another word; just drink this."

The earl pressed the glass into her hand and walked over to the window, leaving her to sip the brandy in partial privacy. Curiosity was gnawing away at him but he didn't want her imminent collapse on his conscience. A host of speculations chased through his imagination. Could she be related to one of his former comrades in arms on whose behalf she was bearing a message? The obvious

mourning she wore promised no good news and he sensed a deep
sadness beneath the surface discomfort under which she was la-
boring. That probably stemmed from the embarrassment to her
modesty of her unconventional appearance at a strange house
without protection for either good name or person. He was still
staring out into the gathering dusk listening for any sounds from
his mysterious caller when Pennystone returned with a tray of tea.

Christopher kept his back to the room while the butler drew up
a table before Miss Llewellyn. Through admirably repressed impatience he discerned the homely sounds of tinkling china and the
pouring out of the tea. Pennystone's murmurs sounded positively
avuncular and presently Miss Llewellyn thanked him in a soft little voice that had a lilt of music in it. The sound of the door closing released Christopher from his self-imposed exile and he
turned to see his guest daintily consuming a slice of bread and
butter before she thankfully raised the cup to her lips. When he
came back into the light of the candelabra, she blinked as if she
had forgotten his presence for a moment. Obviously he was not
having the same peculiar effect on her that her presence was having on him!

"You have been so very kind and thoughtful, Lord Ashleigh. I
did not realize how low and fatigued I was until your butler
brought this life-restoring tea. Thank you so much."

He smiled, convinced that the brandy she had neglected to
mention had probably contributed more to her present sense of
well-being than the tea. The glass stood empty on the tray beside
the Wedgwood teapot. "Now perhaps you would like to tell me
what I may have the honor of doing for you, Miss Llewellyn," he
said, taking the chair across the tea table from his unexpected
guest.

Glowing green eyes looked straight at him from beneath feath-
ery black brows. "I am here today, sir, to fulfill a promise I made
to my father before he died, though I have little expectation that
you will be able to assist me. It seems too great a coincidence to
hope for." She sighed and stared into the fire for a second as if
looking at something in the past; then she moistened her top lip
with her tongue in an unconsciously provocative gesture before
bringing her eyes level with his that had never left her face. "I am
hoping you may be able to tell me how to locate someone who
has the same family name as yours."

Christopher felt the muscles in his face tighten but he kept
control over his voice. "Who is the person you seek, Miss
Llewellyn?"

"We knew him simply as Matthew Cardorette, but he signed the register as James Matthew Adolphus Cardorette, which should be more helpful in locating him." She looked at him hopefully.

A wave of disgust washed over Christopher, leaving him sick and shaken. He had been half-expecting it but still found it galling to accept that this lovely girl was one of Matt's light-o'-loves. Several had come forward in the weeks after his death looking to gouge money from his family, but he'd never before felt personally revolted by the knowledge. Why had it taken her so long to put forth her claim?

Christopher was unaware that some of the disgust he felt must be evident on his face until he saw dismay leap into hers. He consciously adjusted his voice and expression to erase all feeling as he inquired, "You believe I might be able to locate this person for you, Miss Llewellyn?"

"Frankly, no, but when my father saw the announcement of your betrothal in the newspaper at the squire's house he was struck by the surname. Later, when he knew he was dying he made me promise that I would seek you out and request your help in locating Matthew Cardorette."

What a consummate actress she was! If he didn't know she must be an adventuress he'd have been completely taken in by that artistic little choke in her voice and the slight filming of tears in those magnificent eyes when she spoke of her father. Suddenly, memory replayed her earlier words in his head and he demanded sharply, "Did you say this person signed the *register*? What register, Miss Llewellyn?"

"The parish register at his wedding."

"Are you saying you are *married* to my—to Matthew Cardorette?"

"No. Matthew Cardorette is my brother-in-law. He married my sister, Meg."

"And when did this alleged wedding take place, Miss Llewellyn?"

"Five years ago, and there was nothing 'alleged' about it, sir. I was present at the ceremony."

"Five years ago!"

Lord Ashleigh positively goggled at the young woman staring at him in wary bewilderment in the wake of his abrupt reversal from his initial attitude of solicitous concern. She blinked nervously but attempted no further speech.

"If your sister has been married to Matthew Cardorette for five years, how did she come to lose track of him, and why did she send you off to track him down instead of coming herself?"

"My sister is dead, Lord Ashleigh."

"How very inconvenient for your claim."

"Inconvenient!" The girl recoiled as though he had slapped her. She was trembling and pale but her dignity remained intact as she said, "I can see that you do not believe a word I have said, but that does not really signify if you can tell me where I may find Matthew Cardorette."

"Certainly, I can. He is buried in the village churchyard a half-mile from here."

"Dead!" She stared at him in white-faced consternation; then tears welled up in her eyes and spilled over. "Poor Jamie," she whispered, groping for her reticule.

Christopher watched in grim silence as she took out a black-bordered handkerchief and proceeded to wipe her eyes. She hadn't missed a single trick in her well-rehearsed efforts to play on his sympathies. He felt he was merely taking his cue from a fellow cast member in a play as he asked, "Who is Jamie?"

She appeared not to have heard him as she stared into the fire, biting her lip and twisting her handkerchief in her hands. He had to repeat the question before she swung those tear-filled eyes in his direction. "Jamie is my little nephew."

Still with that sense of reading lines in a play, the earl demanded, "The son of Matthew Cardorette and your sister?" When she nodded, he asked, "How old is the child?"

"Jamie is four years old."

Christopher flung himself out of the chair, grimacing as pain shot through his injured shoulder. He took a quick turn around the room, struggling with the notion that his brother could have willfully concealed a legal marriage and a child all these years. "I assume you can produce proof of these assertions, Miss Llewellyn?" he demanded, whirling to face the silent girl.

"Well, the marriage was performed by my father and is recorded in the parish register of his church, St. George's, in Lower Melstrum in Herefordshire. Jamie's birth is recorded too. He was named James for his father and Arthur for my father. Lord Ashleigh, may I ask what relationship you bore to Matthew Cardorette?"

"He was my brother."

She looked at him searchingly. "I thought there was something familiar about you when you walked into the room, though you don't really look much like Matthew. He was bigger and not so dark in coloring. Your eyes are the same hazel color though."

"Thank you. I am aware of what my brother looked like, Miss Llewellyn."

She flushed at the rebuke and fell silent. His impulse was to apologize for his rudeness and he resented it. Nine chances out of ten said this gentle lovely creature was part of an elaborate scheme to extort money from the estate, but naturally her claim would have to be investigated. What bothered him most about the situation was that if her story were true it would mean Matthew had denied his legitimate child. He had known his brother was weak and self-indulgent but he had never questioned his honor.

"Why have you waited all this time to try to find my brother, Miss Llewellyn?"

She looked puzzled. "Sir, we have never known how to set about finding Matthew. We never knew where his home was or anything about his family. He came into our lives five years ago as the result of an accident involving the carriage he was driving. He was injured almost on the doorstep of the rectory, and my father took him into our home. My sister helped to nurse him during his recuperation, and they fell in love. I was only sixteen at the time but I remember that he scarcely ever mentioned his family. My father married them six weeks after he came to Herefordshire. Papa urged Matthew to inform his family about the marriage, but he was reluctant to write to them. It was my impression that he was rather afraid of his father. When he and Meg had been married about a month, Matthew suddenly decided to go to see his family and tell them the news in person. After he left Lower Melstrum, we never saw him again."

The earl was thunderstruck. "Your sister had no further contact with her husband during her lifetime? I find that incredible."

"She received one letter from him written a few weeks after he left. He spoke vaguely of needing more time to prepare his father for the news, which we gathered would not be welcome, and promised to return shortly for Meg. That was the last contact we had with him."

"So he never knew your sister was carrying his child?"

"No."

If there was any truth to this sordid tale, at least it was some small consolation that Matt had not knowingly denied his child. "Why did your father not insist on trying to trace his errant son-in-law?" Skepticism was written clearly on his lordship's features.

Miss Llewellyn said sadly, "My father was a tremendously good man but he was not a worldly person. When he understood how completely crushed Meg was by her husband's desertion and how much she shrank from anything that could be considered pursuit or coercion, he ceased importuning her to call Matthew to account. And then Jamie came into our lives like a blessing from Heaven and Matthew was . . . not forgotten—never that, unfortunately—but no longer of prime importance. It was not until after Meg had died and my father realized that his own health was failing that he began to fret about finding Jamie's father and seeking support for the child. We have very little money, you see, and will have to leave our home when the bishop appoints a new pastor."

Miss Llewellyn was silent. Her tale was told, and a stark and appalling tale he found it. If by any chance it were the truth, then the Llewellyn family had been grievously injured by his brother. A new thought struck him in all its horror, and his voice was harsh with repression as he demanded, "Miss Llewellyn, when did your sister die?"

"She died of pneumonia on the twenty-fourth of January."

Christopher continued to stare at the mournful girl but he no longer saw her. He was trying to cope with the monstrous concept that her story, if true, meant that only his own accidental death had prevented Matt from making a bigamous marriage. His abandoned wife had survived him by a month.

Christopher shook his head to cast off the shadows. All this was still to be proved. Nothing could be achieved tonight. His eyes refocused on the pale and appealing face across the table from him and he could not prevent pity at her plight from softening his expression. She was drooping with fatigue and reeling from his unmerited hostility, but her gentle dignity had not deserted her in these straits.

"Miss Llewellyn, may I suggest that you put all worries about the future from your mind for tonight and let young Chester take you back to the inn now? His father's beds are clean and comfortable and you are sorely in need of a night's rest. I shall call on you in the morning and we will arrange everything then."

She rose at once, obedient to the command in his voice, perhaps even relieved to have someone else assume her burdens for a short time. He escorted her to the door himself and saw her safely into the waiting gig.

Christopher stood in the drive watching the departing vehicle until he could no longer distinguish it from the other shadows in the dusk and the clopping sounds had diminished to faint echoes.

He turned very slowly then and gazed at the lighted house for a long moment as if it might have changed its aspect in the last half hour and become strange to him. It was with reluctance that he directed his steps back inside.

Christopher located George Cardorette in the small family parlor perusing a copy of the *Edinburgh Review* that he lowered to his lap at his cousin's entrance.

"Who was your mysterious lady caller? She must have been comely indeed to keep you occupied all this time."

"She was quite lovely," Christopher replied soberly, not even aware of the other's jocularity. A log snapped in the fireplace with a loud crack during the pregnant second that elapsed before he continued. "As to her identity, if her story can be validated, she is the aunt of the true sixth Earl of Ashleigh, Matt's four-year-old son."

2

As the carriage jolted into a pothole, Miss Brianna Llewellyn's eyes flew open and her hand automatically extended to grasp the strap, but within seconds the springs had accommodated to the jarring and the ride settled into the swaying smoothness that, unbelievably, must have lulled her to sleep. The lengthening shadows of the trees along the edge of the road confirmed that she had actually slept for an hour or two. Recalling with a shudder the dreadful two days of her journey by public stagecoach to Ashleigh Court, Brianna had good cause to be grateful to the earl for her present comfortable situation in one of the Cardorette carriages.

She had been most reluctant to accept so great a favor from someone who obviously thought her capable of participating in a fraudulent scheme to extort money from his family, but even after a decent night's repose in the quiet inn near Ashleigh, she had been no match for the insistent earl. Despite his low opinion of her personally, he had been determined not to be backward in any attention his consequence demanded as fitting for a possible family connection. The protests prompted by her puny pride had been swept away as inconsequential by the earl in the process of insisting on his grand gesture of sending her home in a style she could never have aspired to as the daughter of a poor country pastor. And here she sat, ensconced in a beautifully sprung and luxuriously appointed carriage, on a padded seat of coffee-colored velvet, being driven by a skilled coachman whose livery matched the colors in the Ashleigh crest emblazoned on the doors of the carriage. The driver was assisted by a similarly attired armed guard who had made all the arrangements for her stay at a superior hostelry last night. If all this magnificence were not sufficient to draw curious eyes to her insignificant person, she had also been provided with a female attendant drafted from the earl's household to wait upon her during the journey. The intimidating presence of this silent personage had succeeded in nullifying the enjoyment she might otherwise have derived from the unwonted luxury of her surroundings. Her first tentative attempts at impersonal conversation with the abigail had been met with a freezing civility that had dried up any subsequent overtures. Brianna had retreated into the shell of shyness that all Meg's and her father's efforts over the years to accustom her to a society beyond the rectory had never succeeded in dispersing.

Recalled to the existence of the unwanted companion Lord Ashleigh had forced on her, Brianna angled her head slightly to sneak a glance at the other occupant of the carriage and was rather inordinately pleased to see that the unapproachable Selwyn appeared to be napping. Somehow this little weakness made the abigail less intimidating. As she looked more fully at the sallow, lined visage of the gaunt, gray-haired woman in the unbecoming brown hat, Brianna gave herself a mental shaking. She was being foolish beyond permission indulging in such childish fantasies. Selwyn was not some sort of dragon, for goodness sake; she was simply a dour middle-aged woman who had been jerked out of her accustomed niche in the earl's household to play abigail to a stranger on a tedious journey. Probably she would be shocked to learn that her temporary mistress perceived her as threatening in any way.

An excess of imagination had ever been her besetting sin, Brianna acknowledged with a grimace, turning her glance to the passing scene outside the window. But a woman of one-and-twenty, moreover one who had the sole responsibility for the welfare of an orphaned child, should have progressed beyond such constricting tendencies. One would have thought that this past terrible year, encompassing as it had the successive losses of the two dearest people in the world, would have destroyed forever any lingering remnants of childhood in her bruised spirit. Certainly, last month, she had felt as old as the Welsh hills beyond the border when her father had been laid to rest beside his wife and elder daughter. For weeks she had fought with every ounce of strength to hold him in this world, a world he would have quitted gladly had it not been for the all-consuming fear of what the future might hold for her and his small grandchild. A fear that tortured his every waking moment and kept him from rest. The only thing that could give him any peace—and that merely temporary—in that dark period was her constantly reiterated promise that she would seek out Matthew Cardorette and bring him to a sense of his obligation toward his unknown son. She had repeated her promise as often as her father needed to hear it; indeed, she'd have promised anything that would have eased his mind during his last painful days just as she had earlier promised her dying sister that she would never desert Jamie while he needed her.

Brianna had never traveled beyond the city of Hereford in her whole life and never on a public conveyance, but the rector had been adamant that she must conduct the search in person, averring that it was all too easy to ignore a written request from a stranger. Thus, armed with the latest edition of *Patterson's British Itinerary,* supplied by their friend, Doctor Chamfrey, and refusing to recognize the possibility that her journey could turn into an odyssey before she was successful, she had set out four days ago for the principal seat of the earls of Ashleigh, who happened to possess the surname of Cardorette. This knowledge had been an unexpected gift through the courtesy of the London press on the occasion of the announcement of the current title holder's betrothal in late September. Backed by the modest sum of money her father had realized from selling the collection of books it had been his life's dedication to amass, Brianna had endured all the discomforts of traveling on the public stage, exacerbated in her case by the congenital shyness that made it so difficult for her to deal with strangers. She had arrived at Ashleigh Court in a state of nervous exhaustion bordering on collapse. Her condition must have been only too apparent to his lordship's butler, whose reassuring manner had calmed her misgivings about her intrusion.

The earl too had been wonderfully kind at first, insisting that she recruit her flagging strength with brandy and tea before she explained her uninvited presence in his house. It was only after she had mentioned his brother's name that his manner had hardened toward her. Ordinarily she'd have fled before the dislike and distrust that replaced his initial gentleness, but her solemn promise to her father had stiffened her backbone, aided unwittingly by the earl when he spoke slightingly of her parent and Meg. She had held her ground and pleaded her case despite internal tremors that threatened to disgrace her by becoming visible to her antagonist. Perhaps she had not been able to conceal her perturbation from him as well as she had thought at the time because the ill-disguised hostility had dropped gradually away. When he had proposed postponing any further discussion until morning, he had once again spoken gently and kindly to her, though not with the same warmth he had displayed before learning her errand.

As Brianna sat staring blindly out the window, she wondered at the strange unsettling emotions that had taken possession of her since she had reluctantly set forth to fulfill her father's dying wish. Her original fears that the quest might prove to be a wild goose chase at worst or involve considerably more travel than her father had anticipated, at best, had proved groundless, fortunately. The long mystery of Matthew Cardorette's origins had been cleared up at the first attempt to locate him.

Wildly improbable though it seemed, her former brother-in-law—her *late* brother-in-law—she reminded herself somberly, had belonged to a noble family. She could not decide after much circular reasoning these past two days whether this circumstance rendered his desertion of his young bride more or less heinous in retrospect. That the marriage was a mésalliance from the Cardorette point of view was beyond question. Of gentle but undistinguished antecedents on her father's side and from a cadet branch of a somewhat more prominent family on her mother's, Meg would not have been considered a fitting mate for a son of the nobility, lovely and accomplished and *good* though she was on any scale of natural virtues. The disparity in their fortunes alone rendered the match unthinkable. One could not escape the conclusion that Matthew had been so taken by Meg's beauty and personal charm as to forget for a time what would be expected of the girl he chose for a wife. Once back among his family and away from Meg's potent appeal, he had obviously regretted his rash action in marrying so far beneath his family's estate. Even granting all this, however, Brianna could recognize no moral standard lenient enough to condone his subsequent behavior in choosing to undo his mistake by denying its existence. His cruel and cowardly desertion of a bride who adored him, without even the bare decency to acknowledge the action to her was, quite simply, unforgivable.

Observing Meg's endless disappointment in going through the mail for years after Matthew's departure, Brianna had often longed to lay violent hands on the man who had broken her sister's heart in the most cavalier fashion imaginable. Being a silent and helpless witness to the uncomplaining suffering of a beloved sister was an invidious position that in time warped one's soul. Certainly she had been aware of a corrosive bitterness in herself ever since Meg's untimely death.

Even the maternal satisfaction of seeing her child blossom and grow sturdy had not been enough to offset Meg's deep unhappiness over her husband's betrayal. When she had contracted pneumonia last winter, all Brianna's pleading had been ineffectual in instilling a real desire to get well in her sister. She had slipped out of life as uncomplainingly as she had lived it.

In the inn's parlor on the morning after their first meeting, Lord
Ashleigh had told her that his brother had died in a carriage accident. Even for Jamie's sake, Brianna had been unable to summon
any real sorrow at Matthew's demise. His weakness had ruined
her sister's life and possibly his own, though naturally she knew
nothing of his existence during the years following his desertion
of his wife. Perhaps his nature had been callous enough to permit
him to put the past behind him without regret. She could not deny
harboring a guilty satisfaction that he would not be in a position
to spoil Jamie's life. Meg had worried about this possibility when
she had begged her sister to raise her son to be a man of integrity
and honor like his grandfather.

Was this the source of her present uneasiness? Meg had not desired to discover the whereabouts of her son's father. She had
feared his influence on the boy. While her own father lived, this
was not an issue. Facing his own death and knowing there would
be insufficient funds to educate the boy in a fitting manner, her
father had put aside future concerns about Matthew's moral influence in the light of present necessities. Brianna's action in going
to Lord Ashleigh had revived the issue of undesired influence in
Jamie's life, however. She was somewhat hazy about the legali-
ties involved in the present situation, but a father's right to the
custody of his children was supreme and superseded any claim a
mother might have, even a deserted mother. Unaware of the existence of a child, Matthew could not have made any provision for
Jamie's guardianship, while Meg had certainly entrusted her son
to her sister's care in the event of her own father's death. Whether
this would have any weight in a court of law was a worrisome
question beyond her experience.

As the earl's superb carriage drew nearer to the village of
Lower Melstrum, Brianna's uneasiness grew, replacing the brief
initial satisfaction at having discovered Jamie's paternal relatives.
Lord Ashleigh had been vague about the future, confining his remarks to the immediate necessity for proving her claims for her
nephew's parentage, but this was not a source of concern for her.
She *knew* that this would easily be established. No, her major
concern was to ensure that the boy's moral training did not alter
for the worse in consequence of her action in seeking out his paternal heritage.

An hour later, after she had thanked the earl's servants for their
care of her and after directing them to the best inn in the district,
Brianna found to her dismay that concerns for Jamie's future had
taken on a frightening immediacy in her absence.

"Sick?" she echoed in the rectory's entrance hall as she stared into the tired face of the woman who had been an important figure in her life from earliest memory. "But how can this be, Molly? He was fine when I left and I've only been gone four days!"

"And thank the good Lord for seeing you safely back so soon. He cries for Auntie Bree every time he wakes, poor lamb, and I haven't known what to tell him."

Molly Lloyd, loving nurse, repository of childhood confidences, disciplinarian in the void left by the scholarly minister and his gentle wife, and general factotum in the Llewellyn household for nearly a quarter of a century, took the black bonnet from Brianna's shaking fingers.

"What happened, Molly? There was nothing wrong with Jamie when I left."

"You know what children are, love, up one minute, down the next and bouncing back before the cat can lick her ear, though I must admit I don't like the sound of his cough. It started with him complaining of a scratchy throat the night you left, and he wouldn't eat anything. I wondered at first if he might just be missing you, but the coughing started the next day."

"Has the doctor seen him?" Brianna was stripping off her gloves as she spoke. She gave them to Molly and undid the neck of the black woolen mantle she had worn in the carriage.

"Yesterday and again this morning. He says it is bronchitis."

"*Bronchitis!* That's the way Meg started," Brianna whispered, terror springing into her face.

"I'm not going to say there's no danger of Jamie's developing pneumonia, love, because it wouldn't be true, but now you're back, he'll be more at ease in his mind, and there will be two of us to nurse him. We'll pull him through this, never you fear."

"Yes . . . of course we will, Molly. I'll run up and look at him. Is he awake?"

"He'd just dropped off again when I heard the carriage wheels outside."

As the two women ascended the staircase, the elder repeated, "I'm that relieved to see you back so quickly, Brianna. Did you learn anything from that earl the rector, God rest his soul, was so intent on speaking to? Were you even able to see him?"

"Yes, Molly, and it turns out Matthew was his brother."

"Matthew Cardorette the brother of an earl? *Was*, did you say?"

"Yes. He's dead. I'll tell you all about it later."

They had reached the nursery by then and Brianna hurried inside, moving silently and surely across the room that was lighted by only a single oil lamp on a table a few feet removed from the narrow bed where her small nephew lay. The room was warm, thanks to a coal fire burning in the fireplace, she noted as she peered anxiously down at the curly haired child.

"He looks flushed," she whispered.

Even as her hand went toward his cheek, the still figure began to writhe about and a spell of painful coughing brought him awake. Molly went immediately to the table where she opened a bottle.

The child's head was turned in that direction until he noted movement from the corner of his eye. "Auntie Bree!" he gasped, holding out his arms. "It hurts, Auntie Bree."

Brianna took the little figure wracked by coughing into her arms, tenderly smoothing the damp curls back from his forehead. "I know, dearest, but Molly and I are going to make you well. See, she has a soothing syrup for you that will make your throat feel better. Open wide, my pet."

"I don't like it, Auntie Bree," Jamie protested tearfully, turning his head away from the spoon Molly was extending toward him.

"You may have some honey afterward to chase away the bitter taste, but this will calm your cough, dearest, so you will sleep better and get well quickly. Now, do be Auntie Bree's brave boy and show Molly that you are not afraid to do what is necessary," she coaxed gently.

Jamie opened his pursed lips and accepted the medicine, though the tears still streamed from his eyes. He gagged a little but managed to swallow the dose. Molly had the sweetened drink ready for him and he gulped some of it down before turning his head against his aunt's shoulder once more, weakened by another bout of coughing. Brianna rocked him, murmuring soft nothings while Molly put his pillow into a fresh case and straightened the rumpled bed covers. When his aunt tried to settle him back against the pillow he clung to her. "Don't go, Auntie Bree."

"I'm not going to leave you, dearest, but you must go to sleep now so you will get better quickly. I'll be right here when you wake up, I promise."

As the exhausted child sank back among the pillows with a little whimper, Brianna said, "I imagine you've not had much sleep these past nights, Molly. I'll stay with Jamie tonight. You go to bed." When the older woman protested that she had not been jouncing about in a stagecoach for four days, Brianna laughed softly and described the luxurious accommodations provided by the Earl of Ashleigh. After a short argument she persuaded the weary woman to seize the opportunity to rest while she could. There was a loud silence as both females avoided the implications of that remark. Molly broke it, briskly declaring she would bring a tray up to Brianna before taking advantage of her presence to catch up on lost sleep.

During the three days that followed Brianna's homecoming, the two women took turns in the child's sickroom, with the one not directly engaged in nursing Jamie sleeping or performing those household tasks that were most pressing. One area they did not have to concern themselves with was meal preparation. The late rector's little grandson was a favorite in the village and a number of their neighbors slipped into the rectory, leaving offerings of food without even making their presence known if the inhabitants were not readily visible. Time lost all meaning for the child's devoted attendants during the period he hovered on the brink of pneumonia. Either would have been hard-pressed to name the day if asked, and sometimes the distinction between day and night blurred as they kept a vigil at the boy's bedside. Such communication as existed between Molly and Brianna was limited to practical exchanges regarding Jamie's condition and needs, generally delivered in haste when replacing each other in the sickroom.

There had been no opportunity for Brianna to describe her meetings with the Earl of Ashleigh to Molly, and the whole experience quickly receded so far into the background as to take on a dreamlike quality when it crossed her mind at all. In truth, Brianna had nearly forgotten Lord Ashleigh's existence in the face of constant mind-numbing anxiety over her small nephew.

It was something of a shock, therefore, during one of Doctor Chamfrey's daily visits to the rectory to hear the earl's name fall from the doctor's lips. Brianna, who had been removing a soiled pillow case while he examined Jamie, paused in the act, her eyes staring blankly, her dropped chin holding the pillow against her chest, heedless that the used case had fallen to the floor.

"I . . . I beg your pardon?" she said, blinking rapidly as her arms wrapped themselves around the plump pillow.

The doctor shot her a look from under bushy gray brows. "I said the Earl of Ashleigh paid me a visit not an hour since—"

"Lord Ashleigh here! Why?" Now her eyes were wide open and full of consternation.

"He said you had descended on him last week in an effort to locate Matthew Cardorette. Is that true?"

"Yes," she admitted reluctantly.

"Then you've answered your own question, Brianna, haven't you?" the doctor replied with the familiarity of one who had brought her into the world and seen her through all the childish ailments. "He is here, naturally enough, to check on the veracity of your claim that his brother married your sister."

"You know it is not a 'claim' but the simple truth!" she cried hotly, stiff with resentment, the green of her eyes deepening with temper.

"I do, of course, but why should you get upon your high ropes because the man is making civil inquiries of those in a position to know the truth?" the doctor demanded. "What would you expect anyone to do in his position? It wouldn't be the first time a woman appeared out of the blue to advance a false claim of this nature upon a wealthy family."

"What did you tell him?" Brianna's tones were still laced with resentment.

"I related to him the medical history as I personally knew it of the man known to me as Matthew Cardorette. I also described the aforesaid individual physically to the best of my recollection, including the existence of a crescent-shaped scar near his left shoulder blade. I imagine you didn't know about that, my girl, but the earl certainly did. It was at that point that he allowed that the man who crashed quite literally into the lives of the occupants of St. George's Rectory five years ago was his brother."

"Did he admit that Jamie is his nephew?" Brianna asked eagerly.

"You're going a bit too fast, my dear girl. I was not in a position to satisfy his lordship as to the existence of a legal marriage, though I could confirm this young man's date of birth since I delivered him. I sent the earl to see the squire who, if memory serves, was the other witness to the marriage." Doctor Chamfrey raised those formidable eyebrows in question and Brianna nodded.

"Yes, the squire and I were the witnesses. It's all in the parish register."

"You can't fault the man for being thorough." the doctor said calmly. He held up his hand for silence and bent over to listen to his patient's chest. After asking the boy to cough and then to breathe deeply, he smiled at the youngster and patted his shoulder as he laid him back among the pillows. The smile lingered in penetrating gray eyes as he said, "I do believe the lad has turned the corner. We'll continue with all the medicines though, and you must watch that he doesn't take a turn backward through sheer contrariness, but I think I can say the careful nursing and the medicines have done the trick. Keep him in bed for the next few days, Brianna, and coax him to eat. I'll check in again tomorrow."

Brianna had no immediate leisure in which to give way to a slump of relief at the doctor's good news. She was occupied in settling Jamie down again for a few minutes after the doctor had shown himself out. Presently, when the child dropped off to sleep and she ran out of invented tasks to perform in the sickroom, she could no longer bar the door of her mind against the entrance of the Earl of Ashleigh. Nor could she deny that she was disturbed by the doctor's disclosure of the earl's presence in the village. She reminded herself that she had been well aware that her claims on Jamie's behalf must be verified, but somehow she had never envisioned the lofty earl conducting the inquiry personally. Casting an eye at the sweetly sleeping occupant of the narrow bed, Brianna wandered over to the window that overlooked the quiet street at the end of the village. There was no sign of human activity down there at the moment, the only moving creatures within her field of vision being a fat tortoiseshell cat that suddenly scuttled under a bush and a white-winged dove that flew out of the same bush to safety.

Where was the earl at this moment, she wondered, her brow puckering faintly. Had he gone to question the squire about his brother's "alleged"—that had been the word he had used—marriage? She let the curtain fall back into place. How distasteful the whole business had become. She was passionately glad that Meg had never had to face the insulting disbelief in the eyes of the man who had unknowingly been her brother-in-law. Her sister's marriage had been a tragic mistake in the end, but there had been nothing even faintly improper at the beginning, though it had happened within six weeks of the couple's first meeting. Even at sixteen, she had been aware that Matthew and Meg were rapturously in love. No more than her sister had she discerned the inherent weakness in the character of the friendly young man with the delightful manners who had won their hearts. It was perhaps not surprising that her scholarly and otherworldly parent had also been taken in by his abundant charm and joie de vivre, but neither the squire nor Doctor Chamfrey had hinted that the likeable stranger might be other than he seemed on the surface.

Over the past five years, Brianna had devoted many fruitless hours to unhappy speculation about the tragedy of her sister's marriage. The experience had left her with a profound mistrust of so-called romantic love. That a force that seemed so powerful

could wither so quickly was a sharp lesson against listening to the
call of the senses in choosing a mate. Seeing the disgust that the
earl had not troubled to conceal, however, had introduced an element of sordidness that had never hovered over the affair before.
That had been difficult to bear. It had mined a lode of stiff-necked
pride within herself whose existence she had never suspected. She
almost hated him for daring to ascribe unworthy motives to her
beautiful and virtuous sister and was guiltily aware that her father
would have deplored such an ungenerous—even unchristian—reaction on her part. Truth to tell, she was more than a little shocked
at the strength of her revulsion, especially since her initial response to Matthew's brother had been positive. A picture of a
handsome man with a wealth of black curls and uncommonly fine
hazel eyes rose before her. His manner toward her had been wonderfully kind at first, but that had all changed when she explained
her errand to him. She could not have been more bereft if a life-
saving hand had been extended to her only to be abruptly withdrawn, leaving her to sink back into a raging sea. She had been
prepared to meet with indifference, even coldness. To glimpse
human warmth and then have it instantly withdrawn had seemed
doubly cruel.

Brianna shook her head to clear it of Lord Ashleigh's unwelcome image. Time enough to let him back in if it became necessary to present him to Molly. Presumably, the earl would come to
the rectory to ask to see the parish register either before or after
his interview with the squire. Her fingers found the small watch
pinned to the front of her black bombazine gown and twisted it
until she could read its face. Molly had poked her head into the
sickroom shortly before the doctor's visit to let her know she intended to sleep for a few hours. At this time of day the village
woman who did the rough cleaning would be downstairs, but perhaps it would be prudent to check the state of the family parlor
and the parish office while Jamie slept so soundly. After a quick
look at the child, she noted thankfully the improvement in his
breathing that she had not quite dared to believe before the doctor's recent confirmation. Brianna then slipped quietly out of the
room and headed downstairs, her mind determinedly fixed on
practical housewifely concerns.

3

Christopher Cardorette took out his watch for the third time since he had been ushered into a comfortably furnished study on the ground floor of Powick Towers, the rambling old house belonging to Squire Henderson that he had been directed to by Doctor Chamfrey. Thirty-five minutes had elapsed since the servant who had opened the door to him had left him here to cool his heels while he sent to locate his master wherever he might be on the estate. The waiting had been rendered less onerous by a decanter of as soft a Madeira as he'd ever tasted, brought to the study by another servant, presumably Mr. Henderson's butler. He poured himself a second glass of this nectar and wandered over to a window between two tall glass-fronted bookcases. He'd already studied their contents, concluding that his absent host possessed every book ever written—at least in the English language—on the breeding, hunting, and racing of horses, including some racing calendars he'd never come across before.

Glass in hand, Christopher gazed out at a manicured lawn, with an incipient frown forming on his brow. He was less sure than when he'd arrived of the wisdom of interrogating the squire about Matthew's dealings with the inhabitants of the rectory at Lower Melstrum. Doctor Chamfrey's testimony had certainly satisfied him on the score of identification. He could no longer question that his brother had indeed spent an extended period of time under the rectory roof five years ago. It only remained to discover whether a valid marriage had taken place with the elder daughter of the house. He had every expectation that the parish register would contain such a record. If it jibed with the date of the child's birth—a full term baby according to the physician's own records—that should be sufficient to establish the boy's claim to the title and inheritance Christopher had assumed to be his for nearly eleven months. Inevitably this meeting with the squire would give rise to gossip in the neighborhood, but in fairness to Matthew and to satisfy his own need to understand what happened afterward, he had to try to discover his brother's true motivation for such a rash action.

There was also the vital matter of the banns. After all this time, Doctor Chamfrey could not recall having heard the banns read at St. George's, and of a certainty they were never read in the Ashleigh parish Church of All Souls. He'd checked on that detail before ever leaving for Herefordshire. Without a certificate attesting to the performance of this rite, no minister would have married them except with a special license that could only be obtained from the archbishop or his representative. If Matthew had been recovering from a fairly serious injury, it was at least problematical that he would have been able to secure a license within the time that had been mentioned by Miss Llewellyn and Doctor Chamfrey. Gossip or no, it was his duty to exhaust all avenues in investigating the validity of this hasty marriage.

Christopher was still staring out the window when the door was opened behind him. Turning, he beheld a tall, broad-shouldered man of about forty, dressed in dusty leathers and top boots whom he had no difficulty in placing as the master of the estate. The man was hatless but carried a crop under one arm as he proceeded to strip off his gloves.

"I see my people have taken care of you, my lord," the squire said, glancing at the decanter on the table near one of the several large brown-leather chairs with which the room was furnished.

"Very well indeed," Christopher replied, holding up his glass. As the two men shook hands, each took stock of the other quite openly. Christopher liked what he saw without reservation. The squire's firm handshake and level glance from alert dark eyes which had missed nothing about his unexpected guest's appearance seemed to indicate a forthright, competent individual whom it would be inadvisable to try to bamboozle.

As Christopher introduced himself and briefly explained the circumstances that had brought him to Herefordshire, Mr. Henderson poured himself a glass of the Madeira and topped off his guest's glass. He gestured to one of the leather chairs and seated himself opposite Christopher. Thick sandy-colored eyebrows that matched his cropped head had arched upward in mild surprise.

"Do I comprehend that Matthew Cardorette is dead and that his family was unaware of his marriage until Miss Llewellyn approached you quite recently?" Christopher nodded and the mystified squire asked, "Why on earth did the Llewellyns wait so long to get in touch with you?"

"According to Miss Llewellyn, Matthew had told them nothing

about his family. Consequently they had no idea how to reach him after he left Herefordshire until her father read about my betrothal in the *Gazette* in September and decided to try to trace his son-in-law by starting his inquiries with a family of the same name. His health failed before he could do so, but he extracted a promise from his daughter to pursue the quest after his death."

Seeing that Mr. Henderson was shaking his head in wonderment or disbelief, Christopher asked, "Do you find it a rather unlikely story?"

"On the contrary," came the prompt response. "If you had known the Reverend Arthur Llewellyn, you'd realize that nothing was more likely. The man was a saint, but he didn't belong in this world—no practical sense at all. While his wife was alive she kept the family afloat financially, but the girls were too young when their mother died to take over the job. The rector would give the food out of his children's mouths if a parishioner, no matter how undeserving, came along with a hard luck story."

"Then you don't think he was the type to try to snare a wealthy man for his daughter?"

This time those formidable eyebrows contracted as the squire said bluntly, "I know he was not, and if, as I apprehend, you are referring to your brother, let me tell you that Matthew Cardorette was tail over top in love with Meg Llewellyn, and small wonder. If you've seen Brianna—"

"Who?"

"Brianna Llewellyn. Did you not say she came to your home?"

"Yes, but I never heard her given name before."

"Oh. Well, as I was saying, if you've seen Brianna, then you'll understand when I tell you that she is merely a pale copy of her sister. Meg Llewellyn was the most beautiful girl I've ever seen, and Matthew Cardorette was pantingly eager to get a ring on her finger. He badgered her father into agreeing to a quick wedding."

"How do you know all this? Did you become friendly with my brother while he was in the area? Is that why you served as witness to the marriage?" Christopher hoped he had succeeded in keeping his voice neutral.

The squire's keen eyes studied the younger man for a moment before he said coolly, "No, I didn't become close to your brother. For one thing he was flat on his back recovering from his injuries for the first few weeks of his stay in this neighborhood; for another, I imagine he must have been a decade or so my junior. From what little I saw of him I'd say he had more address and charm than was quite good for him, the kind of good-looking, agreeable chap that gets spoiled by all the ladies, starting with his mother, and grows up thinking the Almighty probably intended that his every wish should be gratified, even if He neglected to write it in stone. There wasn't any harm in him that I could see, but no strength of character either."

While Christopher was digesting this unflattering sketch of his brother with a mixture of instinctive resentment and grudging respect for its accuracy, the squire continued. "I imagine I was asked to be a witness because I was still single then and had at least met Matthew Cardorette."

"Were the banns read?" Christopher asked bluntly.

The squire chuckled with amusement. "Your brother didn't wish to wait that long. He drove off to London to get a special license as soon as he and that high-perch phaeton of his had both been sufficiently mended to take to the road again."

Christopher's expression was pensive as he drove back to Lower Melstrum in the vehicle he'd hired from the inn where he was staying until this business was settled one way or another. At this point the only thing he could think of that would invalidate the marriage would be to discover that the Reverend Arthur Llewellyn was not a duly ordained minister of the Church of England but a lifetime fraud, a wild supposition he did not credit for a moment. Mr. Henderson's hazy recollection of the date of the marriage fit neatly into the framework necessary for the child to be his brother's. Unless he could credit the three of them, the pedigreed squire, the locally respected physician, and the timid Brianna Llewellyn with devising a scheme to give Matthew's name to Meg Llewellyn's child after his death and then waiting until the fortuitous announcement of his own betrothal to advance the claim, he must accept this child as his nephew and true inheritor of his brother's honors.

Christopher's maternal grandfather's considerable fortune had come to him on his twenty-fifth birthday. He had never coveted or expected to be his brother's heir, but there was no denying the situation was damned awkward. His cousin George had been shocked and outraged when he'd related the gist of his meeting with Brianna Llewellyn. He'd never seen old George so put out over anything; in fact, he'd had to laugh at his generally imperturbable cousin's strong reaction. He'd even told him banteringly that one would think it was *his* inheritance that had just been snatched away. George had calmed down then and offered to go to investigate the girl's story in his stead. They'd had quite a lively argument before Christopher had finally insisted flatly that it was his place to see the affair through to its conclusion. He might not have held forth so determinedly except that he could not rid his mind of a picture of the timid Brianna Llewellyn cowering before his large stern cousin. It was nonsense, of course; George was always the gentleman, and lovely, shy-seeming young women had been known to commit fraud and worse, but having said that, he remained strangely reluctant to expose Miss Llewellyn to old George's wrath, even though it would be a civilly contained wrath. In trying to account for the strength of this protective attitude toward Miss Llewellyn, Christopher concluded that it had most likely arisen because his own conscience was none too clear on that point. Obviously he had failed to disguise the upsurge of disgust that had overtaken him when it had appeared that Brianna might be one of Matt's light-o'-loves, for she had recoiled from him, those jeweled eyes filling with alarm. He'd felt akin to a brutish bully who had just slapped a trusting child. Though he'd quickly gotten his emotions under control, there had immediately sprung up a wariness in her manner toward him that he had been unable to dispel then or during their subsequent encounter at the inn the following day.

An hour later Christopher was approaching St. George's Rectory in the village of Lower Melstrum after consuming a better-than-expected meal at the inn where the three members of his household who had brought Miss Llewellyn to her home were still lodged awaiting the outcome of his investigation, although they were naturally unaware of the reason for their prolonged stay in a rural backwater. He rode slowly through the village taking note of the number of cottages in need of repairs as winter approached. The high street was unpaved and not much more than a quarter of a mile long with a straggle of small houses at one end and the manse and the doctor's residence among the few more substantial buildings at the far end. He tipped his hat to two women who paused in their conversation at the well to stare at the stranger. The women and a couple of small children rolling large hoops were the only inhabitants he glimpsed on his way through the seemingly somnolent village that came off poorly in comparison with those near Ashleigh both in terms of prosperity and activity.

The haphazard rectory bore signs of having come down in the world also. His critical eye detected peeling paint around the windows and a missing shutter here and there. The dilapidated gate creaked on its rusted hinges and the front garden was overgrown through neglect, though it boasted an astonishing number of late blooming roses of mammoth size and unexpected sweetness. The roofs had been patched and wanted patching again if he was any judge. On a more positive note, he took in the gleaming brass knocker on the solid front door and, on entering the vestibule at the invitation of an aproned female in a hideous mobcap, he breathed in a pleasant aroma of beeswax, lemon oil, and roses, a heady mixture that delayed and diluted the impression of general shabbiness that was inevitable after a closer look at the time-scarred furnishings of the chamber into which he was guided.

Christopher eyed the spindly legged furniture in the small parlor with misgiving before sitting gingerly on the sturdiest-looking piece, a carved-back settee with Queen Anne legs and an upholstered seat. Surprisingly, it was quite comfortable and he relaxed somewhat, glancing around the room with interest. Lord knew he was no connoisseur of such things, but even he could tell that no two pieces bore any relation to one another in style or period, and he could only deduce that the room was furnished with a motley collection of parish cast-offs. He couldn't venture the slightest guess as to the original colors of the faded upholstery of the settee he'd selected, and the curtains and threadbare carpet equally defied positive identification. A massive arrangement of many-hued roses in a white china bowl scented the air and provided the only clear colors in the room's muted palette but entirely failed to disguise the scratched surface of the ungainly round table upon which it rested. One or two attractive ornaments on the mantelpiece and a choice silver candelabrum on a side table made a brave show of good taste, but Christopher could not help marveling that this shabby gentility could have produced such an exquisite creature as Brianna Llewellyn. He'd never come across that name before it fell from Mr. Henderson's lips this morning but had instantly been struck by the peculiar appropriateness for its lovely owner. He'd had all he could do to keep his tongue between his teeth when the squire had casually dismissed Brianna as a pale copy of her elder sister, so inconceivable was it to him that anyone could fail to discern the uniqueness of Miss Llewellyn's gentle beauty. Others, like his fiancée, might be more immediately striking in terms of coloring or brilliance of expression, but that did not detract from the perfection of Brianna's features or reduce her to the status of a "pale copy" of anyone, however beautiful.

The subject of Christopher's musing walked into the parlor at that moment wearing another black dress. Her head was uncovered in her own home, revealing a wealth of rich chestnut hair gleaming with red highlights leaving him to wonder in what possible way the elder sister could have outshone the younger. Miss Llewellyn's expression was guarded as she greeted him in a low voice.

"How do you do, Lord Ashleigh?"

"What has happened to you? You have even less color than the last time I saw you, and you look . . . exhausted, drained. Have you been ill?"

The girl blinked thick lashes, taken aback at his vehemence. She stopped her progress into the room and clasped her hands together in front of her, swallowing nervously. "I . . . I . . . no, it isn't I who have been ill, but Jamie."

"What's wrong with him? Is it serious?"

"Yes, he's been ill with bronchitis and there is always the danger of sinking into pneumonia with that, you know. It is how his mother died. Molly and I have been alternating in the sickroom, so we are both somewhat tired, but Doctor Chamfrey said this morning that he believes Jamie has begun to improve at last." Her smile was tremulous and radiant, her relief evident.

"May I see him?"

As Brianna hesitated, clearly reluctant to agree to this request, irritation rose in a slow tide within Christopher. He could feel his teeth go tight, but he made the effort to keep his voice uninflected as he challenged, "Do you not think I have a right to see my brother's child?"

"Does that mean you now accept that your brother did indeed marry my sister?"

Christopher's lips softened into a half-smile as he withstood a serious examination from sea-green eyes. "I believe Matt intended to marry your sister with all the authority of church and state behind him. Will that satisfy you until I've seen the register?"

An answering half-smile trembled on her lovely mouth for a second before Brianna said apologetically, "I'm afraid Jamie isn't at his best right now. In general he is a sunny child, but after a sennight in bed with painful coughing and horrid-tasting medicines at regular intervals, he is feeling very sorry for himself at present and is inclined to be a bit irritable."

"I have the hide of a rhinoceros," Christopher assured her solemnly as he crossed in front of her to open the door.

At his gesture of invitation, she passed through the doorway and led the way upstairs without another word. She stopped outside a door and knocked softly before opening it. Christopher obeyed her beckoning finger and followed her into a small bed-chamber. A handsome middle-aged woman with graying blond hair neatly braided atop her head was seated beside the bed. She rose slowly as he approached, lowering the book she was reading to her side. Though aware he was being studied by a pair of large blue eyes, his own passed quickly over the woman to come to rest on the child in the bed.

Christopher inhaled sharply. The unsmiling little boy had Matt's face, his own curly dark hair, and large, heavily lashed green eyes—his aunt's eyes.

Their mutual inspection was interrupted by Miss Llewellyn's soft voice introducing him to the dark-clad woman whom she referred to as her oldest friend, Miss Molly Lloyd. After an exchange of civil bows, Christopher turned back to the child. Brianna had hesitated, evidently unsure how to announce him to the lad. Christopher held out his hand.

"How do you do, James Arthur Cardorette? I am Christopher Edward Cardorette and I am your uncle."

The boy's eyes grew even rounder. "I didn't even know I had an uncle," he said in a hoarse little voice.

"Manners, Jamie," his aunt reminded quietly.

The child obediently offered his small hand and parroted, "How do you do, sir?"

"Very well, thank you, James, but I understand from your aunt that you have been feeling rather poorly just lately. I hope you will soon be up and about."

"Thank you, sir; I am better today. Sir—"

"Uncle Christopher, or Uncle Kit, if you prefer," Christopher interjected smilingly.

"Uncle Christopher," the boy amended, unsmiling in his earnestness. "If you and I have the same name, does that mean that you are my father's brother like Auntie Bree is my mother's sister?"

"That's right."

"Then where is my father, Uncle Christopher? Auntie Bree said he went away a long time ago and he never came back. She doesn't know when he is coming back. Do you know, Uncle Christopher?"

"Jamie, dearest—"

"He won't be able to come back, James, because he is dead, like your mother," Christopher said, overriding Brianna's interruption. "I know that must make you sad because you would like to meet him. It makes me sad too, but it cannot be helped."

"Why didn't you tell me my father was dead?" the child demanded, rounding on the distressed young woman who had taken a step nearer the bed.

"Your aunt didn't tell you because she didn't know until I told her just now," Christopher said firmly, determined to get the inevitable awkwardness behind them as quickly as possible.

"Why did he never come to see me or my mother?" The boy directed this query to his newly found uncle, uncompromising in his search for the truth.

"Jamie, darling, you mustn't talk any longer. It's time for your medicine. Your throat is sore and your chest will hurt again if you do not rest your voice."

Christopher ignored Brianna's attempt to stave off a scene that must occur sooner or later. The child had a right to know as much of the truth as his understanding could cope with. He said coolly, "Your father went away before you were born, James, so far away that he never knew about you. If he had known, he would have wished very much to see you."

"Why did he go away?" Jamie was unrelenting, the clear green eyes very unchildlike in their expression as they fixed themselves unwaveringly on the visitor.

"I don't know the answer to that, old chap, nor does Auntie Bree," Christopher said over Brianna's little caught breath. "Only your father and mother could really answer that question, but one day I will tell you all about your father when he was a boy and show you his portrait. Would you like that?"

For another moment the young earl continued to stare searchingly into his uncle's calm countenance, then a brilliant smile spread across his own, revealing teeth like small pearls and rendering him nearer to his true age than he'd yet appeared, solemn and accusing by turns.

"I'd like that very much," Jamie said shyly, then added as a polite afterthought, "Thank you very much, Uncle Christopher."

"You're quite welcome. And now, my lad, it's time you took that medicine your aunt mentioned to speed your recovery. I need to talk with her now, so we'll leave you in Miss Lloyd's capable hands. Good-bye for a little while, James."

"Good-bye, Uncle Christopher."

Christopher murmured a farewell to the older woman, who had been watching him measuringly throughout the short session. He guided Brianna out the door with a purposeful hand on her arm when she would have lingered. She did not resist, saying nothing all the way down the stairs. Once back in the parlor, however, she found her tongue and pounced on him like an angry kitten.

"How could you be so cruel to a sick child?"

"In what way cruel?" His voice was cool, only his elevated brows expressed surprise at the attack.

"Telling him his father was dead in that bald fashion!"

"He had to learn the truth sometime. What better moment than when he'd expressed a strong interest in the subject? And why did you not tell him yourself? You knew I was in Lower Melstrum. Doctor Chamfrey said he was coming here after our little talk this morning."

"I have scarcely had an opportunity. I arrived home to find him exceedingly ill. Not only that, but I could scarcely predict whether or not you would choose to repudiate the connection." She sounded defensive, but unhappy too, and Christopher lost all desire to spar with her.

"I could tell by his persistence that the boy really wished to learn the story behind his birth. He must know he is different from the other children in the village who have two parents," he said gently. "I told him only what I thought was necessary at this stage. The rest can wait until he is older. Are you really angry with me?"

The hint of anxiety in his voice must have disarmed her because she said hastily, "No . . . that is, I suppose I am angry at the whole situation because I feel so helpless to shield Jamie, but I do realize that none of it is your fault. I am persuaded you did what you thought best for him and I am sorry I snapped at you just now. Please forgive me."

"Anything, anytime," he said promptly, and watched her lashes sink to cover momentary confusion.

"You must wish to see the entry in the parish register," she put in hurriedly.

Christopher allowed himself to be led into the church office where he viewed the pertinent entries in silence, recognizing his brother's carelessly scrawled signature. Matt had signed his full name but not his courtesy title of Viscount Daimley, evidence that he had indeed concealed his identity during his stay in Lower Melstrum. The silence remained unbroken until they returned to the shabby parlor.

"May I offer you some refreshment, sir?" Brianna asked, seeming all at once aware of her position as hostess. "I believe there is still some of the sherry my father liked."

"Thank you, Brianna," he said, deliberately using her name. She looked startled but turned away without comment as she unearthed a bottle and glass from a much-scarred ebony cabinet.

"Here you are, sir."

"Christopher," he said as his fingers touched hers on the stem of the glass. "We are one family after all." She averted her eyes and tried surreptitiously and unsuccessfully to remove her fingers from under his on the glass. "Christopher," he repeated.

"Christopher," she said in a husky voice, and pulled her fingers free, backing away a step. "Please sit down."

He noted the absence of any appellation, but decided not to press the matter at this point. He had no desire to strew difficulties in the path of the upcoming discussion. "Well then, shall we proceed to the next stage?"

"Next stage?"

"Yes. How soon can you be ready? Two days? Three?"

"Ready for what?"

"To remove to Ashleigh, of course."

Her lips parted, but this time she did not echo his words. Instead, after a pause, she said carefully, "Do you mean that you would like us to make you a visit, sir?"

"Certainly not. I was referring to your permanent removal to Ashleigh." Seeing the appalled look on her face, Christopher made an effort to keep from showing his impatience. "Surely you must have envisioned this outcome when you came to Ashleigh?"

"Of course I did not! In the first place, I had no real expectation of ever discovering Matthew's origins; I was merely fulfilling a promise I made to my father. If I thought anything about what would happen if, contrary to my belief, I did find him, I suppose I hoped that he would provide for his son's education for a profession."

Christopher's eyes never left her dismayed face, assessing the sincerity of her passionate denial. "But after seeing Ashleigh Court, you must have realized that Matt's family was well able to assume the responsibility for the boy's upbringing."

"I apprehended that you must be wealthy beyond anything we ever dreamed of, but that doesn't mean that Molly and I desire to become your dependents. If you wish to make Jamie an allowance we shall be very grateful, but there is absolutely no necessity for us to become a charge on your purse also. The three of us shall do well enough remaining in Lower Melstrum, which has always been our home."

"You and Miss Lloyd may wish to remain in Herefordshire. I

cannot compel you to return with me, but Matt's son will be raised at Ashleigh, make no mistake about that, whatever your personal decision."

Brianna's cheeks had whitened at the softly uttered ultimatum and tears sprang to her eyes. She was trembling as she charged, "How can you sit there and threaten to take my sister's child, the only family I have in the world, away from me? Meg gave him to me before she died and I swore to her that I would take care of him!"

"It is my fervent hope that you will keep that promise . . . at Ashleigh. The last thing I desire in the world is to threaten you, Brianna, or part you from the boy. But you must know that no court would uphold your claim to James over that of his father's family. This is a contest you can never win, my dear." As she continued to stare at him in dumb misery, he switched tactics, saying softly, "I am a little pained that you seem so reluctant to give me a chance. I believe we can make all of you comfortable and welcome at Ashleigh."

"Look around you," she cried with an outflung hand that indicated their meager surroundings. "Is it not painfully obvious that I could never fit into the kind of life you must lead? I don't belong on a grand estate like Ashleigh. Jamie doesn't belong there!"

"You are mistaken, Brianna, especially in your last statement. James at least does belong there. Ashleigh Court and everything that goes with it is his."

"Wh . . . what are you saying?" Translucent green eyes pleaded with him to unsay his words while one slender hand crept to her throat in wordless apprehension.

"Have you not yet guessed the truth? Did it never occur to you that I might be *younger* than Matthew? Well, I *am* the younger by four years."

"Then . . . then Jamie . . . " Brianna swallowed and fell silent, unable to force the words from her constricted throat while her nervous fingers made pathetic little scraping motions at the neck of her gown and her eyes clung desperately to his.

Christopher came to her rescue, saying lightly, "James Arthur Cardorette is the sixth Earl Ashleigh and the owner of Ashleigh Court."

4

Two days after his momentous conversation with Brianna Llewellyn in the rectory parlor, Christopher set off in solitude for London. He'd been forced to accept the doctor's verdict that it would be dangerous to subject a young child to the rigors of traveling until he had more completely recovered from his bout with bronchitis. For Christopher this meant a change in his own plans. It had been his intention to escort the occupants of the rectory to Ashleigh, but it really made no sense to linger idly in Herefordshire when there were equally vital matters awaiting his personal attention elsewhere. Prominent among these was the necessity of breaking the news of his disinheritance to his fiancée before any rumors to that effect reached her. He also needed to see his solicitor to set all legal steps in motion for declaring James his father's rightful successor. This being the case, he'd reluctantly left his traveling carriage in Herefordshire to await Doctor Chamfrey's release of his patient. He'd sent the abigail back to Ashleigh by mail coach when Brianna had decided she preferred the extra space in the carriage to accommodate a probably restless youngster to maid service on the journey. He'd ridden to Herefordshire but elected to hire a post chaise on the longer trip to London, especially since it appeared a period of inclement weather was coming in from the west.

Any lingering doubts he'd harbored that Brianna Llewellyn had set out to feather her own nest by seeking assistance from any wealthy relatives her nephew might own had been entirely dispelled in Herefordshire. Utter dismay was not too strong a term to describe her reaction to James's sudden eminence. She had sat there in the faded parlor of the only home she'd ever known with silent tears running down her cheeks, her hands clasped tightly in her lap. He had not known what to say to comfort her, but after a moment she had blurted, "Why could not Matthew Cardorette have been an ordinary man who would have appreciated Meg's loving goodness and been pleased to have a wonderful son like Jamie?"

Before he could frame any kind of answer, she'd looked him straight in the eye and said sorrowfully, "You have every reason to dislike us, sir. I much regret I ever undertook to uncover a past better left buried. We have robbed you of what you had a right to believe was your inheritance."

More touched than he would have believed by her concern, he'd tried his best to convince her that he'd never expected to be his father's heir in the first place and was far from a pauper even now. Certainly he stood in no need of sympathy. He could only hope his words had been effective since he had no desire to figure as an object of pity in her estimation. At least she had offered no further resistance to coming to Ashleigh to live.

As the miles ticked by, Christopher's thoughts winged ahead to what he might expect in London. He banished Brianna Llewellyn's image from his memory and concentrated on the beautiful person of his fiancée, Lady Selina Milliken. On his return to England in August, he'd called on Matt's bereaved betrothed as a matter of form. In a lavender-colored gown of half-mourning which flattered her golden coloring, she had made an immediate impact that was reinforced each time he saw her by the discovery of some new talent or accomplishment. Hers was a vibrant personality backed by a quickness of understanding that lent her conversation a brilliance and wit not often found allied to outstanding beauty of face and form. She sang like a nightingale, shone in a ballroom, scintillated at a dinner table and delighted with subtle promise in a tête-à-tête. Lady Selina was deliciously responsive to his overtures without abrogating in the slightest degree the role of precious object to be won. Her confidence in her powers of attraction was so superb, she was never betrayed into becoming the huntress if he pulled back momentarily from the pursuit. He was captivated and intrigued but not so fascinated that his appreciation lost the element of clear-sightedness that had characterized what he finally admitted was a courtship. He'd known beyond question that whatever she might have felt for his brother was over and done with. The lovely lady was heart-whole and his for the asking, though he did not fall into the error of believing she was in love with him. The more he considered the idea, the more reasons he found to make her an offer. He was seven-and-twenty and had never experienced the kind of love that leads to the abandonment of self, but he found Lady Selina marvelously desirable from a personal point of view, and she would certainly grace the role of his countess and mistress of Ashleigh in the eyes of society. In some sense, he felt he owed her another chance at the position Matt's death had denied her. He questioned whether the lady had a heart to lose, but on the other hand, he was not seeking mindless adoration; at least she would never bore him. That last quality had tipped the scales at the time and he had gone on to make a formal offer for Lady Selina's hand. He had been duly accepted, sweetly by the young lady, and gratefully by her father, the Earl of Ormand, who had two daughters still in the schoolroom to establish and a genteel rather than large fortune.

That was September, only two short months ago, but it seemed as if a lifetime had gone by, for now everything had changed. He was no longer the Earl of Ashleigh; in fact, he had never really held that honor or commanded that fortune even while briefly enjoying the benefits of both. A secret marriage and an unheralded birth had put that eminence out of his reach years ago. Ever since Brianna Llewellyn had crashed into his life, not literally as his brother had done into her sister's life, but with an equal impact, he had been asking himself at odd moments how he felt about this *bouleversement* of fate without emerging any the wiser. Oddly enough, he didn't feel different inside himself in any aspect he could put a finger on, but he couldn't deny the awkwardness of the whole situation was daunting.

There was no getting around the secret marriage, but he owed it to his family name to keep the fact that Matt was planning to marry without ascertaining whether his legal wife was still alive from becoming public. Perhaps for James's sake, Brianna would acquiesce to letting the world believe that her father had at some point told his absent son-in-law that his daughter had died without also telling him of his child's birth. Christopher did not deceive himself that the thought of traducing the character of the father she revered would be other than abhorrent to her. She would hate him for asking it of her, deservedly so, but it did seem the least damaging version of the past for the boy to live with, as well as preserving his family's good name. Perhaps there was some way she could be spared the knowledge of the distasteful necessity to blur the truth of her nephew's background.

Meanwhile, there was the awkward situation awaiting him in London. Lord Ormond could be pardoned any chagrin he might harbor—to put it no higher—at twice having lost a large marriage settlement made on his daughter by the Earl of Ashleigh. He had every right to nullify the agreement even if his daughter wished to go through with the marriage. She was a diamond of the first

water and had been hotly sought after. She was still only twenty,
young enough that another Season was no humiliation, especially
under the circumstances. There was time enough to achieve a
more brilliant match than he now represented. It was, after all,
what she would have done had he not come along during her
mourning period and made the effort unnecessary. On the other
hand, he was no pauper, and she might consider it a case of "a
bird in the hand." Christopher had every confidence that his
strong-minded fiancée wound bend her father to her will when
she made her decision.

Which way would Selina jump? This question and its corollary:
how did he hope she'd jump? occupied his mind for the better
part of two long dull days on the road. Despite her pretty pretense, his betrothed was no more in love with him than he was
with her. He had no legitimate complaint since he had invited the
situation by his own unsentimental actions. It hadn't troubled him
at the time and he'd been telling himself repeatedly that it didn't
trouble him now. Unhappily for his peace of mind, his heart had
begun to reject this statement. A marriage of convenience, even
with a superlatively desirable woman no longer seemed good
enough; he wanted more.

When he'd initiated a lighthearted campaign to woo Selina in
the approved fashion last summer he had not really taken into
consideration the fact that reigning beauties who are courted from
the moment they make their bows to society tend to regard constant adulation as their due. By the time he had gone down to
Ashleigh to set things in order for his marriage, leaving his betrothed to assemble her bride clothes and supervise wedding
preparations, he had already begun reevaluating the advantages
and disadvantages of taking an Incomparable to wife.

And then he had met Brianna Llewellyn and discovered that
this shy girl, for so she seemed in comparison with the sophisti-
cated Selina, though Brianna was actually slightly the elder,
aroused in him a disconcerting emotion that he did not associate
with his betrothed. It wasn't romantic love as he understood the
sentiment from the pens of poets but rather an instinctive desire to
protect her from the cruel buffets of fate. It might be considered a
laudable sentiment if only he could be sure it was sufficiently divorced from any feeling of possessiveness. Even had his reaction
to Brianna been one of supreme indifference, having two young
women with nothing in common residing under the same roof
could not be other than awkward. Being obliged to house someone who aroused personal feelings in one's husband would cer-

tainly be distasteful to a new bride if she were perceptive enough to discern those feelings. Selina, Christopher was persuaded, possessed the required degree of perception. He also judged her capable of making Brianna feel totally unwelcome at Ashleigh in all the subtle ways women had of exerting their superiority over less-favored females. Taken all together, the straws in the wind seemed to bode ill for the success of the odd ménage that recent events had created.

As the post chaise rumbled through the outskirts of the metropolis, Christopher almost found himself hoping his fiancée would decide she could do better for herself than to settle for a mere "Honorable" with a comfortable rather than a large fortune and an estate that could not be described as a showplace and did not include a house in London.

Lady Selina Milliken sat before her mirrored dressing table trying the effect of a hair ornament she had purchased that morning on New Bond Street. She twisted her head this way and that in an effort to assess the effectiveness of the green-and-blue enameled designs against the silver of the high comb and the gold of her hair.

"No, Mamie, hold the mirror more to the left," she bade the tiny maid who was poised behind her with a hand mirror. "Hold it higher and tilt it toward the dressing table. No, that's no good—away from the table. Ah, that's better. Perhaps it would show to greater advantage if the comb were placed in front of the topknot. What do you think, Mamie?"

"I think it's beautiful at the back, my lady. How would you anchor it in front? There's not enough hair there for it to stay put."

"We'd have to make one fat curl in front of the topknot to support the comb. Let's try that, Mamie."

"Now, my lady? Isn't this your 'at home' day? Suppose someone comes to see you?"

"Then 'someone' will have to wait while you rearrange my hair again quickly, and I shall grow impatient and scold you all the while, making you nervous and all thumbs," her mistress said, directing a playful smile up at the skinny young girl still patiently holding the mirror. "Shall we try a fat curl in front of the topknot, Mamie?" she added coaxingly.

The abigail was about to remove the pins securing the carefully disposed curls atop her mistress's head when the bedchamber door opened and Lady Ormond hurried in.

"There you are, my dear. I have a lovely surprise for you. Lord Ashleigh is here. He is in the green saloon."

"Ashleigh here? He told me he would not be back in town much before the wedding."

The expression on her daughter's lovely face was more speculative than welcoming, and seeing the avid interest in the maid's face, Lady Ormond said sharply, "That will be all, Mamie. You may go."

"Yes, ma'am." The girl dropped her eyes, dipped a curtsey and left the room.

The glance Lady Ormond returned to her daughter was a bit troubled as she watched the girl reposition a pin in her hair and give the arrangement of curls a final pat before picking up a hare's-foot brush which she proceeded to dust over her already perfect skin. "Selina, you . . . you do *like* Lord Ashleigh, do you not?"

"Of course I like him, Mama." The brush was suspended as the girl examined her complexion closely and rubbed off a speck of powder. She did not meet her mother's eyes in the mirror. "Why do you ask?"

"Well, I have sometimes thought . . . that is, I know it was a crushing blow when poor Matthew was killed in that shocking fashion just before the wedding last year. He was so devoted to you."

"It was a pretty dismal time," her daughter agreed, reaching for a flagon of perfume.

"You bore up splendidly during those dreadful early months of your mourning when every social activity was forbidden you."

Lady Selina's slim shoulders hunched once in dismissal. "I would not have it said of me that I did not give Matthew's memory its due."

"No, of course not, dearest. That's why your father and I were so pleased when Matthew's brother began to call. No one could possibly criticize you for receiving him whenever he chose to come here. He was practically family, after all, and it was natural that you should console each other. And when he proposed, we were delighted for you to have a second chance at happiness."

"And a title and all the Cardorette money?" suggested the girl brightly.

"Do not speak in that vulgar fashion, even in jest, Selina; it is most unbecoming."

"What is it you are trying to say, Mama? We are keeping Ashleigh waiting."

Lady Ormond was twisting her wedding ring around on her finger. "Only that before he left town, you seemed a bit different with Lord Ashleigh than you were with his brother, rather casual at times so that people might conceivably gather the impression that you are not as sincerely attached to him as you were to Matthew. I know you would not wish to wound him by any lack of those little attentions a man has a right to expect from the woman who has accepted his suit."

Her daughter laughed merrily at the anxious face in the mirror. "Dearest Mama, would it set your mind at rest if I told you that Christopher Cardorette is a very different proposition than his brother? Matthew was wildly infatuated with me and let the world know about it, which can never be less than gratifying to a female's vanity. But Christopher's is a much more reserved personality, and he would not be pleased to have a fiancée who fawned all over him in public."

"But he is in love with you." The statement had the uncertainty of a question, and Lady Selina considered it thoughtfully as she applied perfume to her wrists and throat.

"Is he? It's possible, but not probable, I think. Christopher's feelings are not out in the open for everyone to see. I don't know him well enough to judge if he has any real feeling for me. Oh, he likes me well enough," she added after reading dismay in her parent's countenance, "and he admires my looks and even appreciates my intelligence, which is more than Matthew did. In some ways I actually prefer him to Matthew, and he is even more handsome, though I do wish he were a bit taller so we would make a more striking picture together. He won't be as easy to handle as his brother, unfortunately, being much more intelligent, but it would be a real accomplishment for any woman to bring him round her thumb. I have accepted the challenge," she finished gaily, "so you have nothing to fear, Mama."

Lady Selina stoppered the perfume bottle and put it down with a firm little click before rising gracefully from the bench. She twitched her green-sprigged white muslin skirts straighter about her slender, well-curved form and said, "There, I'm ready. Shall we go down, Mama?"

"Actually, Lord Ashleigh asked if he might see you alone for a few minutes, dearest," Lady Ormond replied, her restless glance skittering over her beautiful, poised daughter to the doorway beyond.

Lady Selina's rounded chin ascended another degree or two, accenting the lovely line of her throat. "A private greeting—how romantic of him," she declared, sweeping out the door her still-uneasy parent was holding open.

Christopher acknowledged an extremely rare case of nerves as he paced about the tastefully decorated room Lord Ormond's butler had shown him into. He'd experienced this same internal jitteriness awaiting Ney's last two cavalry charges up the hill at Waterloo when they'd had barely anything left with which to stop him. He tried to laugh at the comparison that had come unbidden into his mind. The scene about to be played out in this room was scarcely a life-or-death situation as in Belgium. In fact, there was no similarity at all, particularly since he did not even know how he wished the current crisis to be resolved. Still, the unpleasant sensation of his heart beating in the pit of his stomach like a tom-tom made sitting still unbearable, so he continued to pace aimlessly about the room while he awaited the arrival of his fiancée.

He seemed to be doing a lot of waiting about in strange rooms for people these days. He'd had time to read every title in Squire Henderson's bookcases when he was in Herefordshire, and Selina had already kept him pacing for fifteen minutes. As he swung around he bumped into the curved leg of a handsome French side table with a superb marquetry top. He allowed its beauty to impinge on his thoughts momentarily. This room with its rich green damask fabric and intricately patterned Turkey carpet was certainly a far cry from the chilly threadbare parlor in the rectory of St. George's Church in Lower Melstrum. What a depressingly drab setting that had been for a girl as lovely as Brianna Llewellyn. She belonged in a room like this one with its predominantly green color scheme to complement her eyes. It struck him suddenly that it was in this very room that he had made his formal offer to Selina, and his mouth pulled in at the corners. It might well be the setting for the end of their betrothal also.

He heard a light step outside the door and pulled up short. Selina entered and came quickly toward him with a smile on her lips and her hands gracefully extended.

"Christopher, what a lovely surprise!"

He'd forgotten how beautiful she was with her well-delineated features set in a complexion of peaches-and-cream lusciousness. Her figure was luscious too, he recalled suddenly as he accepted the clear invitation in her eyes and pulled her into his arms. Her body was firm and ripely curved with a delectably small waist and long legs. He kissed her upturned lips quickly, aware of a heady scent, sweet but a trifle overpowering at close quarters, and raised his head to smile into large blue eyes only a few inches below his own.

"That was quite a welcome."

She laughed, flicking her lashes down demurely, then up again as she drew herself out of his loose embrace. "I didn't expect to see you back in town much before the wedding, Christopher. I understood there were a number of renovations you wished to personally oversee at Ashleigh. Are you here for good now?"

Christopher's smile had faded as she spoke, and now he said abruptly, "No, something has happened that will affect my—our—future, and I have come to break the news to you."

Lady Selina's smile had frozen at the rare serious look on her betrothed's face. "Shall we sit down?" she suggested, leading him over to a green damask sofa with carved arms. "What is this ominous news, my lord?"

As Christopher related the recent discovery of his brother's secret marriage and the heir he had not known of, he kept his eyes fixed on his fiancée's face. He saw the initial shock she could not disguise in dilated pupils and parted lips, and could only admire the swiftness with which she controlled her reaction. She sat perfectly still, scarcely seeming to breathe as she listened with concentrated attention until he had finished with an account of his investigations in Herefordshire and his conclusion that the long-ago marriage had been entirely legal. "So you see, I have sold you a bad bargain and—"

"Of course you did no such thing," she intervened forcefully. "There is absolutely no question of any blame to you in all this." She met his eyes squarely.

Surprised gratitude welled up in Christopher for her sportsmanship, but he persisted. "Nevertheless, it remains that you agreed to marry the Earl of Ashleigh with all that the position entails. Naturally our agreement is nullified by these revelations, as your father will be quick to point out, and rightly so."

"Let's leave my father out of this for the moment, shall we?" Lady Selina's intelligent eyes had been studying him frankly, almost with calculation. Now she said, "I agreed to marry Christopher Cardorette, not the Earl of Ashleigh. Do you think me such a fair-weather friend as to back out of an engagement for such a reason?" She placed a finger against his lips when they would have opened, and shook her head. "Hear me out please, Christopher. There is only this to add. Unless *you* desire to be released from our engagement, I say we proceed with the wedding, supposing that my father does not disown me, of course."

She smiled at the humor of this absurd thought, and Christopher molded his mouth into a matching smile, knowing she had left him no choice, and unable to say whether he was pleased or the opposite. "It shall be as you wish, my lady," he said in his customary light manner.

"I hope it will be as we both wish," she amended softly.

"Of course," he agreed, wondering at the slight challenge he sensed behind her words.

Christopher was still puzzling over the momentous meeting with his betrothed when he returned to Hanover Square hours later to join her and her parents for an evening at the theater. Before today he would have sworn that Selina was no more in love with him than he was with her, and he'd have bet his entire, greatly-reduced fortune that she'd have availed herself of the opportunity to bow out of the engagement using her father's withdrawn permission as a shield for public consumption to cloak her own desires. She had not done so, which should prove that she did indeed love him, but some extra sense deep inside himself still questioned this explanation for her action. Yet he could come up with no motive other than love that would cause a toast of the town to accept a mediocre match when she could most likely still achieve a brilliant one.

Christopher would have been comforted to learn that the mother of his intended bride, with a lifetime's knowledge of her offspring to guide her, was no less puzzled than he by her daughter's action in persisting with the engagement. Lady Ormond had naturally been shocked at the news of the diminished stature of the man who proposed to marry her eldest daughter, but the greater shock by far was administered by Selina herself when she calmly informed her parent of her intentions.

"But . . . *why*, dearest? You've as good as admitted your attachment to Ashleigh—Mr. Cardorette, I should say—is not very strong," protested the confused matron when her daughter found her in her boudoir immediately after Christopher's departure. "Under the changed circumstances no one will criticize you. We can put it about that your father has forbidden the contract. Why should you persist with the betrothal?"

"Because he *expected* me to renege! I could see it in his eyes!" The golden curls fairly quivered with wrath as Selina tossed her head impatiently.

"Well, of course he did. Honor demanded that he offer to release you, and Ashleigh—Mr. Cardorette—is an honorable man."

Lady Selina was not even listening to her mother as she stalked about the small room, unable to contain her passion. "I have never expended so much effort on any other man before, but obviously he never believed for a second that I had fallen in love with him!"

"What has that to say to anything?"

"*Everything!* Christopher was stunned when I said I'd still marry him. Well, I shall make him fall in love with me if it's the last thing I do. He'll *beg* me to marry him!"

"But you have already told him you intend to marry him!"

Lady Selina stopped her stalking and looked fully at her bewildered parent. The storminess died out of her eyes and she went over and hugged her mother briefly. "Do not mind my temper, Mama. I am an absolute beast. It is just that that odious man put me into such a passion."

She would have left the room on that odd remark, but her mother called out to her, "If you think him odious, how can you contemplate marrying him, especially now? You would do better to part immediately."

Lady Selina had laughed, her good humor partially restored. "As to that, I am not absolutely certain that I shall marry him in the end. We shall see." And she had gone out, leaving her mother more limp and fearful than ever of what the immediate future held in store.

Christopher, not being privy to this illuminating discussion, was left to ponder and seek additional clues to the mystery of the female character, at least as embodied in the person of his fiancée as he was admitted to Lord Ormond's house at half after five to find the family awaiting him in the main drawing room.

Lady Selina dazzled the eye of the beholder in a gown of jonquille silk trimmed with golden ribbons, her burnished curls gleaming like old gold atop her elegantly poised head. She greeted Christopher warmly and reminded her father with a playful tap on his arm that she had forbidden any mention of dull subjects like portions and settlements that evening.

"Miss O'Neill is giving her first performance as Elwina in *Percy* tonight and we must all be in a receptive mood to appreciate her artistry."

Christopher bowed in smiling acquiescence, but his glance met that of his prospective father-in-law over his betrothed's head. "I inquired for you today, sir, here and at your club but had the mis-

fortune to miss you. I shall call here tomorrow morning, if it will
be convenient."

"Certainly, my boy. Nasty business this," the earl added. He
cleared his throat, but his daughter held up a slender hand
adorned with two sparkling rings.

"Not another word, Papa," she warned gaily.

Lady Selina's sparkle rivaled that of her jewelry as she kept
them all entertained on the drive to the Opera House in Covent
Garden with an amusing flow of anecdotes designed to bring
Christopher up-to-date on the social doings in town during the
three weeks he had been away in the country. When they entered
the theater, she took her fiancé's arm to ascend the grand staircase
between the two rows of Ionic columns that framed the Grecian
lanterns hanging between each pair of columns. As they passed
through the antechamber at the top of the stairs, past Rossi's
statue of Shakespeare, toward the entrance to the earl's box in the
lower tier, Christopher was conscious of the many admiring and
envious glances he and his beautiful companion attracted, but apparently Selina had eyes only for him.

Christopher would have had to be a boorish clod indeed to fail
to enjoy the delights that evening offered. The play was entertaining, the performance of the celebrated Miss O'Neill everything
her past successes promised, and one of London's most beautiful
young women was putting herself out to please him. During the
intervals, their box was a popular gathering place for members of
the younger set who were not off hunting in the shires in mid-No-
vember. It was no surprise to see that Lady Selina was the magnet
that drew them. He had not expected her to retire behind a screen
when he left for Ashleigh, especially as her mourning period was
coming to an end.

Christopher felt all the awkwardness of his own altered position, however, when the first visitors greeted him by the title he
no longer could claim, but when he opened his mouth to begin the
tedious explanation that would have the town in an uproar of gossip the next day, he caught the slight negative shake of the earl's
head and thankfully refrained from spoiling the pleasant evening.
Lord Ormond was quite right; explanations could wait until he
had settled the business with his solicitor and the court. He might
even be fortunate enough to escape the town's reaction by delaying any personal revelations until just before his return to Ashleigh. At this thought, he experienced a pang of guilt for the
unenviable position in which his fiancée and her family would be
placed when the news eventually surfaced, but his remaining in

London would not prevent the inevitable gossip about so news-worthy an event.

In any case, remaining in town was out of the question. On his way to London he had written to his cousin George to acquaint him with the outcome of his investigations in Herefordshire and ask him to instruct the housekeeper to have the nursery suite readied for its future occupant and his two custodians. There was no doubt in his mind that George and the efficient staff at Ashleigh would shortly have everything in readiness to receive the young earl, but naturally he must be there to personally welcome his nephew when he arrived, and not just for the child's sake either. Brianna Llewellyn had been very subdued and forlorn when he had last seen her in the faded rectory parlor in Lower Melstrum. She had accepted the necessity of the move with her reason, but heart and spirit had silently grieved at the idea of leaving her childhood home and the place where her dear ones were buried. He had understood this without a word being said by her, and he thought he could appreciate what would be her state of apprehension on arriving at Ashleigh Court. Everything about the Court was bound to seem overwhelmingly large and alien at first, and he wanted to be there to assist her in accustoming herself to the new reality of their changed lives.

Not knowing just how soon Doctor Chamfrey would permit his small patient to travel, Christopher was full of impatience to accomplish his business in London so he could return home in good time to receive the little party from Herefordshire. With luck and goodwill, the newly enlarged family at Ashleigh would have gotten past the initial stage of awkwardness and grown comfortable with each other by the time he brought his bride home.

5

Christopher's session with Lord Ormond on Sunday morning was cordial in tone, though the earl made no bones about admitting that he would prefer another match for his daughter in light of the changed circumstances. He was quick to disclaim any personal animus toward Christopher in this position, a compliment of a sort that was acknowledged by the recipient with a correct little bow. In his turn Christopher explained that these same reduced circumstances compelled him to make a corresponding reduction in the markedly generous marriage settlement they had originally negotiated. Understandably disappointed, the earl pointed out that, as his nephew's guardian, Christopher would continue to enjoy the income from the Ashleigh estate during the boy's minority, but he was ultimately persuaded that the court of Chancery would look askance at having a considerable portion of that income diverted to the use of a woman whose child would not in the expected course of things stand to inherit the property. Christopher was more than ready to guarantee a fixed income, or "pin money," to his wife, however, and this was accepted by the earl, who could not fail to be aware, his prospective son-in-law pointed out gently, that very few women ever received marriage settlements of any kind.

"That might be true for most women, but my daughter can take her pick of the most eligible men in the land," the earl returned with pardonable pride. "She seems set on having you for some reason or other, so there's nothing more to be said. Selina has always known her own mind, and there's never any budging her once she's made it up."

Christopher said all that was proper to the occasion and bowed himself out of the earl's study, relieved to have the most delicate item on his list of pressing business safely behind him.

He was immediately pounced on by his betrothed, who inveigled him into escorting her to church, accompanied, as he quickly discovered—but not quickly enough to recall a pressing engagement—by her mother and two younger sisters. In his former regiment Captain Cardorette had been famous for his even disposition, but he was not partial to the company of school-age females with piercing voices combined with a deplorable tendency to succumb to the giggles at unseemly moments. By the time the noisy party returned to Hanover Square, Christopher felt as if hundreds of critical and curious eyes had bored holes into his back, but he had not managed to muster a sufficient amount of resolution to refuse his betrothed's invitation to lunch *en famille* at the earl's residence.

Fortunately, their father's presence exercised a beneficial quieting effect on the exuberant Miss Caroline and Miss Emily, and lunch passed off quite pleasantly. In due course, a tray of cheese and fruit was placed upon the table. Lady Selina popped a grape into her mouth and turned to her fiancé.

"It is indeed fortunate that you are in town at present, Christopher, because Papa is promised for one of his dull political dinners tomorrow. You will be able to escort us to the theater in his stead, will you not?" She flashed him a confident smile. "They are reviving *The Beggar's Opera* at Covent Garden, a play I have always wished to see."

"*The Beggar's Opera*?" Lady Ormond echoed in tones of disapproval before Christopher could speak. "I do not consider that play at all suitable for the viewing of young ladies, Selina."

"Why, what can you mean, Mama?" The brilliant blue eyes focused on her parent with patent surprise. "It has been one of the most popular theatrical offerings for the last century at least."

"That may be so, but it is still a bawdy tale that I do not consider fit fare for anyone of delicate sensibilities or tender years."

"Oh, Mama, you are too deliciously Gothic!" Lady Selina said on a trill of laughter. "Why, I have heard the songs from *The Beggar's Opera* all my life, and all the girls with whom I am acquainted have read the play," she added.

"Selina, my dear," protested the countess, "I know you are only jesting, but you will give Lord Ash—er, Mr. Cardorette—a disgust of you if you persist in this heedless manner."

"Not on that head, I assure you, ma'am," Christopher promised the harassed matron with a smile of singular charm. "It was ever thus, you know; the younger generation takes a perverse pleasure in trying to shock its elders, but it is mostly show. They like to think themselves awake on every suit, but when it comes right down to actions, they do not wander far from those moral principles they were taught at home."

"Mr. Cardorette is in the right of it, my dear Olivia," the earl said. "*Knowing* there is a certain amount of depravity in the world is a far cry from participating in it. It doesn't do to protect the young from all knowledge of the existence of such things, for then they'd be ill-prepared to resist the false lure of the flesh pots."

"Then, may I go, Papa?" Lady Selina asked eagerly.

"I see no harm in it if your mother agrees."

"May I, Mama?"

Lady Ormond still looked far from pleased but she bowed to her lord's will. "If Mr. Cardorette will be so kind as to escort us, I suppose I must acquiesce, since it means so much to you."

"It will be my pleasure, ma'am," Christopher assured her.

"May we go too, Mama?" piped up Miss Emily, the bolder of the schoolroom pair.

Such foolhardy presumption was depressed by her maternal parent, who speedily disabused her younger daughters of any notions that they were eligible for adult treats. She banished them to their rooms for the afternoon to study their catechism. The girls' mortification aroused Christopher's compassion for the growing pains of adolescence and he gave them an understanding wink as they filed meekly out of the dining room.

Lady Selina recalled her betrothed's attention at this point. "You haven't yet told me, Christopher, if you are to be situated in London until the wedding."

"I regret that this will not be possible. I must return to Ashleigh Court to welcome my nephew as soon as the business of his guardianship is in a way to being settled."

"Shall we be living at Ashleigh Court too?" Lady Selina looked a trifle confused. "This has all happened so recently that I have not thought the matter through."

"Yes, we shall all be situated at Ashleigh, at least until James goes off to school; then, if you should desire it, we might retire to Chelmsley, my own estate, during part of the school year. I am afraid you are being asked to preside over a larger household than most brides, my dear Selina. I'm sorry for that, but it cannot be helped, as things stand."

"I believe you will find Selina will soon get in the way of running a large establishment, sir," Lady Ormond said. "She has been well trained in domestic management."

Christopher bowed in acknowledgment. "I am quite sure of it, ma'am, seeing what a shining example she has always had in you."

Lady Selina, who had been looking pensive, spoke up over her mother's pleased reaction to this graceful compliment. "Just how many persons will be living under our roof—that is, Ashleigh Court's roof?"

"In addition to us and the young earl, there is my cousin, Mr. George Cardorette, with whom you are already acquainted, I believe?" She nodded and Christopher continued. "My cousin acted as steward and bailiff of the estate while my brother lived, and has consented to stay on at least until I learn all the ins and outs of managing a large property."

"Very wise, my boy. It takes time to get the hang of such things," the earl said.

"Is that all?" Lady Selina asked.

"Not quite. James's maternal aunt, Miss Llewellyn, has been in charge of the child since her sister's death. She will continue to oversee his daily routine, and I believe there is also a companion of a sort, Miss Lloyd, though it was my impression that she was actually a confidential servant rather than a gentlewoman."

"I see. Will the aunt expect to dine with us?"

"Naturally."

Christopher's face was a courteous mask that revealed none of the inappropriate resentment he was experiencing at this line of questioning. He was aware that his betrothed had every right to put the questions and he none at all to resent them on Brianna Llewellyn's behalf.

It was Lady Ormond who next asked, "How old a woman is the boy's aunt—Miss Llewellyn, is it?"

"That's correct." Christopher nodded and hoped there had been no significant pause before he added, "I believe she is approximately the same age as Lady Selina, perhaps slightly older."

"So young?" Lady Ormond frowned, and her daughter's eyes narrowed thoughtfully. "Then you will have to get some respectable woman to lend her countenance at Ashleigh until you are married."

It was Christopher's turn to be taken aback. "But there is Miss Lloyd to lend Miss Llewellyn countenance until Lady Selina arrives."

"Not if she is only a servant," Lady Ormond said flatly. "Not in a household comprising two bachelors at present, and not if Miss Llewellyn cares for her reputation. Of course she may not be of a social order that makes such a fine distinction?" The countess's light eyebrows ascended in query as she awaited his response.

"She is a gentlewoman," said Christopher, furious but determined not to show his displeasure at the question. He quickly passed his few female relatives under mental review without much pleasure in the exercise. "Well," he said with discernible reluctance, "my Aunt Hermione would come like a shot at an invitation to stay at Ashleigh. The only problem will be getting rid of her after we are married. She is a very managing female."

"I have the perfect solution!" cried Lady Selina triumphantly. "Mama and I will go back to Ashleigh with you. That way there will be no need of your Aunt Hermione. Mama will be chaperone for both Miss Llewellyn and me."

"It sounds a delightful idea," Christopher lied desperately, "but can your family do without you for so long, ma'am?" Turning from Lady Ormond to his betrothed, he continued, "And are there not still many details—your bride clothes—remaining to be settled about the wedding? And there is Christmas, which will be upon us shortly." He allowed his voice to peter out as he saw that Lady Ormond was influenced by the weight of these objections and was framing a refusal, but her daughter had the bit between her teeth now and she began to persuade her parent.

"We need not stay as long as Christmas, Mama. Once the child has settled into his new home we may come back to town to get ready for Christmas and the wedding. We can bring Miss Llewellyn with us and—"

"Take her away from her nephew at Christmas?"

Shocked disapproval sounded in Christopher's voice, and for a moment the outcome hung in the balance; then Lady Selina said brightly, "Why should they be separated? The boy and the servant may come too. They can all put up at an hotel here in town until after the wedding. I am persuaded the boy and his aunt will love to see all the sights of the capital after having lived always in the country. They may stay here until we go down to Ashleigh after our wedding trip."

"I do not believe all that racketing about would do for a child who has recently been ill," Christopher began, grasping at straws, only to have the props knocked out from under him by Lord Ormond, who had listened with the keenest interest to the discussion.

"I approve the basic idea of seeing how everyone takes to living together at Ashleigh, my daughter as well as the child. Suppose we agree that Selina and her mother shall go back with you for a fortnight or so. Then we can take our time to decide what further temporary arrangements seem most proper for the boy and his retinue?" His lordship pinned his prospective son-in-law with a hard glance, and Christopher knew there was no use trying to squirm out of this hellish visit. All the same, he did make one last weak effort.

"I really should be leaving the city within the next couple of days," he said, addressing himself to Lady Ormond, who seemed the likeliest ally.

This good woman, having finally grasped her husband's unspoken reason for throwing his support to the plan proposed by their daughter, failed Christopher however, saying graciously that she would pledge to have her daughter and herself ready to travel at Mr. Cardorette's convenience.

It was no great comfort to Christopher that he had also read Lord Ormond's hope that an early exposure to the diverse collection of persons at Ashleigh Court might cause his daughter to reconsider her quixotic decision to marry a man who had come down in the world. His own overriding concern was that Brianna Llewellyn would now have no time in which to overcome her initial strangeness and accustom herself to a new way of life at Ashleigh before his bride began her reign as mistress. Some bone-deep intuition told him that any chance of a happy beginning to Brianna's enforced relocation would be erased by the very natural fuss that would attend the arrival of the new mistress by servants and neighbors, for Selina would in effect be the mistress of Ashleigh during the long years of his nephew's minority.

It was in a grim mood, made the more so by the necessity of concealing his feelings, that Christopher took his leave of his promised bride and her parents that day to begin preparations for the fateful journey to his childhood home. Not even on that first trip to Ashleigh after his brother's death when he'd been overwhelmed by the unhappy knowledge that he was the last of his once-happy family left had he been so reluctant to return home.

In Herefordshire, Brianna Llewellyn was no less reluctant to embark on a journey that meant the end of the life she had known and the beginning of a new way of life that would eventually be much enriched for the child she loved but could never be anything but makeshift for her. In time there would be a sense of belonging for Jamie—he was very young, after all, and would gradually forget his first few years spent in relative poverty in a country rectory—but she would always be an outsider at Ashleigh Court. Her presence would be tolerated by Christopher Cardorette because for the next few years at least she was necessary to Jamie's well-being. He had already sustained far greater losses than any child should have to bear. Mr. Cardorette was a kind man—she had sensed this at their first meeting when she had felt so unwell—and he would try to make her feel at home at Ashleigh. He was about to be married, however, and must be wishing another unwanted dependent at the ends of the earth. It was bad enough to have Jamie thrust on him and his new bride, but Jamie at least was still young enough to be relegated to the nursery and more or less forgotten in the day-to-day course of the newly wedded couple's life. They could choose when and whether to interest themselves in the details of the boy's routine. Unfortunately, Brianna was another matter. It was nearly impossible to ignore the presence of an adult in one's home, however unwelcome. The merest civility demanded that some sort of accommodation had to be worked out. Could anything be more uncomfortable than an enforced intimacy between strangers? And when one was also in a dependent position, there was the constant mortification of this undesirable state to be reckoned with. Brianna shrank from the thought but could not escape it.

As she sorted through their personal belongings during the days of her nephew's convalescence, Brianna was buffeted between memories of the happy but forever-dead past and troublesome apprehensions of the future as a perpetual and unwanted guest in another woman's home. Her sympathies went out to the unknown Lady Selina Milliken who was to have what should be the happiest and freest period of her life cluttered with extra persons intruding on that privacy so essential to bride and groom at the beginning of their wedded life. She cringed spiritually from the unpalatable role she had been assigned by a malicious fate but knew she could not avoid it. She had promised Meg that she would not desert Jamie while he needed her. She moved about the shabby, beloved old house of her youth performing all sorts of household tasks for the final time with pain in her eyes and a reservoir of unshed tears in her heart.

Molly Lloyd observed her former nursling's brooding silences with concern during this period, unsure of the exact nature of Brianna's unhappiness, which seemed to have taken on a more acute form than the deep gentle sorrow that had followed the death of her father. Not even to this oldest and most trusted friend could Brianna confide her present misery. When she tentatively mentioned her dread of intruding on the privacy of Mr. Cardorette and his bride, Molly dismissed it with the vague expectation that something could be worked out. Perhaps there was a dower house, she suggested, where they could set up housekeeping with

Jamie if Mr. Cardorette was agreeable to the idea. Certainly she was far more resigned and accepting of the whole situation than the younger woman and less inclined to foresee difficulties ahead. She espoused the belief that "sufficient unto the day was the evil thereof" and was generally content to let tomorrow take care of itself—a philosophy that allowed her to bring all her faculties to bear in coping with each day's problems as they arose, her abilities undiminished by past regrets or anxieties for the future.

Once entered upon, Jamie's convalescence proceeded apace in the usual way of healthy young animals, and within a sennight of Mr. Cardorette's departure from Herefordshire there was no legitimate reason to delay their own any longer. In that short span, all traces of the Llewellyn family's lengthy residence in the rectory had been removed, leaving it spotless, shabby, and soulless to await its next inhabitants. Such family possessions and mementoes that were important to Brianna—pitifully few in number and of more sentimental than actual value—had been packed for transport by carrier to Ashleigh Court. Their personal belongings and clothing would not strain the capacity of Mr. Cardorette's traveling carriage, Brianna estimated, soberly assessing the meager assortment of packages and valises neatly stacked in one corner of the entrance hall as they awaited the arrival of this equipage on the day of their departure. Following Mr. Cardorette's instructions, she had sent a message the night before to the inn where the driver and guard had been domiciled for nearly a fortnight. The squire had dropped in to bid them godspeed, his wife's absence on a visit to relatives having prevented him from giving a dinner for Brianna during this period. They had said their good-byes in the village and taken a regretful leave of Doctor Chamfrey, whose professional services had represented only a small part of the regard in which he was held by all the Llewellyns over the years. The gruff practical physician had been her father's close friend and confidant though their temperaments were diametrically opposed, and Meg and Brianna had loved him dearly from earliest childhood. It was a severe wrench to remove herself from easy reach of his wise counsel and the unfailing good humor that was colored by a bracing knowledge and acceptance of the foibles of his fellow men. So poorly had she managed to hide her distress at leaving and her disinclination to embark on this new life that Doctor Chamfrey, in an effort to stiffen her backbone, had taken it upon himself to read her a stern lecture on the importance of approaching life's inevitable new challenges with courage and clear-eyed optimism. Eventually, he compelled

a promise from her that she would strive to conceal any personal
apprehensions for the child's sake. Indeed, she was fully conscious of this duty in any case.

Brianna was conscientiously mindful of her promise as the
three travelers climbed into the Ashleigh carriage and left the village of Lower Melstrum behind them, but still there was a distinct
difference in the attitudes of the passengers during the first few
hours of the journey. Miss Lloyd appeared as unconcerned as if
she were merely driving to a market town to stock up on provi-
sions, while the child's unadulterated pleasure in a new adventure
was patent in every quivering line of his small body. In contrast,
Brianna's valiant attempts to meet and match her nephew's enthusiasm, though acceptable to an excited child, would not have
passed an adult's scrutiny and were belied by the sadness in her
eyes.

As the hours passed uneventfully, the first flush of excitement
gave way to the monotony of confinement for the boy and it fell
to the lot of his aunt and nurse to keep him entertained in those
stretches between stops to change horses. During these all-too-
brief intervals brimming over with the various sights and sounds
and smells peculiar to a busy posting inn, their only problem was
in keeping a tight rein on their charge. Common humanity demanded that they allow the child to stretch his legs during these
stops, though it was never a simple matter to coax him back into
his rolling cage after brief exposures to the drama of seeing tired
sweating horses unbuckled from all manner of wheeled con-
veyances and led off to the stables while fresh pairs or teams were
substituted between the shafts. Jamie was endlessly enchanted by
the comings and goings in the bustling inn yards: the piles of baggage being strapped on heavy stagecoaches, the seasoned travelers rushing into the inn to try to consume some food or drink in
the few minutes allotted them during the changeover, and, particularly, the noisy sendoffs and welcomes being given some travelers by hordes of friends and relatives. To a child whose short life
had been spent in a sleepy village and whose circle of intimates
had shrunk to just two persons, such goings-on were a revelation
and a constant source of awe. Jamie's bright curious eyes darted
everywhere, absorbing as much as he could from the colorful
ever-changing scene. Small wonder he had to be cajoled back into
the carriage after each stop.

That evening brought even greater delights when the little earl
was permitted to dine with his nurse and aunt in the public dining
room of the splendid inn where Brianna had stopped on her return

journey from Ashleigh Court a fortnight before. They were shown to a private table commanding a view of the entire room for the child, thanks to an accommodating waiter who unearthed a couple of hefty volumes from somewhere to boost him up in the strategically placed Windsor chair. Brianna had been surprised and gratified at the gracious reception accorded them by the innkeeper, not realizing in her naiveté that the driver and guard had made sure their host knew he was housing connections of the earl of Ashleigh. Their smiling landlord could not have improved on his hospitality had he been aware that he had the honor of supplying a trundle bed for the earl himself rather then merely accommodating "connections" to a noble family.

No such worldly concerns troubled the little boy's enjoyment of a unique treat. His sparkling green eyes roved about the dining room, innocently assessing his fellow guests with the disconcerting directness of childhood curiosity. They were rather a disappointing lot that evening from Jamie's point of view, there being no other children present save a bored youth of about fourteen traveling with his tutor. In any case, the diners were not nearly so fascinating to a young child as the silent, skillful waiters who passed back and forth between kitchen and dining room through a door in the rear wall, carrying huge trays which they hoisted effortlessly up over their heads, at times narrowly averting collisions with their fellows or the guests. Jamie gazed after them in wonder, to the detriment of his meal, and had to be reminded more than once to eat the food on his plate before it got cold. Cold or hot was immaterial to him since his attention was never directed to the food long enough to identify what he was putting in his mouth until the fatherly waiter who had earlier provided the books told him with a wink that, if the young master cleaned up his plate, he thought he might discover some of the cook's famous jam tarts in the kitchen. To oblige his new friend, Jamie did just that, and he was rewarded with the promised treat. Brianna's glowing eyes and sweet smile of gratitude were rewards enough for the waiter, who stood gazing after her graceful figure for a moment as the small party finally left the room when the boy could dawdle no longer over his jam tarts.

Only his aunt's inspired though largely imaginary description of the myriad mysteries awaiting exploration in the extensive grounds of his new home induced Jamie to leave the wonderful inn with a cheerful countenance the next morning and he was inclined to be less accepting that day of the dull stretches on the road as they made steady progress. Happily, the stops still provided enough excitement to give the women needed respites from the increasingly onerous chore of keeping the child amused with stories and word games.

They were some thirty miles or so from their destination when boredom suddenly gave way to uncertainty and terror as the carriage rocked to an abrupt stop, throwing Jamie, who had jumped up to look out the window at the first alien sounds, back against the bench with a force that stunned him for a second. Brianna's arms went out in a futile attempt to break his fall, and she received a minor shaking also. Thus it was Miss Lloyd who let down the window and peered out at a scene of confusion. She saw a man on horseback and another dismounting at the front of the coach, both with drawn pistols. Swiftly she pulled her head in again and closed the window. She turned an amazed face to Brianna.

"What is it, Molly? What is happening?"

"Well, if my eyes are to be believed, we are being held up by armed men in broad daylight!"

Brianna's arms clutched Jamie to her instinctively, her eyes going wide with fright. "What can we do?" she whispered.

"Against armed men? Not a thing," declared Miss Lloyd. "The more pertinent question is what are the driver and guard doing?" She turned back to the window, then hissed a warning. "One of them is coming to the door."

The appalling sound of a gun discharging just then was instantly followed by a sharp cry and the frightened neighing of the horses and jingling of harness as the carriage jolted forward, then settled to a stop once more. Before the shocked passengers could gather their shaken composure one of the doors was jerked open and an ugly, unshaven face belonging to a large burly individual appeared in the aperture. Narrow dark eyes beneath heavy black brows assessed them swiftly.

"I'll take the brat," the man said.

Brianna shrank away from the broad hairy hand that reached into the carriage, thrusting Jamie behind her. She stared into the opaque unwinking eyes of the highwayman, too terrified to speak.

"We have no valuables with us and very little money. You might as well be on your way," Miss Lloyd snapped.

The man's eyes never left Brianna's. "I said, hand over the brat," he repeated in gritty tones, paying no attention to the older woman's words. "Unless you'd like me to shoot you first before I take him."

When Brianna still did not move, the man's other hand reached for the pistol stuck in his belt, while his cruel eyes held hers captive.

Suddenly Miss Lloyd launched herself at the highwayman and he staggered back a half pace at the same time that the second thief shouted out, "Joe, someone's acoming up behind us fast!"

After that, things happened with a rapidity that Brianna, from her position on the other side of the carriage from the pair struggling in the open doorway, could only guess at. She could see nothing that occurred outside, being wholly occupied in grasping Molly about the waist and straining to keep her in the carriage as the man tried to pull the older woman out and push her off his body at the same time. After what seemed an eternity but could not have been more than a couple of seconds, the highwayman succeeded in freeing his arms and shoving his attacker backward. Since Brianna was still pulling with all her strength, the two women landed in an untidy heap on the floor of the carriage with Molly on top. Jamie was whimpering and the women were trying to disentangle themselves when a cultured voice spoke from the open door.

"Are you hurt at all, ladies?"

A strong arm assisted Miss Lloyd back into her corner where she could be heard fighting to regain her breath.

Brianna raised her head at the sound of the new voice and found herself staring into a pair of concerned blue eyes whose expression changed to one of wonder as she blinked. Fear and confusion gave way to cautious relief as she felt her arm taken as she struggled up to her knees and then onto her seat. "I . . . I am unhurt, thank you, sir," she said breathlessly. Her eyes sought her friend. "Molly, are you all right? Did he hurt you?"

"Not a bit of it," Molly said cheerfully. "See to Jamie, my dear."

While Brianna gathered the crying child into her arms, Miss Lloyd turned back to the stranger. "Have they gone, the highwaymen? I assume you are not one of them?" she added dryly.

The man laughed. "No, ma'am. I am Sir Harry Paxton and I live nearby. My groom and I had just turned onto the road from my property when we heard the gunshot and came racing to investigate. If you will excuse me for a moment, I do not yet know exactly what has transpired."

The man disappeared from the opening. The ladies took advantage of the lull to soothe the frightened child and straighten their disheveled appearance as best they could, each using the other as a mirror to check the results.

When the man who had introduced himself as Sir Harry Paxton returned a few moments later, he brought the anxious women a mixture of good and bad news.

"The holdup men have gone without trace, ladies. There were only two of them and they cleared off into the woods as my groom and I drove upon the scene, a fortunate occurrence since neither of us is armed. The unfortunate thing is that your guard has been shot through the shoulder." The women exclaimed in dismay at this information and their rescuer gave it as his opinion that although the wound would require immediate medical attention it was not life threatening. "What I should like to propose, ladies, if I may be so bold, is that you permit me to escort you to my home where my sister will make you comfortable while we set about getting a surgeon for the injured man. My groom has already packed the wound, which is all that can be done here at present."

While their rescuer was explaining the situation in his pleasant voice, Brianna took the opportunity to really look at him for the first time. In her perturbation earlier, she had remarked nothing save clear blue eyes in a clean-shaven face, in blessed contrast to the unsavory appearance of their recent attacker. Now she saw a well-set-up man in his early thirties dressed with the quiet elegance of a gentleman beneath a driving coat with a half dozen shoulder capes. He had removed his beaver hat to reveal a finely shaped head of wavy golden hair. His features were good without being in any way extraordinary, but to her way of thinking his outstanding quality was the air of kindness that seemed an essential part of him. She breathed a sigh of relief after her summing up and glanced at Molly for confirmation. Her friend gave an almost imperceptible nod. Since his suggestion appeared to be the most sensible course, the women agreed at once.

Instead of spending their first evening at their new home, the weary travelers found themselves accepting the hospitality of strangers that night—but such kind strangers. Miss Paxton turned out to be her brother's counterpart in every respect, from her fair coloring to the gentle kindness of her speech and manner. She had moved with quiet capability to order rooms prepared for her unexpected guests, while her brother dispatched a message to the nearest surgeon and saw to the accommodation of the horses and driver after two sturdy footmen had carried the injured man to a bed.

There had been one awkward moment when Brianna had introduced herself and her companions. The name Cardorette had been vaguely familiar to the Paxtons and, of course, the earl's crest was on the carriage doors. After a brief hesitation, Brianna merely referred to Jamie as the earl's nephew since she did not feel it was her place to reveal the changed circumstances of the Cardorette family. Because dissimulation was foreign to her character, she felt ridiculously guilty, and this in combination with her natural shyness made her even more reticent than usual at first. It was a tribute to the tact and sensibility of the Paxtons that she had relaxed enough to converse almost with ease by the time dinner was over. Initially, she had been dismayed at the thought of presuming on her rescuer for shelter for the night. She said that they must not trespass further on the Paxtons' hospitality by remaining, but would move on to the next coaching inn and resume their journey the following morning without the guard, who must remain behind for a few days to regain his strength. Brother and sister both waved away all her protests. Sir Harry went so far as to say that he could never have borne to face the Earl of Ashleigh were he to be so cavalier as to allow the latter's family to continue their journey without armed protection after their frightening experience. Since his sister had promptly seconded him on every point, Brianna had given in, convinced that Sir Harry was sincere in his protestations. She must suppress her distaste at being put under further obligation and spend her energies in expressing a proper gratitude to her hosts.

She enjoyed her evening at Fourtrees, the Paxton estate, despite the circumstances that produced it. The surgeon had given a reassuring report of the guard's condition after removing the bullet from his shoulder. Molly had insisted on keeping Jamie with her and had remarked on the pleasant manner of the servants attending to their needs. The genuine friendliness of her new friends succeeded in dissolving the stiffness of manner Brianna affected to disguise her timidity in company and she responded to their overtures with all the warmth of her true nature. Under the influence of their light-hearted raillery as they competed to tell her stories of their youth at Fourtrees, she once or twice unlocked the smile that had been in captivity since Meg's death. The admiration in Sir Harry's fine eyes when they lingered on her face evoked a strange little flutter of excitement in the breast of one who had seldom been exposed to the flattering attentions of young men despite her twenty-one years. Since Meg's tragic marriage and her father's retreat into scholarly seclusion, there had been little social intercourse except of the most casual with the few genteel families in their immediate vicinity.

Joanna Paxton was a few years younger than her brother and shared with him the same quiet good looks and the self-possession of those at peace with their own natures and content with their lives. The loving bond between brother and sister was obvious and heartwarming, and it was delightful to Brianna to feel herself included in the circle of their warmth. In response to their genuine interest, she related a few stories that perhaps more than she intended sketched a picture of what it was like to grow up in a small self-contained family presided over by an unworldly scholar who practiced practical Christianity on an individual level among his humble flock.

As she prepared for bed in the charming blue-and-white guest chamber several hours later, Brianna was left with a sense of contentment. A few moments' reflection produced the surprising conclusion that she could not recall when last she had spent such a pleasant and stimulating evening in agreeable company. The last thought that took possession of her mind before she drifted off to sleep was the tentative hope that living at Ashleigh might not be quite the ordeal she had imagined in her habitual isolation. Perhaps their lives would all be enriched by expanding their tight little circle to include Jamie's father's family.

6

It was shortly after midday when Christopher escorted his fiancée and her mother through a pair of stone gateposts onto Ashleigh land. He was riding Lady Selina's handsome chestnut gelding whose last-minute inclusion in the party had made it necessary to curb their pace and lay over at an inn the previous night. Lady Selina was a skilled and enthusiastic rider, and upon learning that there was no horse in the Ashleigh stables at present suitable for a lady, she had prettily begged Christopher's indulgence in taking her own dear Cinnamon along so she might ride with her betrothed during her visit. It had been beyond his power to deny such a sweetly uttered request from one whose happiness and welfare would soon be his prime consideration, especially when his reason for wishing to refuse was an unreasonable desire to return quickly to welcome another woman to his home.

As he accompanied the Milliken traveling carriage along the beech-lined drive to the house, Christopher was in the grip of a tearing impatience that was nonetheless pressing for the necessity to conceal it from his companions. The two days he had allowed for completing his business in London had stretched to four, and the journey had expanded to two days, during which he had put himself under a rigid discipline to act the courteous host whose only consideration was the comfort of his guests. As he cantered up the drive, however, his thoughts were winging ahead to another woman as had happened all too frequently during the journey.

Unless the boy's convalescence had been prolonged beyond what the doctor had expected, the party from Herefordshire should have arrived a day or two ago with only his cousin's grudging civility as welcome. That stark fact had overshadowed his own journey.

Christopher reined in the chestnut and his eagerness to seek out Brianna Llewellyn. His own inclinations severely held in check, he dismounted and opened the door of the carriage, delivering himself of a gracious welcome to his prospective bride and her parent as he assisted them down. He accepted their initial comments on the beauties of the grounds and the elegant facade of the house with an easy smile while listening to the satisfying sounds of his people springing into action behind him as several footmen came down the steps.

In the next few minutes Lady Ormond's coachman was directed to the stables, the ladies were assured by Pennystone that the carriage containing their abigails and the bulk of their baggage had arrived safely the previous evening, and it was agreed that they would be conducted directly to their rooms to freshen their appearance before a late nuncheon was served. Any tours of the premises would wait until after this repast.

George Cardorette appeared in the open doorway as Christopher, a hand under each woman's elbow, was escorting his guests up the front steps. Cordial bows and salutations were exchanged in the foyer. Christopher cast a swift glance around the high-ceilinged hall while Lady Ormond assured Mr. Cardorette that their trip had been blessedly uneventful.

"Speaking of journeys, George, when did the Herefordshire party arrive?"

"They haven't arrived yet, coz," Mr. Cardorette replied before turning to answer a question put to him by Lady Ormond.

"Not?" Christopher smoothed out the frown that had gathered on his brow when his betrothed turned her beautiful eyes in his direction. "Has any further communication been received from them?"

"No, nothing," said George.

"Well, at least you are here now to greet them when they arrive, Christopher, which I am persuaded was always an object with you," Lady Selina said with a bright smile.

"Er- yes, one doesn't wish to be remiss in these matters," he acknowledged smoothly.

Christopher had cause to be grateful to his cousin for taking up the slack in the conversation at the table a half hour later as they prepared to enjoy a selection of salads and his cook's delicate meat pasties. His own participation was more mechanical than inspired as his initial relief that he was in time to greet his nephew and Brianna gave way to a growing anxiety at their continued nonappearance. Before he had set out for London from Hereford, he had instructed Brianna to send word to Ashleigh if any unforeseen difficulties arose to postpone their departure beyond the agreed-upon time. She had not done this, and his hasty calculations indicated that they should have arrived by yesterday at the latest.

"Do you think it will last, Christopher?"

His fiancée's clear voice broke in upon Christopher's internal cataloguing of possible occurrences that could account for the delay and recalled him to his duties as host. He bent a lazy smile on the lovely blonde seated on his left. "Do I think what will last, my dear Selina?"

"For shame, Christopher! Confess that you were woolgathering," his fiancée commanded with an arch smile. She spared him the disgrace of such an admission by continuing without pause. "I was expressing the hope that this spell of pleasant weather will last long enough for you to show me the best rides in the area."

"I believe we can expect a few more days in this mild pattern, don't you, George?"

"Two or three perhaps," that gentleman concurred, launching into a description of one of the rides he thought might appeal to Lady Selina. Christopher resolved to keep his mind fixed on those present and began a desultory conversation with Lady Ormond.

An hour and a half later, they were all four in the main drawing room when Christopher's acute hearing picked up the faintest sounds of a carriage approaching the front entrance. He excused himself from the company and strolled into the central hall a moment later just as a footman opened the massive door.

Christopher's initial satisfaction at recognizing the Ashleigh coach gave way to surprise at sight of a mounted stranger apparently acting as escort. He came down the steps at a quickened pace but too late to prevent the well-dressed horseman from dismounting and opening the door to the carriage. He was well in time, however, to note and resent the tender gallantry with which the stranger handed down the first passenger to alight. He banished the slight pucker between his brows and made himself smile.

"Welcome to Ashleigh Court, Brianna."

Christopher's voice pulled the young woman's eyes away from the man helping her to descend. He observed the slight rise in color in her cheeks with satisfaction as she extended her small hand to meet his.

She looked better than when he had last seen her, he decided—more rested and with less strain in her eyes. She was still too pale but a few weeks free of the burdens that had weighed her down should see the youthful bloom return to her skin. There was no time to dwell on this pleasant prospect, for the still unknown escort was now lifting down a wriggling small boy, much to the latter's outspoken indignation.

"I can get down by myself," Jamie declared. He caught sight of the man holding his aunt's hand and promptly forgot his grievance. "Uncle Christopher," he cried, hurtling toward that amused individual the instant his feet touched the gravel. "You'll never guess what happened! We were held up by real robbers and I had dinner in the dining room of a splendid inn, and the waiter, who was my friend, brought some of the cook's special jam tarts just for me!"

A laughing Christopher had swooped and hoisted the child up into his arms during this spate. Now the laughter stilled as he held the boy in one arm, the better to read the excited little face. "Are you telling me that your carriage—this carriage—was stopped by highwaymen, James?"

"Yes, real robbers, Uncle Christopher," the child confirmed. "But they didn't steal anything 'cause Sir Harry scared them off. It was a great adventure," he added importantly, but though his uncle's lips quivered at this, his eyes had flashed to the stranger, now assisting Miss Lloyd to alight, and thence to Brianna, who had not spoken since her first soft greeting.

"Is this true?"

Brianna nodded. "I am afraid so, sir—Christopher," she added hastily as his brows climbed and he looked pained.

"When did this happen, and where?" Christopher demanded.

"It happened yesterday afternoon," Brianna replied, "but I am not entirely certain where—"

"The attempted holdup occurred on a stretch of road between Shutmire and East Welty, a short distance from a little-used lane that runs along one boundary of my estate," said the man Jamie had identified only as "Sir Harry." "Happily, my groom and I came onto the road from this lane just in time to hear a gunshot—"

"A shot! Was anyone hurt?" Christopher's eyes winged back to Brianna to assure himself that she was in one piece, but it was the stranger who answered.

"They shot your guard in the shoulder, I fear, but the injury is not too serious. My people are looking after him until he is able to travel again."

"I . . . see. I am deeply in your debt, sir. Your timely intervention may have prevented a far greater tragedy." Christopher thrust out his hand toward the other man. "I am Christopher Cardorette."

"This is Sir Harry Paxton," Brianna intervened before that gentleman could speak. "I beg your pardon, gentlemen; I have been remiss in not making you known to each other, but when Jamie came bursting out of the coach in that wild fashion I forgot my manners in the confusion."

"Not to be wondered at," Christopher said with a laugh, setting his squirming nephew down. "This imp certainly knows the value of a dramatic entrance." He made a smiling bow to Miss Lloyd. "Pray excuse my own lack of manners, Miss Lloyd. Welcome to Ashleigh Court. I hope you will be happy here with us. And now may I suggest that we remove ourselves from the servants' path and go inside. We'll have the whole story of James's 'great adventure' in more comfortable surroundings."

Christopher gave an order for refreshments to the hovering Pennystone before leading the new arrivals inside. Any natural constraint among the oddly assorted members of the procession was held at bay, thanks to the artless utterances of the small boy whose eyes were popping at the size and magnificence of his new surroundings.

"Your house is awful big and grand, Uncle Christopher," he confided, his head tipped back at an awkward angle as he gazed up to the colorful scenes painted on the ceiling far above. "It's even bigger than the squire's, isn't it, Auntie Bree?"

"You had better keep your eyes on where you are going, Jamie, or you will bump into something," Brianna advised him, wisely leaving any correcting of his behavior for a more suitable time.

"It won't seem so grand once you have been here awhile and learned your way around," his uncle promised, ruffling the mop of black curls. Only half his mind was attending to the child's reactions; the other half was still trying to assimilate the disturbing news of the attempted holdup. He opened the door to the drawing room and stepped back to allow the newcomers to precede him into the room.

As she passed in front of him and became aware of three pairs of eyes turned expectantly in their direction, Brianna's step faltered and Christopher cursed his forgetfulness in not preparing her for the enlarged reception awaiting them. The bombshell dropped by the self-possessed child now serenely surveying the company had driven all thoughts out of his head. There was no help for it, so he plunged into the mass introductions.

After a slow start, Christopher's brain was functioning at triple speed again, taking note of the reactions of the various persons present. Lady Ormond's pleasant civility was echoed by Miss

Lloyd and Sir Harry Paxton, who immediately gained the distinction of being the only man Christopher had ever witnessed meet the spectacular Lady Selina without displaying an overt quickening of male interest. Lady Selina herself projected a friendly pleasure in the introductions that threw Brianna's reticence into stark contrast. Christopher knew that a debilitating shyness was responsible for her seeming stiffness and he could only deplore the fact that the others did not share his understanding. It was very odd but right from their first meeting he had felt himself attuned to changes in Brianna Llewellyn's emotional state, an ability he could not yet presume to claim with respect to his betrothed. As for his cousin, despite George's polished civility, Christopher thought he detected a shade of criticism in his attitude toward Brianna. Poor George had desperately hoped she would prove to be a fraud. Perhaps one could not expect him to be well-disposed toward the person who had initiated the disruption in their lives, despite her gentle loveliness. George had looked mildly puzzled at the presence of Sir Harry Paxton but his real interest was in the child standing quietly in front of his uncle, whose hands were on the boy's shoulders.

Christopher had purposely saved the child until last. Those in the drawing room had risen and come forward at the entrance of his guests. After the various introductions had been acknowledged, he smiled at the group and said, "And now I have the honor to present James Arthur Cardorette, sixth Earl of Ashleigh."

"*Earl of Ashleigh!* I beg pardon, but I was under the impression that *you* were the Earl of Ashleigh!" Sir Harry blurted, his expression dumbfounded as he gazed from Christopher to Brianna.

"Miss Llewellyn was unaware that her brother-in-law was my elder brother when she sought out James's father's family recently," Christopher said, coming swiftly to Brianna's rescue. "Unfortunately, my brother never divulged the fact of his early marriage to anyone, and he himself never knew of his child's existence." He ended this brief explanation by turning the boy by his shoulders and facing him toward the large dark man examining him intently. "James, Mr. Cardorette is your cousin George. Make your best bow to him."

The boy obeyed, gazing up at this large new relative with a child's unabashed interest as he offered his small hand. "Do you have any boys like me, Cousin George?"

"Er, no . . . James," the big man replied with a look of blank horror that had Christopher biting back a smile. His own turn to be nonplussed came a second later as the child's attention switched back to him.

"What's a earl, Uncle Christopher?" Jamie asked. As his uncle hesitated, momentarily at a loss, the boy reminded him patiently, "You said I was a sixth earl. I know six. It's this many—He splayed the fingers of one hand and held up the index finger of the other—"But I don't know what is a earl."

"I'll explain later, Jamie," Brianna began, but Christopher interrupted her.

"An earl is not a thing, James; it's an hereditary title." Seeing the next question forming on the boy's lips, he continued, "You are the sixth earl because your father was the fifth earl, and one day your son will be the seventh earl of Ashleigh."

"I did not know I was a . . . an earl," the child said reflectively. "I don't feel any different."

"That's good because you are not any different," his uncle replied with cheerful dismissal. "Now here is Pennystone with refreshments for everyone. Shall we be seated? Ladies, if you will like to share this settee," he added, gesturing Brianna and Molly toward a green damask settee as Lady Ormond and her daughter resumed the places they had occupied before the arrival of the party from Herefordshire and their escort. Brianna gathered the child up between herself and Molly as the men disposed themselves among the chairs grouped around the fireplace.

When Pennystone had left the room after seeing the ladies supplied with tea, the young earl with milk, and the gentlemen with Madeira, Lady Selina leaned across her parent to put a smiling question to Sir Harry, who was seated in a chair at right angles to the settee upon which Brianna sat, "Are you an old friend of Miss Lloyd and Miss Llewellyn, sir?"

"I hope I may indeed claim the honor of being the ladies' friend, but it is a friendship of very recent date, Lady Selina. It was my privilege to be in a position to render them a small service on their journey."

"It was not a *small* service at all. Sir Harry rescued us from a pair of brutal highwaymen who held up our carriage yesterday." The necessity to acknowledge the enormity of their debt to their gallant rescuer emboldened Brianna to raise her soft voice in company, an act requiring more courage than she normally possessed.

The reaction was all that a born storyteller could hope for and Brianna would most dread as all eyes present locked on her pale countenance. Sir Harry came to her rescue again with a firm dis-

claimer of any heroics on his part. It was he who, correctly inter-
preting an imploring look from Brianna, related yesterday's
events from his point of view in response to the others' questions
about the affair. The women were understandably horrified and
sympathetic. The Cardorette cousins expressed astonishment at
the boldness of a daytime robbery on a stretch of road that had
never in their knowledge been considered dangerous, something
Sir Harry was quick to corroborate.

"It's my guess the pair were intoxicated and dared each other to
perform some vainglorious feat," George Cardorette declared.

"I did not really get close enough to either to observe their bodily state," Sir Harry said with an apologetic shrug.

"I detected no smell of spirits on the brute who opened the carriage door," Miss Lloyd said in a deliberate voice, "and we were
actually engaged in a physical struggle for a few seconds."

This, Miss Lloyd's first contribution since her murmured acknowledgment of the introductions earlier, stopped that line of
speculation cold. It was into this pulsating silence that Jamie
flung his second bombshell.

"That bad man was going to take me away with him, but Auntie Bree wouldn't let him touch me, and Molly hit him," he declared with ghoulish satisfaction.

"Is this true?" demanded Christopher, aghast, his eyes flashing
from Brianna to Sir Harry.

"I knew nothing of this, sir. The ladies never mentioned it. I assumed it was simply an abortive attempt at robbery," that gentleman said, his gaze going in mute question to Brianna, who looked
uncomfortable to be the cynosure of all eyes once more.

"He—the highwayman who opened the carriage door—tried to
take Jamie with him," she admitted.

"That bad man said if Auntie Bree didn't give me to him, he'd
shoot her," Jamie added with obvious relish, causing Christopher's lips to twitch even while his heart turned over at the
thought of a gun pointed at Brianna.

"This puts an entirely new construction on the matter," he said
heavily, his brow creased in frowning concentration.

"A ransom attempt?" Mr. Cardorette suggested.

"Presumably, but that presupposes knowledge of James's identity *and* the time when the carriage would be passing the spot the
kidnappers had selected."

"No one at this end could have known when the party would
arrive," his cousin pointed out. "How many people knew the time

of your departure from Herefordshire?" He addressed this question to Brianna who bristled visibly at the implication.

"Everyone in the village knew of our departure, sir, but only the doctor and Mr. Henderson, the squire, were aware of Jamie's identity, and they are above suspicion," she replied with firm dignity.

"Is it absolutely essential to presuppose knowledge of any sort on the part of the highwaymen?" Lady Selina asked. "I presume there is a crest on the carriage?" Christopher, to whom this query was addressed, nodded, and she went on. "If the would-be thieves had spotted the carriage on the road earlier, might they not have ridden ahead to set up an ambush, assuming there would be valuables inside, and only thought of a kidnapping plan later, upon seeing two plainly dressed women and a child inside?"

The three men gave this proposed version their consideration for a few seconds under the bright intelligent gaze of Lady Selina.

"It is certainly not outside the realm of possibility that it happened that way," Mr. George Cardorette conceded, glancing dubiously at his cousin.

It was apparent from his skeptical expression that Christopher did not give much credence to the theory propounded by his fiancée, but he allowed that there was nothing to prove it had not happened in just that way.

"I suppose I must be grateful that you did not condemn my suggestion out of hand as a ridiculous piece of feminine nonsense," Lady Selina said softly with little moue and a flicker of long lashes that were too demure to be believed.

The cousins laughed outright, while Sir Harry protested his innocence of any such biased thinking. Lady Selina tossed them a smile full of challenge, and somehow the subject of the unsuccessful holdup was permitted to elapse, much to Brianna's relief. She was able to retire from center stage for some necessary peace in which to begin to accustom herself to the situation that had greeted them at Ashleigh Court.

The fact of Lady Selina's existence had been known to her before she ever met Christopher Cardorette, but she had not expected to find the young woman already established at the Court on their arrival. Any small hope that she might have time to settle into this alien setting before having to learn how to get along with the new mistress of Ashleigh was at an end. Brianna sat quietly, trying to maintain an air of polite interest as she was treated to a masterly display of the ease with which a clever female can keep the attention of three very different men firmly fixed on herself.

Brianna did not resent this; the last thing she desired was to be
the center of masculine, or, for that matter, feminine attention. As
a rule, nothing was more expressly guaranteed to render her
tongue-tied. Except for at the very beginning of their first interview, she had never felt shy with Christopher Cardorette, however, and Sir Harry and his delightful sister had gone out of their
way to make her feel at ease in their company last night. In fact,
she had begun to hope that her fears this past week of fitting in at
Ashleigh might have been unduly magnified. That was until she
had crossed the threshold of this opulent room and felt herself
being critically inspected by two exquisitely dressed females and
a large, unsmiling dark man. It was clear to her as she listened to
the rapid crossfire of amusing trivialities being exchanged by
Lady Selina and the gentlemen that she did not belong in this
worldly company. She could not imagine herself producing a single amusing comment, even were she to be granted hours of study
and reflection to devote to the project.

Brianna was thankful presently when the housekeeper, Mrs.
Dobbs, entered the room to show the newest arrivals to their quarters. They had traveled no more than thirty miles today—an easy
jaunt—but she was more than ready to experience the privacy
provided by a room with a door that would keep the rest of the
world at bay.

The housekeeper led the two women and the wide-eyed child
up a handsome oak staircase that branched off in two directions
on the first floor. As they proceeded up the righthand branch to
the next level, Mrs. Dobbs's gaze kept returning to the little boy
who skipped along beside his aunt, giving her the benefit of his
first impressions of their surroundings. These were predominantly
favorable, though he confided in what he mistakenly thought a
whisper that some of the people in the paintings they passed along
their route looked almost as mean as the robber who had held up
their carriage. Brianna's eyes met and acknowledged the twinkle
in Mrs. Dobbs's eyes before she gently cautioned her nephew that
it was impolite to criticize people's appearance.

"But they was just pictures, Auntie Bree, not real people."

"They are pictures of real people, dearest. Very likely some of
them are Uncle Christopher's ancestors, and yours too."

"What are ancestors?"

Brianna knew the canny Jamie habitually used questions to divert her attention from a scolding, but on this occasion she allowed herself to be so diverted. Her answer brought them to the
nursery, a large bright room, thanks to several windows through

which the late afternoon sunshine poured. Jamie's eyes fairly popped as they lighted on a low table, its top painted blue, upon which were set up dozens of toy soldiers, their red coats gleaming in a captured sunbeam. He started to run toward them, then checked, sending an eloquent imploring glance at the housekeeper, who chuckled and nodded.

"Yes, they are for you, Master James. Those soldiers belonged to your father and your uncle when they were your age, and your uncle thought you would like to have them now."

"Oh, I would!" the little boy cried ecstatically. "Thank you, Mrs. Dobbs." He cast her a seraphic smile before picking up two of the soldiers to study with the intensity of a scientist. It was plain that for the moment at least he had forgotten his companions' existence.

Mrs. Dobbs turned impulsively toward the other women. "It will be wonderful to have a child in the house again, the sweet lamb that he is. Those black curls put me in mind of Mr. Christopher when he was a lad, but the smile is exactly the same as his father's."

As Brianna bent over the table at her nephew's invitation to take a closer look at the variety in the soldiers' uniforms, Miss Lloyd directed a smiling question to their guide. "You have been at Ashleigh Court for a long time then, Mrs. Dobbs?"

The housekeeper appeared to be roughly the same age as Molly and more comfortably padded. Both were blessed with fresh clear complexions and bright blue eyes. Molly's fair hair was worn in a smoothly braided knot at the back of her head while Mrs. Dobbs's gray-spattered brown curls rioted out from beneath a spotless lawn cap.

"I came here just after Mr. Matthew was born," the housekeeper replied, "as the nursery maid at first. I was thirteen at the time, and I've been here ever since except for the eight years that I was married. Mr. Dobbs, dear good man that he was, left me well provided for when he died but with no child of my own to care for, so when the mistress died so sudden-like when Mr. Christopher was only twelve, and the master begged me to come back and run the house, I was that glad to turn my own silent cottage over to my brother and his brood and came back where there was plenty that needed doing. And I've never regretted it," she declared, pausing for breath. "Not yet leastways, though the old master was a hard man after his lady died, and that's a fact."

Neither Brianna nor Molly permitted herself the indulgence of curiosity at that point and presently Mrs. Dobbs led them first to

the cozy night nursery, which Jamie barely glanced into, so eager
was he to explore the further delights hinted at by the array of
cabinets in the sunny playroom. Miss Lloyd was pleased with the
comfortably furnished chamber close to the nursery that was to be
hers, and the spontaneous admiration she expressed for the pretty
blue-and-rose floral chintz that was used at the windows and for
bed hangings pleased the housekeeper in return.

"I see your bags have already been brought up, Miss Lloyd,
and if I'm not mistaken, that knock will be young Lily, who is the
maid assigned to the nursery suite. I'm sure you will find her
work acceptable, and she should be very good with the child too,
since she has a raft of young brothers and sisters at home. She's a
bit of a chatterbox but a good-hearted girl for all that."

Mrs. Dobbs had gone to the door during this speech and now
she admitted a sweet-faced young girl with masses of wildly curling red hair and round gray eyes, who bobbed a shy curtsey to the
ladies and sent a broad grin in the child's direction, which Jamie
returned in full measure.

"Would you like Lily to unpack for you now, Miss Lloyd?"
Mrs. Dobbs asked.

"Actually, if Lily would care to keep Jamie company in the
nursery for a bit, I would prefer to do my own unpacking," Molly
responded.

Seeing that this program apparently appealed to the maid and
the boy, Mrs. Dobbs said, "Then I'll leave you to it while I show
Miss Llewellyn to her apartment, shall I?"

The plump housekeeper promptly headed for the door, followed by Brianna, leaving Jamie, who had embarked on a chatty
description of his journey for the edification of his new friend, the
appreciative Lily.

7

To Brianna's surprise, Mrs. Dobbs led her past the day nursery and back to the staircase that had brought them to the nursery wing. Slightly at a loss, she followed the housekeeper downstairs into what she took to be the main portion of the house, along a wide carpeted passageway, stopping at a door about halfway down on the right.

"Here we are," Mrs. Dobbs said, throwing open the door and entering with a brisk step.

Brianna followed more slowly and stopped just inside a fair-sized sitting room, her questioning eyes seeking the housekeeper's.

"The bedchamber is through here." Mrs. Dobbs crossed to a white-and-gold paneled door in the fireplace wall, waiting patiently for Brianna's tentative approach before she opened the door and stepped into a luxuriously appointed bedchamber.

Brianna entered on reluctant feet, her startled gaze taking in the mahogany four-poster bed with its graceful canopy and creamy lace hangings, before falling to the silken textured rug at her feet, obviously of eastern make and alive with an intricately patterned design in glorious colors. "There must be some mistake, Mrs. Dobbs," she began hesitantly. "Naturally I expected to be housed near Jamie in the nursery wing."

"There's no mistake, Miss Llewellyn. Mr. Christopher specifically directed that this suite be prepared for you. I know it's a far distance from Master Jamie, but Miss Lloyd is right next to him, you recall. See, there are your bags near the armoire waiting for Hannah to unpack. She will be your abigail. She's not London-trained, of course, but she's a willing girl and has a real gift for dressing hair. I believe you'll find her work satisfactory. That door opens into the same corridor as the sitting-room door and this one leads to a small dressing room."

As she spoke, the housekeeper crossed to a door in the wall by the bed and opened it, stepping back to allow an approach Brianna did not immediately make. She was engaged in trying to conceal her dismayed surprise at the unexpected magnificence of the accommodation Christopher Cardorette had provided for her. Mrs. Dobbs seemed to be expecting some comment. It would not do to enter into an argument with a servant, so she swallowed her objections and said with simple truth, "The rooms are quite beautiful, Mrs. Dobbs, and they sparkle with care and attention. I see you've even had fresh flowers brought in. They are lovely. Thank you so much."

Apparently she had redeemed herself in the housekeeper's eyes, for that lady was smiling at her in an approving fashion. "The best guest suites are along this corridor. Lady Ormond and Lady Selina are across the hall. Their bedchambers are either side of the sitting room that is just opposite yours. The rooms on that side are larger but they look onto an interior courtyard. I prefer the view from these windows. This was my lady's favorite suite after she redid it shortly before she died," Mrs. Dobbs added, a fleeting sadness dimming her features. "The master—the old earl, that is—never wanted people around him after his lady died. Mr. Christopher used to come up here sometimes and sit out there." She indicated the sitting room with a movement of her head. "He'd sit for hours at a stretch, poor lad, just staring out at her garden that summer she died. Both boys adored their mother, who was one of the gentlest creatures God ever put on this earth, and took before her time. Nothing was ever the same around here after she was gone." Mrs. Dobbs let out a gusty sigh and then said with determined cheer, "It will be good to see this old house come to life again, what with a child in the nursery again and soon a new mistress."

A soft knock on the sitting-room door heralded the appearance of the maid, Hannah, and spared Brianna the necessity of coming up with some suitable comment to acknowledge this spate of biographical reminiscence. Instantly Mrs. Dobbs was her efficient self once more as she introduced the timid-looking maid and promised Brianna she herself would return to conduct her to the saloon where everyone would assemble before dinner.

Two hours later, Brianna glanced nervously at the mantel clock in the sitting room of the beautiful suite she had been assigned by Christopher Cardorette's express order. It lacked seven minutes to the hour when Mrs. Dobbs would return to escort her to the room where the current inhabitants of Ashleigh gathered before dinner. For the last ten minutes she had been sitting staring at the same page of one of the periodicals she'd found when she wandered into this room after dismissing Hannah, who had dressed her hair and helped her get ready for the upcoming ordeal. The intervening time since she'd left the others had been woefully inadequate to forge the courage she needed to rejoin the party with a decent show of composure. She hadn't a hope of holding her own in any general conversation; she only desired to avoid disgracing herself and her upbringing by stammering like a ninnyhammer when someone addressed a question to her or, even worse, shrinking visibly under the dark measuring regard of Mr. George Cardorette, whose perfect manners earlier had yet failed to disguise his initial assessment of her as unprepossessing. She could not have said how she knew that Mr. Cardorette found her completely negligible, but she had instantly sensed his—animosity was too strong a term—perhaps contemptuous indifference best described his reaction to her.

Brianna bounded out of the chair, her mental agitation making it impossible to remain seated. The edginess that had attacked her nerves from the moment she'd entered the drawing room this afternoon had not dulled to manageable proportions in the intervening hours. The instant she and Hannah had finished stowing her meager wardrobe in the vast interior of one of a pair of matching armoires in the bedchamber, she had flown back upstairs to the nursery seeking sympathy for her banishment. It had been disconcerting to receive none. She'd found Molly and Jamie cozily established in the bright playroom, reading from one of the books Jamie had discovered in one of the wall cabinets in the room. They'd been pleased to see her, but though Jamie had looked a bit doubtful at hearing that his aunt was situated in another part of the huge house, Molly had greeted the news almost as though she'd expected it.

"Mr. Cardorette is only giving you your due, after all, my love," she'd said when Brianna had worriedly announced that she was being housed right near Lady Ormond and her daughter. "You are as much an invited guest as anyone else here."

"But that is not really true, Molly, and you know it as well as I do. I am here as a necessary evil solely because Jamie needs me. Mrs. Dobbs told me she thinks mine the nicest suite of all, and I feel excessively uncomfortable to be plunked down there in the midst of Mr. Cardorette's invited guests, who, you may be sure, are very well aware of my true position in this household. I feel I am masquerading under false pretenses."

"Fustian, my love," Molly had replied forthrightly. "You are being unfair and ungenerous to Mr. Cardorette in ascribing to him your own description of yourself as 'a necessary evil.' Obviously he wishes his future wife and his household to accept you as an integral part of the family. If you are uncomfortable with that, then I must attribute your discomfort to an excess of stiff-necked pride."

Thus roundly chastised, and suddenly aware that Jamie was listening to the discussion with absorbed attention, Brianna had dropped the subject of her accommodations. But a peaceful half hour with her loved ones had not served to reconcile her to her undesired inclusion among Christopher Cardorette's chosen companions.

As the time to rejoin the others approached, she paced about the suite berating herself for being so easily intimidated in social situations. With the possible exception of Mr. George Cardorette, everyone seemed to be reasonably well-disposed toward her, and in any case, she was not a Scheherazade whose life depended on her ability to entertain. Obviously she was in no position to produce anecdotes featuring the well-connected in London society as Lady Selina and her mama had been doing this afternoon, but she was not dull-witted. Thanks to her scholarly father, she was as well versed in the classics as anyone and had formed her own opinions on topics of general interest.

When she reached this point in her internal debate, Brianna gave a snort of self-derision and her lips curved reluctantly upward. The chances of Brianna Llewellyn delivering herself of one of these opinions in the event the conversation should take a philosophical turn was about equal to that of a snowball surviving an hour in even the coldest reaches of hell. She arrived at this conclusion and the dressing table in her beautiful bedchamber simultaneously. Her eye was drawn to her own reflection though she would have preferred not to be reminded on yet another level of how out of place she was in these elegant surroundings. Even the clever arrangement devised by Hannah that anchored the heavy knot of hair at the back of her head rather than the nape, flattering though it undoubtedly was, could not lift her appearance into the realm of the fashionable. She had done no more than exchange her dreary black bombazine traveling dress for a lightweight black gown with a demurely cut round neckline and short sleeves. Her mourning clothes, hastily made up after Meg's death, were even less appealing ten months later, now too loosely falling from her frame in mute testimony to the pounds she had shed since her father's death. She compressed her lips and turned away from the disheartening vision of herself in the glass. This afternoon Lady Ormond and her spectacular daughter had been wearing perfectly cut garments in the pale muslins that were in vogue, and there was no reason to expect their evening attire to be less costly and eye-catching.

Brianna shivered a little and walked resolutely back into the sitting room. There was no escaping the fact that in the company of the Milliken ladies she was going to look like the proverbial poor relation, which term about described her true status. Since this was inescapable, she had best give her thoughts a new direction. Her sensibilities—and yes, the stiff-necked pride Molly had deplored—were of small consequence at present. The welfare of her sister's orphaned child was what counted, and it was already evident that Jamie would thrive at Ashleigh Court. She had not realized until they had embarked on their journey just how very like Matthew Jamie was in his outgoing temperament. No trace of her own timidity or Meg's reserve had restrained the boy's eager curiosity about each fresh aspect of the journey. She had been struck by his cool self-possession at meeting a number of strangers here at Ashleigh. It seemed he was more his father's child than she had thought, isolated in their small rural village in Herefordshire, and that prospect could never be entirely welcome to one who had witnessed the havoc wrought by Matthew's inconstancy of character. It would be her mission in life to see that the moral values cherished by the Llewellyn side of Jamie's heritage did not get lost in the enjoyment of all this worldly splendor. She'd been thankful earlier to hear Christopher Cardorette's matter-of-fact dismissal of any idea that being an earl should make the boy feel any different. His eyes had met hers for an instant over their nephew's head and she'd had a quick, and therefore possibly erroneous, impression that he'd actually winked at her.

Once diverted to Jamie, Brianna's thoughts took on a happier aspect and she had relaxed somewhat by the time Mrs. Dobbs arrived to escort her down to an apartment somewhat smaller than the formal saloon where tea had been served that afternoon. In here, straw-colored velvet curtains covered the windows and a fire burned busily in a fireplace whose amber-streaked marble surround glowed with reflected light—a pleasant, nonintimidating room. But Brianna's recently acquired composure failed her at the first test: the sight of Lady Ormond and her daughter, both elaborately coiffed and richly gowned and bejeweled, seated together on a sofa. They were laughing at a remark made by Mr. George Cardorette, standing nearby, and did not immediately perceive a new presence. Feeling dwarfed and invisible in her nondescript black, Brianna hesitated, battling an urge to creep silently away.

Christopher Cardorette, who was standing to the left of the fireplace in conversation with Sir Harry Paxton, spotted her before she could translate her cowardly impulse into action. He broke off his conversation and hurried forward with a smiling word of welcome, halting her incipient retreat. Sir Harry followed on his host's heels. From the way the two men set about putting her at her ease, Brianna deduced that she had been less than successful in hiding her foolish panic and she was in quick succession ashamed of her lack of poise and genuinely touched by their gallantry. Determined to do her part, she forced some animation into her voice and gave the men her full attention. Within a surprisingly short time, the need for conscious effort had vanished and she began to enjoy herself in their company.

Brianna's eyes were sparkling and a bubble of laughter had just escaped her lips at some amusing nonsense of Christopher Cardorette's when a clear voice behind her cut across the sound. "For shame, you two men, selfishly monopolizing Miss Llewellyn when we ladies have not yet had even the tiniest opportunity to become acquainted."

Lady Selina's playful remark had the dual effect of strangling the laughter in Brianna's throat and diverting the gentlemen's attention to her own smiling countenance where she sat beside her mother on the sofa, her head tilted to one side in mock reproach.

"My dear Selina, I do apologize," Christopher said promptly, accepting his fiancée's rebuke at face value. "It was indeed ill-done of us to deprive you of Brianna's company. Permit me to atone. Brianna?" he added, turning to offer his arm to the now-silent girl with elaborate chivalry.

Brianna had no choice but to accept her cue and allow Christopher to escort her over to the sofa where Lady Selina made a play of edging closer to Lady Ormand while in smiling invitation she patted the enlarged place beside her. Brianna summoned up a polite smile of her own which, however, faltered a little as the full battery of Lady Selina's charm was aimed in her direction.

"Chris tells me your father was a rector of a village church in Herefordshire, Miss Llewellyn. I do hope you won't find life in a large country house terribly slow and monotonous after such a busy and useful existence."

Instinctively Brianna mistrusted the sweet solicitude in the other girl's voice and countenance without quite knowing why. She was spared the challenge of replying to these sentiments by the timely entrance of Pennystone announcing that dinner was served.

With only six people at table, the talk was general during dinner rather than being confined strictly between immediate neighbors. Given her nature, it was not to be wondered at that Brianna should take advantage of the informal situation, letting the others bear the brunt of the conversation that dwelled mainly on recent political, social, and cultural happenings in the nation's capital. Since there was absolutely nothing she could have contributed from first-hand knowledge, her continued silence was practically preordained and was interrupted only when Christopher Cardorette invited her comments on his chef's offerings during the meal. Her brief appreciative replies to his questions constituted her entire conversational output except for when she was constrained to deny Lady Selina an opinion on the literary merit of a currently popular novel, since she had never heard of, much less read, the work in question. Though unhappily aware of her own conversational shortcomings in this articulate company, at least Brianna found the various topics discussed of more than passing interest. She also enjoyed the vicarious stimulation of two lively political arguments that flared, then subsided at Lady Ormond's tactful intercession.

Alas, the same could not be said of the strained hour the ladies spent together making stilted conversation in the saloon while the gentlemen lingered over their port in the dining room. Initially, Lady Selina had seemed curious about the marriage between Matthew Cardorette and Brianna's sister. After giving a terse, reluctant account of the way the two had met, Brianna had been most relieved when Lady Ormond had frowned down her daughter's subsequent attempts to unearth the reasons behind the ending of the marriage. The discovery that Brianna had never been to London closed another avenue of possible interest. Though the country-bred girl would have enjoyed hearing a description of St. Paul's and other landmarks she'd dreamed of seeing one day, Lady Selina was disinclined to provide any, declaring with a shrug of her pretty shoulders that she was useless at that sort of thing. It didn't take long to exhaust the topic of the weather and accommodations en route to Ashleigh, and Brianna was then reduced to admiring Lady Ormond's skill at embroidery, drawing the older woman out at some length about the intricate altar cloth she was working on while they waited for the men to join them.

Yesterday's attempted kidnapping and the rescue by Sir Harry Paxton proved to be a richer lode when introduced by Lady

Selina. Brianna had no objections to describing the affair in detail and she was perfectly willing to expatiate on the kindness of Sir Harry and his sister in rendering aid to the injured man and showing them such generous hospitality.

"Generous certainly, but not totally disinterested hospitality, I'd wager," Lady Selina said with a knowing smile that brought a puzzled look to Brianna's face.

"I am afraid I do not understand you, Lady Selina. How could it be other than disinterested kindness? We were total strangers to the Paxtons."

"Ah, but it is obvious to a blind man that Sir Harry has great hopes of improving that situation," Lady Selina replied archly.

This pointed observation earned the young lady a disapproving look from her parent, which she ignored, being absorbed in an amused study of Brianna's reactions to the implication.

Confusion, dawning comprehension, denial, and self-consciousness flitted across Brianna's features in rapid succession. The self-consciousness was destined to be longer lasting than the other emotions, thanks to the arrival at that precise moment of the gentlemen from the dining room. As if to prove the accuracy of Lady Selina's speculation, Sir Harry headed straight for the chair beside Brianna, smiling at her with more than ordinary warmth. Brianna carefully avoided any meeting of glances with Lady Selina in her urgent desire not to see the amused satisfaction she was positive would be evident on that flawless face. In fact, until the sudden heat that had scorched her cheeks subsided, she shied away from any visual contact, returning her eyes to her clasped hands whenever anyone sought her glance.

Eventually she was able to overcome her internal cringing and give proper attention to Sir Harry's pleasant discourse. Over the next hour, Brianna had reason to be grateful to her erstwhile rescuer. His patent pleasure in her company, which he frankly monopolized that evening, went a long way toward succouring her spirits, crushed by a feeling of inferiority in the presence of the beautiful and sparkling Lady Selina, who easily held center stage with her lively wit and ready repartee. While seeming no less appreciative of this bravura performance than the other gentlemen present, Sir Harry reserved his warmest smiles for Brianna. The admiration in his blue eyes when they compelled her gaze was balm to her struggling self-esteem. Far from expecting brilliant conversational sallies from her, he was content to accept her genuine interest in hearing about his plans for making improvements on his estate. He welcomed her few comments and was visibly delighted with a minor suggestion she advanced with reference to the rose garden, which was his sister's pride and joy.

Thus the evening she had dreaded passed most pleasantly for Brianna. Her restricted manner of living in Lower Melstrum had never included evening parties graced by charming and eligible members of the opposite sex. Though Meg had attended a few dinner parties with her father before Matthew Cardorette had crashed into their lives, Brianna had been too young at the time for those mild diversions that existed in their locality. The ending of her sister's marriage had effectively ended any remnants of a social life for the Llewellyn family. In her unhappiness and disillusionment Meg had turned inward, relying solely on the companionship of her father and sister. In any case, the rector was not a man who sought the stimulation of social intercourse and since it would never have occurred to Brianna to go to parties without her sister, they simply ceased accepting invitations. With Jamie's birth the Llewellyns' little world had expanded joyfully; he had become the center of their universe, more than compensating for the lack of outside society in their lives.

Brianna Llewellyn at twenty-one had never sampled the heady delights of having an attractive man exhibit a marked predilection for her company until the advent of Sir Harry Paxton. In her absorption in this novel experience she failed to note that Sir Harry's partiality was obvious to every other person present as well. Since Lady Selina's sly suggestion had so overset her earlier, Brianna's imperviousness was providential for it preserved her precarious composure. She went to bed that night in happy ignorance of the fact that Lady Selina's initial amusement had acquired a faint undertone of pique after her efforts to draw Sir Harry into her own orbit had apparently gone unrecognized by that besotted gentleman. Nor was Brianna aware that the cordiality with which Christopher Cardorette had welcomed his nephew's rescuer had stiffened by degrees until it more nearly resembled a frozen formality at the end of the evening.

The next morning brought enlightenment to Brianna in one area. The sense of well-being she had taken to bed with her had still been there when she opened her eyes to sunlight turning the creamy walls a pale gold and accentuating the jewel tones in the lovely oriental rug in the center of her bedchamber. Unhappily, it did not survive the recollection, as she swung her legs over the side of the comfortable bed, that Sir Harry would be returning home soon after breakfast. She knew past any doubt that his gentle conversation and approval had saved her from floundering in

strange social seas last night. Her heart quailed at the thought that
there would be nobody to keep her from sinking without trace in
the future.

As she washed and donned the clothes Hannah had pressed for
her, Brianna tried to keep the door shut against an overactive
imagination. Her days would be spent with Jamie and Molly in
delightful new surroundings in which the child would flourish. It
was only the evenings that would be difficult and they would become less so as she accustomed herself to the company of people
from a world she had only read about. Christopher Cardorette was
disposed to be kind, and she had not sensed any real animosity
beneath Lady Selina's condescension. In time the strangeness
would wear off and they would become easier with each other.

Despite this internal rationalizing, Brianna entered the breakfast parlor in a subdued frame of mind. A quick glance around the
small, sun-filled room showed that neither of the other ladies was
present. Her step slowed, but there was no retreating; the three
gentlemen were already rising. She slipped into the chair Sir
Harry was pulling out beside him as he was seated nearest the
door. In responding to their greeting, she had noted without surprise Sir Harry's welcoming smile and Mr. George Cardorette's
polite indifference. What did give her pause was the look of annoyance that flashed across Christopher Cardorette's face as he
removed his hand from the back of the empty chair beside him.

"Perhaps I should have waited for the other ladies before coming down," she said uncertainly.

"Nonsense, Brianna," Christopher replied. "As Mrs. Dobbs will
have told you, breakfast is always served here at half after eight.
Lady Ormond and Selina are used to town hours. They may
breakfast lightly in their rooms today or wander down later. In a
day or two, they may discover that country air and country pursuits give one a more hearty appetite in the morning." He smiled
but it was a perfunctory effort.

In the next few minutes, Brianna decided the atmosphere in the
cheery room was much less spontaneous than that prevailing the
day before. Sir Harry seemed not to notice that his host's former
cordiality had frozen into a ritual courtesy, but Brianna was puzzled and uncomfortable as she listened to Christopher's short answers to Sir Harry's conversational overtures. She was relieved
when Mr. George Cardorette excused himself to see to some work
awaiting him in the estate office.

"I'll say good-bye now, Sir Harry, and wish you a safe journey
home," he said, coming around the table to shake hands with the

baronet, who had risen from his chair. He nodded to Brianna and left the room after reminding his cousin that he'd expect him later in the office.

Sir Harry settled back into his chair. "Is there any more of that delicious coffee left?" he asked with an easy air.

"Of course." Christopher went to the sideboard and returned carrying the large silver coffeepot. "Brianna?" She held up her cup and he refilled it before doing the same for his guest. "I sent word to the stables to have your horse brought round at a quarter past nine. Plenty of time for a last cup of coffee," he added with impersonal courtesy as he took his own seat again.

Stealing a look at the porcelain clock on a corner shelf, Brianna saw that it was nearly ten minutes past the hour already and she experienced a stab of dismay at the idea of being left without a friend at Ashleigh. Somehow, in the short span of time since their dramatic meeting, Sir Harry had become just that—a friend and champion, someone whose interest in her welfare was real and personal. As her eyes left the clock, they encountered the enigmatic gaze of Christopher Cardorette. She wrenched them away from his intense hazel-eyed scrutiny to seek the safety of Sir Harry's smiling gaze.

"I would like to thank you once more for your crucial intervention the other day, sir," she began with a rush, conscious of time running out. She held up a silencing hand against his automatic disclaimer. "That vicious highwayman would have taken Jamie, and I shudder to think of what might have happened if you had not appeared. I won't embarrass you further by falling on your neck in tearful gratitude," she added with a little smile that contained an element of mischief, "but I am fully cognizant of the enormous debt I owe you. Please convey my thanks to your sister for her gracious hospitality. I shall write to her, of course."

"I should like to bring my sister to call upon you in a sennight or so, after you are settled in at Ashleigh Court."

"I regret that might not be possible," said a cold voice from the end of the table before Brianna could express her delight at the prospect of a visit from Miss Paxton. Two heads turned toward Christopher in surprise. "Lady Ormond and Lady Selina are here for a short visit only," he explained. "Miss Llewellyn will not be able to remain here without a chaperone, so Lady Ormond has kindly suggested bringing Miss Llewellyn and my nephew to London with her until after my marriage takes place."

"And that will be when?" Sir Harry asked.

"The wedding is set for the last day of the year," his host replied.

"My sister and I would be more than delighted to have Miss Llewellyn and the child as our guests at Broadhurst during the interim."

"I'm afraid that is out of the question," Christopher said, summarily disposing of Sir Harry's offer.

Before Brianna could voice her increasing dismay at hearing her immediate future discussed and disposed of without any consultation of her wishes, Pennystone appeared in the doorway.

"One of the grooms has just brought Sir Harry's horse to the front entrance, sir."

"Ah, thank you, Pennystone." Christopher rose and came down the length of the table, leaving the other two with no choice but to emulate him. "And Sir Harry's valise?"

"Already in the hall, sir," replied the butler.

The trio strolled out of the breakfast parlor. She and Sir Harry were being herded like stupid sheep by an all-powerful shepherd. Brianna raged impotently, walking in rebellious silence toward the entrance hall. They reached the back of the hall just as Lady Ormond and Lady Selina descended the main staircase.

"I shall write to you soon," Sir Harry said in an aside to Brianna under cover of the greetings being exchanged between Christopher Cardorette and the ladies from London.

Brianna nodded, still bereft of words to express her outraged sensibilities. But had she been as articulate as a barrister pleading in the courtroom, she would not have been granted the opportunity for argument amidst the ensuing confusion of leavetaking. She murmured a hurried farewell to Sir Harry in her turn, and stood mute and furious as she watched Christopher dispatch his guest with suave civility.

Christopher turned to Lady Ormond the second the door closed behind Sir Harry. "May I conduct you and Selina to the breakfast parlor, ma'am?" he asked solicitously.

As the countess refused, stating their entire satisfaction with the fare that had been brought to their suite, Lady Selina put in eagerly, "I am simply dying to see something of the estate, Chris. It's a beautiful day for a stroll about the grounds."

"Yes," he agreed with a smile, "the house can wait. We should take advantage of the sunshine to wander through the gardens. You will join us, Brianna?"

To Brianna's quivering sensibilities there was an overtone of command implicit in the invitation, which was all of a piece with the cavalier attitude Christopher had revealed in the breakfast parlor. Suddenly, it seemed of the utmost importance to escape that dominating presence until she had considered what her own reaction should be to his assumption that the ordering of her life was within his province, as though she were no older than Jamie.

"Thank you, but I have not even seen Molly or Jamie yet this morning, sir," she said in a voice she kept even by dint of repressing her seething emotions.

She smiled at the ladies and had one foot on the bottom step when Christopher said carelessly, "We'll be happy to delay our outing until you have checked up on the nursery, Brianna."

Her teeth went tight for an instant before she said, not without a private satisfaction at thwarting him in some small way, "I am sorry, but you see, I am accustomed to spending the greater part of the day with Jamie and I must not disappoint him, especially when everything at Ashleigh Court is so new and strange to him. I beg you to hold me excused, sir."

Brianna cast a sweet false smile at her tormentor and continued up the stairs, her back ramrod straight beneath the plain black gown.

8

Despite her stated intention of joining her young nephew, Brianna did not go directly to the nursery but veered away from the back staircase and presently entered her own apartments where she dropped onto one of a pair of charming bergère chairs covered in a gold-and-white floral brocade fabric. If she did not wish Jamie or Molly to see her in this agitated state, she would require a spell of privacy in which to sort out her impressions of what had occurred in the last hour.

The lingering charm of the late fall gardens beneath her window had no appeal for Brianna at that moment. Her thoughts were far less pleasant than the view and confirmed her instinctive reluctance to come to Ashleigh Court. The knowledge that she was virtually dependent on the charity of a person unrelated by the ties of blood or affection could never be less than galling to her pride, but her first objections when the question of residing under Christopher Cardorette's roof arose had been mainly concerned with the permanent inconvenience to him and his bride in having herself foisted onto them. Her fears of intruding in their lives had been stronger than concern over the constant subjugation of her own spirit and independence inherent in the arrangement. After less than twenty-four hours at Ashleigh, however, her own selfish concerns had already become of paramount importance following that eye-opening demonstration in the breakfast parlor that she would no longer have the freedom to choose her own friends. As the master of Ashleigh Court, Christopher Cardorette naturally had the final say as to who was welcome. It was not for her to question this, no matter how she might deplore his summary dismissal of Sir Harry's request to bring his sister to call without even the courtesy of an indefinite promise for the future that would have cost him nothing. It was not the action so much as the manner of its execution that had struck a chill in her heart. Obviously her own wishes in the matter had been of less than no importance in his arbitrary decision to discourage a continuation of the acquaintance.

Brianna was gnawing at her bottom lip as she sat in a tense posture of rebellion gazing blindly through the window. After a few unproductive moments of railing against a fate that had cast her into this disadvantageous position, her shoulders slumped and the stubbornness softened from her jawline. There was nothing she could do to assert her independence in this area, hamstrung as she was by her promise to Meg that she would not desert Jamie. She must do her best to fit in here as unobtrusively as possible while Jamie's need of her existed. It was disappointing to discover that the kindness she thought she had detected in Christopher Cardorette at their first meeting had been no more than the good manners of a host, but she would survive the disappointment. She had not suspected him of having a domineering nature even when he'd been adamant about bringing his nephew under his personal supervision—that was understandable—but his handling of Sir Harry's request this morning had been enlightening, to her deep chagrin. Sir Harry was taller, broader, and older than his host, but in her eyes Christopher had appeared the dominant personality during the brief farewell ceremony.

Brianna sighed deeply for the loss of the promising friendship with Sir Harry and his delightful sister as she rose and prepared to report to the nursery. Her green eyes were shadowed when she checked her appearance in the beautiful Venetian mirror in her sitting room, and she had to remind herself once again of Molly's sharp admonition to keep her own reservations hidden from the child who must be allowed to settle into his birthright smoothly. For her part, she would simply keep the greatest distance possible between herself and the rest of the Cardorettes. After all, there was nothing new in subordinating her own personal life to the needs of her family. It had been thus ever since Matthew Cardorette's advent into their lives and must continue so at least until Jamie was old enough to go to school.

Brianna anchored her heavy knot of hair more securely at the back of her head and hurried up the back stairs to the nursery wing, a determined smile pinned to her lips. The smile became real when she heard childish laughter coming from the playroom before she was halfway down the corridor. Her quiet entrance a moment later went unnoticed at first since the attention of everyone in the nursery was riveted on a complicated structure of wooden blocks being constructed in the middle of the room by the young earl with the assistance of the maid, Lily, who handed over the blocks from a nearby cabinet at the boy's command. Brianna's eyes found Molly sitting near a window, a forgotten heap of sewing on her lap and a little smile on her lips, before returning to the engrossed partnership. The Cardorette brothers must have had very indulgent parents if the huge quantity of blocks in evidence was a fair indication of the supply of toys here, Brianna mused idly, her gaze also transfixed by the structure arising in the center of the floor. It was already taller than its creator, whose assessing eye never left his masterpiece as he gingerly placed a block and held out an imperative hand to his assistant.

"Another block, please."

His accomplice demurred, "I dunno, Master Jamie. That last block made the whole thing shiver. Mayhap you didn't see it, but I did. Don't you think it's tall enough now?"

"Another block," commanded the architect, scorning to acknowledge this craven female utterance. "I am going to use every block in the cupboard for my castle."

"Lawks, Master Jamie," Lily squeaked, handing over another piece, "there's dozens of 'em still in there. That castle's agoing to fall down for certain afore you use up all these blocks."

Intent on the placement of the piece in his hand, the boy ignored the doomsayer. Brianna caught Molly's eye and the two women exchanged a quick smile before their attention was irresistibly drawn back to the unfolding drama. Overcome by the suspense of the moment as the little boy eased the block into place with agonizing slowness, Lily stirred minimally from her kneeling position just as Jamie withdrew his hand. The perilous structure seemed to tremble for a fraction of a second before it collapsed inwardly, reduced in an instant to an untidy heap of blocks at the child's feet.

In the next instant Jamie whirled on his companion, his cherubic features distorted by rage. "*You* made my castle fall, Lily, when you moved!" he charged.

Brianna spoke above the maid's protestations of innocence. "Now, Jamie, you know it is very unfair to blame someone else when things go wrong. If you start with a wider base next time, you will build an even bigger castle."

At the sound of his aunt's voice the little boy abandoned his ruined enterprise and ran to greet her, wrapping his arms tightly around her hips. "Where have you been, Auntie Bree? I've been up for hours, but Molly would not let me go to find you."

"There were things I had to do, dearest," she replied, smiling down at the trusting little face that made all her sacrifice worthwhile. Before Jamie could challenge her vagueness with a child's inflexible determination to discover the reasons behind everything that happened in his world, she continued gently, "Tell Lily you are sorry for blaming her for the collapse of your castle, dearest."

Thoughts of mutiny clouded the small face briefly while he assessed the degree of his aunt's determination, then a sunny smile replaced the clouds as Jamie capitulated. "I am sorry I yelled at you, Lily," he said, giving her an angelic smile before adding craftily, "P'haps your skirt just brushed a *little* against the castle when you moved."

Brianna mentally debated the advisability of demanding an unconditional apology from the boy, then decided to allow him his partial victory. Rome wasn't built in a day. Jamie's childish rages never lasted long. Even at four he showed promise of becoming a reasonable person. In any event, Lily had hastily agreed that mayhap her skirt *had* brushed against the block structure, so this was obviously not the ideal battlefield on which to ram home a moral lesson.

"You did not come up to read me a story last night before I went to bed like you always do, Auntie Bree," Jamie said with a steely stare. "Molly don't read as good as you."

"That's gratitude for you," Molly said *sotto voce*, resuming her sewing.

Brianna grinned at her friend before turning to face her accuser. "Last night was our first night at Ashleigh Court, sweetheart, and I did not quite know what the schedule was for the grown-ups' meals, but I'll find time to read to you every day, I promise. Would you like me to read a story now?" The child assenting with an eager nod, she went on, "While you are putting away your blocks, I'll look in these cabinets for a new book."

"Lily can put the blocks away," Jamie said. "I'll find a book."

"You know the rule, Jamie. You must put away the toys you take out before you go on to something new."

"Lily took the blocks out, not me," the child pointed out, standing his ground.

Brianna disciplined a smile. "Even so, they were for you to play with, which means the responsibility for putting them away is also yours."

"What means that word—responsibility?" Jamie asked, never loath to employ delaying tactics.

"It means it is your duty, your job to put the blocks away," his aunt replied implacably. As Jamie still hesitated, weighing whether to continue his protest, Brianna, mentally reflecting on how often child rearing seemed to be an exercise in the art of compromise, added on an inspiration, "Lily may help you put them away if you ask her nicely."

This face-saving offer appealed to Jamie, who smiled widely at his young attendant. "Will you help me, please, Lily?"

"O' course, Master Jamie." A smiling Lily began gathering blocks together, and the little boy joined her in the task.

"Crisis averted, victory in doubt," Molly muttered as Brianna opened the cabinet to the left of the window in search of a book.

Brianna chuckled. "I am just beginning to gain a true appreciation of your efforts in raising Meg and me, Molly. Was it one continuous struggle to avoid losing the upper hand?"

Molly smiled reminiscently. "Meg was easy to raise, compliant, gentle, and dutiful. You, on the other hand, had your moments of rebellion like this young man."

"I don't recall that you were ever in danger of losing control of the reins."

"Oh, no," Molly agreed, smiling at the dryness in the other's tones. "The best of children will become tyrants if they are permitted. It is not their fault. What's worse, such children never learn self-discipline or develop a sense of fairness. I pity the folk that have to deal with them as adults."

Brianna barely had time to receive Molly's assurances that she had slept very well in her attractive new quarters before Jamie finished his chore and demanded his story. She gathered him onto her lap in the capacious rocking chair in a corner of the room and proceeded to explore the world of fantasy with her beloved little companion.

Brianna spent a happy morning with her nephew, sending Lily down to the kitchen eventually to tell the cook she would share nursery lunch. Molly glanced rather sharply at her former nursling but made no comment until Brianna had tucked Jamie in his bed for a nap over his heated protests.

When the younger woman returned to the playroom, Molly put down her sewing and said bluntly, "Why did you not go down to eat lunch with the others?"

"I thought Jamie needed my presence on his first day in this huge house full of strangers."

Molly's next question ignored this plausible statement. "Don't you like them, Mr. Cardorette's cousin and his fiancée and her mother? Are they unfriendly or condescending to you?"

"N-no. They have all been pleasant and civil to me."

"But?" Molly asked.

"These people are not like us, Molly. They come from a world we know nothing of, so it is perfectly reasonable that they should find me dull and uninteresting. We have nothing in common."

"I should think human beings could always find some common ground if they seek it. You have to live among these people, so the sooner you try to find that common ground the better off you will be. Hiding out in the nursery won't achieve much."

There was a sustained silence while Molly went back to her sewing and Brianna wandered restlessly about the large, sunny room, unaware that her friend's glance keeping track of her meanderings contained all the sympathy that had been absent in her practical advice. At length, Brianna turned and said slowly, "I am persuaded it is for the best to keep my contacts with the others here to a minimum. That is very likely what Christopher Cardorette would prefer. This morning when Sir Harry Paxton said he would like to bring his sister to call on me soon, Mr. Cardorette brushed aside his request with some tale of my going to London with Jamie when Lady Selina leaves because there will be no chaperone here until after his marriage."

Molly lowered her work to her lap again, looking thoughtful. "I confess I had not considered that aspect of the situation, what with a houseful of servants and myself here also, but he's correct of course. Though I'd think it would make more sense to bring in some respectable woman to stay with you rather than uproot Jamie a second time."

"It wasn't just that, Molly," Brianna said in a rush. "I could tell by his brusqueness to Sir Harry that he intended to discourage any continuation of the acquaintance. He doesn't mean me to have any friends except of his own choosing despite his fine talk of my being a member of his family. I shall have no more independence of action than the youngest scullery maid at Ashleigh—less, for she at least is permitted the companionship of the other servants."

Molly folded her sewing, her eyes intent on the precise movements of her capable hands, before she rose from her chair with an air of decision. "Now, do not allow yourself to wallow in self-pity," she recommended in firm tones. "It's a sheer waste of time and energy. Besides, it's early days yet to be making sweeping judgments. I am going to put my feet up for an hour while that young rascal sleeps. I suggest you do the same. When he wakens you can take him outdoors to explore the grounds. The fresh air will do you both good. I'll see you later."

Brianna looked on with a sense of frustration as her oldest friend and confidante went quietly out of the nursery. Molly had

listened to her troubles as always, but this time she had offered no
wise solution. In essence, she had merely advised Brianna to reserve judgment and try to find accommodation with these alien
people, sensible counsel no doubt but nothing that could materially improve the restrictive conditions under which they must
dwell here at Ashleigh Court.

Dissatisfaction with her lot sat heavily upon Brianna as she left
the nursery in her turn, heading with reluctant steps toward her
own suite for lack of any more appealing choice. She had no intention of following her friend's example of lying down upon her
bed, however. In the ordinary way, Brianna never felt tired, and
lying down would only result in more idle time to devote to her
unhappy thoughts. Instead she used the interval to unpack all the
personal bits and pieces she had brought from her home. It was a
bittersweet undertaking; each item brought back cherished memories of the past and underscored her present loneliness. She shed
more than one tear in the next hour as she unwrapped the precious
oddments and repeatedly toured her new domain for suitable
places to display them. The miniature of her mother, painted before her marriage, that had always held pride of place atop her father's chest of drawers she placed on the elegantly styled
mahogany dressing table with its beautiful mirror. The leather
volumes of poetry inscribed to her by her father went on the bedside table, where they would always be near to hand. For want of
a nail and, truth to tell, the courage to put a hole in the gold-and-
white striped walls in the sitting room, Brianna stood the rather
clumsily framed sampler Meg had stitched when she was ten
years old on the mantelpiece. After some deliberation she removed a porcelain figure of a shepherdess from the narrow table
below the Venetian mirror, replacing it with the small easel that
held a pencil sketch her mother had done of her two smiling
young daughters, each with an arm about her sister's waist. She
had been thirteen and Meg fifteen, Brianna mused, as she made a
small adjustment of the easel. Her mother had done the drawing
as a surprise for her husband's birthday shortly before her own
untimely death from a sudden violent stomach disorder.

Glancing around the rooms with a critical eye when she had
finished arranging her personal treasures, Brianna had to concede
that some of the additions may have detracted a bit from the former visual perfection of the decor, but at least she now felt more
at home in the apartments Christopher Cardorette had personally
assigned to her.

Her mood had improved for the better with this assertion of her own individuality and she was quite cheerful when she proposed a walk to Jamie after his nap. The rest of the afternoon passed happily in exploring the grounds in the immediate proximity to the house. To a child used to playing in a small garden all his life, the seemingly unending sweep of gardens, lawns, ornamental water, and pastures, with mysterious woods beckoning from a distance, was nothing short of an earthly paradise. Jamie could scarcely contain his delight in this expanded world, darting from one place to another that afternoon, ever eager to see around the next corner. His joy was infectious and communicated itself to his aunt who willingly tramped along in his erratic wake.

The hours sped by and it was not until Brianna began to feel a lack of warmth in the sun's rays that they turned their steps back toward the house. Even then, Jamie had to be coaxed and cajoled with a promise that they would continue their exploration the very next day to soften his resistance to going back indoors. The excited child was so eager to describe his wanderings to Molly that it took ages to settle him into a receptive mood for his supper.

When she returned at last to her own rooms, Brianna had barely time enough to wash her hands and jump into the dress she had worn the previous evening if she were to avoid the solecism of a tardy appearance in the saloon. She waved off Hannah's offer to redo her hair, grabbed a shawl and a clean handkerchief from the drawer in the dressing table, and hurried downstairs, unaware that the hours spent outdoors had given her clear porcelain skin a delicate tinge of rose. Likewise, her glance in the mirror had been too fleeting to detect all the tendrils of hair that had escaped from her once-neat chignon while she was playing hide-and-seek with her nephew in the shrubbery. A cursory hand swept over her hair as she ran lightly down the stairs discovered a couple of tresses on the back of her neck and, with a muttered oath, she slowed her step while she quickly repinned them into the mass with more hope than expectation that she had restored her customary neat appearance.

It seemed her hopes in this direction were unfounded. As Brianna entered the saloon, still wrestling with the knitted shawl that had slipped from her shoulders during the repinning operation, Lady Selina said gaily, "Goodness, it must be more draughty in the corridors than I thought. Were you blown in by a high wind, Miss Llewellyn?"

Uncomfortably aware that she was now the focus of everyone's attention, Brianna let her resentment overcome her timidity as she answered more sharply than was strictly polite. "No, I simply lost

track of the time this afternoon and had to hurry over my changing. I apologize if I present a disheveled appearance."

"I would rather call it an enchanting disarray," Christopher
said, presenting Brianna with a glass of sherry, his smiling eyes
lingering on a reddish curl caressing the side of her neck behind
her ear.

"How gallant of you, Chris," Lady Selina said lightly, while
Brianna sank onto a chair and took a sip of her sherry, praying
that the heat this compliment had brought to her cheeks was not
visible to the company. The last thing she wanted was to blush
like a schoolgirl in front of these people who were used to exchanging this sort of badinage as a matter of course.

"I am a gallant person, my dear Selina. Have you not found me
so?" Christopher protested with a wounded look.

"Upon occasion," the blond girl allowed, smiling up at her fiancé in what Brianna, watching the pair from under lowered
lashes, could only term an intimate fashion. Which was perfectly
fine, she assured herself hastily. The couple was betrothed and
could be expected to engage in behavior that exhibited their natural partiality for each other. What threw her off stride was something resembling intimacy that she occasionally saw in Christopher's eyes when he looked at herself. She must be mistaken.
She was no doubt too inexperienced to distinguish real emotion
from the purely automatic masculine gallantry to which Lady
Selina had just referred. Her reading indicated that worldly persons affected odd mannerisms and subscribed to artificial pat-
terns of discourse foreign to the simple country people among whom
she had always lived. Would she ever really comprehend these
people?

"We missed you at lunch today, Miss Llewellyn," Lady Selina
said now, scattering Brianna's thoughts. "And at tea, which
Mama and I enjoyed in solitary state in the drawing room. Were
you three off gallivanting about the estate?" she asked, including
the men in her laughing question.

"I lunched in the nursery as I generally do," Brianna replied,
noting that Christopher Cardorette was listening with narrowed
eyes to her response, "and had no tea at all. Jamie was so en-
thralled to be exploring the grounds this afternoon that I could not
induce him to go inside until nearly his suppertime."

"And I was in the estate office almost all day slaving over
some accounts," Mr. George Cardorette explained.

"Poor George, no time for gallivanting on this lovely day,"

Lady Selina exclaimed with mock pity. "You are a slave driver, Chris!"

"I protest the injustice of the allegation. I myself spent the afternoon supervising the mending of some fences," Christopher said in his own defense. He then turned to Brianna. "Now that James's first day in new surroundings has been successfully accomplished, I expect it will be a simple matter to arrange to be free to take tea with the other ladies in the afternoon."

The words were spoken with exquisite courtesy but the command behind them was crystal clear to Brianna. Before she could give voice to rebellion or acquiescence (and when reviewing the conversation later before going to sleep, it was impossible to recall which had been nearer the tip of her tongue), her decision was preempted by Pennystone's announcement of dinner.

The cousins did not linger in the dining room that evening. Their early return to the saloon was welcomed by all three ladies with unadmitted relief, for the younger two had developed no very easy manner with each other as yet, and Lady Ormond was bored with trying to elicit more than a minimal response to direct questions from Miss Llewellyn, surely the most tongue-tied girl it had ever been her misfortune to try to engage in conversation.

The problem of how to get through the rest of the evening before the tea tray was brought in was solved by George Cardorette who requested that Lady Selina give them the pleasure of hearing her sing.

Pleasure it certainly was. For the next hour Brianna existed in a cloud of enchantment, thrilling to the most beautiful music it had ever been her privilege to hear. Meg had possessed a sweet though limited voice, but her sister had never sung again after Matthew left Herefordshire. Lady Selina's trained and powerful soprano was of another order entirely.

Hearing the sincerity in Brianna's praise of her daughter's performance and the eagerness with which she appealed for yet another song each time Selina proposed to end her impromptu recital, Lady Ormond's heart warmed to the shy country girl. Miss Llewellyn's awkwardness in company was the natural result of her restricted upbringing and could be overcome with increased exposure to a wider society. She was not at all deficient in understanding, and she possessed a sweetness of expression that Lady Ormond suspected was more a reflection of her basic nature than the strict training young ladies received to advance their chances on the marriage mart. Of course, she could not hold a candle to Selina, who was an Incomparable by any standard of judgment, but Brianna Llewellyn was a taking little thing and something could be made of her after her period of mourning was over. If Christopher Cardorette was willing to provide Miss Llewellyn with a modest dowry, she might even achieve a respectable alliance. Between them, she and Selina might be able to fire her off successfully next autumn, which would remove her from this household, an end devoutly to be desired. It never did to have two women under one roof, particularly when the second one was pretty and unattached. It was not casting aspersions on Christopher Cardorette's honor to recognize this salient fact. It merely acknowledged the weakness inherent in the masculine nature when confronted by temptation in the form of a pretty woman and propinquity, especially when there was not present that degree of mutual affection between husband and wife that was required to offset the temptation and sustain the marriage. On Selina's side, there was the question of an element of conquest present that had troubled her mother from the beginning, though a stranger learning that Selina had not backed out of the betrothal when offered her freedom might reasonably conclude that she was animated by the purest affection. As for Christopher, the countess could not pretend to a deep understanding of his character on such short acquaintance, but she had looked in vain for a certain light in his eyes when they dwelled on Selina. She'd seen admiration, respect for his betrothed's intellect, liking, even an amused delight in her wit, but never that . . . that yearning with which a man looks at the woman he longs to make his own. On the contrary, after little more than twenty-four hours at Ashleigh Court, she'd wondered more than once if she'd spotted that telltale yearning in his eyes when they gazed at Brianna Llewellyn. The countess was not so blinded by maternal partiality as to dismiss the idea that any man could prefer another and lesser female to her lovely daughter. Romantic attraction between men and women was a mysterious force, not to be explained by reason or logic. It struck without warning and often took no account of honor.

Lady Ormond had already decided, when she shepherded the two young women upstairs an hour later, that if her daughter persisted in going through with this marriage it was going to be a matter of the first priority to remove Miss Brianna Llewellyn from beneath Selina's roof.

Brianna went to bed in a music-induced state of contentment that evening, unaware that yet another unrelated person was proposing to take over the ordering of her future.

9

"I've found you, Auntie Bree! I win!"

The triumphant words, delivered in a ringing treble, drifted into the estate office through a partially opened window and reached the man writing at the large desk. His attention captured, Christopher Cardorette raised his head from the note he was leaving for his cousin. A woman's soft laugh harmonized with the child's exalted shouts.

The line of Christopher's mouth widened as he envisioned Brianna indulging her little nephew in his insatiable passion for hide-and-seek in the shrubbery surrounding this wing of the house. He remained unmoving until even the faint echoes of the sounds had faded away; he bent forward then, the tiny scratching noises made by his pen the only sounds to disturb the late-afternoon stillness. When he'd completed his message he did not immediately leave the office but sat back in the chair staring at the pen he was turning between his fingers as if searching for cracks. Actually, the motion was automatic and his eyes were unfocused as he mentally reviewed the past sennight.

Matt's son had settled in contentedly—nay, that was too tame a word to describe the small boy's joyous embrace of his ancestral heritage in toto. Pennystone reported that James had been seen exploring various corners of the house on several occasions when he'd eluded his keepers for a half hour. Evidently he already had the kitchen staff wound round his thumb and had made friends with both footmen, as well as having learned the names of all the indoor servants within a few days. Christopher's lips softened and spread as he recalled his nephew's delight when he'd brought him to visit the stables, and the dozens of questions he'd fired at his uncle. By the time the nursemaid, Lily, had appeared to lead her protesting charge to the nursery for lunch, Christopher had been worn out with explaining, not to mention improvising tactful delays in granting James's repeated requests to be put on a horse posthaste and allowed to gallop off into the distance. He must see to acquiring a pony for the boy as soon as feasible. Perhaps George would know of a suitable animal in the neighborhood.

Christopher added a line to his message and put down the pen, coming out from behind the desk, his eyes making a slow survey of his surroundings. There was little enough to engage his interest. Apart from the ornate desk, the room's furnishings consisted of a nondescript table whose scarred top held a decanter and glasses, a wing chair for visitors, and a tall, four-paneled wooden screen painted with a hunting scene placed across one corner. He still did not leave the office but walked over to the window instead. There were no longer any human sounds to be discerned among the rustlings in the shrubbery, nor any sight of a living creature, not even a bird. James and Brianna must have taken themselves elsewhere in their rambles. He'd been astonished to learn just how much territory a fragile-looking young woman and a small boy could cover on foot when he'd had a number of farm workers and villagers smilingly report meeting the new earl in various places, some at quite a distance from the house. He must remember to caution Brianna about the caves located near a line of cliffs on the western border of the estate, though he would hope that area was well beyond their reach, certainly on foot. So far, though she admitted to riding in her youth, Brianna had not availed herself of his offer to mount her, refusing each invitation to ride with the excuse that she had promised to do something or other with her nephew.

Christopher's eyes narrowed and his forehead creased as he allowed himself to consider Brianna Llewellyn. If he were to be completely honest with himself, something that had been habitual in the uncomplicated past, he must own to being quite irrationally disappointed not to have advanced in friendship with Brianna after having her under his roof all this time. Most of the hours he could spare from estate affairs, and some he couldn't spare, were spent in the company of his fiancée, which was only to be expected. He walked with Selina in the gardens, rode with her over the estate, and had even called at the rectory one day when their ride had brought them to the village.

Brianna had refused every invitation to join them in any activity. She had not come down to breakfast since that first morning, electing as had his fiancée and her mother to take her morning meal in her apartments before going up to the nursery where she persisted in remaining for lunch. She had, he acknowledged grudgingly, presented herself for afternoon tea following his strong hint to that effect, but most often he was still somewhere about the estate at that hour. The evenings were spent in general conversation, which meant that Brianna spoke only when directly addressed, or in musical activity, which meant listening while Selina entertained them with her music. Brianna had firmly denied possessing any voice at all the first time Selina had deferred to her, insisting with patent sincerity that she was never so happy as when listening to Lady Selina's vocal renditions. He never tired of hearing his fiancée's lovely voice either, but the fact remained that such a program insured that he should have no opportunity to improve his acquaintance with Brianna.

Too honest to deny that the frustration this state of affairs produced was eating away at his good nature and his patience, he was disliking himself very much indeed for not being able to overcome this personal hankering, which increased in intensity as the days passed. He told himself repeatedly that Brianna Llewellyn was nothing out of the common run of females, certainly not to be compared in the same breath with his betrothed when it came to physical beauty and social accomplishment. Conceding for the sake of argument that the particular arrangement of features, coloring, form, and texture that was uniquely Brianna added up to a strong appeal to his senses, this was all superficial. There was nothing in her personality or character as far as he had been able to fathom either, what with all the defenses she threw up to prevent a real understanding, that should make her company seem more desirable to him than that of his affianced wife.

Yet desire her he did, against his will and his honor, and thus the frustration and self-loathing. This torturous thinking only fed his self-indulgence. What he must do was cut her out of his thoughts entirely. Grimacing with disgust at his weakness, Christopher stalked out of the estate office.

The following day Christopher went up to the nursery before lunch. Brianna and Miss Lloyd looked up in faint surprise from their sewing. Miss Lloyd's face warmed into a smile but Brianna's expression remained wary. This he noted in the split second before his nephew, who had been absorbed in setting up two opposing armies of toy soldiers, spotted him and jumped to his feet.

"Uncle Chris, Uncle Chris, can I ride the horses yet? I'm bigger now, and I ate all my vegetables yesterday, didn't I, Auntie Bree?"

"Did he, Auntie Bree?" Christopher parroted, hoping to surprise a smile out of the lovely young woman watching him gravely.

She did smile, barely, but directed her reply to the child. "You're not big enough to ride yet, Jamie, and you must not tease your uncle about this every time you see him or he will think you badly behaved indeed."

Completely unabashed by this reprimand, Jamie promptly adjusted his sights to a more attainable goal. "Well then, will you toss me in the air again, Uncle Chris?"

Christopher laughed and obliged, tossing his small nephew up and catching him over his head. Jamie's squeal of delight did not quite drown Brianna's little gasp of fright. Seeing the challenge in the man's eyes, she bit off the protest he knew she wished to make against such rough play, choosing to avoid confrontation. Jamie demanded another toss, but Christopher avoided goading Brianna further, electing to divert the child's attention to the package he had put on a table when he came into the room.

Jamie's eyes grew round. "A present for me, Uncle Chris?" He proceeded to rip off the wrapping paper, uncovering a pile of books. "Are all these books really mine?"

"All except the big one on the bottom. That is for your aunt," Christopher replied, taking the volume in question over to the speechless young woman whose eyes were almost as round as the child's as she glanced from the book in his hands to his face. "This had just been published when I was last in London," he explained. "I thought you might enjoy it."

"For me?" There was a husky note in her voice and the movements of her hands to accept the volume he was holding out were tentative at first. She recovered from her first surprise, and read the title aloud. *"Picturesque Views of Public Edifices in Paris.* Oh, what lovely drawings, and they are so beautifully aquatinted! Thank you so much, sir. No one has ever given me anything so wonderful before."

She made an unconscious little gesture of hugging the book to her chest as she gazed up at him with a radiant smile, her green eyes glowing like emeralds.

It was over in a minute. Jamie's voice sought his attention. Brianna turned to hold out the volume for her friend's inspection, and the next time she looked in his direction the cool mask behind which she dwelled when addressing him was securely in place once more. He might almost have imagined those few seconds of deep rapport.

But he hadn't imagined it. For an instant of perfect communion their two souls had been isolated in the universe, purposely and willingly divorced from the rest of humanity. And that was why he made a solemn promise to himself as he left the playroom that he would not again seek Brianna out. Such a moment could not be permitted to happen again now that he knew the extent of his infatuation, for that was what this must be, this overwhelming desire for the company of one person only. His heart had been beating like a drum gone wild back there when she had looked up at him with those beautiful eyes softer than he'd ever seen them. It was unfair to Selina that he should feel this way about another woman. He could not help his feelings, but his behavior he could and would control. As he made his way down to the dining room for lunch, Christopher was still shaken by the experience he'd just undergone and sobered by the knowledge that his honor demanded that he avoid similar situations in the future.

It took every ounce of concentration he possessed to act the role of host and prospective bridegroom at lunch. Happily, the ladies were full of the dinner party that evening that would introduce them to the people who would soon be Selina's neighbors. He had invited all the genteel families within a comfortable distance to meet his future bride. It was unfortunate that the news of his brother's secret marriage and heir had not been allowed to die down before he presented Selina, but he had every expectation that she would have the county elite eating out of her hand in short order once their curiosity had been satisfied on the other count. He was going to have to be on his toes, though, if he was to conceal the recent date of Meg Llewellyn's death. No doubt some of these people had been aware of Matt's engagement to Selina Milliken, although the marriage had been scheduled to take place in London, as was his own. He doubted it would be possible to keep Brianna forever in ignorance of Matt's intention to marry bigamously without hiding her away like a skeleton in the closet, and this he would not do. If she would not agree to keeping silent about the date of her sister's death in order to protect the name Matt had dishonored, then they would simply have to ride out the scandal.

He had let his fiancée and her family assume that Matt's wife had died years ago and that her father had concealed the fact of the child's birth from his son-in-law. They had not questioned this plausible story, and so far, Brianna and Selina had not reached a stage of intimacy where the subject might arise between them. At this point, a casual comment from anyone's lips could bring the whole house of cards down and send the buried scandal boiling to the surface. He and George would be walking a tightrope tonight, indeed had been walking one from the moment the two young women met. Sooner or later one or the other would fall off. At present he'd be hard-pressed to decide whether he disliked the idea of scandal or the constant hypocrisy more. Richly though Matt may have deserved that his double life become public knowledge, Christopher knew he could not voluntarily destroy his brother's memory, for James's sake if no other reason. Even accepting that Selina and Brianna must learn the truth eventually, he had not been able to divulge the disgraceful secret to either woman up to the present moment, though he could not delay much longer.

Christopher could scarcely be said to be in the proper frame of mind for a party when carriages began arriving at Ashleigh that evening. His fiancée's exuberant spirits irritated him, to his shame, and Brianna's not entirely unexpected attempt to withdraw annoyed him more. He was at great pains to conceal both reactions and his general malaise, but the continued tension was extremely wearing.

As anticipated, Selina's spectacular looks and animation assured her instant success, and not exclusively with the masculine element either. His fiancée was too clever to make enemies of members of her own sex. As in London, her poise was unassailable; she seemed always to know just what to say to the dowagers and even to jealous mamas of the girls who were cast in the shade by her mere presence at the same assembly. What an asset she would be to a man hoping to carve out a political career for himself. His admiration for her performance that evening was sincere and ungrudging, and if he secretly questioned her own sincerity or wondered if it was anything beyond a well-learned role she played with consummate skill, it was his own cynicism he should and did deplore.

Christopher was pleasantly surprised to note late in the evening that Brianna too had apparently been approved by her new neighbors. When she had come downstairs tonight in the same obviously inexpensive black gown unrelieved by the smallest fashionable detail that she had worn almost every evening at Ashleigh, he'd railed inwardly against the conventions that prevented him from arraying her in a manner befitting her loveliness, hating that she would appear a mere shadow beside Selina's gold-and-white brilliance. Cheap clothing could not conceal the porcelain purity of her pale skin or dim the lustre of jewel-toned eyes with their dense black lashes, but he feared that, combined with her native shyness, the dull costume would make it easy for people to relegate her to the background. He had charged his cousin with the task of supporting Brianna and protecting her from falling into the clutches of possible scandal-seeking matrons desirous of uncovering any sordid details of Matt's marriage from the only source with firsthand knowledge. George's good offices had not been too much in demand, luckily. It might be that Brianna's timidity touched a chord of sympathy in some of the older ladies, or mayhap her sweet diffidence was actually a relief after Selina's intimidating mastery of her present environment. Whatever the reason, Christopher was relieved to see Brianna chatting comfortably with several of his mother's old friends when the men returned to the ladies after dinner. While he had been supplying his male guests with port, snuff, and cigars in the dining room, half of his mind had been busy worrying about whether the women had succeeded in ferreting out his brother's secret during the all-female conclave in the drawing room.

He'd determined on music as the safest post-dinner program since it limited the amount of conversational interaction. Under Lady Ormond's skillful direction, the rest of the evening passed enjoyably for the guests. By sheer good fortune, the two young ladies and the trio of gentlemen who sang and played before Selina were sufficiently talented not to be retroactively overshadowed by his fiancée, whom Lady Ormond wisely kept to last. It would have needed a superbly confident performer to willingly follow an artist of Selina's caliber.

By the time his guests began to make their farewells, Christopher was more fatigued than after a day's forced march through the Pyrenees. He was convinced he'd discovered the true meaning of a contest of endurance. Everyone expressed seemingly genuine thanks for a superb dinner and an enjoyable evening. Since his chef had outdone himself, Christopher supposed that part was true but wondered passingly how many of the smiling faces prating of enjoyment were as deceptive as his own. He pulled himself back from this irrelevant reverie, knowing he must maintain his alertness just a bit longer.

The last to leave were Mr. and Mrs. Amphlett, whose property marched along the estate on the south. Mrs. Amphlett had been his mother's closest friend and he would always remember her kindness to two motherless boys with gratitude. A sudden impulse led him to bend and press a kiss on her smooth cheek after he'd shaken hands with her rotund spouse.

"It is always good to see you, ma'am."

The small woman with apple cheeks beamed a smile up at him. "It has been all too seldom of late years, my dear boy. I trust we'll have the happiness of seeing a lot more of you and your lovely bride in the future." She turned to offer her hand to Lady Selina. "It has been a pleasure to meet you, Lady Selina. I wish you joy in your coming nuptials and will look forward to calling at Ashleigh in the new year when you are at home to visitors."

"Thank you, ma'am. I too shall look forward to improving my acquaintance with my new neighbors."

Mrs. Amphlett then turned to Brianna who hovered on the edge of the group, prevented from escaping by Mr. George Cardorette's bulky presence. "I shall hope to see you even sooner, Miss Llewellyn, and I must meet that young nephew of yours. From what you have told me, he sounds remarkably like his father and uncle, who were lively scamps at that tender age. How much I wish that dear Felicity could have lived to see her grandson. She would have been so grateful to you, my dear child, for taking such loving care of him all this time."

"Indeed, ma'am, you give me too much credit. I did but continue what my sister began," Brianna protested.

Christopher cut in, "Brianna is too modest. I am persuaded you and I would agree, ma'am, that it is her constant devotion that is primarily responsible for the fact that James is a healthy and happy child today."

In the little silence that rang out before his fiancée slipped a hand under his arm, saying brightly, "Yes indeed, it is a tribute to Miss Llewellyn," Christopher had time to wonder if there was not in his voice more fervor than might be reasonably accounted for in his role of grateful uncle. He'd jumped in just now, driven by a sudden conviction that Brianna was about to disclose the fact that her sister was not long deceased. Mrs. Amphlett's benevolent smile was unchanged, however, and she took her leave after exacting a promise from Brianna to bring James to call when her grandchildren came to visit in ten days' time.

A weight slid from Christopher's shoulders as the door shut behind the last of his guests. He'd been dreading this first encounter with his neighbors since Matt's marriage and parenthood had come to light, but it had been a good idea to get it over with in one fell swoop. Hopefully, any drama surrounding James and Brianna's arrival at Ashleigh Court and his own upcoming marriage was now and forever dispelled by the tranquil domestic picture they had all tried to present this evening. His smile, young and carefree for the moment, swept over the members of his household. "Shall we partake of a last cup of tea and discuss the neighbors behind their backs?" he suggested with a glint of mischief.

Lady Ormond smiled but insisted that she and the young ladies were more in need of their beds than a gossip session at present. Brianna had already sidled over to the staircase. Lady Ormond and her daughter joined her presently, leaving the cousins to drink brandy in masculine solitude in the study.

The momentary euphoria at having gotten through the evening with no embarrassing revelations had quickly drained out of Christopher, leaving an aftertaste of deceit in his mouth that brandy could not dissipate. He stared at the amber liquid in his glass with a jaundiced eye.

"We brushed through the evening without incident, but it cannot go on indefinitely, George. Even if we can keep Matt's bigamous intentions from becoming public knowledge, Selina and Brianna have to know the truth sometime. They will soon share a roof permanently. It is whistling in the dark to expect that the subject of Selina's engagement to Matt will never come up."

George raised his serious dark gaze from his glass to his cousin's face. "Are you so certain then that those two will actually share more than a temporary roof?" he asked quietly.

"What do you mean?" All expression had vanished from Christopher's face.

"I must admit I was . . . surprised when you wrote from London that Lady Selina intended to go through with the marriage," George replied. Then he added, "No need to poker up. I am well aware that what is between you two is none of my affair, but her father might well have withdrawn his permission in the circumstances. Then, since you've been back—" He broke off and resumed staring into his glass.

Somewhere in the house a board creaked and the ticking of the mantel clock became audible in the lengthening silence.

"Yes?" Christopher prompted, a hint of impatience in his voice. "Since I've been back?"

"Best not go on," his cousin said, waving a dismissive hand. "You might not appreciate my frankness."

"Now that you've started, you might as well get it out of your system, George. I'll survive the frankness, and I daresay you'll survive being told to mind your own business." Christopher's tone was wry, but his eyes drilled into his cousin's.

"Very well then." George drank the last of his brandy and lumbered to his feet. "As I said, it was something of a surprise that the betrothal was to stand. Naturally one assumed the reason to be a strong mutual attachment, but there's been precious little evidence of any romantic attachment between the pair of you since

your arrival." George paused here, but his cousin continued to
stare at him, his face a closed book. The big man proceeded more
slowly, feeling his way. "From the point of view of an onlooker,
I'd say all the blame lies at your door. Selina is too clever to wear
her heart on her sleeve, but she has given you opportunities to
wax sentimental in the time-honored style of suitors if you should
be so inclined, opportunities you've studiously ignored. She is no
fool and it won't have escaped her notice that your eyes follow
Brianna Llewellyn's every movement more closely than mere civility would dictate. In the hall just now she intervened to distract
Mrs. Amphlett from making a similar observation."

When his frowning cousin still did not respond, George walked
over to the door, turning to add, "If it is your wish to end your betrothal, I'd say you are going about it in the right way. In that
case, should there be any need for either girl to learn of Matt's intention to commit bigamy? Do not torture yourself over this, Kit,"
he went on, this time not inviting any comment. "From my long
knowledge of Matt, I'm inclined to believe that he'd entirely forgotten about that early marriage by the time he fell in love with
Selina."

"*Forgotten!*" Incredulity was in every rounded line of Christopher's face.

"It's not so incredible when you consider Matt's propensity for
ignoring bad news and refusing to see obstacles in his path. You
will concede that he always had great difficulty in accepting that
matters might not fall out the way he desired them; he was always
genuinely astonished when he lost one of his preposterous wa-
gers. In some ways he was like a child, with a child's tendency to
believe what it wants to believe and forget what will negate its
rosy vision. When he couldn't summon the courage to tell Uncle
Herbert about his marriage—and he was deep in debt at the
time—what was more likely than that he simply put it out of his
mind? He ignored the situation until he was actually able to forget
the marriage happened. You stare, but you might try looking at it
in that light. Good night, Kit."

Christopher did not move when his cousin left the study, but
sat sprawled in his chair, his legs apart and his glass balanced on
his stomach while he stared broodingly into its depths as if seeking knowledge or advice. In only one respect had George's per-
spicacity surprised him. He'd honestly tried to conceal his
burning interest in Brianna, knowing he owed it to his fiancée, but
evidently his eyes had betrayed him, at least to his cousin. At that
moment he saw himself as the lowest species of worm. He had

gone into this engagement with cool deliberation, taking advantage of the previous connection with his brother to cut out a number of would-be suitors during Selina's period of half-mourning. By dying, Matt might be said to have wronged her unintentionally; though his death before he got her to the altar had prevented a far greater wrong, did she but know it. Matt's brother could not compound the iniquity by trying to wriggle out of this betrothal, not without abandoning his honor forever. Even his bone-deep conviction that Selina did not really love him could not alter the case. If she desired this marriage, he owed it to her to do all in his power to fulfill her expectations.

George had pronounced no judgment upon his actions, but if the reference to his interest in Brianna had been an oblique reminder of how a gentleman should conduct himself toward the woman he had asked to become his wife, then he must profit by this advice. He must redouble his efforts to please Selina and never lower his guard when Brianna was present.

Christopher got slowly to his feet and set his glass and his cousin's on the tray on top of the cabinet that held the liquor supply. He checked that the coals were scattered in the fireplace and extinguished the oil lamps before exiting the room. All his careful movements reflected a heaviness that was foreign to his normal decisive manner. He felt decades older than the man who had returned to England four short months ago and blithely set about selecting a wife to grace his new position.

10

In the days that followed, Christopher made a conscientious attempt to banish Brianna from his thoughts entirely. He put himself at his betrothed's disposal, riding with her whenever the changeable late November weather permitted and practicing duets in the saloon when they were confined indoors. He personally conducted her on a tour of the house that included every corner of every wing from attics to cellars. He invited her opinions and listened receptively to the intelligent suggestions she made for refurbishing a number of rooms that had grown somewhat shabby over the years. He kissed her in the rose garden one afternoon and found her almost more responsive than he was prepared for. When voices close by necessitated breaking off the embrace, he tried, unsuccessfully, to persuade himself that the feeling that washed over him was disappointment rather than relief.

This incident left him more shaken than he could ever have predicted. What was the matter with him that he could not simply enjoy the charms of the most beautiful and accomplished woman he had ever known? He had not lived the life of a monk. He'd enjoyed intimate relations with a number of women in England and abroad. Some were mere dalliances with available females, it was true, but there had been a few liaisons of longer duration with women for whom he had felt a measure of affection while the affair lasted. No scruples or hesitation at taking what was offered had troubled him then. Why should he be less wholehearted about enjoying the promising response of the woman who would shortly be his wife?

Christopher's malaise during this soul searching increased tenfold when he relived the scene and recalled that the voices that had disturbed his tryst with Selina had belonged to Brianna and James, playing one of their interminable games in the shrubbery. Sweat broke out on his brow and his palms as he confronted the probability that he had felt guilty, as if in kissing his fiancée he were betraying Brianna. At that juncture in his painful reflections, he'd launched himself out of his chair like one of Whinyates's rockets and taken himself out of the house for a salutary gallop in the rain. That had cleared his head and shown him that it was only going to be a matter of accustoming himself to making love to his prospective bride. She was everything that was desirable in a woman, and once he was removed from the spell Brianna had obviously cast over him, he'd find himself more than content to have Selina in his bed.

The folly of taking Brianna and James to London had become apparent during his soul searching. It was infinitely preferable to keep her out of reach at Ashleigh while he got over what he now recognized as a classic example of infatuation. The result of this decision was that he wrote immediately to his great-aunt Hermione whose unwelcome presence in his home as chaperone was going to be required for a time. Maybe, he thought with bleak humor, he could entrust the delicate task of dislodging her after his wedding trip to his future bride. He'd yet to see the situation that could daunt Selina. He'd back her to get rid of an unpleasant old woman without turning a hair or creating ill feeling in the family.

Two days after the interrupted kiss in the garden, Christopher and Lady Selina were returning from a morning ride when he spotted the small figure of his nephew skulking around a corner of the stableyard. James was not permitted the freedom of the area, so Christopher assumed he'd evaded his hard-pressed keepers again. Knowing this was the first place they'd look for the boy, his uncle decided to prolong his freedom by pretending not to have seen the truant. He and Lady Selina continued toward their waiting grooms.

When a flash of black and tan impinged on his peripheral vision, Christopher instinctively pulled Rufus's head around before his brain had made sense of a low growling and assimilated the danger. Seeing a large dog streaking toward the spot where James had vanished, Christopher spurred his horse and burst around the side of the yard.

The child had frozen, petrified at the furious sounds **and** frightening spectacle of the advancing animal. Christopher measured the angle of the dog's approach, knowing it would be a close-run thing whether he could arrive before the vicious animal. In the next instant he caught sight of Brianna racing toward the child from the direction of the kitchen garden.

"Run inside the tack room, Brianna, and shut the door," he shouted, his voice hoarsened with fear.

Christopher pulled Rufus up between the child and the advancing dog and swung himself off. The snarling dog was perilously close as he grabbed his nephew and threw him up on Rufus's back. "Hold on to his mane, James," he ordered, and called "Steady boy," to the well-trained horse, not having the luxury of time to see whether his commands were obeyed. His eyes were searching the immediate area for something he might use as a club when he heard Brianna's clear voice.

"Down boy, *down*, sir!"

Christopher's heart lurched. A picture of what the savage animal might do to her white throat flashed across his mind as he whirled around.

The sight that met his starting eyes filled him with relief while it strained his credulity. Brianna stood on the far side of the horse, her hand on the head of a huge, ugly, and wary dog. The tension drained out of Christopher, leaving him limp as he stood staring stupidly. He was dimly aware of the sounds of people approaching. He took a couple of steps toward the pair, and the dog began a low growling noise deep in its throat. Christopher stopped.

"Quiet, boy," Brianna said calmly, and the growling stopped, though the dog's fierce eyes remained fixed on the man. "Are you all right, Jamie," she asked anxiously.

"O' course I am. I am riding Rufus, Auntie Bree," the boy replied jubilantly.

Christopher had possessed himself of the reins in an automatic gesture by now, so his nephew's claim was not strictly true. But, glancing from the slender young woman effortlessly controlling as savage an animal as he'd ever laid eyes on to the unruffled child perched atop a large horse for the first time in his young life, Christopher had the odd impression he was meeting the intrepid pair as strangers again. He had no time to refine this impression, however, as he suddenly became conscious of an audience consisting of Lady Selina, still mounted, and a number of stable lads and grooms.

"Where did that animal come from?" he demanded of his groom, indicating the dog that still glared at everyone with ferocity.

"It belongs to Symonds, Mr. George's groom," Whitby replied.

"Well, lock it up and send Symonds to me."

Whitby hesitated and Christopher said impatiently, "Well?"

"Begging your pardon, sir, but the brute won't allow anyone near him except Symonds. He's bitten two of the lads already and would have done worse, had his master not pulled him off."

Whitby's eyes held awe as they focused on the young woman holding the dog by her side with a hand on its head, but he made no move toward the beast.

Christopher thrust Rufus's reins into the groom's hands and again approached the dog, who appeared to be gathering his muscles for a spring, that low rumble starting in its throat again as it bared its teeth.

Lady Selina gasped out, "Take care, Chris!"

Brianna said hastily, "Perhaps I had better put him somewhere, sir, until his master returns. He does not seem to be a very friendly dog." She again restrained the animal's antics, quieting it with a firm voice and hand.

"An understatement if ever I heard one." Christopher's voice was dry as he kept advancing and seized the dog's collar, twisting it tightly when the animal tried to bite him.

"Here's Symonds now," one of the stable boys called out as a man in a moleskin vest and top boots rushed up to the group.

Christopher was controlling the snarling dog by brute force and having no easy time of it when Symonds took the collar from him. Instantly the dog stopped struggling. "I'll lock him up, sir," the groom said. "I don't know how he could have gotten out."

Christopher directed a hard stare at the man but said only, "Report back to me in fifteen minutes," before addressing his next remarks to the assembled horde, who had begun chattering in sheer relief. "The excitement's over and no harm done. Back to work, lads. Take care of Rufus, Whitby, after you hand master James over to his aunt." He had walked over to his betrothed as he spoke, and proceeded to assist her to dismount. "I'll escort the ladies to the house and return to see Symonds, Grimstead," he added, speaking to his head groom who was directing his minions back to their various tasks.

"Are you part witch, Miss Llewellyn, that you can soothe such a savage beast?" Lady Selina asked, only half-joking, as the quartet set off for the main house a moment later. "I vow I have never seen the like. I do not scruple to confess that I was paralyzed with fear of that vicious animal, even sitting safely atop a horse."

"Dogs always mind Auntie Bree," Jamie said matter-of-factly.

"Do you cast a spell over them?" Lady Selina persisted.

"I do not do anything special," Brianna replied with a little hunch of her shoulders, looking squarely into the curious face of the blond girl. "It's simply that dogs have always obeyed my commands. Much better than a certain young man," she added, fixing her skipping nephew with a stern look. "You know you are not to go down to the stables by yourself, Jamie. It was very naughty of you."

Jamie shot a glance at his equally grim-faced uncle and saw no help there. "I only wanted to see the horses," he offered in weak defense of his conduct.

"When you deliberately disobey orders, don't compound the crime by making excuses, James. Take your punishment like a man," his uncle advised with a snap.

"Yes, sir." A subdued Jamie slipped his hand into his aunt's.

The small group continued toward the house in an uneasy silence that lasted until Lady Selina, in a praiseworthy attempt to lighten the atmosphere, spoke again in a bright voice. "All's well that ends well. That was a very brave thing you did, Miss Llewellyn. Christopher might have been badly bitten."

"*Brave!*" Christopher's fiery glance flicked from his fiancée to Brianna. "Say foolhardy rather. I was wearing gloves and a heavy coat. I told you to get inside the tack room."

Stung by the unfairness of this harsh criticism, Brianna put up her chin. "Considering that I have been able to command obedience from dogs all my life, sir, I refuse to accept that my action today was foolhardy, or brave either, but entirely normal."

"For all you knew to the contrary that dog might have been rabid," Christopher countered sharply, his eyes flashing. It seemed as if he might continue in this caustic vein, when he pulled up and made a jerky bow. "If you will excuse me now, ladies, I shall get back to the stables."

Both women watched Christopher's abrupt departure, then their eyes met over the child's head.

"Do not look so shocked, Miss Llewellyn," Lady Selina said with a little smile. "My mother has always held that when a man has had a fright his natural reaction is to vent his anger on some innocent object. You might look upon Christopher's incivility as a measure of his concern for your safety just now. I feel sorry for that man—Symonds, was it?—when Christopher calls him to account, though I must say I found the man as unprepossessing as his savage pet."

"Yes, he was a brutish-looking individual," Brianna agreed, anxious to leave the subject of Christopher Cardorette's recent behavior. Fortunately they had almost reached the path to the kitchen garden where she and James would leave Lady Selina.

For the rest of the day Brianna gave Christopher a wide berth. She remained in the playroom instead of going down to tea, and made sure there was no opportunity for any quasi-private speech

between them in the saloon before dinner by attaching herself to
Lady Ormond's side. Brianna had known nothing save loving
kindness from her gentle parents all her life. Though she and Meg
had had the usual sibling squabbles during their childhood, they
had been closer than most sisters and remarkably harmonious,
thanks mainly to Meg's generosity of spirit and lack of temperament. She herself possessed a quick temper, but it was all but impossible to quarrel with her sweet sister. Her restricted upbringing
had shielded her to such an extent that she was ill-equipped to
deal with angry gentlemen. Her eyes slid all around the room
rather than meet Christopher Cardorette's glance, for she suspected that his urbanity masked a still-smoldering anger.

Christopher cornered her after dinner, interposing himself between Brianna and his cousin and Lady Selina who were engaged
in a lively argument over music. Lady Ormond, busy hunting in
her work bag for something, was too preoccupied to rescue her.

"I would like to apologize for my shortness toward you this
morning, Brianna," Christopher said softly.

Brianna looked timidly into a pair of intensely alive hazel eyes
and felt herself being drawn inexorably away from safety into an
unnamed danger. She blinked and looked away, breaking the
spell. Relief that he was no longer angry with her, a desire to
scramble back to safety and sheer nerves loosened her tongue and
she blurted, "Lady Selina explained to me that gentlemen tend to
become angry when they have been frightened—that it was fear
for my safety that caused you to fly out at me today."

"Selina said that, did she?" Christopher's eyes narrowed but his
face was devoid of expression.

"Yes, or rather she said that it was something Lady Ormond
holds to be true. I fear I know very little about the way gentlemen
think or act. There was only my father, you see, and he, I believe,
was not quite like other men."

"You knew my brother," Christopher said with a lazy smile
that faded as her face tightened.

"All I learned from knowing Matthew was to distrust so-called
romantic attachments between the sexes." Her tone was laced
with bitterness.

"Were you in love with my brother too?" Christopher demanded.

"Certainly not!" Brianna snapped. "But I admit to being as
taken in by his declarations of undying love as my sister was. I
did not suspect that his love for Meg was as rootless as a mush-
room and could not even survive a return to his family."

"Matt was always afraid of my father," Christopher began and stopped.

"And he knew your father would condemn such an unequal match," Brianna added quickly, "but this knowledge did not prevent him from ruining my sister's life while his infatuation for her lasted."

The others broke in on their tête-à-tête at that moment and Christopher was spared further useless defense of his brother's reprehensible conduct, but he could not get this conversation out of his mind over the next few days.

The frightening episode in the stableyard stayed with him, haunted him as he compulsively relived that moment of stark terror when he'd heard Brianna's voice commanding the attacking dog. The scene had developed so rapidly from his first inkling of potential danger for his nephew that he'd not been able to monitor Brianna's movements after he'd yelled to her to dash inside. The realization that she'd disobeyed him and was confronting a vicious animal had produced a sickening sensation of cold fear that he hoped to God he never had to experience again. Nothing he'd felt or witnessed on a number of battlefields had come so close to incapacitating him. Sheer dread of what he'd find when he turned around had weighted his limbs and placed some sort of resistance between his need to act and his ability to do so—at least so it had seemed at the time. He still counted it as nothing short of miraculous that she had escaped a clawing or worse from that evil beast, despite the evidence of his own eyes to support her claim to being able to command obedience from dogs. Never would he willingly allow her to put this reputed ability to the test again if it meant facing down a savage animal. He'd shoot the beast first.

Despite his cousin's plea on behalf of his groom, Christopher had ordered Symonds to remove the dog from his property. He would not take the risk of having it get loose a second time. He'd had all he could do to keep his hands off the man's throat, when, far from being apologetic, Symonds had had the effrontery to argue that it was the stable hands' taunting of the dog in his cage that had enraged the beast past endurance. A weak hinge had given way on the gate under the dog's repeated onslaughts to reach his tormentors. Christopher had been in no mood to accept the man's assurances that the dog would not attack anyone without provocation, and had made it clear that the animal must go if Symonds wished to remain employed at Ashleigh. The groom had sullenly accepted the ultimatum, but the look he'd shot at Christopher on leaving the room had lacked nothing of his pet's fierceness. When he'd asked his cousin later how he could stand having someone around whose normal mien was barely this side of surly, George had shrugged and said Symonds was good with the horses and he hadn't hired him for any charm of manner. Christopher had pointed out that a vast gap existed between a dearth of endearing qualities and downright insolence, after which George had promised to give his man fair warning that an improvement in his attitude was expected.

There the matter rested. Brianna and James had dismissed the incident as soon as it happened. George obviously thought his cousin had overestimated the potential danger in the original situation and had subsequently reacted too harshly in his handling of the affair. Except for Symonds, whose sullen resentment was palpable whenever they met, Christopher was the only person who could not regard it lightly. He kept reliving that terrible moment when he'd thought Brianna would be savaged.

That had been the moment when he'd recognized that what he felt for Brianna was not an uncomplicated lust for a woman who was beyond his reach. Neither was it infatuation. He had not mentally invested Brianna with all the desirable feminine qualities; he did not see her as the embodiment of the perfect woman. He saw her and had seen her from that first meeting as the woman he wanted to protect and keep by his side for the rest of his life. He could no longer deny or demean what he felt for her; he loved her, it was as simple and as hopeless as that. Only a few days remained of his fiancée's visit and there was no sign that she regretted her decision to continue with the betrothal. Indeed, she was full of plans for renovating the house and entertaining his neighbors. There was no way out of this proposed marriage consistent with maintaining his honor.

Christopher knew he was behaving badly in the days that followed the incident in the stableyard. He was edgy and short-tempered about the estate and prone to falling into abstracted moods in the house. Despite continual self-prodding to play his part more convincingly, he was merely going through the motions. He must guard his eyes whenever Brianna was near lest he betray his love and longing, and at the same time simulate an interest he did not feel in Selina when they were together. It had not been easy even when he'd believed matters would improve once he and Selina left Ashleigh and Brianna behind for the scene where their courtship had taken place. It was all immeasurably more difficult now than he knew it was not a question of opportunity or lack of it, of place or propinquity, but the simple difference between loving and not loving.

Coming up from the stables to the house three days after the incident with the dog, Christopher was intent on his unpleasant thoughts. In no hurry to meet the members of his household over the teacups, he detoured through the gardens, conscious of a desire to stay out in the sunshine a little longer. December would be here in less than a sennight. There would not be many more of these deceptively mild days; winter was nearly upon them.

He left the gravel path to examine a white rosebush blooming profusely in defiance of the calendar. These small sweet roses had been among his mother's favorites, he recalled suddenly. A familiar pang of loss assailed him as he stood staring down at a half-opened flower, pale and perfect like Brianna's complexion. He touched the petals gently. Smooth and silky, delicate but so much stronger than its appearance promised . . . like Brianna. A picture of her racing in defense of the child she loved flashed before his eyes. How strange that in the heat of the moment some corner of his brain had still noted the speed and grace with which she had moved, even hampered by skirts. Like these roses she was much tougher than her fragile appearance indicated.

Christopher shook his head to clear it of a persistent vision as he stalked away from the roses. He must put Brianna out of his mind permanently. It was an indulgence he could not permit himself. He was frowning as he rounded a corner and stepped swiftly onto another path. Someone was sitting on a stone bench a dozen feet ahead. His rapidly beating heart recognized the object of its desire almost before his eyes identified Brianna's slight figure wrapped in a black shawl. She was absorbed in reading something, her back half-turned toward him.

He could swerve onto the path intersecting his before she became aware of his presence. The hedges would conceal him before he'd taken two steps. He'd walk on the grass and she'd never know her privacy had almost been disturbed.

His frowning eyes on the sheet of paper in Brianna's hands, Christopher continued on the gravel path, making no effort to diminish the sounds made by his boots on the stones.

The girl on the bench turned swiftly. "Oh, you startled me, sir. I didn't hear you coming." The paper she'd been reading slid from her loosened grasp and over her knees to the ground. Brianna bent down to retrieve it but Christopher's fingers were there before hers. She straightened her knees, rising to her feet and extending her hand for her property.

There was the slightest hesitation before Christopher handed her the folded sheet of paper. "A letter, Brianna?"

"Yes," she replied, tucking it into a pocket of her gown. She added with a touch of defiance as she met his questioning eyes, "It is from Miss Paxton in reply to my letter of thanks for her hospitality."

"I see. And does she express a desire to continue the acquaintance that began so unconventionally?"

"Yes, she does hope that we may become friends." Brianna looked a challenge at him.

"Do you not mean rather that it is her brother who desires this?"

"Sir Harry has already expressed his desire to improve our acquaintance, as you will no doubt remember. His sister speaks only for herself in this letter. Why do you frown? What is your objection to the Paxtons?"

"I did not say I had any objection to the Paxtons," Christopher retorted. "The truth is that I do not know anything about them. Naturally I would not wish to see you commit yourself to a friendship until I have checked on them."

"Checked on them? You speak as though you thought them fly-by-night tricksters. Sir Harry and Miss Paxton have lived all their lives in a lovely home in a settled community. What could be more respectable?"

"Things are not always what they seem on the surface. I won't have anyone taking advantage of your . . . inexperience."

"We have human nature in Herefordshire too, you know, sir. The idea that—"

"Christopher."

Interrupted in full spate, Brianna blinked. "What?"

"My name is Christopher," he said with barely controlled annoyance. "We are members of the same family and I find these constant 'sirs' of yours exceedingly aggravating."

"I'm sorry. Christopher then," she amended. "As I was saying, the idea that the Paxtons wish to take advantage of me in some way is ludicrous. You must see that."

"Why must I? I have not checked into their background. Until I do, I must ask you not to encourage their advances."

"They are not making 'advances' as you put it. Sir Harry and Miss Paxton have merely expressed a desire, shared by myself, to continue the acquaintance that began when they rendered me, and your nephew, I might remind you, a singular service."

"A service for which they have been adequately thanked."

Brianna goggled at the closed face staring aloofly down at her. "There is no adequate thanks for the service Sir Harry performed," she said with quiet dignity. "I am persuaded he saved Jamie's life. Am I to cut the acquaintance without cause? Is that the way you would have me repay the debt?"

"Perhaps you think the only sufficient thanks would be to bestow yourself on Paxton in marriage?" he suggested sarcastically.

Two spots of color flared in Brianna's cheeks but her words were still measured. "Who said anything about marriage? Are you not making a rather fantastic leap from embryonic friendship to marriage?"

"I'll take my oath it's what Paxton has in mind, but if you think that marriage to him would mean you could remove James from Ashleigh, you may think again. My brother's child stays right here, and if you desire to remain in his life, you stay here too."

"I have already accepted that I must sacrifice any personal life while Jamie needs me," Brianna said, meeting his angry eyes with no hint of shrinking, "but I must say that I find it rather oppressive to be denied even the privilege of friendship."

"I do not recall denying you any such privilege," he said through gritted teeth. "The other night this house was full of people with whom you are welcome to form friendships. I heard Mrs. Amphlett invite you to call on her with James. I hope you will accept her invitation."

"Ah, *I* see," Brianna said on a pronounced note of discovery, her eyes opening wide. "I am to be permitted to enjoy friendships with those persons approved by you. How . . . how *paternal* of you, sir, to treat me in the same way you would treat Jamie." She realized she had gone too far when twin flames leapt into hazel eyes. She took a step backward but not fast enough to escape his wrath.

Christopher seized her by the shoulders and shook her once, hard. "How dare you suggest I am treating you like a child!" he said with quiet menace. "You prefer to be treated as an adult? Shall I treat you as an adult, Brianna? Shall I? Like this?"

The uncomprehending girl stared dazedly into glittering hazel eyes, her field of vision shrinking as his head blotted out the sun, and then as he came closer, to nought but two eyes that were no longer angry but held a feral excitement. She closed her own eyes in self-defense just as his mouth fastened onto hers with cruel pressure. She didn't struggle in his tight grasp but moaned as her head was bent back at an uncomfortable angle. Even that was only transitory as Christopher released her arms to enfold her in a close embrace at the same time that the pressure on her lips lessened and his began to move over hers in an entirely different manner. After a second or two, Brianna moaned again and tore herself out of his arms. She was shaking all over but seemed not to notice that her shawl had fallen to the ground during her struggles. Wounded green eyes searched his hot ones; she seemed unaware that her trembling fingers had gone instinctively to her lips.

"What have I done that you should treat me with so little respect?" she cried brokenly, tears filling her eyes.

When he did not immediately answer, Brianna spun around and ran toward the house without another word.

Christopher stood where he was for a few seconds longer, getting his ragged breathing under control. His eyes fell on the black shawl on the ground and he bent to pick it up. He looked at it for a moment, undecided, then folded it with deliberate movements before setting off for the house himself, his steps slow, and the shawl in one hand.

Behind him, the figure standing in the shadow of the hedges at the intersection of the two paths withdrew silently, lifting her skirts to avoid grass stains on the light-colored muslin.

11

Brianna did not put in an appearance at tea or dinner that evening, citing the preeminent feminine excuse of a headache as her reason for seeking seclusion in her own apartments. Lady Selina, on the other hand, was even more vivacious than usual and looked magnificent in a deep-blue silk gown that set off her lush figure to perfection while intensifying the color of her eyes. Though quick to compliment his fiancée on her lovely appearance, Christopher was somewhat slower to respond to her charm and wit than was his wont. Lady Selina did not allow his want of spirits to dampen her own. Abandoning her betrothed to her mother's civil platitudes, she proceeded to enlist the feminine resources at her command to entertain Mr. George Cardorette. In this she succeeded very well indeed. George's serious dark eyes were warmly admiring and his rare laugh was heard on several occasions that evening.

All three ladies came downstairs to breakfast the next morning for the first time since the visit began. Brianna, having refused all sustenance the night before, was in need of more nourishment than chocolate and bread and butter, and the other two came because Lady Selina had chivied her mother into it.

Brianna entered the room almost on the blond girl's heels. Her general greeting, barely above a murmur, was all but drowned out by Lady Selina's cheerful voice calling out gay greetings to the surprised gentlemen.

Glancing at Brianna, Lady Selina was instantly all solicitude, saying in a concerned voice, "My dear Miss Llewellyn, should you have left your bed so soon? You still look sadly pulled."

Indeed, the contrast between the two young women was more pronounced than ever. Lady Selina, attired in a charming dress of pink and white muslin that enhanced her pink and gold coloring, was the epitome of healthy young beauty at its zenith, with her sparkling eyes and rosy-tinted lips and cheeks. Today, Brianna's habitual pallor was nearly corpselike, a comparison cruelly accentuated by the all-black dress that seemed to hang from her slight frame. There was a strained look in her eyes, whose color more nearly resembled murky waters than emeralds today.

Aware of all eyes on her, she mustered a wan smile and addressed Lady Selina. "Thank you, I am much better this morning."

"Those migraines can be the very devil, I comprehend," Lady Selina said sympathetically. "I am most fortunate in being immune to them myself, but my aunt Fanny is a martyr to migraine. Even when the pain is gone, it seems to take her days to recover her normal spirits, does it not, Mama?" Not waiting for corroboration, she went on with a little grimace. "The poor dear seems always to be sinking into or endeavoring to come out of the megrims. One feels for her distress."

"Happily, headaches are a rare occurrence for me," Brianna said with unusual firmness. "I shall be fine after a short walk in this brisk air."

"Do not stay outside too long or you will take cold," Christopher cautioned her. "There is a dampness creeping into the atmosphere at this time of year."

Brianna's glance flickered toward him and away again, but she said nothing, lowering her eyes to her plate.

Lady Ormond embarked on a tactful change of subject at that juncture. Soon the conversation became general, though Brianna's contribution was less than ever, while Lady Selina shone by virtue of her quick wit and high spirits. George Cardorette hung on her every word, his dark eyes devouring each swift change that flitted over her expressive countenance. Lady Ormond gazed on her daughter with fond maternal pride, and Brianna, too, was fascinated by the lovely young woman who could hold an audience captivated by the power of her charm and personality.

Christopher Cardorette wore a slightly abstracted air this morning even while responding readily to his betrothed's amusing chatter. His vagueness vanished at the end of the meal, however, when Lady Selina requested a few minutes of his time just as everyone was preparing to leave the breakfast parlor.

"Of course, my dear Selina. Shall we adjourn to my study?"

A few minutes later, Christopher turned to face his fiancée after closing the study door. He smiled easily, though his eyes were intent. "What may I have the pleasure of doing for you, my dear?" he asked, not moving from his position near the door.

Lady Selina was smiling too as she glided over to him, her eyes holding his. "I'd like you to kiss me," she replied without preface or hesitation.

There was a tiny surprised pause before Christopher, still wearing a determined smile, reached out to gather her into his arms. She was unsmiling now, her eyes never leaving his as he bent to comply with her request. What ensued was no token kiss but a firm full meeting of their lips.

When he broke off the contact at last, Christopher's eyes sought his betrothed's but hers were veiled for a time by downswept lashes as she proceeded to release herself from his embrace without haste. He did not try to prevent this but remained still, waiting for her to look at him again, which she did a second later with all her usual self-possession. Beyond that he could read nothing in her expression, not rapture or revulsion, nor anything in between, unless there had been a flash of something akin to regret. If so, it was gone too quickly to pin down.

She stepped away from him and said politely, "Thank you. I was nearly sure, you know, but under the peculiar circumstances, I thought it essential to remove all doubt, as I am persuaded you will agree." She paused expectantly.

"I am sure I would," he replied, equally polite, "if I knew what doubts we are discussing."

"Doubts about whether or not you are in love with me."

Christopher's countenance must have betrayed his discomfort because she now said, gently mocking, "Just recently I have discovered a weakness in my character that I had not hitherto suspected."

"A . . . weakness?"

She nodded. "I discovered that I am far too selfish and possessive to knowingly marry a man who does not love me madly."

Christopher felt heat sear his throat, and his cravat was choking him all of a sudden. "My dear Selina," he began, "I—"

"No, do not, I beg of you, perjure your soul to maintain the character of a gentleman. I would so much rather you trusted me with the truth as one rational being to another." She regarded him quizzically.

"I have used you very badly," he said, attempting no defense, "and I deserve to be horsewhipped, but indeed I never meant to hurt you, Selina."

"And neither have you," she shot back, reverting to the society beauty as she elevated her chin before her mouth twisted wryly. "It would be more to the point to admit that we have used each other badly. You offered for me and I accepted you for reasons that seemed quite adequate at the time. It was only after coming here and seeing the way you look at Brianna Llewellyn that I have realized just how little chance a marriage between us would have of success."

"You are being incredibly generous."

"Far from it. As I told you, I am much too selfish to accept less from the man I marry than the—dare I say *blind* devotion you have so gallantly striven to conceal?"

Christopher's eyes narrowed as he caught the hint of disparagement in her oblique reference to Brianna, but he was too monstrously grateful to her for releasing him from the betrothal to begrudge her a little feline satisfaction. She really was magnificent, and if he had never met Brianna they might have made a true match of it in time. Voice and eyes were warmly admiring as he assured her, "I have no slightest doubt that there are dozens of better men than I eager to offer you their heart's devotion. You have only to choose the one to whom you feel able to entrust your own heart."

"If indeed I possess a heart," she said with a self-deprecating little moue.

"I hope you will believe that I speak the unvarnished truth when I assure you that you do indeed possess a heart, a very generous one," he said gently.

Again a shade of something that might have been regret passed over Selina's lovely face to vanish instantly as she laughed. "I believe there is often a trace of awkwardness in the situation in which we now find ourselves," she said briskly.

"I am completely yours to command, Selina. Everything must be as you choose."

"Well then, if you have no objection, I should prefer to keep this between ourselves until after my return to London. Papa will send an announcement to the papers."

"As you will." He bowed his acquiescence.

"It's too late to leave today, but perhaps we might go tomorrow? We were originally slated to stay only two or three days beyond that time. I should not think it will be remarked on if we go a bit earlier."

Christopher hesitated. "I do not wish to press you, my dear, but if you would delay one more day, my great-aunt Hermione is to arrive tomorrow to play propriety. I had already decided not to uproot James again by taking him to London with us."

"Oh, I had forgotten that plan," Selina said blankly, "but really, Chris, there is no need for you to escort us personally. I am persuaded George would be glad of a couple of days in London. In the past he has been used to coming up at least once or twice a month."

"I am sorry to seem disobliging, my dear, but your father entrusted the care of yourself and Lady Ormond to me. He would have every right to judge me a blackguard if I delegated the trust to another."

"Oh, dear," Lady Selina sighed. "Very well, then. We'll go the day after tomorrow. So much for having matters arranged just as I choose," She added with a rueful smile.

"No, if your heart is set on leaving tomorrow, George shall deputize for me with Aunt Hermione. I only hope her sharp tongue may not have driven him into hiding before I return."

"Is she such a dragon?" Lady Selina's crystal laugh rang out. "Actually, it might be quite diverting to meet Great-aunt Hermione as long as she remains ignorant of the ephemeral nature of our acquaintance. We'll leave the day after tomorrow then."

The entire conversation had taken place a few feet from the study door. Now Lady Selina whisked herself around her former fiancé and opened the door before he could do it for her.

"Selina," he said softly, waiting until she looked over her shoulder to add, "Thank you."

She smiled but made no answer as she left the room, closing the door quietly behind her.

A long minute ticked by before Christopher moved a single muscle, then he slowly relaxed the rigid control he had imposed to prevent his great relief from becoming obvious to Selina. He had no desire to wound her by letting her see that he felt like a condemned prisoner who has received a royal pardon seconds before his scheduled execution. He'd been caught in a trap of his own making and must consider himself the most fortunate man alive that he would not now have to pay the price for monumental stupidity.

It was not until after dinner that evening that the rest of the household received any notice of the changes about to occur. The engaged pair had resumed a good-natured argument about the merits of *The Beggar's Opera* that had started before dinner, and had agreed finally to disagree on this subject, neither being able to change the other's opinion in the slightest degree.

"I cry quits," Lady Selina said gaily. "You are not to regard this as capitulation, mind you, Chris, but we are boring Mama and George and Miss Llewellyn to tears. We may resume the discussion on the journey to London on Wednesday if you can think up any more convincing argument in the interim," she challenged, wrinkling her perfect nose at him.

The other three looked startled at this casual reference to leaving Ashleigh. Neither of the ladies had recovered before George Cardorette said sharply, "How is this? I thought you expected to remain for another three or four days yet."

"So we did," Lady Selina replied with a mischievous smile, "until Chris informed me that Lady Hermione Withers arrives tomorrow to play propriety for Miss Llewellyn while we are away, and I suddenly bethought myself of all the hundreds of details awaiting our attention in London. So if you do not object, Mama, I told Chris I would prefer to leave a little sooner than planned."

Lady Ormond murmured her willingness to fall in with her daughter's wishes, but George looked thunderstruck. "Great-aunt Hermione!" he cried, horrified. "Have you taken leave of your senses, Kit? Once she steps foot in the place, you'll never get rid of her."

"I feel sure you underestimate my powers of persuasion, my dear George," Christopher replied with a sweet smile.

"This is all rather sudden, is it not?" George continued, looking searchingly at his cousin, who remained completely at ease. "I thought there was some idea of taking Miss Llewellyn and the boy to London when Lady Ormond and Lady Selina returned?"

"A tentative plan only. I could not quite like the notion of uprooting James again so soon, and when I sought Miss Lloyd's advice, she agreed that the wiser course would be to have my aunt come here instead."

"You asked Molly's advice?" Brianna said, startled. "She never said a word to me about this."

"Did she not?" Christopher replied with an indifferent air that stopped Brianna in her tracks. She grew hot at the fear that her question might be considered presumptuous and subsided at once.

It suited Brianna's book at present to hold herself aloof from events occurring at Ashleigh. Though they were nearly of an age, she had not developed a true ease with Lady Selina during the course of their short but close acquaintance. She did not dislike the young woman who would soon be mistress of Ashleigh, she assured herself; there was much to admire in Lady Selina, but the very catalogue of her perfections was daunting in itself. Nor could she formulate a legitimate complaint about the other girl's treatment of herself, which had been unfailingly amiable and pleasant. If she detected a thread of condescension and superiority in the other's manner, that could well be her own stiff-necked pride

talking. The simple unpalatable truth was that Lady Selina *was*
her superior in every trait and accomplishment by which women
were judged in society. She herself must have a contemptibly
jealous nature to be so determined to find fault after a short interval of living under the same roof, she conceded in an unhappy
mood of self-revulsion. The recollection of the ease with which
she and Joanna Paxton had taken strides toward real friendship
within a few hours of meeting rose up to sting Brianna's conscience. Somehow, despite her good resolutions formed almost
daily to overcome her own moral shortcomings, she had not managed to get closer to Lady Selina as time passed. She could not
even dissuade herself from the suspicion that beneath her surface
friendliness, Lady Selina maintained an emotional distance that
her own poor efforts could not hope to diminish. Brianna casti-
gated herself for clinging to this suspicion; it was just as likely
that her own feeble attempts at getting upon warmer terms with
Lady Selina were seen as forced and insincere by the other girl.

Another and worse inhibiting factor, guilt, had been added after
the kiss Christopher had forced on her in the garden. After an agonizing period of examining her conscience, Brianna had honestly
absolved herself of complicity in this misdemeanor. There had
been nothing provocative in her behavior to warrant the liberty he
had taken, but she had not known how to face Lady Selina following the incident without betraying her agitation and a persistent sense of guilt that all her arguments had failed to rationalize.

She could not hide forever, and when she emerged reluctantly
from the sanctuary of her apartments it was to find Lady Selina
being kinder than ever to her, thus heaping coals of fire upon her
remorseful head. Her own simmering anger against Christopher
for putting her in such an indefensible position *vis-à-vis* his fiancée was denied the relief of any outlet. He gave her no opportunity to snub him as he roundly deserved; in fact, he did not even
glance her way for long enough to detect the coldness with which
she was resolved to treat him. If anything, he and his betrothed
seemed more *en rapport* than ever, from which Brianna could
only conclude that his nature must be inherently deceitful. Obviously, he could cheat his affianced wife out of what should be
solely hers without turning a hair. No sign of strain or hint of re-
morse shadowed his countenance or troubled his conscience. He
was completely despicable.

She'd been deceived in Matthew Cardorette's character five
years before, and it appeared his brother's was cut from the same
flawed cloth. Perhaps all men shared the same tendency toward

infidelity that she as a woman could only deplore. Perhaps faithfulness was a virtue to which the stronger sex only paid lip service. She was positive her own father had never been disloyal to her mother, but she had always known that he was not quite like other men. Did Sir Harry possess the same weakness as the Cardorette brothers? Would Jamie grown up flawed in the same way now that his uncle had influence in his formative years?

Brianna's observations and conclusions were such as to have a profoundly lowering effect on her spirits as the time for Lady Selina's removal to London grew short. When next she returned, it would be as the mistress of Ashleigh. They must find a way to dwell together in harmony if not true friendship.

Lady Hermione Withers's arrival the next day was not an event that promised a lightening of Brianna's gloom. When she'd inquired of George Cardorette if his great-aunt was a maiden lady or a widow, he'd told her testily that the gentleman who had bestowed his name and estate on Lady Hermione under the mistaken impression that he had found a good mother for his orphaned children had quickly recognized his error and had had the good sense to cock up his toes some three years later, no doubt in a desire to find a lasting release from her overbearing ways. His unfortunate offspring had made their escape from her domination at the first opportunity that presented. Mr. Withers's heir had lost no time in banishing his stepmother to the dower house on attaining his majority. His two sisters had escaped into marriage and had been loath to admit their stepmother over their thresholds ever afterward. Though the widow's jointure was deemed handsome by all of her acquaintance, Lady Hermione considered it paltry for one born the daughter of a marquess and promptly set out on a round of visits to her hapless relatives in an effort to live as much at others' expense as possible. Since her unamiable disposition was combined with a ruthless determination to seize the reins of each establishment she entered, it was not surprising that she rapidly wore out her welcome everywhere she went. When matters reached a head and she was asked by the most resolute member of her current host family to curtail her visit, she would repair to her own residence until she succeeded in wangling another invitation.

Brianna had listened to this testimony with a sinking heart that the elderly widow's subsequent arrival did nothing to lighten. Lady Hermione was an imposing figure, tall and deep-bosomed with steel-gray hair beneath a voluminous cap and a stentorian voice that would not have disgraced a sergeant-major. Her opaque black eyes darted continually about her surroundings as if searching for something upon which to exercise her managerial talent. She was enveloped in a mud-colored pelisse lavishly trimmed in sable, and she carried a huge muff of the same fur. The maid, Hannah, told Brianna later that Lady Hermione's carriage had three trunks strapped on the roof as well as an assortment of lesser baggage in the charge of a harassed abigail.

The ladies were in the formal drawing room when Lady Hermione descended upon them, still in her outer wraps and clutching Christopher's elbow with one gloved hand while the other wielded a gold-handled ebony cane. She acknowledged Christopher's presentation of Lady Ormond with a curt "How d'you do," and paused to inspect Lady Selina through a lorgnette she pulled out of the sable muff hanging around her neck on a long ribbon. "There's nothing wrong with your eyes at any rate," she observed to Christopher as Lady Selina dropped a smiling curtsey. "The gal's a honey pot right enough."

While Lady Selina contrived to look modest, Christopher indicated Brianna. "May I present Miss Llewellyn, Aunt? She is my late sister-in-law's sister."

Snapping black eyes swept over Brianna and dismissed her as the girl curtsied in her turn. "So she's the one who upset the applecart. A bad business that."

Brianna's surprised, "Ma'am?" was lost in Christopher's cold reply. "I must always be grateful to Brianna for her care and devotion to my nephew who is in his rightful place at last."

"No need to take that tone with me, young man; you won't make me believe you enjoyed setting the *ton* by the ears and losing out on the succession to boot."

"Shall we sit down?" Lady Ormond said hastily, seeing by the tightening of his mouth and the flare of his nostrils that Christopher was disposed to engage in verbal battle with his aged relative.

Possible unpleasantness was averted by the timely entrance of Pennystone carrying the tea tray, and George Cardorette, who had been summoned by his cousin to present himself without delay when Lady Hermione's carriage had been heard on the gravel drive.

The evening that followed could not have been judged a success by even the most lenient of standards. Lady Hermione came down to dinner, her tightly corseted bulk clothed in a purple satin gown whose décolletage was filled with a diamond parure that would have benefitted from a cleaning and did little to disguise her wrinkled neck despite its vulgar dimensions. She was hung all over with a profusion of shawls and draperies and proceeded to change her chair several times before dinner to escape draughts that no one else detected. She took over every conversation that arose before dinner, expounding at length on topics as varied as the misguided efforts of the parliamentary reformers to effect a change in the system of criminal penalties to the dissolution she claimed to see in the morals of the present generation of young matrons once they had secured the succession. In response to an anguished look from Lady Ormond as the ladies were filing out of the dining room, the gentlemen heroically cut short their post-prandial interlude to rejoin the ladies in record time. Lady Ormond's thin nostrils were quivering with dislike as she sat with a rigid back while Lady Hermione critiqued her embroidery uninvited. Brianna had taken refuge in muteness as she sat huddled in a corner of a sofa staring fixedly at her own fancywork. Only Lady Selina was impervious to Lady Hermione's outspoken remarks, remaining good-tempered and cheerful even when, having acceded to Christopher's request that she sing for them, she was stopped in her tracks on the way to the pianoforte by Lady Hermione's flat statement that she was not at all partial to music as after-dinner entertainment.

"Then I should not dream of inflicting any on you, ma'am," Lady Selina said with a sweet smile. "Are you fond of cards? Would you care for whist or perhaps a game of piquet or cribbage?"

Lady Hermione allowed as how she enjoyed a rubber of whist occasionally. It was her intention to dismiss the young ladies from consideration, but Lady Ormond foiled her by pleading a headache. Lady Selina offered herself in her mother's place before the widow was well-launched on what promised to be a lecture on the foolishness of giving in to minor physical discomfort. Brianna was obviously rendered ineligible by the look of sheer horror in her eyes at the idea of playing cards, so Lady Selina was perforce accepted by Lady Hermione. As it turned out, the young woman gave a good account of herself at the card table and did not once lose her pleasant expression even while being taken to task—erroneously in some cases—by Lady Hermione for misplays during the course of the contest.

Lady Ormond's maternal instincts forbade her to take the easy way out by retiring with her alleged headache, though it was soon apparent that her redoubtable daughter stood in little need of support. The countess made a few conscientious attempts to engage Brianna in conversation, but the rector's timid daughter had been driven into full retreat by Lady Hermione's bullying manner and could scarcely raise her voice to be heard. Thankfully, Lady Ormond subsided with her maligned embroidery and Brianna made a pretense of doing the same, though she was actually studying the cardplayers as she waited for the dreadful evening to come to a merciful end.

It was during one period of idly watching the expressions of the players that Brianna became aware that George Cardorette's eyes dwelled more often on Lady Selina's lovely face than was called for by their partnership against Lady Hermione and his cousin. She noted further that when his great-aunt criticized the girl's play, Mr. Cardorette's square jaw firmed with repression as he clenched his teeth against leaping to his partner's defense. His reaction was much more marked than that of Lady Selina's betrothed or the victim herself, who took the criticism in good part. Brianna saw Christopher exchange a merry look with Lady Selina during one of his great-aunt's harangues. At this point George Cardorette was gripping his cards with a force Brianna had no doubt he would like to transfer to his outspoken relative's diamond-encircled throat. Brianna had known from her first day at Ashleigh that Mr. Cardorette infinitely preferred Lady Selina's company to her own. There was nothing extraordinary about that. Being a fair-minded girl, she understood that Lady Selina, with her beauty and animation, possessed far greater attractions for gentlemen, but now she wondered if it were more than just a mere preference. By the end of the card game, she had satisfied herself that George was in love with Lady Selina, and her heart was wrung with pity for him. His position at Ashleigh was going to be terrible indeed when Christopher brought her home as his bride. Difficult though her own position was *vis-à-vis* Christopher Cardorette, at least she did not have to endure the added torture of being in love with another woman's husband.

By the time she went to bed that night, Brianna's despondency had spread beyond her own unenviable situation of being dependent on someone who had tried to flirt with her even before his marriage to another, to include living at close quarters with the most disagreeable old woman she'd ever met, and having to witness the suffering of a man hopelessly in love with his cousin's affianced wife.

12

L ady Selina and her mother left after breakfast with Christopher riding beside the carriage. They planned to do the trip in one day this time, sending Lady Selina's horse with the slower coach carrying the abigails and most of the baggage. Christopher informed his great-aunt that he would stay over one day in London to rest his own mount before riding home on the third day, and promised her she could repose her entire confidence in George, who would see to everything in his absence. This diplomatic way of trying to forestall any meddling in Ashleigh's domestic routines on Lady Hermione's part did not prevent the widow from ordering the time of dinner brought forward to conform closer with country hours, but Pennystone refused to be intimidated by her ladyship's high-handed manner, informing her with his usual dignity that Mr. Christopher did not permit tampering with the chef's schedule and she would have to take up the matter with him personally on his return.

Brianna had watched the glossy dark-blue carriage with the Ormond crest on the door roll down the gravel drive with a bewildering mixture of emotions stirring in her breast. At the last, she had been sorry to see Lady Selina go, in part because the prospect of dancing attendance on Lady Hermione without support was so patently alarming. Brianna had no illusions about her ability to handle the overbearing and opinionated old woman with anything resembling the skill and good humor Lady Selina had displayed. She might not find Lady Selina as compatible in outlook as Miss Paxton, but they should be able to rub along together well enough and might in time become friends.

After making Lady Ormond a curtsey as the women were about to enter their carriage, Brianna had turned to the younger, saying impulsively, "May I wish you every joy on your wedding day, Lady Selina? I am going to miss our musical evenings quite dreadfully." A tiny spark of impishness appeared in her smile as she added, "Although it is fortunate for me that Lady Hermione doesn't care for music, or I fear I'd find myself demonstrating my lack of accomplishment in that area willy-nilly."

For once, Lady Selina's ready smile was absent as she looked rather searchingly at Brianna. "Thank you for your good wishes, Miss Llewellyn." She glanced at George Cardorette assisting her mother into the coach, then leaned closer to Brianna, saying in a low voice, "In my opinion you are a very fortunate woman, Miss Llewellyn. Pray remember I said that, will you?" She bestowed one of her dazzling smiles on the puzzled Brianna as she straightened and gave her hand to Mr. Cardorette, whose dark countenance wore a forbidding expression as he bade Lady Selina a formal good-bye before handing her up into the carriage. Brianna had turned away, convinced he would not welcome her sympathy for his pain, and would fiercely resent her knowledge of it. She had bidden Christopher the coolest of farewells, which he had barely seemed to notice, and she had stepped back onto the grass as the earl's coachman gave his team the office to start.

Life at Ashleigh was less complicated with Christopher and Lady Selina away. Brianna and Jamie continued their exploration of the estate, roaming at will for hours at a stretch. Taking the child's increasing stamina as proof that he had made a complete recovery from his bout with severe bronchitis, Brianna was quite content to follow this healthful program while the good weather lasted. Her days passed happily, revolving, as they always had, around her sister's child.

The evenings were another matter. Brianna duly presented herself for tea on the first day, her extreme reluctance disguised by the consideration for the elderly that her mother had drilled into her daughters from an early age. A minister's home must always be accessible to his parishioners, and there were in every parish a number of lonely souls or busybodies who took full advantage of this to impose on the hospitality of the rectory. She made every effort to think of Lady Hermione as belonging to this sisterhood, but the widow's simple belief in her own superiority, coupled with a rampant curiosity to know every intimate detail about those persons who crossed her path—a curiosity, moreover, unchecked by any considerations of delicacy or regard for her victims' privacy—stretched Brianna's civility and tolerance to their limit. Having no wish to hide her family's circumstances, she willingly described the village, the rectory, and the manner of living obtaining there, but she flatly refused to satisfy Lady Hermione's intrusive desire to probe the details of her sister's marriage. Those persons who equated Brianna's personal timidity in social situations with strangers to a lack of moral courage or backbone soon learned their error, Lady Hermione among them. Her bullying tactics failed to elicit any information beyond the bare facts that Matthew Cardorette had met and married Brianna's sister, that the marriage had not been a success, and he went away without ever learning of the child's existence. Repeated questions brought repeated stony-faced refusals to discuss the subject and left the stymied interrogator with a fast-growing detestation of the insignificant country miss who should have been reduced to a quaking compliance in the presence of the true aristocracy but instead kept steadily at her sewing with no sign of discomfort at having merited her ladyship's disapproval.

Lady Hermione blatantly ignored Brianna at dinner that night, much to George Cardorette's dismay when he found himself the sole object of her attention. His attempts to bring Brianna into the conversation did not save him from a series of questions from Lady Hermione about his father's death ten years before that broadened into a homily on the evils of gambling, the wanton waste of one's patrimony, and the beggaring of one's children that reduced her great-nephew to a state of impotent rage. Hearing the snap in his curt, discouraging replies and reading in his dark eyes the urge to personally strangle his aged relative, Brianna threw herself into the fray, requesting Lady Hermione's help in matching an odd shade of green silk in her embroidery work. Mr. Cardorette took instant advantage of this diversion to excuse himself on the plea of some unfinished work. The next evening he did not put in an appearance in the saloon after an uncomfortable dinner hour spent in small talk for the sake of the servants, interspersed by periods of unfriendly silence. At one point, his great-aunt commented acidly on the inordinate number of times his wine glass was filled, a comment that was responded to by nothing save a darkling look from under thick black brows drawn into a straight line. The two women spent an hour sitting together in the saloon, mentally isolated with their individual handwork, exchanging no more than a half-dozen brief remarks, before Lady Hermione ended the ordeal by retiring early, much to Brianna's relief.

On the morning of Christopher's scheduled return, Brianna entered the breakfast parlor with a lighter step. It was not that she felt a personal desire for his company, far form it; his occasional attempts at gallantry or flirtation—in her ignorance she knew not how to characterize his behavior toward herself—produced a state of fearful anticipation in her, but at least he represented an additional ally against Lady Hermione.

A swift glance around the room reassured Brianna that the formidable dowager was absent this morning and she slipped into her chair with a spontaneous smile and greeting for George Cardorette. A salutation consisting of an unintelligible grunt and a hooded look from under heavy eyelids conveyed no slightest degree of fellowship, and Brianna retreated to a contemplation of her own breakfast, although her well-disguised interest remained with the man across the table as she studied him beneath her long lashes.

This morning Mr. Cardorette did not have the appearance of a man who had risen well-rested from his bed. He was dressed with his usual impeccable neatness in a brown coat of the finest wool and a snowy cravat tied in intricate folds, but his rich olive complexion looked pasty gray and his eyes were dull and shadowed. This had been obvious at first sight and, combined with his lack of appetite—as evidenced by the gesture of extreme disgust with which he waved away Pennystone's offer of kippers—led her to wonder if he might be ill. Further observation showed that he was holding his head stiffly, all his movements slow and deliberate as he drank black coffee and swallowed an occasional morsel of dry toast. Clearly, his head ached abominably. Out of the blue, Brianna's memory produced a detailed picture of Mr. Algernon Gossett, a parishioner of her father's, after one of his notorious bouts of drinking. Just so wan and deliberate had Mr. Gossett appeared on numerous occasions in the village. Whether from unhappiness over Lady Selina's coming marriage to his cousin or simple bad temper after being grilled and having old wounds probed by Lady Hermione, Mr. Cardorette had most likely overindulged in spirituous libations last night and was paying the inevitable price this morning. Out of common humanity Brianna avoided adding any weight to his cross, refraining from all comment and conversation and pretending an inordinate concentration on her own repast.

Except for the clink of cup against saucer, silence reigned in the sunny breakfast room until Mr. Cardorette, staring broodingly into his coffee cup, said, "I never thought she'd actually go through with it. Naturally she could not pass up a second chance at the title and fortune; that was understandable, but afterward? And why now?"

Brianna said nothing as it was obvious that Mr. Cardorette was indulging in a private dialogue, but his words initiated a rapid chain of conjecture in her mind. *Who* was this "she" who could not pass up a second chance at the title and fortune? It was not a random shot to substitute Lady Selina for the unnamed woman; she was probably haunting Mr. Cardorette's thoughts at present. He'd said a *second* chance. Did that mean Lady Selina had had a chance to marry another titled man before Christopher? Why had she not done this? Brianna sat very still as memory repeated Mr. Cardorette's words in her mental ear. He had referred to a second chance at *the* title and fortune, not *a* title and fortune. It must be the *Ashleigh* title! Brianna's unwinking stare remained on her fingers clutching the cup halfway to her lips as she made the logical mental leap. Her eyes winged to Mr. Cardorette.

"Was Lady Selina ever betrothed to Matthew Cardorette?" she asked bluntly.

He blinked at the sound of her voice and shot her an unreadable look before his eyes were veiled again. She thought that he was not going to answer, but at last he took another gulp of his coffee and said, "Yes."

Brianna's brain was still reeling from the implications and she gave voice to her perplexity. "But how could he know that Meg was dead?"

Mr. Cardorette's cup crashed into its saucer and he pushed back his chair from the table. "You must refer any questions on that subject to my cousin, Miss Llewellyn," he said curtly as he rose. "Excuse me, I have work to do."

Brianna's eyes followed Mr. Cardorette's large frame as he hurried out of the room, but without really seeing him. Questions were whirling around in her brain as she struggled to assimilate the information she had just received, information that must have been kept from her purposely, else she would surely have discovered something so basic to the situation here at Ashleigh before now. She reached for the silver coffee pot and poured out a third cup of the strong brew. She would indeed have a number of questions to put to Mr. Christopher Cardorette on his return from London.

Nursing her coffee, Brianna's thoughts pursued a different direction as she tried to put herself in Lady Selina's place. Had the beautiful blonde loved Matthew Cardorette and grieved deeply for his death? Did she love Christopher more than she had loved his brother? Had she loved either man at all or was she merely interested in making a splendid match? If this last were true, would she not have broken the engagement when Jamie's claim overset Christopher's succession? Or would society have looked askance at such an action? Must the fiction of a love match be maintained in a milieu where marriages were often arranged for reasons that had more to do with economics and social connections than mutual affection? These were all questions that a country-bred girl could not hope to answer correctly, and she knew that delicacy of mind must always prevent her from asking those in a position to answer them.

One thing of which she was persuaded regardless of her personal feelings, Lady Selina would always act in a manner consistent with the strict codes of behavior obtaining among the *ton.* Brianna's mien grew more thoughtful when she reached this point in her cogitation. The earl's daughter would not have accepted Christopher's offer—nor for that matter would he have made it— had it not been sanctioned by society. Therefore, the mourning period must have been observed.

Again Brianna froze into immobility as a thought almost too shocking to be contemplated with calm bobbed to the surface in her mind like a pinecone that had been pinned under the water and suddenly released. *Had* Matthew Cardorette known of the death of his abandoned wife? Brianna put down her cup, dawning horror in her eyes, and rose abruptly out of her chair, her nerves too stretched to sit still any longer. She scarcely knew how she would contain her agitation until Christopher's return this evening. On the threshold, she halted suddenly. There was one fact she could ascertain without waiting for Christopher to satisfy her burning curiosity. He had said at their first meeting that his brother was buried in the village cemetery.

Several hours later Brianna stood in the shelter of a magnificent oak tree, holding tightly to her nephew's hand as she read the simple inscription on a handsome new headstone: JAMES MATTHEW ADOLPHUS CARDORETTE, FIFTH EARL OF ASHLEIGH, VISCOUNT DAIMLEY, BARON RUFFIELD. *Beloved by all who knew him.* At her side Jamie stirred.

"You are hurting my hand, Auntie Bree."

"I'm so sorry, darling." Brianna released the child's hand.

With a small finger Jamie traced the writing on the stone. "J . . . A . . . M . . . E . . . S . . . James, like me. Is this my papa's grave, Auntie Bree?"

"Yes, dearest," Brianna said in husky tones.

Jamie went on with his tracing and read out slowly, "March fourteenth, 1784. What is this big word, Auntie Bree?"

"December."

The child continued to trace out the numbers. "December fifteenth, 1814. Is that when my papa died?"

"Yes, dearest." Brianna struggled to keep the bitterness out of her voice. "Your papa died on December fifteenth, 1814."

James was enjoying himself trying to read a few simple words on the tombstones in the peaceful, well-tended cemetery of All Souls church. There was no one around to find his behavior objectionable, so Brianna did not hurry him away. She needed a breathing space in which to subdue the surge of rage and resentment that had flooded through her entire being as she had read the proof that Matthew Cardorette's villainy had not ended when he'd abandoned wife and child. Only his own death had prevented him from committing bigamy. As she gave somewhat abstracted answers to Jamie's many questions, Brianna speculated uselessly on whether Christopher had kept Lady Selina in ignorance of the fate she had escaped. Did the neighbors know the whole truth? Was she the only person who had been kept in the dark about her erstwhile brother-in-law's infamy?

Now that she knew the truth, one or two puzzling remarks made to her at the dinner party last week assumed a different meaning. Mrs. Amphlett, after laughing at the story of one of Jamie's antics, had remarked that Matthew would have delighted in such an enterprising offspring and wasn't it a shame that Brianna's father had not told him about his son. Brianna had opened her mouth to explain that her father had never been able to tell his son-in-law about his child when George Cardorette had interrupted with a question that had led the conversation away from Jamie.

Brianna glanced down at the eager little face of her sister's child and wondered if he would ever have to know about his father's dishonor. Christopher must have put out some lying tale to protect his brother's good name. If it were not for this innocent child she would take great delight in exposing the lies and letting the whole world know what kind of man the fifth earl of Ashleigh had really been. She could only be grateful that Meg had never known of her husband's final betrayal and pray that Jamie would never discover his father's worthlessness.

The afternoon was waning when Jamie and Brianna set off through the splendid stand of pinewoods that bordered the road leading to Ashleigh Court from the east. It was a wonderful place to walk or ride since the underbrush was kept down. It was a favorite venue for Jamie who liked marching in and out among the tall sentinels and playing some of his hiding games. The woods paralleled the road for some distance, generally separated by a wide grassy verge but coming right down to the road in some places.

Jamie was skipping ahead of her today, weaving in and out of

the trees, covering twice as much ground as his aunt, which was
not at all unusual. He was singing a little marching song he'd
learned from his uncle as he went. Sometimes he vanished from
sight for a while in his digressions, but Brianna could always hear
his chirping voice. He'd been out of her line of vision for a
minute or so and she speeded up her pace when the tuneless
singing became fainter. She caught sight of his blue jacket off to
the left where the woodland approached the road and she headed
in that direction. She was still some little distance away when she
saw him stop and bend over. In the same instant the unmistakable
sound of a gun firing rang out. For a split second of sheer terror
she thought the boy had been hit.

"*Jamie!*" she shrieked, running like the wind toward him, but
he was already straightening up, unconcernedly holding out
something for her inspection. She came up to him, catching him
protectively in her arms, straining to hear any sounds in the sepul-
chral silence of the woods.

"See the nice smooth stone I found, Auntie Bree."

"Yes, dearest," she replied, glancing not at his prize but scanning the area for the person with the gun. There had been a sort of
thwacking sound almost simultaneous with the discharge. Her
eyes searched the trees in their immediate vicinity, dimly aware
now of hoofbeats approaching from the direction of the road just
out of sight.

As the front door of the Millikens' London residence was
closed behind him by the porter, Christopher stood on the top step
for a moment, adjusting the angle of his beaver hat atop his un-
ruly black curls. He started down the steps, pulling on his gloves
as he went. He did not look back as he reached the pavement and
set off in the direction of Oxford Street.

His engagement to Lady Selina Milliken was over except for
the official notice that Lord Ormond would send to the papers tomorrow. It had ended as it began, on a perfectly civilized note devoid of any emotional trappings. Selina had informed her mother
of her decision in the carriage on the trip up to London, and Lady
Ormond had said everything that was proper to the occasion,
nearly but not quite managing to conceal her heartfelt relief at her
daughter's safe delivery from a situation little conducive to her
ultimate happiness. Lord Ormond hadn't bothered to hide his satisfaction that the visit to Ashleigh Court had produced the desired
result. A diamond like Selina could aim higher than a man who
was no better than the manager of another's estate.

Everyone was happy, not least of all himself. He hadn't felt this sense of promise and adventure since the time he'd struck out on his own and joined the army. The thought of having Brianna near him every day and yet as forbidden as the apple in the Garden of Eden had filled him with a reckless unhappiness that had challenged his honor daily. Life would have been a constant battle with no reward possible save the comfortless knowledge that he had done his duty and avoided temptation for one more day. There were still no guarantees that she would ever come to love him as he loved her, but future problems had no power to dampen his present elation. From their first meeting, he had wanted to take her burdens upon himself and protect her from all of life's vicissitudes. He could truthfully say that those feelings had existed before this aching desire to possess her, body and soul, that now possessed him to the point of madness. She *must* love him; he would find a way to show her that they belonged together, that their union had been ordained since the beginning of time.

Christopher sauntered along the streets of Mayfair concocting plans for the future and mentally devising a schedule of things to be accomplished during his short stay in the metropolis. For tomorrow his tentative schedule included such diverse activities as visits to a jeweler, a fashionable modiste, and a bishop. There was still the whole evening ahead of him. Tired though he should be after a long day in the saddle, he had no intention of retiring early and hiding from all his acquaintances. He was feeling too alive to wish to court the oblivion of sleep. He hadn't packed formal evening gear in his small portmanteau, not have any desire to spend an evening doing the pretty to a lot of females, which at present would doubtless mean lying about his wedding plans, in any case. Yes, he decided as he checked into a hotel after having retrieved his bag from the stables where he'd left Rufus, tonight would be much much more enjoyably spent in masculine company.

Accordingly, Christopher dined well at Grillons and took himself off to his club where he had the unexpected good fortune to meet a former comrade in arms whom he'd not seen since Paris in the summer. Jack Wrexham was a likeable rattle of limited intellect, whose optimistic nature had survived the horrors of war almost unscathed. He was only newly arrived in England, a decided advantage from Christopher's point of view since Jack knew nothing of his friend's engagement and accepted the news of an unknown nephew who had displaced him in the earldom with only passing interest and a cursory expression of sympathy before the talk turned to military matters and memories. It was just the respite Christopher needed after a month fraught with drama and seesawing emotions. Thankful to be able finally to let down the constant guard he had had to impose over his words and expressions of late, he relaxed completely in his comrade's undemanding company and spent a thoroughly contented evening. They parted company when Jack had to leave to keep an after-theater appointment, and Christopher readily agreed to join his friend at a discreet gaming club the following evening.

Since the announcement of the termination of his betrothal would not appear in print until the day he was scheduled to leave London, Christopher was untroubled by any curiosity on the part of any chance-met acquaintances as he went about his business the next day. He was more than pleased with the results of his exertions and began to experience an impatience to be on his way home. He looked forward to the evening as a way to kill time before he could take his leave. Although he enjoyed a game of cards and all kinds of sporting contests, gambling for its own sake had never held much allure for him, probably because so much of it occurred in crowded, airless rooms where one spent long hours sitting still. Physical confinement of any sort was distasteful to him, but tonight anything would do to pass the time.

The games themselves could not hold his interest for long. After a couple of hours sitting at a faro table, he felt an overwhelming need to stretch his legs and excused himself, pocketing his negligible winnings as he strolled about the too-warm room. Jack was still engrossed in watching a little ball spin at a roulette table, so Christopher ambled into the adjoining room and straightaway bumped into a man who looked vaguely familiar, but whose name he could not recall.

"Ah, it's Ashleigh's brother, is it not?" the man said, helpfully identifying himself as Wainright, a former classmate of Matt's. "Is your cousin with you?"

"George? Why no, George is at Ashleigh Court."

"I thought he might have brought you here, this being a favorite haunt of his," Wainright explained.

"No, I came with a friend. I gather this place is all the rage right now," Christopher said with a little smile, "but I'm afraid I have never really found this sort of thing entertaining for more than an hour or two."

"Lucky you," Wainright said feelingly. "I wish I might share that attitude; I'd no doubt be a happier and wealthier man today— your cousin too, I daresay."

"Does George like deep play?"

Christopher had kept his question casual, but Wainright back-tracked hastily. "As to that, I really couldn't say, not from personal knowledge at least."

"But the word in the clubs has it that my cousin plays deep?"

"Well, yes, especially this past year since Matt died," Wain-right confirmed.

The next day on the long ride home, Christopher pondered the information he'd stumbled across regarding his cousin's propensity for gaming. Strictly speaking, it was none of his affair how George chose to occupy his leisure time. For that matter, neither were his cousin's finances any of his concern, even if he'd still been the head of his family. George wasn't a green stripling to be advised how to spend his money. Come to think of it, he had never known exactly how well or badly off his uncle Martin had left his only child fixed, having been himself still at Eton when George's father had died. It had been understood in the family that Martin Cardorette had been all to pieces, having accumulated heavy debts over a lifetime of gambling excesses. George, who had just come down from Oxford, had shortly sought a position, but whether or not something had been salvaged eventually from the estate, Christopher had never known. He was aware that his own father had left a modest bequest to his nephew. For all he knew to the contrary, George might have repaired his fortunes by now or even won a real fortune at the tables, though he had received the opposite impression from Wainright last night. He had not liked to press the man, who had obviously regretted his loose tongue almost immediately. A month ago, Christopher might have done something for his cousin if he were indeed in trouble, but it was a different matter now that he was responsible for preserving his nephew's estate.

Christopher was lost in a frowning reverie, debating whether or not to raise the subject of finances with his cousin as he approached the boundaries of Ashleigh in late afternoon, but his mood lightened radically at the thought of seeing Brianna again without the wall that had been his betrothal between them. His feelings had been fettered for so long he would have to take care not to pounce on her and send her scurrying behind that other wall of deliberate reserve she had erected between them since her arrival at Ashleigh. He accepted that he was going to have to rein in his impatience and woo her slowly until he had reversed the distrust that disastrous loss of control in the garden had roused in

her. He must have gone a little mad that afternoon when he had
first forced a quarrel on her and then forced a bruising kiss on her
unwilling lips. The constant strain of repressing his feelings for
Brianna had brought him to a pitch of frustration where anything
might set off his temper. Jealousy, quick and flaring, over her
championing of Paxton had provided the spark and he'd released
the feelings in a manner guaranteed to rebound to his discredit
with a girl of strict moral principles. If she now thought him a
hardened libertine, it was no more than his action merited. He
could not expect leniency or perfect understanding from a shel-
tered girl who had never had to wrestle with a similar moral
dilemma.

The pure elation that had filled him when Selina released him
from the betrothal had been quickly dissipated by the awkward
reality of the situation between himself and Brianna. The problem
would be to keep an irrepressible spring of optimism from bub-
bling up and swamping his carefully considered plan to proceed
slowly.

Without preliminary warning from any of his senses the silence
of the late fall afternoon was shattered by the sound of gunfire, a
single report only, followed instantly by a woman's scream. His
heart pounding with the awful knowledge that it had been Brianna's voice he'd heard, Christopher left the road, urging Rufus
toward the woods from where the sounds had come.

"Brianna, where are you?" he yelled.

"Over here, Uncle Chris!" James called back.

As Christopher approached through the woods from the road,
the child broke out of his aunt's embrace and ran to meet his
uncle. Christopher leaned out of the saddled and scooped him up
in one arm, to James's intense delight.

"Brianna, are you all right? What happened? I heard a shot."

When the young woman did not move or even look at him,
Christopher set his nephew down and swung himself off Rufus,
holding on to the reins as he put a hand on her shoulder. "What
happened?" he said again, his eyes following the direction of her
fixed stare.

His presence seemed not to have made any impression on the
shaking woman. All thoughts scattered and he reacted instinctively, putting his arms around her. She was rigid in his hold and
she didn't look at him as she pulled away. He looked again where
she was staring and this time noticed a white gouge in the trunk of
a large pine. He strode over to the tree, squatting down on his
haunches to examine the mark.

"The shot I heard, is this where it went?"

"I . . . I think so." Brianna's voice was a mere thread of sound.

"Did you see who it was? What was he shooting at?" When she didn't reply but remained where she had been since his first glimpse of her, he repeated, "Brianna, did you see the shooter?"

She shook her head.

"So you don't know if he was shooting at a rabbit or what?"

"Not a rabbit. I . . . I think . . ."

As Christopher waited, Brianna's eyes fastened on the little boy who had gone over to join his uncle by the tree. Seeing their sick expression, Christopher found it difficult to control his own voice. "You don't mean—?"

"I saw Jamie bend over and I feared for a moment that he'd been hit, but he was only picking up a stone. He was standing right here where I am now. The . . . the height of the mark on that tree . . ." Her unsteady voice became wholly suspended and the child ran back to wrap his arms around her legs.

"What's the matter, Auntie Bree? Are you cold?"

"Yes," Christopher answered for her. "It's getting colder in these woods. How would you like to ride home on Rufus, James? Your aunt and I will walk beside you."

Nothing could have pleased the child more, and they proceeded on their slow way to the house along the road this time. Christopher attempted to question the boy in a casual manner but it was quickly evident that James had not heard or seen the person who had shot the gun. He'd been too busy searching for stones. Neither had he seen any rabbits or pigeons during his walk in the pinewood. Any fears or questions about what had happened had been driven clean out of his mind by the inestimable joy of riding Rufus. James enlivened the walk home with spontaneous comments on the passing scene from his high vantage point and gave voice to frequent expressions of unbounded delight in the adventure. Brianna was almost totally silent, and since she and Christopher had placed themselves on opposite sides of the horse for safety's sake, he could not study her countenance for clues to her present state of mind. Though she had succumbed neither to vapors nor hysterics, he'd known how upset she was by the stark horror in her eyes and the trembling she had not been able to control. She'd found no comfort in his arms; indeed, she had stiffened and pushed him away almost immediately. Much as he longed to soothe away her fears, it would not do to make too much of the affair in the child's presence. James was happily oblivious to the danger he'd been in. Brianna would recover presently when they could talk about the incident without alarming the boy.

Three hours later, Christopher had to concede that he'd been overly optimistic in thinking he could restore the tone of Brianna's mind. After turning James over to Molly, she had joined him in the office at his request so that they might have the benefit of George's opinion. His cousin had agreed with him that the shooting had most likely been done by a poacher who had been too fearful of reprisals to identify himself when he heard Brianna's scream and realized that there were people in the woods. However, their combined efforts had failed to convince Brianna that the episode had been a freakish accident. She had been calm and composed throughout the interview but she would not back down from her claim that Jamie's bright blue coat could never have been mistaken for game of any sort, feathered or furred, and that only his sudden bending to pick up the stone had saved him from being hit. In vain had they pointed out that, not having seen or heard the shooter, she could not be positive of the direction of the ball and that James had most likely blundered into the field of a shot at the wrong moment. He'd been singing the whole time, she had stated, angry at what she saw as their obtuseness. She could not be brought to accept that the idea of wishing to harm a child was so preposterous as to guarantee that the shooting must have been accidental. She even dragged in the attack on the carriage that had brought the Herefordshire party to Ashleigh in support of her suspicions that her nephew was in danger. Christopher had commissioned his cousin to question everyone who worked on the estate about their whereabouts this afternoon and about anyone they might have seen who did not belong here, not because he believed any light would be shed on the matter but to placate Brianna whose nerves were clearly overset by the frightening experience.

As expected, George's report to him when he joined him in the saloon before dinner was entirely negative—everyone in the stables and all the gardeners claimed to have been going about their legitimate business that afternoon, and no one had seen a stranger, with or without a firearm.

Christopher could tell by Brianna's listless acceptance of the result of the inquiry that she had expected no more. Behind the wall of reserve she maintained in his presence, she was clearly unhappy, and, just as clearly, there was absolutely nothing he could do to reassure her that her fears were groundless. Only time would calm these fears and erase her suspicions.

Meanwhile, the homecoming he had anticipated so eagerly when he had set out from London at the crack of dawn was spoiled. Owing to the circumstances of his having subscribed to several of the London dailies when he returned to Ashleigh, his own news, seeming somewhat anticlimactic now, could not be kept back for a more propitious moment. His great-aunt devoured the society news even if she read nothing else in the papers.

13

" So she wouldn't have you in the end?" Lady Hermione said. "I suspected she was a flighty piece behind that oversweet manner of hers. Mark my words, she's hanging out for a bigger prize than you turned out to be. You are better off without her in that case." There was more satisfaction at having her dark suspicions confirmed than sympathy for her great-nephew's disappointment in the widow's ringing tones.

They were all four seated in the small drawing room, the men having just returned from the dining room. Brianna, stunned by Christopher's terse announcement of his broken engagement, glanced rapidly from one protagonist to the other. Christopher's face, which had revealed none of his thoughts when he reported Lady Selina's desire to be released from her promise to marry him, was now darkened by an expression of fastidious distaste as he fixed his undiplomatic relative with a piercing stare.

"On closer acquaintance, Lady Selina was persuaded our temperaments would not suit after all. It was a difficult and courageous decision and I honor her for it."

Under his steely regard, Lady Hermione harrumphed and declared that in her day girls didn't go about breaking their pledged word so easily, but this new freedom was all of a piece with the general decline in manners and morals.

To avert what promised to become a lengthy digression on this apocryphal decline in morality, George interceded with the formal offer of sympathy the occasion demanded. Christopher thanked him and looked at Brianna, his brows slightly raised.

"I . . . I am sorry for your . . . disappointment, sir," she managed, taking refuge, as had his cousin, in the conventional. Christopher's eyes narrowed at her wooden response, then he turned back to his aunt and proceeded to entertain her with an amusing recital of the current *on dits* making the rounds in the capital.

Brianna took no part in the ensuing conversation, sitting in her corner of the long sofa and employing her sewing as a shield behind which to indulge in her own furious speculation. Christopher's startling announcement had merely capped what had been a hideously difficult and disturbing day that had begun with George Cardorette's unwitting revelations at the breakfast table. She had been in a rare state of seething anger ever since, retroactive anger directed at Matthew Cardorette on behalf of his despised wife, and a strange consuming anger toward Christopher for his base deceitful nature that encompassed the sly covering up of his brother's iniquities at her sainted father's expense and his dastardly betrayal of his betrothed by his unwelcome gallantry toward herself. The strength of her revulsion almost frightened her, though that was nothing to the fright she had sustained in the pinewood this afternoon when Jamie had come so close to death. Christopher's casual dismissal of her fears and suspicions concerning Jamie's safety had been the final straw. She had never detested anyone so thoroughly in her life, and the passionate nature of her feelings alarmed her, nearly threatening her reason.

Brianna was in no mood to sympathize with the jilted fiancé; indeed, her first reaction had been a queer little leap of her heart that she attributed to her own malicious satisfaction at his supposed pain. On one level she was ashamed of her own un-Christian lack of compassion, but her anger and disgust remained. The only thing that had changed was her initial impulse to confront Christopher with her knowledge of his deception regarding his brother's bigamous intentions. By the end of the day, cooler judgment had prevailed. An emotional tirade would achieve nothing beyond a temporary relief of her pent-up anger. Brianna told herself she could not bear to listen to whatever defense of his reprehensible conduct he might mount. In truth, she preferred to have no more contact with such an unadmirable character than was unavoidable given the exigencies of her position in his household.

Over the next sennight or so, Brianna adhered rigidly to this resolution. In vain did Christopher seek out opportunities to avail himself of her company. She became adept at evading his overtures and eluding his presence, spending no more time with the other inmates of Ashleigh than was required by common civility. With no music to provide entertainment, the evenings deteriorated into a three-sided exchange of banalities interspersed with longwinded homilies by Lady Hermione when she disagreed strongly with either of her nephews' views. To all Christopher's requests and cajolery that Brianna allow them to teach her to play whist or

piquet, she returned a cool refusal couched in polite but definite
language that left no room for hope that she might experience a
change of heart. When Lady Hermione, irritated by such an unco-
operative spirit, said that in her day no well-brought up young
woman would have dreamed of setting up her own preferences in
opposition to the wishes of her elders, Brianna replied with a
sweet false smile that she thoroughly endorsed her ladyship's sentiments, explaining that her refusal to play cards was the direct result of having been raised in a minister's household where such
activity was frowned upon as tending to lead to moral laxity. She
then offered to read aloud to Lady Hermione from a book of ser-
mons she had recently come across in the library. It was at this
point that the cousins elected to play chess on those evenings they
did not remove to the billiards room after dinner.

Honesty forbade Brianna to deny that she knew how to play
chess, especially when her conscience already pricked her for
overstating her father's objections to card playing. Her determined efforts to avoid playing chess with Christopher were
stymied eventually by his equally determined and infinitely more
good-humored efforts to draw her into a match. Having run out of
acceptable excuses, she gave in with poor grace, furiously aware
that her reluctance looked positively churlish beside his exemplary courtesy and patience. That didn't stop her from prohibiting
all extraneous conversation during the contest, however, blandly
claiming her level of skill to be so low that she could not afford to
have her concentration distracted. Brianna actually won the game,
but the conviction that Christopher had allowed her to win only
added to the resentment she felt at being manipulated by him.

Brianna knew she was behaving badly. Even had she been as
lacking in sensibility as Lady Hermione, who seemed to have no
idea that the frankness upon which she prided herself went more
often over the line into gratuitous insult, Brianna had earned the
sharp censure of her oldest friend for what Molly termed her callous disregard for Christopher Cardorette's feelings. Christopher
had appeared in the nursery one day and proposed a jaunt to the
nearest market town for herself and Jamie, an invitation Brianna
had unhesitatingly turned down with—according to Miss Lloyd—
a transparently flimsy excuse and no proper expression of gratitude for the kind thought. After Christopher had bowed himself
out, accepting her blunt refusal with unaltered politeness, an astonished Molly had not spared her former charge the rough edge
of her tongue, telling her without roundaboutation that she had
never thought to be so ashamed of her manners.

Brianna did not make the mistake of trying to defend what was indefensible conduct in Molly's eyes, preferring to accept the scold because not even to this close confidante could she enumerate all the reasons for her present behavior. Molly knew how she chafed at her dependent position with its accompanying restriction of her freedom of choice in a matter of personal associations, and she had listened gravely to the story of Matthew's planned bigamous marriage. To Brianna's chagrin, her friend had not entered completely into her own feeling of rage at Christopher's daring to whitewash Matthew's betrayal by letting people believe his father-in-law had told him at some point of his wife's death, while concealing the fact of his son's birth. To be sure, Molly had sadly deplored any action that must tarnish the Reverend Arthur Llewellyn's sterling character, but she had stunned Brianna by suggesting, though with a troubled countenance, that her father would have gladly sacrificed his good name in this respect if by so doing he could have spared his grandson the shame the knowledge of his father's dishonor would bring. After some painful deliberation, Brianna had reluctantly conceded the truth of this but had still passionately condemned Christopher for taking it upon himself to sacrifice her father in his brother's behalf without either consulting or informing her of his intention. Molly had readily recognized the justice of this complaint, but Brianna could not think that her friend appreciated the full extent of the wrong, especially since she continued to censor Brianna's conduct toward Christopher. Molly might have been less ready to preach forgiveness and charity had she known of Christopher's deplorable lack of loyalty to his former fiancée, but for some inexplicable reason, Brianna could not bring herself to tell her friend how Christopher had flirted with her and *used* her in his disgusting betrayal of Lady Selina's trust. This coerced complicity was the real wellspring of her consuming rage, a rage that would not admit of prudent compromise for the sake of appearances.

Thus Brianna continued to treat all Christopher's friendly overtures with the same chilly formality, blind to the danger inherent in such unnatural behavior as she was willfully blind to the hurt look that sometimes came into his eyes following one of her rebuffs. She derived a fierce satisfaction from denying him any crumbs of friendship. It was only in those unguarded moments before sleep overtook her that her disciplined mind relaxed its strict vigilance enough to permit her to wonder fleetingly what her parents would say about such a mean-spirited campaign as she was waging. Actually, she knew very well how deeply they

would disapprove of harboring such spiteful feelings for the sake
of her own soul's welfare. In these nocturnal justifications she argued that she could not afford to worry about her soul; she was
waging a desperate battle to keep from falling into the same trap
that had spoiled her beautiful sister's life and led to her early
death. She fell asleep each night reconfirmed in her resolution.

Brianna and Molly were sewing in the nursery one cold clear
day when Jamie, who had been out walking with Lily, burst into
the room, his green eyes alight with excitement.

"Auntie Bree, Uncle Chris has a surprise for us down at the
stables. He said I was to tell you the . . . honor of your presence
is re . . . requested."

Both women laughed at the little boy's relief in successfully
parroting the message entrusted to him, but Brianna, staying in
character, demurred. She smiled at the expectant child and said
with manufactured regret, "I am sorry, my dear, but I am too busy
to go down to the stables just now. Lily shall take you and I'll see
your surprise another time."

"But Uncle Chris said the surprise was for *both* of us. Please
come, Auntie Bree."

"You are not hurting the man but the boy by this childishness,
Brianna," Molly said in a sharp aside.

Brianna flushed under the rebuke and got up from her chair.
"Very well, Jamie, but you must wait until I get my warm cloak.
The wind is biting today." To Molly she said disparagingly, "All
this fuss will probably be for nothing more important than a new
litter of kittens."

Brianna could not have been more wrong in this prediction.
She insisted on having Lily accompany them, with some idea of
satisfying Jamie by a token appearance before she returned to the
nursery, leaving the maid to supervise him. As the three approached the stables, Jamie ran on ahead, impatient with the
ladies' dawdling pace. Before Brianna and Lily rounded the corner of the stableyard they could hear his rapturous voice.

"Oh, he's beautiful! Is he really mine, only mine, Uncle
Chris?"

The sight that met their eyes was guaranteed to melt the stoni-
est-hearted guardian, and Brianna was decidedly not that. Under
the smiling regard of his uncle and several of the stable boys,
Jamie was hugging as much of a shaggy gray pony as his short
arms could enfold. Observing the child's ecstatic hugs and caresses and the animal's exemplary patience in receiving this tribute, Brianna's lips curved irresistibly upward. She kept her eyes

on her nephew, well aware that Christopher was trying to compel her glance as she walked up to the happy pair and patted the pony's nose at the boy's urging.

"Isn't he the most beautiful pony in the world, Auntie Bree?" Jamie demanded, leveling shining eyes on her for an instant before returning all his attention to the object of his admiration. "Uncle Chris bought him just for me. *Thank* you, Uncle Chris!" he cried, turning to the man who had stepped closer to his aunt. "What is his name?"

"He's called Smoky, but you may change his name if you wish," his uncle said, relieving the stable lad of the pony's bridle.

"Smoky," Jamie repeated, testing the sound. He displayed all his pearly teeth in a delighted smile. "I like the name, don't you, Auntie Bree?" Again he gave her no time to answer before demanding of his uncle, "May I ride Smoky now, Uncle Chris?"

Now Brianna directed a warning look at Christopher before addressing the boy. "Your uncle and I will have to talk about this, Jamie. You are rather young for riding lessons yet."

"I'm *not* too young to ride, Auntie Bree, I'm *not*!" Jamie blazed. "Uncle Chris wouldn't have bought Smoky if I was too young, would you, Uncle Chris?"

Sympathy for the boy's frantic appeal was evident on his face but Christopher said, "Whoa, there, James. That's no way to speak to your aunt." He paused and waited silently until James mastered his temper and, seeing no sign of relenting in his uncle's face, swallowed hard.

"I'm sorry I yelled at you, Auntie Bree, but Uncle Chris doesn't think I'm too young to ride, do you, Uncle Chris? I rode Rufus, and Smoky's *much* smaller and . . . and I'm getting bigger every day and . . ." His voice petered out and he glanced from his aunt's troubled face to his uncle who took pity on his distress.

"Smoky has to rest today, James, because he has come a long way, but tomorrow you may have your first riding lesson if you promise to obey all the rules." Christopher contrived to present a stern, no-nonsense expression.

"Yes, yes, o'course I will. *Thank* you, Uncle Chris." The delighted child completely forgot about his aunt's objection as he turned to croon to the pony about what fun they would have together.

Christopher's laughing gaze encountered flinty resentment when it swung back to Brianna. His smile vanished but his words were soft and his tones conciliatory. "You cannot keep him a baby forever, Brianna. He's ready and eager to spread his wings a bit. Don't be concerned that he'll hurt himself; he'll be well taught."

She looked at him steadily without favor. "Obviously my wishes in the matter have no weight with you at all."

"Be fair, Brianna. Of course your wishes for James's welfare count, but in this instance I believe I am better able to judge the situation. You saw him happy as a lark up on Rufus, who is a large horse. Smoky is small and placid and well-used to children, an ideal first mount. If you are honest, you'll concede that James is absolutely fearless and eminently ready to begin riding."

There was a friendly challenge in Christopher's eyes. Brianna glanced away to see her nephew urging Lily to pat his pony before she said evenly. "You told me in Herefordshire that the court would make you Jamie's guardian, so whatever I may think is immaterial, is it not? If you will excuse me, I'll return to the nursery now."

"Just a minute if you please, Brianna. Smoky was only part of the reason I asked you to come down to the stableyard." All the warmth had left Christopher's voice. He turned and called a short command to a groom hovering in the opening to the barn.

Jamie and Lily were busy discussing Smoky's points but silence prevailed among the adults for a long uncomfortable moment. Brianna kept her eyes on the entrance and her back ramrod stiff until the groom reappeared leading a neat bay mare who approached with bright-eyed interest and dancing steps. The mare's coat shone with brushing and she held up her head like an acknowledged beauty greeting her courtiers.

"What do you think of her?" Christopher asked.

"She's beautiful," Brianna conceded with reluctant honesty. She was feeling too raw to accommodate her antagonist more wholeheartedly.

"She's yours," Christopher said with equal brevity.

Jamie and Lily had deserted Smoky to admire the horse, a diversion that gave Brianna a little time to recover from her surprise and decide on her course of action. Meeting Christopher's expectant glance she said politely, "Had you consulted me before embarking on a search for a mount, you would have been spared the time and trouble, not to mention the expense, involved. I gave up riding a number of years ago. I hope you will be able to return the mare," she added indifferently before turning away from the man staring at her in angry bafflement to tell Lily she was going back to the house and leaving Jamie in her charge.

Christopher caught up with her in the garden before she could reach the house. "Just a moment, Brianna," he called out as she passed the stone bench where they had already enacted one unpleasant scene.

She condemned as sheer cowardice her instinctive desire to increase her speed and seek the safety of other people's presence. Instead she halted, recognizing as she did so the strategic error in granting him any privacy in which to persuade her to change her mind. There was no encouragement in the stiff expression and bearing she presented to the man approaching soft-footed and swift, with a dangerous gleam in his hazel eyes as he surveyed her drawn-up figure dispassionately.

"At least James thanked me for my efforts on his behalf," he observed in a neutral tone.

"I agree it was very remiss of me not to express proper gratitude. Please accept my apology," she said, cutting that ground out from under him.

There was no softening of her stiffness, and puzzlement gained the upper hand in Christopher's eyes for the moment as they searched hers. "Did you ever hear of cutting off one's nose to spite one's face, Brianna?" he asked softly, a whimsical quirk to his well-cut lips.

"If you are going to talk in conundrums, sir, I fear you will have to excuse me. There are things I must attend to in the nursery."

Christopher sighed, conceding defeat. "Very well then, let's talk plainly, shall we? You have been upon your high ropes ever since I returned from London. What grievance are you cherishing so tightly that you can barely bring yourself to be civil to me these days?" When his invitational pause produced no immediate reaction beyond a quick flaring of thin nostrils and a firming of her lips, Christopher went on relentlessly. "You prefer to make a guessing game out of it? All right, I'll play. My guess is that you are still fuming over that ill-advised kiss. If it is an apology you wish, it is yours. I should not have kissed you like that. I lost my head and I apologize. Please forgive me."

This time the silence was of the deafening variety. It was Brianna's turn to search the face of her antagonist, but if she sought some sign of true repentance she did not find it. There was nothing save impatience to be read in his handsome countenance. She backed up a half step, and reading her intentions, Christopher shot out a hand to grasp her forearm.

"Have you nothing more to say? You might at least tell me that you accept my apology," he grated through clenched teeth.

"Perhaps I don't feel I am the injured party, at least not the principal one. Have you apologized to Lady Selina?" she flared, trying without success to tug her arm out of his tightening grip. She ceased this undignified and unequal struggle, standing quietly while revelation swept over his features. For the first time Christopher looked uncomfortable and he dropped her arm abruptly. Brianna, with an opportunity to escape, stood her ground, her eyes steady and accusing on his.

Christopher took a shallow breath and expelled it before saying with some difficulty, "I do not attempt to defend my conduct, which was improper, but I think you cannot have a full understanding of the situation that existed between Selina and myself."

"Did she break her engagement because of me?"

The blunt question forced a quick decisive "*No!*" from him, but before he could expand on this, Brianna said, even more bluntly. "I do not believe you."

"It is the truth in the most important sense," Christopher insisted. A muscle twitched in his cheek as he read disdain in her eyes. He caught her arm again as she would have left him. "Having come this far, I think you owe it to me to hear the full story of my betrothal," he said quietly. "Please sit down." He indicated the bench behind them, but Brianna shook her head and continued to stand, her steady gaze inflexible as she waited for his explanation.

"I met Selina shortly after my return to England last August after six years in the army. My brother was dead and I was suddenly, so I believed, the last of my family. In that situation, a man begins to think of his own mortality. I decided it was time to look about for a wife and settle down to a normal existence. When Selina crossed my path I was as struck by her beauty and charm as most men must be. I was not in love with her," he said, looking deeply into Brianna's eyes, "and I knew she did not love me either, but we liked each other very well. She had all the qualities one thinks of as gracing the position I thought I held, and on her side, she thought I had a title and fortune to offer her."

As a look of disgust crossed Brianna's face, Christopher said coolly, "You want the truth, Brianna. I am not denigrating Selina in any way by implying that worldly consideration was a factor in her decision to accept my offer. You cannot be so naive as to believe all, or even most marriages are pure love matches. Selina and I might have made a successful thing of it in time, had I not met you."

Brianna tried to pull away from him again, but Christopher held her effortlessly. "I had no intention of telling you this so soon, but obviously only the truth will serve now. The air must be cleared between us." Her hostility did not lessen but he went on doggedly. "I did meet you, however, and everything changed for me. Consider my plight; I could not in honor draw back from my betrothal but another woman filled my thoughts. I tried—my God, how I tried—to convince myself that I was not in love with you; and when that didn't work, I tried to ignore you, but I am no saint, Brianna. The temptation was always there, and at times I could not deny myself the pleasure of looking at you, talking to you, touching you. I am trying to be completely honest with you," he insisted as she turned her head away in disgust. "I don't know what would have happened if Selina had gone through with the marriage. I swear on my honor that I did not consciously try to get her to break the engagement, but when she did, I cannot deny that I was the happiest man alive."

"Did she break it because of me?" Brianna repeated, fixing relentless eyes on him.

"Only in the sense that she finally realized she wanted more from the man she married than I could offer her, than I *had* offered her. Please don't turn away from me, Brianna," he pleaded, taking her shoulders into his hands and drawing her a few inches closer. "I've told you all this today because it was vital to have complete honesty between us. I love you with all my heart and wish to marry you, but I won't rush you. Don't take all hope away from me," he added as she stood limp and unresponsive in his grasp.

She looked up at that. "I must," she said dully, impassive now. "I will never marry you." She averted her eyes from the stricken look that came into his and steeled herself to resist any further entreaties.

"Don't say that, Brianna. You must feel something of the attraction between us—I *know* you do. I won't press you. I am willing to wait until you know your own heart."

"I know my own mind which is more important," she replied, shaking her head. "Please let me go, Christopher. I won't change my mind about marrying you."

"How can you be so sure? Is there someone else? Paxton?"

"There is no one else. I won't marry you because I have no intention of making the same mistake my sister made. It is that simple and that final."

"Simple perhaps, but wrongheaded," he retorted. "I am not my brother and you are not your sister."

"I am certainly not as foolishly trusting as Meg was, but you are very like your brother, Christopher, just as willing to swear eternal fidelity to get what you want at the moment, and equally dishonest with the one you profess to love."

Christopher's skin lost some of its rich coloring at the bitterness in her words and voice. "That's unfair and untrue!"

"Is it? In my view Matthew was dishonest in concealing his background from my sister and dishonorable in writing to assure her he would return for her. You have been equally dishonest in concealing from me the fact that your brother would have made a bigamous marriage with Lady Selina except for his accidental death. But you were not content with simply concealing something discreditable to your family, were you? You must compound the dishonesty by telling people it was *my father's* fault that your worthless brother never knew he had a son!"

Long before this bitter speech ended, Christopher had released Brianna's shoulders and stepped away from her. She suspected the haughty mask he adopted covered an anger as active as her own but his words were measured. "It's apparent that you have built up such a case against me in your own mind as would not admit of reversal by even the most persuasive advocate, but for the sake of getting the truth out in the open, I will say only that I had every intention of telling you the whole story when there had grown more trust between us." He gave a harsh little laugh. "I hope you appreciate the exquisite irony of such simplistic reasoning in the circumstances. As for letting people believe that your father had concealed James's birth from Matt, I deeply regretted the necessity of maligning one who I am persuaded was a fine man. I rationalized it with my conscience by telling myself that I did it more for James's sake than Matt's. I don't know whether that is completely true or not." He shrugged. "There you have it, the sum of my crimes against you for which I humbly apologize. None of it was done to hurt you. I wish you would believe that at least."

"Then there is nothing left to say." She turned away, bent on escape.

"Wait, Brianna. None of this detracts from the validity of my love for you. Don't confuse one thing with the other."

"Please, Christopher, we've been all through that," Brianna protested wearily.

"Scarcely that," he said with a grim little smile. "I've bared my soul to you and you've judged me wanting in character and otherwise unfit to aspire to your hand. Tell me, Brianna, will the man you marry have to be a paragon of all the virtues?"

Stung by the criticism, she retorted, "No, but it is essential that I respect him above others."

"Respect is admirable, but it is no substitute for love, my dear, especially on a cold winter's night, unless you have ice water in your veins instead of blood."

"My sister chose love. With her example before me, I choose respect." Brianna's head was held at a proud angle and twin flames lit her green eyes as she defied his taunting.

"I am persuaded your calculating little brain would agree that it is essential to know what you are turning your back on in order to make an informed decision," Christopher said in purring tones that alerted Brianna to danger.

She reacted a split second too slowly in her backward leap. Christopher grabbed her arm and hauled her up against the length of his body. Only when his other arm had wrapped around her back and gripped her shoulder did he release her arm in order to raise her chin to kissing level.

Their first kiss had been akin to an assault, at least in the beginning. This one was pure seduction from the start. Brianna tried to resist, keeping her lips pressed shut, but his nibbled along the line of her mouth, placing little kisses at the corners while his thumb caressed her cheek and jaw. Her protesting brain was betrayed by the involuntary softening of every part of her body that came in contact with his. Her knees wobbled and Christopher shored her up, wrapping both arms around her now as his lips took full possession of her willing mouth. Wild unknown tremors ran down her body and she instinctively pressed closer without a clear idea of what she sought. All thought of resistance had long since fled and she was a quivering mass of sensation when Christopher suddenly broke off the kiss, putting her away from him with his hands on her upper arms. Brianna shivered in the cold air and stared at him dazedly.

"Do you still prefer respect to love?" he demanded, his eyes gleaming.

It might have been the shock of cold air where the heat of his body had been a moment before, or perhaps it was the triumph glittering in his darkened eyes that was responsible for jolting Brianna's faulty thinking mechanism back into operation, but she rapidly converted appalled dismay at the treachery of her own body into anger against the man who had caused the betrayal.

"Don't *ever* touch me again!" she hissed when she could force a sound from between trembling lips. "I hate you."

Christopher looked at her with contempt. "You've called me a liar before, so you should not object when I return the compliment. That was not hate I felt in my arms just now. You are resolved not to repeat your sister's mistake. She may have picked the wrong man, but at least she had the courage to accept love when it was offered. You'd prefer to make a bigger mistake with your eyes wide open. You'd rather refuse love in your cowardly determination to protect yourself from potential pain. As if anyone's happiness was ever guaranteed in this life! Meg probably knew more of the real joy of life, even if briefly, than you'll ever know."

"And more of unhappiness!" she shot back. "You don't really love me. You say you're not like your brother, but look at yourself! For a brief time you wanted the same woman your brother desired, and like him, when your wandering fancy lighted on someone else, you did not let honor prevent you from pursuing the new object. Oh, how I wish I'd never come to Ashleigh. I'd do *anything* to get away from this place and you!"

This time when Brianna backed away from him, Christopher made no attempt to restrain her. She spun around and dashed for the house as if all the fiends in Avernus were in pursuit of her.

14

When his leather breeches split while he was checking on some of his cottagers' repairs the next morning, Christopher swore with creative fluency, though he apologized quickly before making his way back to the house to change. It was as he was coming down the main staircase ten minutes later that he heard the door knocker, followed by Pennystone's stately tread coming from the back of the entrance hall. He arrived at the bottom just in time to witness Sir Harry Paxton's request to see Miss Llewellyn.

"I'll take care of it, Pennystone," he said, coming forward to offer his hand to Sir Harry.

"Very good, sir."

Christopher led the baronet into his study, noting as he did so that Sir Harry was turned out in trim fashion, his burgundy coat cut by a master tailor to mold to his shoulders, his cravat the epitome of understated elegance. No careless country gentleman this, everything about him was prime from the shine on his tasseled Hessians to the gold signet ring on his finger and the discreet ruby pin nestled in the folds of his neckcloth. Christopher took all this into account in a quick survey as he offered his uninvited guest a glass of Madeira, an offer that was smilingly declined with a wave of one well-cared for hand.

"Thank you but no. I did not expect to find you in at this hour, sir. I really came to see Miss Llewellyn."

"How unfortunate that Brianna should be spending the day with friends outside the area," Christopher said smoothly. "Had we had more notice of your visit I am persuaded she would have altered her plans and you would not have undertaken a three-hour drive for nothing."

Sir Harry's disappointment was patent as he stood in the middle of the room obviously pondering his next move. Severe discipline enabled Christopher to maintain an easy stance and a relaxed noncommittal air while the other man came to a decision.

Sir Harry's pleasant features took on an aspect of determination as he looked squarely at his host once more. "I believe that Miss Llewellyn is of legal age," he began, allowing an infinitesimal pause at this point that Christopher did not elect to fill, before continuing, "so there is no question of seeking permission to pay my addresses to her, but as a matter of courtesy, I should like to inform you that it is my intention to ask her to become my wife. I realize this may seem a bit precipitate on such a short acquaintance, but—"

"I don't think it precipitate at all; in fact, I regret to inform you that your offer is too late. Miss Llewellyn is already betrothed . . . to me." Christopher's countenance remained impassive as the older man looked thunderstruck by this announcement.

"But how can this be? I understood that you were betrothed to Lady Selina Milliken!"

"Apparently you missed the notice of the ending of that engagement in the *Gazette* a sennight ago."

"Yes, I did . . . I . . . don't know quite what to say . . ."

Chagrin had robbed Sir Harry of his customary address, and Christopher said to ease his embarrassment, "I quite understand that the conventional message of congratulations is . . . difficult in the circumstances."

"Yes," Sir Harry agreed, his eyes dulled by disappointment, "But I do congratulate you, of course. She is a lovely young woman. You are a fortunate man indeed."

"I could not agree more." Again Christopher offered his nonplussed caller refreshment, but Sir Harry, gathering his composure about him, said all that was polite in refusing. Christopher saw him out to his waiting phaeton, himself assisting the disappointed suitor into his driving coat. They exchanged a few civil clichés and Sir Harry drove off with his groom sitting beside him.

Not until the phaeton disappeared from view did Christopher abandon his careful pose of conscientious host. His straight black brows were drawn together in a forbidding line and his booted feet sounded loud on the tile floor as he headed back to his *sanctum sanctorum,* though he admitted with a flash of mordant humor that the room might be described more accurately as the devil's den after this morning's work. Fortified with a glass of brandy, he stood by the window staring moodily out at the leaden skies. He was not devoid of sympathy and fellow feeling for Paxton's disappointment; in fact, his conscience was giving him merry hell at present, but he could not regret the lies he had told in this room not fifteen minutes earlier. Given the same set of circumstances again, he'd react in exactly the same way—*dishonorably* in Brianna's eyes, and near enough to that as made no difference, in his own. He'd scented danger at the first sound of Paxton's unwelcome voice in his ears and had resolved to keep him from meeting Brianna even before he'd crossed this threshold. The man had made his interest in Brianna too plain on that first occasion to find a warm welcome at Ashleigh.

After the disastrous quarrel in the garden yesterday, he would not put it past Brianna to accept Sir Harry's offer out of a desperate and misguided effort to get away from himself. He judged her capable of any foolhardy gesture in her panic-driven desire to expunge that passionate embrace from her memory.

Christopher's pulses raced and he swallowed a mouthful of brandy as he allowed himself to relive those charged moments when his fragile-appearing and stubbornly unwilling little love had nearly driven him beyond the bounds of control with her ardent response to his lovemaking. He'd managed to resist the burning desire to take her right there in the garden, but his subsequent handling of the mortified and panicked girl had left a lot to be desired, thanks to the complicating factors of raw nerves and a throbbing body. He'd guessed how she must be hating herself for succumbing to the unsuspected power of the senses. He'd recognized the unreasoning anger she'd whipped up against him for what it was, but the knowledge had not prevented him from making a mull of everything in their final quarrel.

Brianna had hidden away in her apartment for the rest of the day, refusing to come down for dinner, and he'd not set eyes on her so far today. He knew her well enough to be sure she had resurrected her toppled defenses against him by this time. She would be hating him like fury for revealing her own weakness to her. It would have been fatal to allow her to receive Paxton's offer in her present frame of mind.

Christopher downed the rest of the brandy in one gulp and put the glass back on the tray. He did not go directly back to the fields when he left the study but first sought out Pennystone to instruct his loyal retainer not to mention Sir Harry's visit to anyone. As he strode toward the stables five minutes later, his facial muscles were tight with disgust at the realization that he was doing his best to confirm Brianna's low opinion of his character. Despite a heroic effort not to inflict his bad temper on his dependents as he went about his business, Christopher could not help but be aware that a number of people were carefully curtailing their dealings with him for the rest of the day.

Brianna came out of hiding for dinner but she was wan and subdued and did not once meet his glance during the evening. She attached herself to Lady Hermione like a limpet, encouraging that garrulous lady to expand on her favorite theme of the loose morals obtaining among today's youth. After a few minutes, a defeated Christopher had no hesitation in accepting George's challenge to a game of billiards.

It was foreign to Christopher's nature to accept permanent defeat in anything, however. During the long night, further reflection on the present unhappy state of affairs between Brianna and himself kept coming back to one salient point: Brianna's current rage and misery might very well be considered a measure of her emotional involvement. Had she been personally indifferent to him, her anger over what she saw as his duplicity would have been much less impassioned. He had sufficient experience of females from several nations to recognize when a woman's heart was involved in her dealings with a man. For all Selina's willingness to encourage his lovemaking, there had been a vital element missing in her reaction. Conversely, Brianna's frantic determination to remain unresponsive to him had been unavailing. She had come to blazing life at his touch. Heart and body had betrayed her brain's intention of remaining aloof. It was impossible to guess how much of her expressed anger had been manufactured as a self-protection against falling in love with him, but surely it would be stupid to despair at this point. When Brianna had leisure to consider everything he had done in the context of the extraordinary circumstances in which he had found himself, surely her present condemnation would be tempered by mercy and understanding. It might take some time, of course, and that vital time was what he had fought for by lying to Paxton.

When morning came, Christopher wasn't thinking as much about the sins weighing on his conscience as he ought. No, his thoughts sought happier themes, such as the inevitability of Brianna's intellect accepting what her heart knew already: that she belonged to him. He wasn't even fazed by her absence from the breakfast table, not having expected that she would relinquish this new grievance too quickly. He was beginning to gain some understanding of the steely strength of purpose behind the timid exterior she presented to the world, exasperating in the present instance but still adding to her fascination for him.

"Good morning, George," He took his seat with a smiling nod

in his cousin's direction that was met by a long look full of speculation.

"Your outlook seems to have improved materially overnight, coz."

"But, of course, on such a lovely day," Christopher replied blandly, indicating the blue sky beyond the oriel windows with a wave of his hand.

"Better enjoy it while you can," his cousin advised. "Symonds says we're due for some wet weather very soon, and he is generally correct in his predictions."

"Another skill to be chalked up in Symonds's favor," Christopher said dryly, "though in no way sufficient to make up for his surly nature. I see murder in his eyes each time our paths cross. It queers me why you put up with him."

"Since I'm not the one he'd like to murder, the question doesn't arise," George returned with a grin that faded as he sent a penetrating look at the younger man busily devouring a heaping plateful of ham and eggs that had been supplied by Pennystone before he left the room. "It strikes me that Symonds is not the only one around here whose disposition is less than equitable lately. You cannot deny that your own spirits have been a trifle . . . unequal since your return from London, and one never knows when that dreadful girl will subject the household to her sulks and silences."

Christopher's head came up at that. "I had better warn you, George, that you are speaking of the woman I love." The words were soft, but the expression that accompanied them was not.

George, however, was too discomposed by the meaning of the words to heed the clear warning. "You cannot be serious in preferring Brianna Llewellyn to Lady Selina!" he expostulated. "Oh, she's pretty enough in a vapid way, but she has no countenance or conversation. You'll be bored with her within the month!"

"There's no accounting for tastes, George," Christopher said evenly, getting slowly to his feet. "I have every intention of making Brianna my wife as soon as may be. If you find that unacceptable, the remedy is in your hands." He left the room on the words without bothering to gauge his cousin's reaction.

Over the next few hours, Christopher's temper cooled considerably. He could not regret his defense of Brianna but he need not have stalked off in high dudgeon without giving old George a chance to apologize for his hasty words. He would not have chosen to make an announcement of his intentions at this critical stage of his rocky courtship. That had more or less been forced out of him by his cousin's disparagement of his beloved. He could have contented himself with a mild defense under the circumstances, even had his temper not been aroused.

As he rode about the estate checking on the various preparations being made for the winter that would soon be upon them, Christopher's thoughts kept returning to the current complications in his life. In retrospect, he was amazed that he could ever have assumed that he was simplifying his existence by abandoning the military lifestyle for the land. From the moment he'd laid eyes on Brianna, his well-regulated personal affairs had begun to tangle. Actually, the process had most likely begun even earlier when he had proposed marriage to a woman he did not love. Hopefully, the successful resolution of that complication had paved the way for a happy conclusion of the rest, but there was no denying the difficulties that lay ahead in the immediate future. George's attitude had merely added to those revolving around Brianna's lack of trust in himself. The one aspect of the situation that had presented no problem was his relationship with his nephew. Before the discovery that Matt had left an heir, children had never come very much in his way, but somewhat to his surprise he found he liked the boy and was increasingly intrigued by the eager questing intelligence contained in that small person. Once he and Brianna reached an understanding he had great hopes that they would become a real family.

Thinking of James recalled Christopher to the question of the child's safety on the large estate. He and Matt and George had roamed freely over every inch of the place in their boyhood, but the hilly area near the western boundary had always held great attraction, appealing as it did to the sense of adventure in all boys. Now that James was learning to ride, it was likely that he would be tempted to explore in that direction, so his uncle might as well take advantage of the good weather to check that there had not been any weakening in the crust that covered some of the deeper caves. In the past there had been occasional collapses that sealed up portions of the underground areas following particularly severe weather.

It was fairly late in the afternoon when Christopher headed Rufus west. He had not been back to the house all day, having shared the lunch provided by one of his tenant's wives. He was tempted to leave his inspection for another day, but a glance at the sky convinced him otherwise. The bright day had slowly deteriorated during the afternoon and it seemed likely that Symonds's weather prophesy would come to pass in the next few hours. They could have several days of rain to endure. He might as well get this chore behind him now.

As if the thought had conjured up the man, Christopher caught a quick glimpse of his cousin's groom out of the corner of his eye as he turned westward, letting Rufus canter a bit now. That was twice today he'd seen the man in the distance. No doubt it was the scene at breakfast that had brought the unpleasant groom to mind where he had not consciously noted the identity of the other employees he'd passed in the course of his perambulations today.

An hour later Christopher stood on the edge of a flat-topped hill looking out on a pleasantly wide vista undulating below him in grassy folds that rayed out from the cliff bottom like the graceful folds of a velvet cloak from a woman's shoulders. This had always been a favorite spot when they were lads, perhaps because a boy could imagine himself master of all he surveyed from this eminence. To his right the sweep ended abruptly in thick woods, but the view to the left was extensive as the land fell gradually away to a rippling stream in the valley floor and rose again gently to another small rounded hill, and beyond, a string of hills fading away in the distance. Ten yards behind him was a grove of trees where he'd tied Rufus. Immediately beneath his feet was thick springy grass, still green; farther below was the roof of the largest of the caves they'd explored as boys. The opening to the cavern was at the bottom of the cliff. He'd inspected it and several others in the vicinity in the past hour, a bit disappointed to find them so much less impressive than in his memory, but relieved that they still seemed structurally intact. He'd climbed back up here from the left side where the slope was less precipitous and been drawn to the very edge where the hill fell away in a nearly sheer drop for about five-and-twenty feet to the sandy path that passed the cave's entrance. This spot offered the premier view, though this was not the best time of year to appreciate it. The sky had become totally leaden now, covering the watery sun, and he shivered with a sudden chill as the dampness in the air made itself felt now that he was standing still.

Without warning Christopher was struck a stunning blow between his shoulder blades. The shock of it drove the air from his lungs and sent him staggering to his knees, but there was no ground left upon which to kneel. With a sharp cry, he hurtled over the edge of the cliff. He made an ineffectual grab at the outcropping stone before landing on the path. Pain exploded in his body.

* * *

Brianna stopped and looked around her, deliberately taking in every detail of her surroundings, turning around completely to include the direction whence she had come. It was no use; nothing looked remotely familiar. She was ignominiously lost. She made herself say the words aloud in a calm tone. Curiously enough she *was* calm. The worst that could happen was that she would have to find some shelter for the night. She was warmly dressed in her heavy hooded cloak, and it would not kill her to miss a meal. She would be missed by dinnertime, and even if it were too late to send people out to search for her before the light failed, there were sure to be searchers out by dawn.

She was not frightened so much as mortified by her own stupidity. She had been restless and regrettably abstracted of late, too wrapped up in her own problems to be any good to Jamie or Molly. It had been Molly who had suggested—nay, ordered her to take herself off for a long ramble this afternoon to shake the fidgets out of her system. Throughout her girlhood she had delighted in being out of doors in all weather. Often she would bring some food with her and spend an entire day in a solitary scramble over the foothills with only the grazing sheep for company. Today had been reminiscent of those happy occasions, though her mind had been too full of the tense situation between herself and Christopher Cardorette to properly appreciate the natural beauty around her. Had she paid proper attention to where her feet were taking her, she would not have landed herself in this embarrassing predicament.

Brianna shook her head to clear it of extraneous thoughts. She could make better use of the waning daylight than to stand around berating herself for what was already done. Her eyes surveyed the area again. She dismissed the woods she could see ahead from her consideration. Unless she absolutely knew that was the way back to Ashleigh she'd do better to remain where she could see farther ahead. The path to her left was rising fairly steeply. She headed for the high ground, hoping she might be able to orient herself better with the expanded view from a hilltop. She had seen no sheep today, but there might be some sort of cottage or dwelling visible where she could ask directions or seek shelter.

It took some time for Brianna to reach the top of the hill and she arrived slightly breathless from the ascent that had been more climb than walk in places. She rubbed her hands together to get the dirt off her gloves as she headed for the rim of the hill. It was a pleasant spot and the view was lovely and peaceful—too peaceful. Her searching eyes discerned no signs of habitation; not even the rudest hut proclaimed the presence of any human than herself. A kestrel circled overhead, then flew off. She followed its soaring flight, reluctant to lose the only animate creature with whom she shared this small corner of the universe.

Brianna stepped a little closer to the edge of what appeared to be a steep drop-off, testing the ground beneath her feet and finding it firm. Her casual glance swept the area below the cliff on which she stood and her heart lurched in her breast. For a split second her intellect refused to credit what her eyes had identified, but those were indeed a man's booted legs lying on the path below, unmoving. She leaned out farther to increase her field of vision. The next instant she leapt back from the edge, a cry of dread escaping her lips as she whirled and headed back the way she had come at a dead run.

Wordless prayers and promises streamed through Brianna's mind and onto her lips as she half-slid back down the hill, careless of her own safety in her haste to reach that prostrate figure. She was driven by fear, for there could be no room for doubt about the identity of the man on the path. She had recognized the dark curls so like Jamie's.

It was Christopher lying sprawled on his back, one bent arm partly across his chest, and pain knifed through Brianna as she fell to her knees beside his still form. He was so white she feared he was dead. She was unaware that she had been repeating the single word "Please," over and over while she approached. She continued to mutter this pathetic litany as she stripped off a glove and thrust a trembling hand inside his coat.

She couldn't feel his heartbeat! She fought back panic as she placed her fingers on his lips. They were cold as marble but she thought—surely there was a slight warmth on her finger tips under his nose. He was still breathing! She closed her eyes in weak relief and two tears squeezed out from under the lids. Brianna ignored them as she took his wrist in her fingers. His pulse was faint but discernible.

Christopher was alive but obviously injured. Methodically, Brianna set about trying to determine the nature and extent of his injuries. His arms and legs seemed normal to her inexpert touch. Except for an oozing cut on one hand she could see no blood anywhere, but she was afraid to move his head. The fear that he might have broken his neck or back turned her weak, but she forced herself to consider all the possibilities. Seeing him from above she had assumed that he had fallen over the edge of the cliff, but that need not be true. He might have met with some accident right here. She had no way of knowing how long he had been unconscious, but he was very cold and that was dangerous. On her knees beside Christopher, Brianna gazed about her, looking desperately for some sign of another human being. There was nothing, but her roving eyes discovered a gaping break in the cliff wall behind them. She jumped to her feet, excitement stirring. A cave would mean shelter.

Glancing back at the injured man every few seconds as if fearing he would vanish when her back was turned, Brianna made a swift exploration inside the opening. There was a fair-sized cave under the cliff and it seemed dry enough to promise some shelter for the night. Though it was no warmer inside at present, the temperature would certainly drop out here when night came. Brianna agonized over whether she might be aggravating Christopher's unknown injuries if she moved him inside, but he was already so cold she was inclined to think it would be more dangerous to leave him outside for a whole night. There was no question of going for help. Apart from not knowing which direction to take, it would be dark within the hour, and what was worse, rain seemed imminent. Praying that she was making the right decision, she returned to the unconscious man and gingerly placed her hands on either side of his head. There was no reaction when she moved his head slightly to one side, then the other. She froze when she noticed blood under his head, but her exploring fingers found the cut on the back of his head. She breathed a sigh of relief to find it superficial. Her probing fingers located a lump on his head too. At the very least he must have a concussion to be so deeply unconscious. It was the fear of spinal injuries that prevented her from dragging him inside the cave, but the first raindrops ended her dithering.

Christopher moaned when she pulled backward on his shoulders. Biting fiercely on her bottom lip to keep from adding her moans to his, she moved him by inches while slow tears slipped silently down her cheeks. It was a torturous process to pull a full-grown man some fifteen feet, and Brianna was sweating and trembling with fatigue by the time she got him far enough back in the cave to be safe from the rain that continued to fall. She had put her cloak over him for protection. Though rain-damp herself, she was actually warm from her exertions for a while. But by the time the last light had faded from the sky outside, Brianna was thoroughly chilled and her teeth were chattering.

Christopher had ceased moaning when she'd stopped dragging him. There was no return of consciousness, but she thought—

hoped—he was a bit warmer. She removed her gloves and felt his neck under her cloak. Surely his skin was a bit warmer than before? No colder certainly. She had removed his cravat earlier and folded it into a pad that she placed under his head, a pitifully inadequate gesture, but she did not dare remove his coat to make a pillow. He needed warmth more than comfort at present. Instead, she took off her petticoat and added this meager thickness to the other pad. For a while at least, there would be some warmth from her body under his injured head.

She got up from where she had been sitting near his head with her back to the wall of the cave and began stomping around in the limited space, swinging her arms to warm herself, trying to avoid banging into the stone walls in the darkness. She wasn't normally nervous of the dark but here it seemed almost to smother her. No use thinking about it. The blackness near the mouth of the cave was less opaque and she headed there, drawn by the monotonous splash of the rain on the rocky floor. The rain had increased in volume. She found the unvarying sound of it unbearably mournful.

Brianna shivered violently in her damp dress and groped her way back to Christopher. She could avoid the decision no longer. If she was to keep the helpless man and herself from freezing tonight she would have to conserve their bodily warmth. She lifted her cloak from Christopher and carefully spread one long edge on the stone floor just under his left arm and leg. She fitted herself closely alongside him on top of the cloak and drew the rest of it back over them both, trying to tuck as much as possible under him on his right side, no easy task from within her cocoon. The word comfort didn't apply to the result of her manoeuvres—stone does not make an agreeable mattress—but her shivering stopped gradually. She tried as much as possible to lie on her side, pressing against him everywhere she could, but she was afraid to put her left arm across his body in case her weight aggravated some unknown internal injury. Christopher had made no sound or movement since she had dragged him into the cave. In cruel contrast to the pulsating strength and heat that had radiated from him during their last embrace, there was no reaction from his inert body to her present closeness.

On the instant of identifying his unconscious figure at the foot of the cliff, Brianna's willful ignorance of her feelings for Christopher had been replaced with the searing knowledge that she loved him. No longer would she be able to deny or misname her total response to his presence. She still did not believe in the permanence of romantic love, but she could no longer deny its power over those in its thrall. The world had stopped for her when she'd feared that Christopher was dead.

This self-knowledge brought Brianna neither relief nor happiness. She did not wish to be in love with Christopher Cardorette; he was too much like his brother to be a safe person to whom to entrust her heart. If she had to characterize her emotion at this moment of discovery, she would have to call it *fear*, fear that she would be unable to resist his importunities in the future, and fear that her mind would not be able to command her yearning heart and body much longer.

Not that it should make any difference to her decision not to marry Christopher. If a diamond like Lady Selina could not hold his interest for six months, how could an ordinary female like herself hope to keep him for a lifetime? Better to be vaguely dissatisfied all her life than to be wildly happy for a short time and then be plunged into a bottomless quagmire of misery when his interest strayed as it was bound to do sooner or later. Besides, she would be free to leave Ashleigh Court when Jamie went off to school in four or five years. Perhaps in time she would learn to love someone else in a sane and sensible fashion.

The hours crawled past for Brianna in that cave. When her aching bones cried out in agony at the hardness of her resting place, she walked around and stretched a little. Beyond the cave's entrance the steady splash of rain on rock continued in her ears.

When she came back to Christopher she arranged herself along his right side this time. He remained unaware of any change. Only once did he emerge, and that briefly, from the deep unconsciousness that held him suspended in time. He moaned and Brianna laid her arm over his chest.

"Sshhh, my darling; it's all right," she whispered.

"Brianna?" the name was more sigh than sound.

"Yes, I'm here. Go to sleep."

"Pain . . . my head . . ."

"I know, but it will be better directly. Go back to sleep, my love."

He did slip back into his coma and eventually Brianna dozed fitfully, castigating herself as she drifted off for permitting herself the indulgence of endearments. He would never know, but it was unwise all the same.

Brianna's eyelids lifted to a strange murky grayness over her head. Her left arm felt cramped beneath her and when she turned onto her back to release it, pain—and awareness—came to her simultaneously. She was lying on the stone floor of a cave, her body one complete ache. She clenched her teeth to keep back a groan as she turned her head to study the still face of the man she loved. She put out a tentative hand to his cheek and rejoiced to find it no colder than her own.

She had to lift the cloak to ease herself up and away, never taking her hungry eyes from that beautifully sculpted countenance, dimly perceived in the gray gloom of their surroundings. Something seemed different as she staggered to her feet, triumphing over her protesting muscles, and a moment later she realized it was the silence that was odd; the rain had stopped during the night. She recovered Christopher with the cloak and went out of the cave, shivering slightly, to greet the day.

With no break in the cloud cover it was impossible to tell what hour it was beyond the fact that it was full daylight. Brianna stood in the mouth of the sheltering cave, briskly rubbing her arms to stimulate warmth while she stared bleakly at the empty landscape. She had clung to the hope that morning might reveal something she had missed yesterday, perhaps smoke from a fire that would point to a nearby dwelling of some sort. She was aching and hungry and cold, but most of all she was afraid of making the wrong decision for Christopher's sake. Should she set off immediately to get help or remain with him to keep him warm and trust that his people would soon find them?

As Brianna stood in the cave opening, a prey to indecision and fear, the question was answered for her. Muted sounds from the woods to the right disturbed the morning silence. She turned and strained to distinguish the noises, all her senses on the stretch. A long moment later, her heartbeat quickened with joy and relief at the sight of a party of horsemen emerging from the woods.

15

"There is no getting around it; you will have to marry the girl!"

Lady Hermione followed her brisk announcement into the darkened bedchamber. Both were received with a singular lack of enthusiasm by the man in the tester bed.

Christopher had been conscious long enough to assimilate the fact that he was in his own bed, which surprised him, and to become aware of an excruciating pain in his head that intensified with the slightest movement. The only movement he made now was to close his eyes which had flown open as his aunt's strident voice assaulted his ears. This simple ruse failed utterly in its object of getting rid of the source of the noise.

"You need not pretend to be still unconscious because I know you are awake at last. I met that snippy valet of yours outside this door and he told me. He had the impertinence to try to fob me off, claiming the doctor ordered that you must remain perfectly still and proscribed all visitors for forty-eight hours. Harrumph, *doctor!* I imagine I know how to rate the professional skills of someone calling himself a medical man who cannot even predict how long a person will remain unconscious after a blow on the head."

"How . . . long?" Christopher was appalled by the effort it took to produce a thin thread of voice. He gave up the attempt, closing his eyes on his great-aunt's actions in selecting the most comfortable chair in the room, which she proceeded to place near the bed for her use.

"Do you mean how long have you been unconscious? According to that girl, she found you some time before nightfall yesterday, and you've been unconscious until a few minutes ago, but naturally that is what she'd say." Lady Hermione's massive bosom swelled in concert with the disbelief written clearly on her taut features.

Christopher frowned in concentration, trying to make sense out of the words raining down on his head. Even this slight exertion of facial muscles increased his discomfort. "What time?" he whispered before giving in to the pain, trying to keep very still while it rolled over him.

"What time is it now? Nearly four in the afternoon. They brought you back on a litter before noon and sent for the doctor, who is even more mealymouthed than most of his profession. Refused to commit himself on how long you'd be laid up, intoned all sorts of dire possibilities, even while admitting that your pulse was near normal and the only real injury you had sustained, apart from a knock on the head, was a cracked rib or two, which he had bound up."

Christopher now had an explanation for why each breath was pure torture. He took comfort from the information provided by his aunt, though nothing in her manner indicated a desire to render comfort. He closed his eyes again.

"I have no more desire than you to prolong this interview, so you need not think to get rid of me by pretending to be tired. I'll leave as soon as I've said what needs to be said. You were alone with that girl in a cave overnight, and it's no use arguing that you were unconscious the whole time—which I take leave to doubt, though she swore to it with that butter-wouldn't-melt-in-her-mouth look of hers, since she colored up red as fire as she swore it—because it's neither here nor there! It doesn't make a particle of difference whether you were or whether you weren't. I had the whole story from George just now. When he and the grooms found you two this morning you were lying in a cave with her cloak on top of you and her *petticoat,* of all the brazen things, folded under your head! If you think that pretty tale won't be all over the neighborhood in a trice, then all I can say is you don't know how servants gossip. You've ruined the girl, whether intentionally or not is beside the point. No one with the least claim to respectability would receive her now, so there's nothing for it but to marry her. It's not what one likes, and alliance with such a low family, but that's what comes of that quixotic gesture of yours of taking in the aunt with the child. You should have sent her packing from the start. And there's no use your looking daggers at me only for some necessary plain talking either. I'm sorry for it but you either marry the girl or I wash my hands of you."

"Such an inducement tempts me to repudiate the marriage, madam, but it just so happens that the dearest wish of my heart is to marry Brianna." Christopher's anger had lent him the strength to strike back at his uncharitable kinswoman, but the cost was great. Sweat stood out on his brow as he rode a wave of renewed pain. He neither heard Lady Hermione's furious declaration that she would not remain another night under a roof where she was subject to such insults, nor saw her stamp out of the room with her cane striking the floor in hammer blows. He could no longer differentiate the hammer blows to his head from outside noises.

When his cousin came to see him that evening, the pain had receded somewhat, thanks to some helpful powders the doctor had left with his valet, Johnson, and a restorative sleep of several hours duration.

"How are you feeling now, coz?" George inquired with more sympathy than Lady Hermione had displayed earlier.

"My head still aches like the devil but I no longer feel queasy with it, which I can tell you is a great relief," Christopher replied from a flat pillow in compliance with the doctor's orders.

"You sound weak as a cat, but you don't look nearly so pulled as when we got you home this morning. Miss Llewellyn insisted that we carry you on a litter, and I must say I think she was right to urge that precaution. You groaned at every uneven step as it was. Heaven knows what would have happened if I'd slung you over the back of a horse," George remarked with a smile.

"My aunt told me that Brianna found me, but not *how,* or perhaps I mean *why,*" Christopher said, looking intently at his cousin who had drawn up a chair to his bedside.

"I can well imagine that was not the sum of what our esteemed great-aunt had to say," George replied, taking in his cousin's compressed lips and fiery eyes. When Christopher had nothing to say to this delicate probe, he turned his attention to the question. "Miss Llewellyn went for a long walk yesterday and became lost. It was pure happenstance that she should come across your nearly lifeless form in front of one of the caves when she was seeking some shelter for herself. She dragged you inside before the rain really set in and kept you from freezing during the night. That's the story in a nutshell.

"Then I owe my life to Brianna."

"I rather think you do," Mr. Cardorette replied softly, his expression inscrutable. After a moment while both men thought their own thoughts, he inquired, "What happened to you, Kit? Miss Llewellyn did not seem to know."

"I don't know either. I was standing on top of the cliff after inspecting the caves for safety when something hit me from behind and I fell over the edge."

"Some-*thing* or some-*one*?"

"I don't know. Where is Rufus? I had him tied in the grove of trees on top of the hill."

"He got loose somehow and came back to the stables last night. That's how we knew you had met with some kind of accident. Miss Lloyd had already reported Miss Llewellyn missing when she did not return to the nursery to read to the boy before dinner."

"How is Brianna after her ordeal?"

"According to Pennystone, she slept most of the day. She seems not to have taken the slightest chill from the experience. I begin to believe I have underestimated Miss Llewellyn. Symonds tells me she faced down that ferocious dog of his, which is a thing I would not care to do myself. There is apparently more to her than meets the eye."

Christopher nodded, taking this as an oblique apology for his cousin's uncomplimentary remarks about Brianna at the breakfast table the day before. "She has amazing physical courage and stamina, but she is easily overset by unkindness, and I don't want Aunt Hermione badgering her."

"Our dear aunt makes no secret of her opinion that the girl has been compromised," George warned him.

"You know I wish to marry Brianna, George, but I won't have her coerced into agreeing to it as a nasty result of her heroic action in saving my life."

"Do you think it would require coercion to get her to accept you?"

"Yes," Christopher replied shortly. "She hasn't a very high opinion of my character at present."

George looked intrigued but his cousin had no intention of satisfying his curiosity. Christopher made him the bearer of a message to Miss Llewellyn conveying his compliments and his earnest desire to thank her personally at her earliest convenience.

It was not until late in the afternoon on the following day that Brianna saw fit to comply with Christopher's request, and when she finally presented herself in his bedchamber, she was accompanied by Lady Hermione wearing her usual look of sour suspicion of her fellow humans. Brianna had assumed a quite creditable composure, not avoiding his glance as had often been her practice in the past, but this false assurance was betrayed by the white-knuckled clasp of her hands in front of her as she stopped several feet from the big bed. After consuming a sustaining lunch, Christopher had overborne the protestations of his valet and disobeyed his doctor by causing himself to be raised up by the placement of a profusion of pillows behind his back. His head still ached abominably but he felt more capable of dealing with the difficult personalities residing under his roof, the chiefest of whom were facing him now.

"I hope you are feeling stronger today, sir, but should you be sitting up so soon?" Brianna's soft voice was tinged with anxiety, something that pleased him enormously.

"I am much better today, thank you. I'll be out of this bed by tomorrow," Christopher promised, smiling at her in a manner that caused the color to rise in her cheeks.

She seemed disposed to argue with his announcement, but Christopher forestalled this, turning his attention to the straight-backed dowager radiating silent disapproval from just inside the door. "It was kind of you to come to inquire for my health, Aunt," he said with a silky disregard for her real purpose in thus inflicting her unwanted presence on him, "but now I would like to speak with Brianna alone."

"Such a thing would be most improper," declared Lady Hermione haughtily. "The sole purpose of my presence in this room, against all personal inclination after your unpardonable rudeness yesterday, is to remove any stigma of the illicit from this meeting with Miss Llewellyn."

"I have yet to learn that there is anything improper in a young woman's receiving an offer of marriage in private," Christopher said in icy tones.

"It can never be acceptable for an innocent female to hold private converse with a man in his bedchamber," Lady Hermione retorted.

"Since you have not scrupled to air your conviction that Brianna's selfless act of heroism has compromised her reputation beyond all repair short of marriage, I fail to see that the locale of the actual proposal can have any further importance. Please be so good as to remove yourself from this room, madam."

"*Please,* Christopher," Brianna begged, wringing her hands in distress.

"I'll remove myself from this *house*!" his incensed relative declared. "I have never been subjected to such treatment in my life." Before Brianna could go to her, she stormed out of the room, slamming the door behind her.

"Don't go, Brianna!" Christopher cried as the agitated girl took a step toward the door. "You must see that we have to talk."

"That was badly done of you," Brianna said, turning back to him. "Much as she may have deserved a setdown, she is an old woman whose sense of propriety has been greatly offended."

"I know," Christopher sighed, pushing two fingers against his temple as he sank deeper into his pillows, "but I find her gross insensitivity insupportable. She has no regard at all for the human feelings of the victims of her cruel tongue. Please, let us forget Aunt Hermione for the moment, Brianna. I must thank you for saving my life the other day—"

Brianna was shaking her head from side to side. "I promise you it was nothing so dramatic as that. I did only what anyone would have done in the circumstances, which was pitifully little."

"I shall not allow you to make light of what must have been a terrifying ordeal requiring sustained courage and endurance, not to mention strong nerves."

"It was no more than anyone would have done," she repeated stubbornly.

"Somehow I cannot picture Symonds, for instance, expending the same measure of devotion to keeping me alive," Christopher said dryly.

"Why do you say that?" Brianna had come closer to the bed and was looking searchingly into his eyes.

"Because he hates me, that's why. Brianna, were you up on top of that hill at all the day you found me?"

"Yes, I had climbed up to see if I could recognize any landmarks to lead me back here. That's when I saw you lying down on the path below. Did you fall over the cliff, Christopher?"

"I was near the edge and I . . . stumbled," Christopher replied briefly, guessing that George had not talked to her about the accident. "Did you see Rufus? I had tied him to a tree in the grove up there."

"Why no," she said slowly, unaware that he had reached out and taken one of her hands in his as she considered the question, "but I did not really give the grove of trees more than a cursory glance. He could have been there, I suppose, without my noticing him unless he made a noise." She would have removed her hand then, but Christopher pulled her closer.

"In the past you have displayed a persistent desire to escape from my presence," he explained with a self-deprecating twist to his mouth. "It is most unencouraging to a man in love, but this time I cannot permit you to run away, my darling. Loath though I must always be to admit that any of my great-aunt's antiquated notions of propriety have validity today, this time I must agree with her. Marriage is the only means by which I can restore your reputation in the eyes of the world, unfair though it undoubtedly is. Look at me, Brianna, please." When she reluctantly raised her eyes to his at last, he said, "Let there be no misunderstanding between us. You are aware that I have loved you from the start and that I desire nothing more than to make you my wife, but I would not have had this happen for the world. Do you believe me, Brianna?" His hand tightened on hers.

Deep green eyes stared intently into hazel ones for half an eternity, then Brianna said simply, "Yes."

Christopher relaxed perceptibly. "Thank you, my dear. You are generous. The marriage should be performed as soon as may be, but I give you my word as a gentleman not to make it real until you are ready."

Alarm had appeared in her pale countenance at the first part of this speech but it faded somewhat by the time he finished. "Th . . . thank you," she said with an unflattering fervor that he tried hard not to resent.

"Perhaps if I abase myself sufficiently to produce a handsome apology, my aunt may be persuaded to lend the happy event the countenance of her presence. The trick will be in retaining enough stiff-necked reserve so that she does not entirely forgive me, not enough to desire to prolong her visit at any rate."

This audacious speech had the desired effect of calling forth a real smile from the flustered girl at last. He desired to discuss their proposed wedding in detail, but noting the shadows of fatigue in his face, Brianna was firm in persuading him to rest. He raised her small hand to his lips and they parted on more amicable terms than might be expected, given their past history of conflict.

Christopher and Brianna were married by the vicar of the Ashleigh parish church within the week. The frightening—to Brianna—speed with which the affair was brought to this conclusion was made possible by the possession of a special license that Christopher had had the foresight to purchase on his most recent trip to London. His possession of this necessary item, which enabled the traditional reading of the banns to be circumvented, raised a few eyebrows in his household, not least among them, his prospective bride's. Insulated by his happiness from the normal embarrassments that might be held to attend on the forced nature of the marriage they were contracting, he had no hesitation in admitting that his hopes of winning Brianna's hand had led him to obtain the license, knowing that her bereaved state would have prohibited a wedding celebration for many months to come. Lady Hermione had consented to witness the marriage, more from a natural desire to be able to recount the entire episode when she returned to her home than from any wish to accommodate her marginally repentant great-nephew, whom she persisted in treating with frigid reserve during the remainder of her stay at Ashleigh. The only other persons actually present at the brief ceremony were Miss Lloyd, the young earl, and Mr. George Cardorette, but news of the impending nuptials had gotten abroad in the indefinable way of country parishes, and there were a number of persons loitering in the vicinity who appeared on the doorstep to offer their felicitations to the bride and groom when they left the church.

Brianna looked beautiful at her wedding, thanks to the contrivance of her bridegroom and her oldest friend. She had been astounded to learn that Christopher had had the effrontery to order a complete wardrobe for her on that same London trip and had flatly refused at first to accept any part of such irregularly acquired finery. She could scarcely credit that Molly had actually been a willing participant in the scheme, recruited to supply measurements and advice on colors and styles. Christopher had wisely left the persuading of his reluctant bride-to-be of the propriety of the gesture to his accomplice, who had the clear advantage of a lifetime's knowledge of Brianna's character to guide her efforts. While conceding that the purchase by a gentleman of clothing for a female not yet his wife was somewhat irregular, Molly had argued that Christopher's wife would have a position in the area to keep up and it would be awkward and impractical for Brianna to hide away from her neighbors until she had succeeded in procuring a suitable wardrobe locally in which to receive them after her newsworthy marriage. When Brianna had indignantly pointed out that Christopher had been betrothed to another woman when he departed for London, which made a mockery of that argument, Molly had further astonished her by claiming to have discerned Christopher's marked partiality for Brianna at their very first meeting in Jamie's sickroom. She said she had been expecting the betrothal to Lady Selina to come to nought and had had confirmation of this from Christopher's own lips when he had approached her with his odd request.

"You still had no way of knowing I would ever agree to marry him, Molly," Brianna had protested, her temper understandably ruffled. "No one could have foreseen that unlucky accident to Christopher, and I assure you I had not the slightest intention of accepting him before that!"

Molly had eyed her sternly then and replied, "You may have deceived yourself that you were not languishing for love of Christopher Cardorette almost from the moment we came to Ashleigh, but you did not deceive me into believing anything of the sort." She had shrugged shapely shoulders and added, "If you had remained adamant about spurning his offer, though I cannot conceive of such foolishness, the clothes would have been packed away and nobody the wiser."

Brianna had goggled at her frugal mentor's calm acceptance of such prodigal waste but her arguments grew more feeble, and Molly eventually prevailed upon her to accept the wardrobe if for no other reason than to do her bridegroom credit in the eyes of his friends.

The period before the wedding had seen two deliveries for Brianna of the fruits of Christopher's London orgy of shopping. Her scruples notwithstanding, she would have been a most unnatural female indeed to have remained unimpressed by the thoughtfulness and good taste that had gone into the selection of so many beautiful clothes. The garments were of a quality she had never even seen until her recent intercourse with the Milliken ladies, and certainly never expected to possess. Most items were in conformance with Molly's insistence that Brianna would not soon be persuaded to depart from the observance of her mourning, but Christopher had obviously allowed his own luxurious preferences free reign in the selection of petticoats, negligees, chemises, and nightwear fit for a royal bride. Protest and embarrassment had nearly overcome Brianna when she showed Molly these intimate garments, but her fingers were unconsciously stroking the filmy silken fabrics all the while, an action not lost upon her practical friend, who declared they were no more than what any girl would choose for herself were she in the fortunate position of being able to afford the no doubt astronomical prices attached.

"That is precisely my objection, Molly," a scarlet-cheeked Brianna had pointed out. "I could never have afforded such costly trifles, and even if I could, I did not select them; they were chosen for me by a *man*, which you cannot deny is most improper."

"Now you are simply being missish, my dear. For whom, pray tell, will you be wearing most of these items if not for a man?"

Brianna had been silenced, but only because she did not care to embark on another round of arguments that had as their core her ineradicable reluctance for this marriage. She and Molly remained poles apart in their views on the desirability of marriage to Matthew Cardorette's brother, the older woman seeing her reluctance as a childish cowardice rather than the simple prudence she herself knew it to be.

So, Brianna had forborne to argue with Molly's well-meant ad-

vice to place her trust in her bridegroom whose love would carry
them past the awkwardness of the present situation. She selected a
charming dove-gray dress and pelisse in which to be married. The
matching high-crowned bonnet was ornamented by three curling
black ostrich plumes and tied under one ear with black velvet ribbons. With her alabaster skin she presented a picture of ethereal
loveliness in this costume on her wedding day, the only spot of
real color being provided by her deep green eyes. For the most
part she succeeded in hiding her misgivings behind an expression
of sweet gravity, but her black-gloved hand trembled on her
bridegroom's arm as they stood together on the steps of the
church accepting congratulations from people who were no more
than kindly strangers to her.

To her intense surprise when she finally recognized the fact
days later, Brianna slid immediately into a comfortable pattern of
leaving all awkward matters in Christopher's capable hands, starting on the steps of the church where he presented her to villagers
and friends with an air of devoted pride that could not be other
than extremely gratifying to a nervous bride. He held her to his
side with clasped hands as George assisted Lady Hermione into
her carriage and they all bade the dowager a civil farewell less
than an hour after the wedding ceremony. George then absented
himself tactfully by accepting an invitation to dine with the Am-
phletts.

The newlyweds dined in Brianna's sitting room that evening at
Christopher's instigation. She had raised an instinctive protest
when he proposed the arrangement but her alarums had been
soothed by her bridegroom's careful explanation that they needed
more privacy than the dining room provided in which to discuss
some of the mundane household arrangements that might need al-
tering in future.

A nervous dread of being private with Christopher was laid to
rest after the wedding super. Brianna's composure, as brittle as
glass initially, was not threatened by unwelcome displays of
ardor. Christopher was charming and attentive to her comfort, entertaining her with descriptions of the places he had seen during
his years of military campaigning while the elegant little meal
was served them by Pennystone wearing a benevolent air. By the
time the butler withdrew, after removing the small table that had
been set up for their repast and leaving a dish of comfits and a
bottle of champagne, Christopher had extracted a promise that
Brianna would make use of the beautiful mare and resume riding
again.

Not until she was curled up in the corner of the gold settee sipping her champagne, did her husband inform her that he had had his things moved into the bedchamber next to her dressing room for the sake of convention. Any protest she might have felt called upon to utter was checked when he went on to say that he'd been persuaded she would prefer that to joining him in the huge master suite his parents had shared. Feeling more of a fraud every moment, she had accepted the arrangement and the details he now provided of the very generous settlement he was making her. To his credit he tried to dispel her troubled sense of obligation, dismissing the whole business of finances as "the customary arrangements," which, considering that Matthew had never provided a penny for Meg's support from the moment he left Herefordshire, struck Brianna as far from a universal practice. Before she could offer any comment, he mentioned that Mrs. Dobbs would meet with her the next morning to discuss any ideas she might have for changes in the household routines. He laughed outright at her horrified denial that she could wish to institute any changes in the smoothly running management of Ashleigh, predicting teasingly that the time would come when she would laugh at her own reticence in these matters. His offer of a small wager to this effect completed the process of returning her nerves to a more equable state.

Not until just before he took his leave of her did Christopher depart from his impersonal agenda. She had been persuaded to accept a second glass of champagne and was sitting perfectly relaxed in her corner, smiling up at him as he refilled her glass. His eyes darkened suddenly and his own smile stiffened for an instant before he returned his gaze to the bottle, pouring with great concentration. As he replaced the bottle in the bucket, his gaze swept around the room, lighting on the framed pencil sketch on the side table.

"What is this?" he inquired, strolling over and picking it up from its easel. "How charming. You and your sister I presume?"

"Yes, my mother did that sketch the summer I was twelve."

He studied the drawing intently. "Your mother possessed considerable skill as a portraitist. You and your sister were very much alike, were you not?"

"Yes, our coloring was identical, which you cannot tell from the sketch of course, but Meg's hair curled naturally, like Jamie's, while mine is poker straight, I'm afraid." She wrinkled her nose in rueful acknowledgement of this defect.

His lips parted impulsively, then closed as he returned the

sketch to the easel with great care. "I wouldn't change a hair on your head, straight or not," he said lightly, coming away from the table but halting several feet from her. "You are looking tired after such an eventful day. I'm a brute to keep you up so late. I'll wish you pleasant dreams and take myself off. Good night, Brianna."

Brianna blinked at the suddenness of his leaving. "Good night, Christopher," she said a little uncertainly.

Christopher had one foot in the corridor before he looked back over his shoulder at the young woman sitting big-eyed on the settee, a forgotten glass of champagne in one hand. "I want you to be happy here, Brianna," he said, no trace of lightness remaining in his demeanor.

"Th . . . thank you," was all the bemused girl could think of to respond to this impassioned wish, though it was doubtful he even heard the softly spoken words before he closed the door firmly.

Brianna tossed off the contents of her glass with something akin to bravado as she told herself that she was indeed very tired and relieved at the abrupt ending of her strange wedding day. In defiance of this sentiment she continued to sit in her corner for some little time, mentally reviewing the events of the last few hours, her intellect too busily engaged to permit drowsiness.

16

A flash of brilliant light streaked across the night sky but impinged only minimally on the consciousness of the girl lying in the big bed inside a nest of pillows, reading by the light of the branch of candles on the bedside table. The crash of thunder that followed in a few seconds, however, wrested her attention from the town of Meryton where Elizabeth Bennet's youngest sisters were happily and indecorously flirting with anyone in a red coat. Brianna had come upon Miss Austin's novel in the library yesterday and was enjoying the satirical tone of the work immensely, but now she put the book aside and swung her legs over the edge of the bed. The fire still burned low in the grate and the room was warm enough that she did not bother with the pale green peignoir that matched the filmy excuse for a nightrail that had been among the delectable items purchased by her husband in London.

As she padded over to the window in her bare feet, Brianna tasted those words on her tongue. Christopher did not really seem like a husband. True to his word, he had not pressed her to consummate the marriage. His demeanor toward her had been all that was friendly and kind and, now that she considered it, rather more formal in its courtesy than before their wedding when he had often sought her out. In the five days since the wedding he seemed to find her company at meals and in the early evening sufficient to his taste. George Cardorette shared their mealtimes in the main dining rooms. There had been no repetition of the delightful private dinner of their wedding night. Nor had there been any repetition of that smoldering look he had given her while refilling her champagne glass; in fact, it was her impression that he never looked at her for more than a split second at a time, and then impersonally. It was indeed fortunate that she had never given in to his importunities because it was obvious that he had already tired of her in the romantic sense. She must congratulate herself on her foresight and caution; except for this policy, she would most likely be bewailing his coldness by now.

As it was, she had spent a happy few days getting to know her spirited new mare, Mirrabelle, and rediscovering the joys of riding. She had also witnessed Jamie's rapid progress in learning how to sit his pony. Her nephew had been intrigued at first to learn that his aunt was to marry his uncle, but after a barrage of questions about the consequences of such an unknown act, had concluded that the only change was the invisible one of his aunt's now sharing his own surname. This discovery tickled him momentarily, after which he promptly lost interest in the affair.

Standing by the window staring out into the blackness, Brianna could only concur with her nephew that her change in surname was the sole result of the marriage until she recalled that Lady Hermione's absence was the indirect result of the affair and must be counted as a signal blessing. And soon, when the neighbors felt the newly wedded couple had been granted a sufficient measure of privacy, there would be visits exchanged and she could look forward to some sort of social life for the first time since Meg's marriage. The increased activity would certainly dispel this inexplicable restlessness that was afflicting her of late.

The rumbles of thunder in the distance had been coming closer and the skies parted at that moment to pour down rain in torrents. Brianna listened intently, peering out into the dark night though she could barely make out the nearest tree except in the intermittent flashes of lightning. Suddenly there was a streak that illuminated the night sky with an eerie light that briefly revealed every detail of the hedge and skeletal trees nearest the house. Filled with a wild elation at the awesome spectacle, she pressed closer to the window until the loudest clap of thunder she'd ever heard nearly shattered her eardrums. Gasping, she jumped back instinctively and her shoulder knocked against the small watercolor painting hanging to the left of the window, sending it crashing to the floor. The rug did not reach to the wall, and the glass in the frame shattered on impact with the bare wood.

Brianna stood stock still, annoyed at her clumsiness and reluctant to attempt walking back to her bed barefoot when she could not see where the glass had flown. Except during the brief streaks of lightning the room was dimly lighted by a dying fire and the three candles on the far side of her bed. She was debating her next move, her feet growing rapidly colder, when the door to the dressing room was flung open.

"Brianna, what happened in here?" Christopher demanded,

coming into the room carrying a candlestick. She saw his eyes go first to the bed and then make a swift circuit of the room until they located her shadowy form by the window. "What are you doing over there? I heard glass breaking. Did the storm break the window?"

"No, I was watching the lightning when that tremendous peal of thunder startled me so much I jumped away and knocked a painting off the wall. Don't come any closer unless you are wearing slippers," she warned hurriedly as he came toward her. "There is glass all over the floor."

"I have slippers on but I can see that you do not," he replied, sounding impatient. "Don't move a muscle while I put this candle down."

"Why are you doing that? I need the light," Brianna complained.

"I am going to lift you over the broken glass," he said calmly, setting his candlestick down on the mantleshelf.

"*No!*" she cried, then added in placating accents, "I mean, that isn't at all necessary. Just bring me my slippers, please Christopher. They are right beside the bed."

Her husband ignored her hurried words and kept advancing, his eyes roving over her body, scantily covered by diaphanous draperies. She had begun to feel chilled before Christopher came into the room, but now heat flooded through her at the boldness of his gaze, and her knees weakened at the same time. She sagged just as Christopher, crunching glass shards underfoot, scooped her up into his arms. He was wearing a dark velvet dressing gown that smelled faintly of tobacco, though Brianna had never seen him smoke. She clenched her fingers into fists to prevent them from stroking the soft velvet and kept her eyes down, clearing her throat to try whether her voice still functioned. It did after a fashion.

"You can put me down now, Christopher. There won't be any glass this far into the room."

"You are half-frozen in this delectable but inadequate costume. I am putting you right back into your bed."

"I must clean up that broken glass first," Brianna said. "I'll put a robe on and my slippers. If you will be so good as to build up the fire a little bit on your way out, I'll be warm enough. Really, Christopher," she added, risking a glance at his face when he stopped near the bed without releasing her.

"I have no intention of allowing you near that window again tonight. It's too dangerous," he said firmly, sitting down on the edge of the bed with Brianna still in his arms. Knowing the greater danger to be right here, she gave a tentative wriggle to free herself, but his grasp tightened. His voice sank to a throaty thread as he whispered. "As for the fire, I'd say you have built up a tidy blaze already with that transparent gown and your beautiful hair sliding out of its prim braid." While he was speaking, Christopher slipped the fingers of his left hand through her hair to complete the loosening of the braid that she affected for sleeping. Her scalp tingled in the wake of his progress, and when his hand returned to cup the back of her head she shivered convulsively and moaned a protest. Unhappily for the delivery of said protest, she had turned her head to face him. Her nose brushed his jaw and though she pulled back instantly, his hand kept her head imprisoned. Their lips were only an inch apart, a distance erased by Christopher in the next instant when he kissed her.

A small corner of Brianna's brain recognized this kiss as different from the ones that had preceded it. It was gentle, even tender, and it sought nothing from her. It was over before she could even respond. Her lashes lifted and she gazed into slumberous dark eyes with golden lights in them. His skin too had taken on a golden hue in the flickering candlelight. It was firm and finely grained skin, and her fingertips itched to explore it.

These illicit thoughts were derailed as she felt his chest expand beneath her shoulder with a deep intake of breath. "My beautiful Brianna," he murmured, "I have honored my promise not to rush you into consummating this marriage and I shall continue to do so if you wish, but I think . . . I fear you will have to *tell* me to leave you, for I cannot muster the required resolution . . . and stupidity on my own."

It wasn't *fair* to lay such a burden on her, Brianna raged rebelliously. He was cruel and tormenting and teasing, and she would like to *hit* him, after she told him what she thought of such despicable behavior. She opened her lips to do just that but it seemed she had deliberated too long. Christopher's right arm tightened around her hip and the hand cradling her head exerted pressure to draw her closer. She could easily resist that gentle pressure, but before the thought could become deed he was kissing her again and this time his mouth was demanding everything from her.

Brianna was not slow to comply with her husband's wordless demands. Her capitulation had all the fervor of her previous resistance, and Christopher's exclamation of mingled triumph and delight set the stage for a night of enchantment and discovery for both. While the thunderstorm raged outside, Brianna's ardent re-

sponse to his lovemaking amply confirmed his suspicions that her
social shyness masked a passionate nature. There was no sign of
shrinking as she accepted his caresses and followed eagerly where
he led, her soft sighs and quickened breath conveying her pleasure in the journey. She dimly realized that Christopher was restraining his desire for release in order to better prepare her to
receive him, and she gloried in his consideration for her. The
thrilling knowledge that she had the power to afford him extreme
pleasure carried her through the initial discomfort of his possession. His tenderness afterward made Brianna feel like the most
cherished creature on the face of the earth as he tucked her under
his arm for sleeping.

There was not actually a great deal of sleeping done that night.
Eventually, Brianna drifted off under the soothing influence of
her husband's whispered endearments. She woke up some time
later on encountering an obstacle when she tried to turn over.
Confused, she pulled back instinctively, her eyes flying open as a
restraining arm curtailed her movement. A loving murmur from
out of the velvet darkness chased away the confusion, replacing it
with a tingling awareness that spread rapidly throughout her
being, disposing of the remnants of languor. Her body came to
glowing life under the magical influence of Christopher's wandering hands. With the element of uncertainty removed, she
matched him step for step in a slow rising excitement culminating
in a frenzied explosion that spun them off together into a sublime
void of diminishing sensation. Never in her adult existence had
Brianna felt so carefree and weightless, almost as if she were a
disembodied spirit lost in a delicious lethargy. Christopher's declarations of love as she hovered on the brink of sleep were less in-
tellectually comprehended than internally accepted as part of the
incomparable joy of this mysterious experience. She lay quiet in
his embrace, happy that her hair and her shoulder were objects of
veneration to him but too mindlessly content to contribute anything in the form of word or deed. The only part of her that had
any weight was her eyelids, which refused to stay open.

Brianna awoke to full sunshine and a sense of euphoria that
suffered only a minor eclipse upon finding herself alone in the
bed. Naturally Christopher would be gone; she had slept to a disgraceful hour, well past breakfast. For another long moment she
remained quiescent, lazily savoring a sweet sense of well-being,
her eyes dreamy and unfocused as they roved about the sunny
room. On an impulse she slid out of the bed and crossed the room
to stare into the mirror, a little disappointed to find that she was

still herself, not the ravishingly beautiful creature Christopher had
described last night as his lips and hands had explored every out-
ward inch of her. The memory alone caused a wave of heat to
steal into her face, while her fingertips unthinkingly traced the
outline of her mouth. The hair he had stroked and buried his face
in was a tangled chestnut mass streaming over her shoulders this
morning. She grabbed a brush and restored some order to it before tying it at her nape. Feeling more presentable, she climbed
back into bed and rang for Hannah, who arrived bearing coffee
and hot muffins that gave off an enticing aroma of cinnamon
when she bit into them.

While waiting for her bathwater, she read the letter from Doctor Chamfrey that had been carried up on her breakfast tray. Her
father's old friend recounted the small happenings in the village
since her departure and demanded news of Jamie's health and
their lives at Ashleigh Court. Guiltily aware that she should have
written before this, Brianna promptly decided to postpone her
morning ride in favor of penning an immediate reply informing
the kind doctor of her marriage.

It was well after eleven when Brianna, completed letter in
hand, knocked softly on the study door before going in. She had
not really expected to find Christopher indoors at this hour but
disappointment pulled down the corners of her mouth anyway as
she crossed to his desk and began to rummage in the drawers for
some sealing wax. The righthand drawer seemed to contain only
papers, but she slipped her hand underneath the stack, feeling for
a stick of wax on the bottom. She was unsuccessful, and in with-
drawing her fingers, disturbed the papers somewhat. She was
about to straighten them when her own name jumped out at her
from one of them. Without conscious thought she pulled the sheet
out, surprised to discover a letter directed to herself from Sir
Harry Paxton. No premonition of disaster touched her as she automatically read the missive.

It was quite short, consisting of a rather formal expression of
regret on finding her away from Ashleigh Court for the day when
he had called, followed by a punctilious extension of felicitations
on the part of his sister and himself on the occasion of her betrothal to Christopher Cardorette. Her brain still drugged with
happiness, Brianna found the note merely puzzling at first. She
had never been away from Ashleigh since the day of her arrival
under Sir Harry's escort. And when had he called that she had not
been informed of this event? Thinking she had misread something
the first time, she reread the note, but Sir Harry's large legible

script offered no other interpretation or information. Her eyes returned to the date at the bottom of the sheet and remained fixed there. *6th December, 1815!* The paper trembled visibly in Brianna's hand as she sank onto the chair behind the desk, her brain scrambling to reconstruct the events of the recent past.

After she slipped Sir Harry's letter back into the desk drawer, she left the study a few moments later still carrying her own letter to Doctor Chamfrey. Brianna's face reflected her troubled spirit and all the lightness had left her step. There was no room for doubt about what had happened. Sir Harry's letter had been written on the day of Christopher's accident, so he must have called no later than that very day—certainly before she and Christopher had become betrothed. Brianna's eyes grew somber as she put the facts together. There was only one explanation that could account for this letter. Christopher had lied to Sir Harry about her supposed absence from Ashleigh, and he had lied to him about a nonexistent betrothal; he had kept the fact of Sir Harry's visit from her, and finally had suppressed the letter the baronet had written to her on his return to Fourtrees. This fresh evidence that her husband intended to limit her contacts to those people of his choosing, by whatever disreputable means it took to achieve his end, had robbed Brianna of the quiet contentment that had followed the passionate night of lovemaking. The last thing she desired was to jeopardize her precarious happiness, but she could not ignore Christopher's disposition to reduce her to the status of a child, every aspect of whose life could be controlled by its guardians. The more basic issue of his conspicuous lack of integrity in his personal dealing was something she could not even bear to contemplate at present. There was so much about her husband that was lovable, including his marvelous way with Jamie and his good-tempered and evenhanded treatment of the servants. There was no meanness about Christopher in any sense of that word. And the expression in his eyes when he looked at her dragged her heart out of her breast and sent it straight into his keeping. If she did not love him, these flaws in his character would not trouble her so greatly. This then was the other side of loving, the dark side Meg had known only too well.

Brianna was in a markedly sober humor when she checked the time as she left the house. Jamie would be finishing his riding lesson about now. She had not been dressed in time to see him before he went down to the stables. There was not enough time for a visit with Molly before lunch and, in any case, she did not wish to meet her old nurse until she had herself well in hand again. Molly was too quick to spot her moods. She was used to confiding all her thoughts and emotions to her friend but she was strangely reluctant to reveal anything that must lower Christopher in Molly's esteem. Besides, from now on her first loyalty must be to her husband. Meanwhile, she would set her mind on more cheerful matters.

Brianna turned her steps toward the stables with the intention of accompanying her nephew back to the house to give him an opportunity to boast of his increasing prowess on Smoky's back. The day was wonderful for mid-December, brisk and clear, the sky a nearly cloudless azure. She soon saw that last night's storm had left its mark in broken branches, leaves and debris scattered about the lawns and paths, and it was still quite wet underfoot. She picked her way carefully along, wondering a little that the gardeners should not have begun to clean up the mess yet and concluding that there must be worse damage elsewhere. She bent her head to avoid a broken branch dangling down from a laburnum tree, glancing up at the trees farther ahead to see if there were more hazards of a like nature to avoid. A flash of bright blue high up caught her eye and she stopped, shielding her eyes from the midday sun as she looked up, her glance trailing along the Italianate balustrade that adorned the roofline and was topped at intervals by huge stone urns with domed lids that stood out against the blue sky. After a moment she located the blue area again, moving away from her, and she squinted to bring it into better focus. It was a man moving toward the corner of the house, stopping now and crouching in the shade of a tall chimney stack, blending into the shadow.

Recognizing the man on the roof as her husband, Brianna's lips parted to hail him when her ears detected approaching sounds on ground level. That would be Jamie on his way back to the house from the stableyard, she thought, discerning faint snatches of a little marching tune. Sure enough, her nephew rounded the corner slowly, kicking pebbles as he came. Brianna was watching his erratic progress with a smile when some movement at the corner of the roof drew her eyes upward again.

"*Jamie, run!*" she shrieked in terror as something came hurtling down from the roof. She was racing toward the child even as she screamed.

Some divine providence must have been operating at that instant because the little boy had broken into a run upon spotting his aunt. They met a scant few feet from where a huge chunk of stone landed, half burying itself in the ground behind Jamie. Brianna had dropped to her knees and caught the running child in her arms just as the mass struck the ground. Both were showered with dirt and leaves from adjacent shrubs partially crushed beneath the chunk of rock. There was a roaring in Brianna's ears and her arms lost their strength while she battled against faintness. Jamie took advantage of her slackened grasp to pull away to examine the fallen stone.

"Did this big stone fall down off the house, Auntie Bree?" he asked, his curiosity untainted by fear as he examined the chunk from all sides.

"Yes, dearest." Brianna, overcoming her faintness, struggled to her feet and looked up to reassure Christopher that they were unhurt. Her puzzled glance scanned the balustrade but no one was looking down at them. She stepped back from the path onto the lawn to get a better look at the roof, absentmindedly brushing dirt and leaves from her black pelisse as she did so. The question of what had fallen off was answered as she noted that the decorative stone urn nearest the corner no longer wore its carved domed lid. Also missing was any sign of a human presence.

Brianna took Jamie's hand in hers and headed for the same entrance she had come out of a few moments before, expecting at any second to see Christopher come dashing toward them to check on their condition. There was no sign of him, however, and by the time they reached the staircase her temper had begun to sizzle. She sent Jamie up to the nursery for his lunch and headed toward the informal dining parlor.

The cousins were already seated when she strode into the room, declaring with a scowl, "That chunk of stone from the roof balustrade missed killing Jamie by this much!" Her outflung arms indicated a distance no greater than two feet as she glared at her husband.

Both men expressed shocked concern.

"Something fell off the roof?" Christopher asked. "I was fearful that last night's storm might have done some more damage to the roof; in fact I told George at breakfast that I planned to go up there tomorrow to check on everything, did I not, George? I wish now that I had not put it off."

Brianna's jaw sagged in shock, but Christopher, who had come forward at her impetuous entrance, had looked back over his shoulder at his cousin as he spoke, and he missed her thunderstruck expression. She clamped her teeth together against a moan as a wave of nausea churned in her stomach and filled her mouth with saliva. Christopher, full of concern for her whiteness, shoved her into a chair. "Put your head down, darling; you've had a terrible fright, but you'll be better in a minute. George, pour her a glass of water."

Brianna, her head down, was waging a desperate battle to contain and conceal her distress. She paid no attention to her husband's soothing words. Certainly she derived no comfort from his concern and had to ball her fists to keep from slapping his hands away from her shoulders. She accepted the glass of water and sat back up, shrugging away from his hovering hands, making the glass from which she took tiny sips her excuse to avoid looking at him. From some stern core of her being she summoned the strength to master the nausea and sit through the hellish meal, though she could swallow nothing except the water. She even managed to describe Jamie's brush with death in wooden tones, leaving out the fact that she had seen her husband up on the roof at the time of the "accident."

By the time she reached the shelter of her apartments where she was escorted lovingly by Christopher despite her protest that she was capable of getting there on her own, and had dispatched a concerned Hannah, whom he had summoned to her side, by letting the maid think she intended to rest for a while, Brianna was near screaming pitch from abraded nerves. The grim control she had imposed on herself to keep from betraying her knowledge that her husband had tried to kill the nephew who had supplanted him in his inheritance had taken a large toll. When the door closed behind the maid, however, she did not give way to the terror clamoring for release, as she had feared she might in the dining room earlier, after witnessing Christopher's lying performance with her own eyes. She had known he had deceived everyone to protect his brother's name, and Sir Harry's letter was proof positive that he had lied to keep her from forming a friendship with someone not under his sway, but her heart would never have accepted that he was capable of such evil had she not seen his pretense of ignorance of the near-tragedy today. Obviously, he had not seen her from the roof and had been unaware that she had seen him in the bright blue coat that he was still wearing.

The most frightening thing was that she had needed the evidence of her own eyes to believe ill of Christopher. He was so convincing as an amiable man, fond of his nephew, and flatteringly in love with his wife, a woman who could never have competed with his former fiancée but who was infinitely preferable for his purpose, being easier to deceive. To him, she also had the advantage of being alone in the world; no well-connected family

would come galloping to her aid. At this point Brianna forced
herself to ignore her own pain. There was no time to wallow in
grief for a lost innocence; the situation was too desperate. This
had been the third or fourth attempt on Jamie's life. She must remove him from Ashleigh at once before Christopher suspected
that she was no longer a willing dupe to be kissed into abandoning her ability to reason clearly.

Brianna devoted herself to careful planning in the next half
hour before she left the house to head for the stables where she
had one of the young stable boys saddle Mirrabelle for her. She
smilingly declined to take a groom with her and had the satisfaction of knowing her calm facade had not aroused any undue interest in this unusual action.

It was nearly two hours later when Brianna entered the nursery
where Lily and Jamie were again building a complex structure of
blocks.

"Where have you been all day?" Molly demanded, rising from
her chair. "What is this about Jamie's almost getting squashed by
something falling from the roof? I sent Lily to look for you this
afternoon but you were not in your room."

"I went riding," Brianna replied. "Let us go to your room
where we can talk without being interrupted, Molly."

After one long look at the strained young face, Molly followed
her out of the nursery without another word. "What is it?" she
asked when they attained the privacy of her bedchamber.

"We have to leave Ashleigh at once, Molly, and secretly. I
have been making the necessary arrangements this afternoon. I
rode to the nearest posting inn and hired a post chaise and pair
which will meet us at the crossroads beyond the north entrance tomorrow morning at first light. We'll have to walk to meet it,
which means we'll only be able to take one small bag each.
Thank goodness Jamie is a strong walker for his age; it's over a
mile from here."

"Never mind the 'arrangements' for the moment," Miss Lloyd
said from the foot of the bed where she had dropped at Brianna's
first words. "Tell me instead what has driven you to this fantastic
proposal." She listened without interruption to Brianna's detailed
listing of the attempts on Jamie's life, culminating with today's
incident. Her color faded when Brianna described Christopher's
pretense of ignorance of the falling stone, but even this denial of
his presence on the roof failed to persuade her that he was behind
the series of accidents. "He was nowhere in the area when the
coach was held up," she reminded Brianna.

"He could have hired those highwaymen to follow us when we left Herefordshire."

"The attack by the dog must have been an accident. There were too many people around to rescue Jamie. It had no chance of succeeding. There is no real proof that Christopher was behind any of these incidents."

"Perhaps not, but don't you see, Molly, that Christopher is the only one who will profit from Jamie's death? We cannot afford to wait for proof, not after today." Fear looked out of Brianna's eyes.

Molly shook her head. "Something doesn't ring true, Brianna. I cannot believe that Christopher Cardorette would kill a child for any reason, much less to enrich himself or gain a title. He is genuinely fond of Jamie and he loves you."

Brianna set her face in hard lines. "He wanted to keep me a prisoner, to tie me to him so I could not accuse him of a crime later. He was a soldier, he's killed people before. Perhaps he is insane. It doesn't really matter whether it makes sense. The fact remains that we cannot take the chance with Meg's child's life at stake. The next "accident' might succeed. I cannot wait for that to happen, Molly. We *must* leave here!"

Molly's fine blue eyes were full of sadness as she studied the cold determined face of the girl she had helped to rear. "Very well, Brianna, we'll leave Ashleigh Court, but where shall we go and how are we to survive?"

"There is enough money left from the sale of Papa's library to pay the post charges to London. When we get there I will sell the pearls Christopher gave me; they are very valuable and should support us until I find a solicitor who can help us to get some sort of allowance from the estate. There must be something we can do legally."

"I hope you are right, my dear, but that is for the future. The immediate problem is to get away unseen. Would it not be less risky to leave at night after the house goes to sleep? We would have a much longer start before being missed."

"I thought of that, but there is no moon at present and it strikes me as almost impossible to get a sleepy child that distance in the full dark."

"Yes, of course." Miss Lloyd ceased her arguments and they got down to detailed planning.

Brianna returned to her suite to dress for her last dinner at Ashleigh and her last night as Christopher's wife. She would not dare to pack until she came back upstairs in case Hannah should notice that her small valise—fortunately still reposing in the bottom of one of the armoires—was no longer empty. She allowed the maid a free hand with her toilette that evening, though refusing to own to any desire to look her best. Her brief marriage was at an end, but for her pride's sake she refused to leave an impression of a pathetic little mouse behind her.

It was the strangest evening Brianna had ever spent at Ashleigh or anywhere. Never would she have conceived of the possibility that she would ever be called upon to break bread with someone capable of the murder of a child. Oddly, she felt no anger toward Christopher. Somewhere, firmly locked in the darkest recesses of her mind was a crushing sense of loss, but the only way she could perform the role assigned to her was to refuse to allow thoughts of Christopher into her active mind.

Her all-engrossing consciousness of the task in front of her had the unlooked for effect of preserving her from the lingering shyness natural to a bride meeting the man who had newly taken her virginity. For his part, Christopher treated her with a gentleness that would wring tears of regret from her soul when she looked back on this part of her life, but she could not think about that now. It occurred to her after a while that Christopher's attention was not wholly fixed upon the present either. Once or twice at dinner she noted his serious gaze fixed on his cousin for longer than was warranted by the topic of the moment and he answered somewhat absently at times. She took advantage of this to lay the groundwork for retiring early. She let him see her kneading her temples during dinner and finally admitted to a headache back in the saloon, gathering up her embroidery with a wan smile well before the tea tray usually arrived.

Brianna experienced a moment of pure panic that she fought to conceal when her husband got to his feet when she did, but it seemed his intention was merely to walk to the door with her. He opened it and bowed over her hand with a caressing expression in his eyes that drove down her lashes.

"Good night, my dear. I hope your headache will be gone by morning."

"Thank you. I shall tell Hannah to let me sleep until I ring for her tomorrow."

"As I did this morning," Christopher murmured teasingly, bending his head to kiss her.

Brianna kept her lashes down to conceal the tears in her eyes as her lips involuntarily clung to his for a moment. She did not look at him again, turning swiftly to leave the room. She dashed the tears away with impatient fingers as she climbed the stairs, striving for composure. There was still the final scene with Hannah to play out before she could pack a few necessities and lie down upon her bed. There would be ample time for weeping during the sleepless hours that must pass before this chapter in their lives could be brought to an end.

17

As Christopher approached the estate office, Pennystone was entering the short hall from the other end. "Good morning, sir. You did not come down for breakfast. Would you like something now?"

"No, thank you, Pennystone. They gave me a sandwich in the kitchens earlier. I was down at the stables early this morning. Is Mr. George in?"

"I believe so, sir."

"Keep everyone away from here for a while, will you, Pennystone?" Christopher knocked once and walked into the office.

"Good morning, coz. I missed you at breakfast." George's welcoming smile, receiving no return, stiffened as he watched his grim-faced cousin settle into the wing chair, an uncharacteristic heaviness about his movements. After an unnerving few seconds of being silently examined by a pair of penetrating hazel eyes, he spoke again. "Is anything wrong?"

"It's over, George," Christopher said tonelessly. "I should have tumbled to it much sooner—Grimstead was never satisfied that my curricle had not been tampered with that time when the wheel came off—but I've had a lot on my mind lately. I should have known after the shot that nearly hit James in the woods—by then I'd found out about your gambling—but I was prevented from seeing the obvious by a strange reluctance to accept that someone I'd known all my life was capable of trying to kill me, let alone a helpless child."

"You can't know what you're saying, Kit! On the basis of a couple of accidents you are actually accusing me of attempted murder?" George half rose out of his chair.

"Stow it, George," Christopher advised wearily. "Outraged innocence might have worked until yesterday, but not now. You see, the more I thought about that wild storm the other night, the more concerned I became to check for possible damage on the roof, concerned enough that I changed my work plans. I was on the roof yesterday morning, George. I *saw* you push that broken urn top over the balustrade, but I had no idea until Brianna screamed that anyone was below. I could have killed you with my bare hands at that moment."

George Cardorette had fallen back into his chair during this speech, his eyes shifting away from the glittering hazel stare being directed at him. "But you said nothing at lunch when Brianna reported the incident, or later," he said in accusing tones.

"I didn't wish to upset Brianna any further and I wanted to investigate the earlier incidents more thoroughly before taking action. I cannot prove that Symonds shot at James in the woods, though he was seen carrying a gun by one of the stable boys earlier that day, nor can I prove he shoved me over that cliff, though I saw him as I headed into that country, but I don't *have* to prove anything to a judge and jury. You are fortunate that I would prefer to avoid an open scandal, but I want you and your vicious henchman off Ashleigh property before nightfall."

"I fear that would not suit my plans at all, Kit." George rose from his chair as he spoke, his glance directed over his cousin's head.

The hair stood up on the back of Christopher's neck as he felt rather than heard the movement behind him. Instinctively he launched himself sideways out of the chair, thus avoiding the full force of the blow aimed at his head by the man who had obviously been hiding behind the paneled screen during the entire interview. As he reeled under a blow from something heavy and sharp that landed between the side of his neck and his shoulder, it flashed through his mind that he'd heard and stupidly dismissed the sound of a chair scraping back while speaking to Pennystone outside the door. Before he could aim a blow at Symonds, his assailant, his cousin's fist connected with his jaw, knocking him back across the arm of the chair. He must not have entirely lost consciousness because he was dimly aware that his hands were being bound behind his back despite his feeble resistance, and his feet were being tied together at the ankles. When the red haze cleared from his eyes, he was back in the wing chair and Symonds was behind him knotting a handkerchief that had been placed across his mouth to keep him quiet. He glared furiously at his cousin who was now back behind the desk, but George addressed his next words to the groom.

"Fetch the boy here. Tell him his uncle wants him; then bring a horse around to these French doors. Circle around through the shrubbery so you aren't seen. We'll throw the two of them over the horse's back and take them down to the lake."

Symonds nodded his understanding and left the room, and George's eyes came back to his trussed-up cousin glaring at him over the makeshift gag. George sat at ease behind the desk, his bent elbows on the desktop and his fingers loosely linked below his chin.

"As you seem to have discovered, though I cannot imagine how, I have no better luck at the tables or the track than my father had, a regrettable weakness handed down in our branch of the family perhaps. Had my luck been better or my creditors less pressing, this drastic course of action would not have become necessary. Yes, I understand that all those violent head movements are meant to convey your belief that another remedy might be found. I credit you with a generous heart like Matt's. Very likely you would pay my most pressing debts, but it really would not serve except in the short term. You would probably require a promise that I would cease all gaming forever, a fair return for your largesse, and though I would naturally give it, my better knowledge of my weakness tells me that I would not keep it. Sooner or later we would be right back at this same point but with a crucial difference. I would no longer be in the advantageous position I now hold to reap the whole Ashleigh fortune and honors. I think you will agree that I have looked after the estate very devotedly."

George paused and elevated his eyebrows, but his cousin stared steadily back, his head now still. "Certainly my custodianship was an improvement over anything your brother might have achieved. It was Matt's untimely death that first put the idea of inheriting the estate into my mind."

As Christopher's body jerked spasmodically, then stiffened, his large cousin smiled and gave a slight negative shake of his head. "No, Matt's death, though as untidy as the rest of his life, was entirely accidental; you have my word on that. You can see that with you off in the middle of a bloody war with huge casualties, the succession became all at once a real probability instead of the remote possibility it had always been. Certainly the expectation made it an easy matter to obtain credit. I must admit that I took rather too great advantage of this fact in the months before your safe return. And that, to round off the tale, made today inevitable, though I am indeed sorry that the matter could not have completed with two swift clean 'accidents' and the victims none the wiser." He shrugged his bulky shoulders. "However, the nature of accidents is unpredictable to say the least, and it is time to bring the uncertainty to an end. Yesterday's failure set me to thinking that a double 'accident' would be the most efficient method of accomplishing the task. You have merely speeded up the process by your action today. You will be glad to know that your role, though necessarily tragic, will be a heroic one, Kit. You will drown trying—I need not add, unsuccessfully—to rescue your nephew from that fate."

Christopher listened in growing horror to this calm confirmation of the blasphemous accusations he had leveled earlier. The serene rationality with which his cousin discussed what would be unthinkable to any but the most debased character, added immeasurably to the horror. He must talk, argue against a deed that would remove the final core of humanity from one capable of performing it. Christopher rubbed his face frantically against the right wing of the chair that served as his prison, trying to rid himself of the handkerchief that prevented him from speaking.

"Stop that, unless you wish to be knocked out!" George's hands dropped to the top of the desk palm down, and he half rose, then sat back as Christopher's antics subsided. "That's better."

Christopher's eyes trailed to his cousin's to the mantelshelf clock. He had no idea how long Symonds had been gone, but he'd better make use of what time remained before the groom's return to figure out how to avert the impending catastrophe. Something sharp had been sticking into his right hip since he'd leaned over to try to dislodge the gag. Now he wiggled experimentally, confirming that some small but weighty object shared the large chair with him. He'd already tried to struggle out of the cords that bound his wrists without success, but with his options and time severely limited, returned to that task while his eyes roved cautiously about the room looking for anything that might serve as a weapon. Other than the cut-glass decanter on the side table several feet away, nothing immediately registered as a possibility. George was talking again, half to himself, working out his plan to transport his intended victims through the woods to the lake where he would dispose of them. Scanning the desk for inspiration as he continued to strain against the cords, Christopher noticed several books leaning haphazardly against one another. His glance passed over them, then returned to the oddity, noting that one of a pair of brass bookends in the shape of couchant lions was missing, causing the upright books to tip over. Quickly he removed his glance lest George see where it was directed and put two and two together as he had done. The missing bookend must

be the object Symonds had hit him with, and he'd stake his life—
perhaps was already staking his life—that it was now digging into
his hip. Under the impetus of reviving hope, he redoubled his
covert efforts to stretch or break the cord around his wrists but
with no better results.

As George's eye lighted on him again, Christopher forced his
muscles to relax and was surprised to feel more slack in the cords
than before. Trying to keep his shoulders still so as not to betray
his exertions, he moved his wrists experimentally in all directions
and made the pleasing discovery that he'd been hurriedly tied
with his wrists side by side. If he could manage to maneuver one
hand behind the other instead, he might be able to slip out of the
bindings.

Time now became his enemy. Christopher had achieved only
partial success in repositioning his wrists when Symonds strode
into the room alone.

"They're gone!" he announced. "All three of them."

George had come halfway from behind the desk at Symond's
hasty entrance. "Gone where? How can they be gone?" He held
up a hand. "Wait," he said to Symonds, his eyes flashing to his
cousin, wrapped in total stillness in the wing chair. "Did you
know about this?" As Christopher shook his head decisively,
George turned back to his black-avised groom. "How do you
know they are not somewhere on the estate? I assume you are referring to the boy's aunt and nurse, too?"

Symonds nodded. "I went up to the nursery and saw it was
empty the minute I opened the door. I went down to the stables
looking for the boy, but he had not been there at all today, so I
went back up to the nursery. This time I noticed there was a table
all set for breakfast, food and all, but nothing had been touched.
While I was deciding where to look next, that maid came in, the
redheaded wench who comes to the stables with the brat. She said
no one had been there when she brought the food up much earlier,
but she'd assumed the woman and boy had gone down to the
aunt's room to visit. When no one rang to have the trays collected
she finally went back up there on her own. I made her show me
where they slept, all three of them. All the beds had been slept in,
but some of the boy's clothes at least were missing."

"That means they've only been gone for a few hours, but we
have no time to waste. Someone will be coming here to report to
my cousin as soon as they stop squawking in the servants' hall
and collect their wits. Go get that horse now; we'll have to take
him away immediately. If we can't come up with them today, it

will have to be a single accident for him and we'll do the boy later. Go now, out this way, and have the phaeton sent up to me right away. I'll meet you later and we'll go on from there."

A perspiring Christopher had been desperately maneuvering his hands within their cords during the discussion, aided by the fact that the two men were paying him no attention. He managed to slip his right hand free just as Symonds went through the French doors his cousin had opened. He couldn't bother about his ankles; there was only one chance at this juncture and that was to stun his cousin long enough to get free. His right hand closed over the bookend as he surged silently up from the chair. While George was closing the door with his back turned, Christopher took careful aim and threw the heavy statuary with all his strength.

The brass object hit George Cardorette just behind the right ear and sent him to his knees, his shoulder crashing into the doors, which shuddered with the shock but held. Praying that Symonds was too far away to hear the noise, Christopher hopped awkwardly over to the bell pull to summon Pennystone before he began to work on the cords binding his ankles with fingers made clumsy by the need for haste and the fact that he kept one eye on his writhing cousin while he fumbled at the knots. After a few frustrating seconds, he remembered the paper knife that was always on the desk top and hopped over to seize it just as George tried to pull himself to his feet using the ornate chair as a prop. Christopher succeeded in snapping the last cord as his cousin, bleeding profusely down the right side of his neck, lunged at him with murderous intent, though his eyes were glazed with pain.

Christopher leapt aside and George fell heavily across the corner of the desk, the air whooshing out of his lungs. Before the big man could straighten up in his dazed condition, Christopher repaid the blow his cousin had dealt him earlier by landing a flush hit on his jaw that snapped his head back. Neither had spoken a single word since Christopher had thrown the bookend, nor did they now. George uttered a guttural groan of pain and simply collapsed in place. For a moment Christopher stood over him, alert and wary, but his cousin was clearly unconscious.

Pennystone entered the room at that moment, stopping short at the sight of his elegant master, a rope twisted about his left wrist and a handkerchief hanging under his chin, standing over the recumbent and bleeding body of his cousin.

"Send one of the footmen down to the stables immediately," Christopher ordered. "Tell them to stop Symonds. Knock him out if necessary, but don't let him get away. Tell the other male ser-

vants to hide themselves in the shrubbery outside this window in
case he has already left the stables. They are to overpower him as
he tries to enter this room. Make sure everyone understands that
he is to be held physically and brought to me. Go, man, now!" he
shouted when the generally imperturbable butler hesitated for a
second.

An hour later, having arranged the temporary but separate confinement of his cousin and the ugly groom, and having learned
what little was known in the household about the disappearance
of his wife and nephew, Christopher set off in search of the run-
aways. He was taking his curricle, Whitby his groom, his pistols,
a change of linen in case they could not catch them up today, and
plenty of money. The twenty-four hours that had elapsed since
he'd crouched behind one of series of chimney stacks, mistrusting
the evidence of his eyes as the cousin he'd known all his life
coldly tried to crush the life out of an innocent child had been a
period of unrelieved anguish, and it was far from over yet. Brianna had no less than a four-hour start, and he had no idea where
she was heading.

When he allowed himself to contemplate the terror that must
have motivated her desperate flight, disgust at his own insensibil-
ity rose up in his throat to choke him. She had been understandably upset by the attempted kidnapping. In the wake of that
incident, the shot in the woods had terrified her, and he'd dismissed her fears when a cursory investigation failed to turn up a
stranger or someone with a gun in the vicinity of the pinewood
that afternoon. It had still seemed plausible then that the culprit
was merely a clumsy poacher understandably reluctant to identify
himself. His own assisted fall from the cliff, though, should have
alerted him to danger, but he'd been too involved with his hasty
wedding to give the larger problem the attention it merited. However, there was no excuse at all for not talking the whole affair
out with Brianna after lunch yesterday. He'd been so concerned
with his own sense of betrayal and the need to act quickly that
he'd ignored Brianna's anxiety, thinking he could wait until he
could tell her that the need for fear was over.

A few words from him would have allayed her fears and he
would not now be setting out on a blind chase immediately after
undergoing one of the more unpleasant experiences in his life,
and in less than top physical condition. With no clues as to how
she had left the house, his only recourse was to start with the
nearest posthouse and stagecoach office and questioned everyone
who might have come in contact with her, if indeed it was Bri-

anna who had made the arrangements. Christopher's face was drawn into forbidding lines and fear was his closest companion when he set his horses to a brisk pace as the curricle emerged from Ashleigh property onto the public road.

In the one private dining room the Spotted Cow could boast, Brianna paced back and forth from the door to the fireplace, six paces over, then six paces back, swerving each time to avoid the table set up in the middle of the room containing the remains of a nuncheon to which she alone of the three had failed to do ample justice. The little earl, having been awakened before dawn and hustled out into the dank chill December air, leaving his uncle and his beloved pony behind, had, not surprisingly, tried the patience of his loved ones considerably in the hours that followed their stealthy departure. He whined at the discomfort of the jouncing job chaise and periodically demanded an explanation for the sudden trip, as well as information about their destination. The disjointed and fragmentary replies to his reasonable questions that he received from his aunt had left him unsatisfied and querulous. At the moment, he was partially appeased to be well fed and on solid ground, as he sat on Miss Lloyd's lap, being read to from the one storybook he had been permitted to take from Ashleigh Court. Molly was the only member of the little party whose spirits had not been visibly affected by the events of the day. Her serene voice reading aloud continued smoothly until Brianna, on one of her frequent passes, burst out, "What can be taking so long? They should have had that wheel repaired ages ago. Do you realize, Molly, that it is already midafternoon and we have completed less than four full stages?"

"Yes, my dear. The carriage breaking down so unexpectedly as it did was indeed unfortunate. On the other hand, we had very little more than a mile to walk to this pleasant inn, and the weather, though rather cold, was not inclement. The luncheon too was better than one might have expected in a hostelry that does not cater to the needs of those traveling post as a regular thing."

"I had rather see us thirty miles farther on our way than being regaled with the best meal England has to offer!" Brianna declared fretfully.

She had stopped to fix her companion with an impatient look, but now she resumed her restless pacing. Their absence would have been discovered hours ago, and if the person from whom she'd hired the post chaise remembered her sufficiently to match a description, then Christopher was probably hot on their trail at

this moment. She had found, to her dismay, that she was required
to state her destination when engaging the chaise. Perhaps it
would be wiser to leave at the next changeover and switch to the
stagecoach to throw him off the scent. That would mean more
money expended though, and the public stage was notoriously
slow and uncomfortable. Thanks to this wretched breakdown,
they would not reach London in daylight even by post. If only she
knew what to do for the best! Brianna put kneading fingers up to
her temples to discourage the headache that was threatening to
develop, and continued pacing. She had almost reached the fireplace when a knock sounded at the door.

"At last!" she cried, calling out permission to enter. She
stepped forward eagerly, then stopped in consternation when, not
the postilion but her husband came striding into the room, attired
in a many-caped driving coat of drab.

"Thank goodness Whitby spotted the broken-down chaise or
we would have continued on the post road," Christopher began,
stripping off his gloves.

Brianna could feel the blood drain from her head as she leapt to
Molly's side and grabbed her nephew, thrusting him behind her.
"*Don't hurt him!* Please, Christopher, let us go," she begged
piteously. "We'll never cause you any trouble, I promise—" She
broke off, the sound strangled in her throat, and she knew with
abysmal surety that she would forever be haunted by the effect
her pleading words had on her husband. If she'd run him through
the heart with a sword, Christopher could not have looked more
anguished. For a heart-stopping moment their eyes locked, hers
full of shamed knowledge, his showing the awareness of betrayal.
Neither was capable of going forward, but the excruciating im-
passe was mercifully ended by the little boy who wrenched free
of his aunt's grip and dashed headlong to throw his arms around
his uncle's thighs.

"Uncle Chris, I don't want to go to London. I don't like London; I want to go home to Ashleigh with you!"

The bleakness in Christopher's eyes lightened somewhat as he
glanced down at the temporarily temperish but trusting little face
looking up at him. He forced a smile. "And so you shall, James.
We are all going home presently." His gaze skimmed past his
stricken wife to rest upon Miss Lloyd, who had come to stand
with her arm around Brianna's waist. He aimed his quiet words at
the elder lady.

"You need not be afraid any longer. My cousin has admitted
that he was behind the series of incidents that have occurred

lately. I had begun to suspect the truth, but there was no proof until yesterday when I saw him push the stone off the roof. In a way I invited that near-tragedy by telling him I intended going up on the roof today. It put the idea into his head. If James had been hurt, I'd have been equally guilty."

"But if you hadn't seen what you did, the danger would still be hanging over his head," Molly said in the pause that ensued, "so we must be eternally grateful to you for bringing matters out in the open. I do not understand why Mr. Cardorette should wish to harm Jamie."

Christopher still did not look at Brianna as he said shortly, "There were a couple of attempts on my life also. George was my heir until James was found. He is also deeply in debt."

"The cliff!" Brianna exclaimed, her eyes flying to her husband's, but she was not to learn if Christopher would speak to her because a knock sounded at the door just then. It was the postilion reporting that the chaise had been repaired.

Within five minutes Christopher had paid their shot at the inn and they were on the road again, the post chaise being escorted by the curricle. Inside the chaise, Jamie was jubilant that he was returning to his pony, his high spirits in stark contrast to his aunt's unhappy mien. Earlier in the day, Brianna's unhappiness had been masked by her desperate need to put as much distance as possible between themselves and Ashleigh. Now it might be thought that the release from the awful dread of imminent harm to her sister's child and relief that the perpetrator of the evil scheme was not her husband would combine to lift her spirits into the boughs. Instead, she sat huddled in a corner, a perfect mass of misery, mentally heaping strong terms of condemnation on her bowed head for her lack of trust in Christopher's innate goodness. For the most part, Molly diverted Jamie's advances, taking it upon herself to amuse the child, which gave his remorseful aunt abundant leisure to indulge in an orgy of self-loathing.

At one point, Molly did look up from her game of cat's cradle with the little boy to say gently, "He will understand that you regard Jamie's welfare as a sacred trust and that you could not permit your personal feelings to influence your decision to leave Ashleigh for the child's sake."

Dulled green eyes turned toward her in despair. "I know you mean well but it's no use, Molly. My personal reaction was to judge him guilty. You saw how he looked when he realized that. I wounded him beyond forgiveness. I don't deserve to be forgiven."

"Nevertheless, he will forgive you," Molly persisted, "and you must also forgive yourself."

Brianna turned away, two tears trickling down her cheeks.

They saw nothing of Christopher during the changes of horses, nor did they get down from the chaise again until they reached their destination. It was already dark when they arrived at Ashleigh. Molly bustled the exhausted child off to the nursery and Brianna found herself alone and uncertain. Christopher had handed her down from the chaise without even looking at her before going to confer with the postilion. With some relief, she allowed Pennystone to fuss over her, promising to send tea up to her suite immediately as he escorted her to the foot of the main stairs.

Hannah, too, seemed disposed to cosset her mistress that evening. Not one for unnecessary words ordinarily, she was positively garrulous as she brushed Brianna's hair with long soothing strokes while she recounted the dramatic events of the day. Brianna's stupefied reaction to the tale of her husband being overpowered by his cousin and Symonds and miraculously achieving his own unaided escape, knocking Mr. George out in the process, was everything a storyteller could wish. She started in horror as the maid went on to tell how the male servants had hidden in the shrubbery outside the office and swarmed over that villainous Symonds when he brought a horse around to carry away the master's body and dump it in the lake. Even allowing for the servants' tendency to expand and embellish a story, it was clear to Brianna that Christopher had undergone a dreadful ordeal and exhibited great resourcefulness and courage in thwarting a foul plot to murder himself and his nephew. And after this accomplishment, he had been compelled to fare forth on a search for the faithless wife who had betrayed him almost as cruelly as the cousin to whom he had been so generous.

Brianna had thought she'd plumbed the depths of self-hatred when she had seen the pain her distrust of him caused Christopher this afternoon, but the story Hannah told deepened her gloom. She longed to make amends, wipe out the injury she'd done him, and take away the pain of his cousin's betrayal. She looked forward to their first meeting with eagerness and dread.

She let Hannah dress her hair high on her head in an elaborate coiffure that was undeniably flattering and very unlike her usual style, and she allowed the maid to array her in the loveliest of the London gowns: an exquisite black lace confection that made the most of her figure. When Hannah left the room Brianna surveyed herself in the mirror. Beneath a purely feminine satisfaction at looking her best, she identified a deep-seated reluctance to employ any arts of seduction in seeking her husband's forgiveness. She could not bear to be forgiven only because he wanted her in his bed. She needed to be so much more to him than that.

The twenty minutes it took to restore her old unfashionable image made Brianna late for dinner, but no one was offended, save the chef, since she dined in solitary state. Pennystone presented Christopher's compliments and explained that the master was engaged in some urgent matters that would prevent him from joining her that evening. For the sake of the butler's sense of fitness, she went through the motions of eating and even managed to send what she hoped was an informed message of congratulations to the chef for his superb offerings, but not even to maintain the farce of a normal evening would she sentence herself to several hours of solitude in the saloon. Instead, she went up to the nursery to see Molly. She found Jamie fast asleep and her old friend on the point of retiring herself. Molly did indeed look worn after a disturbed night and a day full of strain. Brianna embraced her swiftly and returned to her own apartments.

There was no hope of sleeping until she had spoken to Christopher. She dismissed a startled Hannah, who stared in disbelief at her mistress's altered appearance, and resigned herself to waiting for as long as it took to unburden her conscience.

Brianna did not change into her night things for the same reason she had refused to go down to dinner fashionably dressed. She was afraid she would not hear Christopher in his room if she stayed in the sitting room, so she left the dressing room door open and settled on top of her bed with her book. A fatalistic calm took possession of her. Christopher might reject her apology and herself. All along he had been the one to chance rebuffs, unconditionally stating his love for her while she had played the coward, refusing to acknowledge that she could love someone who didn't meet her exacting standards of conduct, when the truth was that she had fallen in love with him as quickly as he with her. She owed him the truth at last even if it was too late to matter to him. She could only pray that it was not too late.

It was nearly midnight before Brianna heard faint sounds from the next room. Knowing Christopher never allowed his valet to put him to bed, she slid off her bed and twitched her skirts into line as she headed through her dressing room and knocked on the far door. For a moment that stretched beyond the reasonable, there was dead silence. Brianna's heart sank; it hadn't occurred to her that he would refuse even to give her a hearing. She pulled in her lips, moistening them with her tongue in a nervous gesture and clasped her hands in front of her to keep them from shaking. Her courage was failing and she had almost accepted defeat when Christopher opened the door at last. He had removed his cravat but was still wearing his coat. He said nothing, merely looked at her, his face as still and remote as the Greek statues he resembled.

"May I speak to you, Christopher?"

After a brief hesitation, he stepped back and Brianna walked past him. She stopped a few steps into the room whose appointments she did not notice as she turned to find him standing with his back to the door, waiting.

"I could not sleep until I had apologized to you for . . . for ever thinking you capable of wanting to harm Jamie." Her halting words produced no change in his shuttered expression but she plunged on. "I know how deeply that hurt you . . . I saw it in your eyes and I felt . . . like a monster." Her voice failed her then and she bit her lips and stared beseechingly at the man who drew in a harsh breath.

"I always knew you held my character in contempt, of course," he said in a deadened voice. "You had never concealed the fact that you could not respect me, but it still came as a . . . shock that you believed me such a fiend as that."

Brianna closed her eyes briefly, cringing from his mingled pain and anger. "It wasn't like that at all, Christopher! I was always drawn to your kindness, right from that first night in your study. I refused your first offer because I was precisely the coward you called me in the garden. I don't believe my heart accepted that you could harm Jamie, but how could I take a chance with his life when I had seen you on the roof just before that stone fell?" Voice and eyes were pleading for understanding.

"*What?* You *saw* me up there?"

"Yes. I swear it didn't occur to me that you had deliberately pushed that stone over the edge, but when I looked up to tell you we were unhurt, you were gone. It wasn't until you lied about it in the dining room that I . . . I . . ." She swallowed hard and her voice sank to a whisper. "I *had* to put Jamie first, Christopher. I had to listen to my intellect and ignore my heart."

"So that's why you looked so sick in the dining room! My poor Brianna!" Christopher's voice and eyes had come back to life as he walked up to her and stopped a half-pace away, regarding her soberly. "It seems I reaped what I had sown. I saw George on the roof but not you or James below. He had not seen me and I was not quite ready to act; there were things I needed to check on first. It haunted me during that hellish chase today that I had not spoken to you to calm your fears at some point yesterday."

"It must have been hellish, especially after the ordeal you had suffered here. Hannah told me the terrible story." She shivered convulsively. "Your cousin has betrayed you and I have failed you badly. I hope you will be able to forgive me, Christopher."

"As I told you once in the rectory parlor, anything, anytime." A tender light came into his eyes as he murmured, " 'Love is not love which alters when it alteration finds.' I meant it when I promised to love you forever, Brianna. I wish you could believe that my nature is not like my brother's."

"Oh, Chris, your generosity shames me!" Tears welled up in Brianna's eyes. "At first I could not admit to myself that I had fallen in love with you because of Lady Selina. Even when she ended your betrothal, I continued to deny my feelings out of sheer cowardice, but I do love you, and it was mean and downright dishonest to conceal it from you since our marriage."

Christopher had taken her into a gentle embrace at the beginning of this speech, his eyes darkening with passion. There was still some distance between them as she finished and he kept her away when she would have put her arms around his neck. "That word 'dishonesty' brings to mind something I had better confess," he said with a wry twist to his mouth. "Sir Harry Paxton came here to see you—"

"I know," Brianna interrupted, placing her fingers on his lips. "I found his letter in your desk yesterday when I went to look for sealing wax, and I had every intention of calling you to account— it seemed important at the time—but that was before I saw Jamie narrowly escape death."

"It is still important, my darling, and I always knew there would have to be a reckoning. Paxton came here with the intention of making you an offer the day after our quarrel in the garden. With your declaration that you hated me and would do anything to get away from here still ringing in my ears, I was afraid to let you see him for fear I'd lose you. I am not defending my action, which was dishonorable, merely explaining that when it comes down to a question of you or my honor, my choice must always be you. I fear love has not had an ennobling effect on my character so far. Quite the contrary, but I will strive to do better."

"It was very bad, of course," Brianna said with a whimsical look, "but you do seem to have hit upon the one exception that could sway the judgment of the most rigid moralist, at least if she

has the undeserved good fortune to be the object of your affec-
tions."

Christopher laughed and wrapped her tightly in his arms, his
relief at the pitfalls averted matching hers. "That this terrible day
should end like this seems to me nothing short of miraculous," he
muttered on a sighing breath as they savored the joy and comfort
of their two hearts beating together.

Brianna shivered and clung closer. "What is going to happen,
Chris? About your cousin, I mean."

"That is what kept me engaged this evening. As of an hour ago,
George is gone from Ashleigh and soon will be gone from England. I made this a condition when I agreed to pay his gambling
debts. I also required that he write a detailed account of his responsibility for the series of attempts on James's life and mine. It
will be kept with the solicitor and made public should any unex-
plained accident befall either of us in the future. And now, my
darling, let us leave all unhappy topics for tonight." He put her a
little away from him, seeming to notice her attire for the first
time. "Why are you fully dressed after midnight?"

"I had no intention of going to bed until I had begged your forgiveness." Her eyes fell under the burning light in his.

"It is much too late to disturb Hannah," her husband said softly.
"May I offer my services as abigail in her stead?"

To his great delight, Christopher's brash suggestion found
favor with his timid wife. Glowing emerald eyes met his bravely.
"Only if you will accept me as your temporary valet," she replied,
blushing at her own temerity.

"Done," Christopher said, scooping her up in his arms and
heading toward the dressing room. "We'll help each other."